Finding Luke

Escaping the Past: Book Two

by

Suzie Peters

First Published in 2017
by GWL Publishing
an imprint of Great War Literature Publishing LLP

Produced in United Kingdom

ISBN 978-1-910603-37-6 Paperback Edition

GWL Publishing
Forum House
Sterling Road
Chichester PO19 7DN
www.gwlpublishing.co.uk

Dedication

To S.

Chapter One

Luke

I turn the key in the lock and open the door, trying to be as quiet as possible, so as not to wake Will. I can do without 'the look', the guilt-trip, the lecture, the inevitable argument, followed by the drawn-out silence, which if previous experience is anything to go by, could go on for days. Just because he's not getting laid… I shake my head. *No, that's not fair.*

The house is in darkness, thank God, and I make my way over to the kitchen to grab a glass of water. Opening the refrigerator, the bottles in the door clink together and I 'shush' them, placing my finger against my lips, then take the water jug and carry it across to the countertop by the sink. I get a glass from the cupboard, fill it with ice cold water and drink it down in one go, before re-filling it again.

"Thirsty?"

I jump, spilling water on the floor.

"Jesus, Will. What the…?"

"Where the hell have you been?" he asks from the hallway, turning on the main light. I wince against the brightness and put down the glass. He's standing, bare chested, shorts hanging low on his hips, leaning against the wall near my bedroom door, with a disappointed look on his face. "On second thoughts, don't answer that," he adds. "I know exactly where you've been, and with whom. Can't you have a little bit more self-respect, Luke? You and I both know why you do this, but don't you think…"

That's it. I've had enough. "Stop it! Stop acting like my goddamn mother," I yell and he stares at me just for a moment, his face white. *Shit! Way to go, Luke.* I've really excelled myself this time. "Will, I'm sorry," I call to his retreating back. I can't leave it – it'll eat away at him. I follow him down the hallway toward his bedroom at the far end, but he slams the door in my face. I wait outside for a minute, breathing deeply, before opening it and standing on the threshold. Inside, he's sitting on the edge of his bed, his elbows on his knees, rocking slightly. He looks like he's twelve years old all over again, like the intervening sixteen years never happened. He's still my little brother; he'll always be my little brother, and I want to go over to him and tell him everything will be okay… but it's never been okay for him, well not since he was twelve years old.

"She was *our* mother, Luke," he whispers. I walk over and sit down next to him.

"I know."

"Then don't talk about her like that."

"I'm sorry, man, okay? I just get sick of explaining myself."

He turns to look at me. I don't like the expression in his eyes. It cuts a little too deep.

"Well, if you didn't screw around so much…"

It's true… I can't deny it, but… "It's my life, Will."

"I know it is," he relents and hesitates, opening his mouth and then closing it again.

"What?"

"I just wish I thought you were happy, that's all."

I was happy enough an hour ago when I was buried in… what was her name? Monica? No, Michelle. No… Damned if I can remember her name. *Yeah, I was happy enough then…* But am I ever *really* happy these days?

"I'm fine," I say out loud, not wanting to admit the thoughts that are running around in my head – to him, or myself.

He continues to stare at me, like he can see right through me. It's uncomfortable.

"It was Matt and Grace's wedding, Luke," he says at last. He's really laying on the disappointment this time.

"No… it was *after* Matt and Grace's wedding. There's a difference. And we went back to her place…" *Whoever she was.* "It's not like I was screwing her on Matt and Grace's deck, while they were saying their vows; or in one of their guest rooms during the speeches." He grimaces.

"Sorry," I say.

I shrug off my tux. I've got no idea where my tie ended up – it's probably still at Mandy's house… No, it wasn't Mandy… I know it began with an 'M', though.

"I'm going for a quick shower," I say, standing up again. "Then I'll get a few hours' sleep." I make my way over to the door.

"Are you going to see Melanie again?" he asks just before I leave. Melanie! That's it. I turn and look at him.

"No," I tell him. That's not how it works with me, and he knows it. "And how did you know her name?"

"She introduced herself before the ceremony," he explains. "She saw you with Matt and asked me if I knew who the best man was."

I nod my head, keen to escape, and wander down the hallway to my own room. Once inside, I close the door and lean back against it.

'Best Man'. I let my head drop to my chest. It hardly feels like the right title for a guy who can't even remember the name of the woman he's just made scream with pleasure, three… no, four times.

I guess that must be the reason why I feel like such a shit right now.

I douse my head under the shower. The water's hot and harsh, and it's good to feel something for a change. I stand, just thinking. I've lived like this since I was eighteen… Thirteen years of doing exactly what I please. No questions, no strings, and no commitments.

I've never dated a woman, not conventionally. One night stands are my specialty. I don't like the idea of relationships; someone asking questions, wanting to know everything about me. I've never been in love and I certainly don't like the idea of a woman being in love with me. I can't do the whole obligation, responsibility thing. I'm just not that kind of person. In a way, I admire those who are. I can see how Matt's changed since he met Grace and that's great… for Matt, but it's not for me.

I'm not a complete asshole. I'm sure there are a few women out there who'd beg to differ, but I'm always upfront. I let them know that for me, it's just about the sex, about having a good time together, and I'm not interested in a relationship; I always use protection and I never sleep with married women. Even I have boundaries.

I turn to face the cascading water and run my hand up over my chest, recalling Melanie's fingernails scraping across my skin a few hours ago. She was exactly what I look for in a woman: hot as hell, and experienced. She knew what she wanted and she made it very clear at the wedding, she was only interested in me for tonight. She practically threw me out when we were done; no phone numbers, no contact details. That suits me fine. It was just sex; good sex – not great, but good. So, why do I feel like there's an absence of something? And what's the 'something'?

I shake my head, splashing water off the white tiled walls. What the hell is the matter with me?

"How was the honeymoon?" I look across the desk. Matt's tanned and grinning. "Actually, I don't want to know. It's written all over your face."

"Jealous?" he smirks.

"Of course." Grace is beautiful; any man with a pulse would be jealous. The door opens behind me. I turn and the lady in question enters. Her tan is slightly darker than Matt's. Her hair has also changed color, lightened by the sun. Her eyes are alight, satisfied and contented. Matt's a lucky man. I stand. "Hello, Grace," I say and go across to her, planting a kiss on each of her cheeks and placing my arm around her shoulders as we walk across to Matt's desk. "You look fabulous, as ever."

"Hi, Luke," she replies, giving me that 'look' she always does, which tells me she knows I'm flirting, she accepts it, and she's not at all impressed by it. I grin back. We get each other.

"The Cayman Islands agreed with you both, clearly."

"It was spectacular," Grace sighs, taking the seat next to mine, and across from Matt. She catches his eye and they share a look. I love the fact that they're happy, finally settled after everything they've been through in the last few months, but right now… I don't know… something's eating at me.

"Great," I say, wanting to break the spell that's binding them – not for long, just long enough for me to get out of their presence and back to my own world. *Yeah, my own world, where I'm so damn happy.* "Everything's been going well in your absence."

"I know." Matt leans forward, dragging his eyes from Grace and across to me. "I read your e-mails."

"At least you didn't reply to them."

"I was on my honeymoon, remember? And I trust you to run this place…" I know he does, but it's good to hear him say it. "So, production's at full capacity in both factories now?" he asks.

"Yes." We purchased a second factory site at the beginning of the year and it's now completely up to speed, producing our sportswear and lingerie ranges. Orders have been flooding in and business is doing great.

"We just need to discuss the launch of the new range," Matt says.

Grace had been working hard on this with Paul, our senior designer, right up until the wedding. Since moving here from England just before Christmas, Grace has been much more involved in the business, and with this new range in particular, and Matt and I have taken a back seat while we got the new factory up and running.

"Paul and I have come up with a new idea," Grace adds.

"Okay…"

"We've decided that, rather than having three or four girls modeling the range, we should have a 'face of' model. One girl, who we feel typifies the style of that season's designs. She'll do all the photography, and the promotional work and she'll lead the shows in September."

I think it's a really good idea. It fits in with where we've been taking the products, in terms of their exclusivity.

"I like it," I say. "Are we going to use a well-known face? Someone the public will recognize?"

"No," Matt says. "We want the exact opposite. We want someone new and fresh. Someone no-one's seen before."

"Paul worked out a short-list of models while we were away," Grace adds. "Ones who best fitted the styles. And Matt and I made the final choice this morning. She's a stunning girl. We've got the whole shoot arranged. Paul and I have worked really hard on the look and feel for this season's designs…" Why do I feel that there's a 'but' coming round the corner and it's aimed straight at me?

I look from Grace to Matt.

"The thing is," he says, "the shoot is going to take place on location."

"Not in a studio?" That's a departure.

"No," Grace sits forward in her seat and turns to me. "You've seen the designs, Luke. They're exceptional. I came up with the idea of shooting the photographs outside, in places that reflect, or represent the styles. Paul thought it was a good pitch, and we put it to Matt."

"And I agreed." *And where's this leading exactly?*

I sit waiting for whatever it is to fall on me. Almost certainly from a great height.

"The locations are all in France."

"France?" It makes sense, I guess. France is beautiful. I've spent enough time in Paris over the last few years to know that.

"Yes." She turns to Matt again. He gets up and comes around to our side of the desk, leaning against it, his legs outstretched and crossed at the ankle, his arms folded across his chest.

"The thing is…" he begins, "we feel that one of us should go on this shoot. The model we've selected – Megan – she's never done anything like this before…"

"Never? Not at all?"

"No. I said, I wanted someone completely new."

"There's new, and there's a modeling virgin. Guess you went for the modeling virgin."

"Yeah… Look, I need you to go, Luke."

"Surely, Grace should go," I say. "It's her idea."

"Grace can't go right now," Matt says, looking down at her. "She's got a new project to work on."

I'm not that surprised. I don't interfere with the early design processes. It's Matt's company and he's 'hands on' in all departments; I only tend to get involved later on, when we're looking at sales and marketing strategies.

"Paul's been doing some initial work on a range of maternity lingerie," Grace explains. "He's moved it along while we've been—"

"I'm sorry," I splutter. "Did you just say 'maternity'?"

"Yes." I'm vaguely aware of Matt letting out a deep sigh, even though I'm looking at Grace.

"Maternity?" I repeat.

"Yes, Luke. Maternity. Pregnant women are allowed to look sexy too, you know." Her British accent is much more noticeable when she gets mad. She's not all the way there yet, but it's brewing.

"Yeah," I can't hide the doubt in my voice. "Yeah, sure they are."

"The designs are good," Matt puts in. "Look," he says, more seriously, "the point is, Grace can't go."

"Someone is going from the design team though, right?"

"Yeah. Paul's decided that Emma can handle the artistic side, so she'll be going along too." Emma's a really nice girl, good fun, very pretty, and very married to Nathan, who's a firefighter. She's also a great designer, so she'll be useful to have around. "But with an inexperienced model, I need someone there who can handle Alec. Emma can't do that."

"We're using Alec?"

"Yes." *Damn.* "He knows what we need, Luke. I know he's difficult, but he's a good photographer." 'Difficult' is an understatement, but he is good at what he does. "I need someone with seniority on this trip. I can't go either; it has to be you."

"When is this happening?" I ask.

"You'll need to leave at the weekend."

At least he didn't say 'tomorrow'.

"And how long is the shoot?"

"We've allowed just over three weeks," Grace says.

"Excuse me?" I turn to her. "Three weeks?" A studio shoot is normally completed in a few days.

"Twenty-four days, to be precise." She twists in her seat again. "There are six ranges to be photographed. We've allocated two days for each shoot, but then there's traveling, finding precise locations at each venue, checking for lighting... All of that will be down to Alec, but you'll have to drive between locations and some of them might take a day, maybe longer, to get to. And then there's a contingency of about four to five days, in case you have bad weather and can't work."

"And if we finish up early and don't need those extra days?"

"That's up to you," Matt says. "Alec can send the images back electronically. So you can either get an earlier flight home, or stay on over there and have a short vacation."

"Working with Alec, I'll have earned it."

Grace has gone back to her office and Matt and I have finished discussing everything else that happened while they were in The Caymans.

"This new range," I say to him. "Maternity... Are you sure about that?"

"The initial drawings are good," he says. "Why do you have a problem with it?"

"We're getting a good reputation for tasteful, sexy lingerie... I just can't equate maternity with sexy, that's all."

"Are you serious?"

"Absolutely."

"But, can't you imagine how incredible it would be to have the woman you love carrying your child... caring for it inside her, nurturing it? Hell, I think that's about as sexy as it gets."

I stare at him... He's *really* changed. Admittedly, it's a change for the better, considering where he was a couple of years ago, but... Hang on a second... "Grace isn't pregnant, is she?"

"No." He hesitates for a moment. "But, we're trying."

"You are? Already?"

"Yes, already." He shakes his head at me, but he's smiling. "We made the decision the night I proposed…"

"How romantic."

"There were reasons," he says, pauses and then continues, "Grace has some medical problems, it might not be that easy—" He stops. I had no idea.

"Sorry, Matt." I feel like a jerk now. "Is this to do with her first husband?" The guy raped and beat Grace for years before he had the good sense to get himself killed. It's a wonder she's as together as she is – and she's about the most together person I've ever met.

"Yes. He got her pregnant. It went wrong." He looks up at me. "I can't go into details, but she could've died." I can see the fear in his eyes. "It's her story," he says. "It doesn't feel right…"

"You don't have to tell me anything, except that she's okay." I don't need details, but I do care about Grace.

"In terms of her general health, she's fine. In terms of getting pregnant and carrying it to term…? We don't know, but we'll find out, hopefully quite soon."

I can't imagine being where he is… Grace means everything to him. We sit in silence for a while.

"Are you sure you're okay with this photo shoot?" he asks out of the blue. "I'm sorry to throw it at you. I know you never really enjoyed doing them, but Grace needs to be here… And so do I, for obvious reasons." He grins at me. I get it now.

"Sure," I say. "It's fine. How bad can it be?"

"With Alec?"

"Yeah, okay. It could be bad."

"Grace will go through the locations with you tomorrow. She's got everything mapped out; flights, car hire, hotels, everything. Grace and Emma have arranged it all already… You just have to turn up, make sure everything runs smoothly and Alec doesn't cause too much trouble."

"Okay. This model… Megan, was it? How old is she?"

He opens a document on his computer and reads. "She's… twenty-two."

"That's young."

"It's one of the reasons Grace wanted Emma on the shoot. It'll be some female company for her, but she's also a really good fit with the styles. I'm just waiting for the final contract to come back from the agency."

"And then she's ours for three weeks?"

"Yes, but only professionally."

"Of course."

"Luke," he says, his voice sounding the warning note I'm so familiar with.

"Yeah, I know. No fooling around with the models… or model, in this case."

"Alec's a bully, and you'll need to look out for her, but your responsibilities end at her bedroom door… got it?"

"Got it, boss." It's his golden rule, and one I've never broken.

In any case, there's more to this shoot than the model… and, if my previous experiences of French women are anything to go by, maybe the next three weeks won't be so bad after all.

Megan

"You do understand, don't you?" The woman's voice on the phone is persistent, like she's talking to a three year-old.

"Yes." Nothing she's said so far has been that hard to grasp.

"If you accept this job, you have to commit to this photographic shoot, and the fashion shows in the fall." She's going to repeat it all anyway… because I'm clearly three years old.

"Yes, that's fine."

"So, you're happy with the arrangements?"

"What will I be modeling?"

"Well… they're sportswear designers, dear… I've told you this already." Her sarcasm isn't lost on me.

"I know, but it's not too revealing, is it?"

"It's sportswear," she huffs.

"Yes, right."

"So, can I tell them you agree? I have to get the contract back to them."

I think for a moment… and it only takes a moment. The job is very well paid. It's worth more money than I could have dreamt of earning working at Dexy's bar. I can't afford to say no. "Yes, that's fine." I say.

She hangs up, telling me she'll be in touch.

I twist my phone round and round, turning it over in my hand, staring at the blank screen. Have I just made a huge mistake? I gave up my job at Dexy's a month ago because I couldn't handle any more drunks trying to get into my pants. I'm more than familiar with drunks – I lived with one for too many years – but I'd had enough. I wanted to find a job with one of the museums in the city, but there's just nothing available, and I need to pay the rent, and send my dad some money, or I'll have to move back with him… and I can't do that. This will work… It's just a temporary fix to a temporary glitch. Three weeks' work now… another three or four weeks in the fall, and I'm set for six months… which leaves me plenty of time to find the job I really want to do. It all makes perfect sense.

I hear the front door open, then close and Erin appears. She's a little shorter than me, thin, with shoulder-length auburn hair and just enough freckles to look cute. She's already found a 'proper' job, at an elementary school near the city center, but she doesn't start until next semester, so she's taken part-time work in a pizza restaurant just around the corner. We've known each other since our first day at college; we moved into this small apartment at the end of our first year and we're best friends.

"Well?" she says.

"I got it."

"You could sound a little more enthusiastic."

"It's not exactly my dream job, Erin."

"No…" she comes and sits down next to me on our tiny couch. "But it'll pay the rent and keep you fed for a while."

"Us… It'll keep us fed." She gives me a hug.

"And it'll get your dad off your back…"

"I know. Just as long as he doesn't find out where the money came from."

"How's he ever going to find out?" She has a point. He'll just take whatever I give him, and then ask for more, like he usually does. "So, what do they want?"

"I've got to go to Europe," I tell her.

She turns and stares at me. "Are you serious?"

"Yes." I can't help but smile. "It's incredible, isn't it? Europe! As long as I can cope with the flight, I'll be fine."

"What's wrong with flying?"

"I don't know… I've never done it. I've always been a bit scared of it though."

"You'll be fine. You need to try new things. Besides, it's the chance of a lifetime. Whereabouts in Europe are you going?"

"France."

"Wow… How long for?" she asks.

"Three weeks."

"When do you go?"

"I'm leaving on Saturday. And they're sending one of the women from the company, as a kind of chaperone, so it's all perfectly okay."

"I told you this would work out. And to think, I passed it up." Erin saw the advertisement calling for models, in a magazine last week. It was a local agency and at first, we laughed it off, but I was having no luck searching for work, and money was already getting a little tight, so I went to see them. They signed me up and told me they had the perfect job for me, on the spot. It seemed too good to be true, but so far, it's all working out fine.

"The company I'm going to be working for are in sportswear."

"Oooh… lovely. Lots of Lycra. At least you've got the figure for it." She laughs and jumps up off the sofa. "Coffee?" she offers.

"Hmm, please. And I suppose I'd better think about what to pack."

"I've decided to turn my phone off," I say to Erin as we pull up outside the departure building. "I can't risk my dad calling while I'm over there… Just in case he overhears someone speaking in French or something. You can text me if there are any problems and I'll switch it on each evening and check my messages."

"Don't worry, just enjoy yourself. You don't get to go to France every day."

"I'll be back on July 2nd at the latest."

"I've got your flight details in my diary."

"And if my dad calls on the landline…"

"I'll just tell him your phone's off because you're working, and you'll be there to see him… when?"

"July 19th, as planned, but—"

"I won't say a word about where you are, or what you're doing. Just stop worrying, Megs, and go have a great time." She kisses my cheek and I hop out of the car, grabbing my bag from the back seat.

"Bye!" I return her wave as she pulls away.

It's a warm, sultry, overcast day, and I welcome the air conditioning as I enter the building and pull the piece of paper with all the details on it from the pocket of my bag.

It says I'm supposed to meet Emma Conway and a guy called Luke Myers by the Delta check-in desk. I've got no idea what they look like, but hopefully the agency will have sent them my photograph, so they'll find me.

It's fairly busy inside but I find the desk easily enough. There's a pretty blonde woman standing to one side, searching the crowds.

"Are you Emma Conway?" I ask her.

"Yes. And you're Megan Ford." She shakes my hand. "Wow. Your photographs don't do you justice," she says.

I know I'm blushing but she either doesn't notice, or is polite enough to ignore my embarrassment.

"I hope I haven't kept you waiting," I reply eventually.

"No. We've only been here a short while. Luke will be back in a minute. He went to get coffee."

I nod my head. She's a very cheerful-looking, bubbly person. She's shorter than me, but then a lot of people are, being as I'm five foot ten. She's wearing jeans and a red check shirt, with sunglasses perched on her head, holding her hair back from her face.

"You may as well check your bag in," she says. "We've already done ours."

"Oh, okay." I go up to the desk and go through the procedure, then return to her.

"I think Luke went to pick the damn beans himself," she says. "Either that, or he's found some poor, deluded…" I've stopped listening. Her words are just white noise, because behind her, out of the corner of my eye, I've noticed the most gorgeous man I've ever seen, walking through the concourse. He must be around six foot three or maybe four inches tall, broad shouldered, with a narrow waist. His toned muscles are evident through the tight white t-shirt that's plastered to his body, and his long legs are encased in light stonewashed jeans. He's carrying three large paper cups in a cardboard tray. For a brief moment, I manage to tear my eyes from him and notice that every other female in the vicinity is also staring at him, some with their mouths open. I wonder if he knows how good he looks and how much attention he's getting. Then I look back at him… Of course he does.

He stops for a moment, then stares in our direction, a confused expression on his face. It seems like he's forgotten something. He waits for a minute or two, then almost seems to shake his head, before he slowly moves toward us…

Chapter Two

Luke

I never thought I'd say this, but I'm actually relieved to be here, and I'm looking forward to the trip. There have been a few last-minute changes but we're all set now. Two of the venues for the photography pulled out, so Grace had to find alternates, then the agency kicked up a stink over the fee, because we want to take the model overseas. They knew that all along, but suddenly it became an issue. They're a royal pain in the ass.

Will had to go away a couple of days after Matt and Grace's wedding. He only came back yesterday and we didn't really get to sort out our differences. I don't like leaving him alone at the best of times, but when we're barely talking, it's even worse. Still, after the week I've had, it's nice just to be at the airport and ready to go… except the model isn't here, or she wasn't when I got bored waiting and went to buy the coffee. That said, I don't have a clue what she looks like. Emma does – she's seen the photographs, but I've been busy in meetings, clearing my desk ready for the trip, preparing the marketing strategy for the new sportswear range, going over sales figures and checking through details with Grace.

The best part of the trip so far is that Alec isn't with us. He took a flight out yesterday, and we're meeting him at the hotel in Paris. We're booked to stay there for one night, then we hit the road. At least we'll get this part of the journey to ourselves – a few less hours spent with him has got to be an advantage.

The concourse is busy and I'm trying real hard not to drop the coffee, or spill it over anyone, especially as people keep stepping out in front of me. I've bought one for Megan, hoping she likes coffee, because it would be awkward if I got back, she was there and I hadn't got her anything. Plus it would only mean I'd have to go and join the end of that long queue again.

I can see Emma at the check-in desk. She's got her back to me, but she's talking to… *Damn.* I stop in my tracks, and the guy behind swears at me. Who the hell is Emma talking to? I can only see the top half of her face but she's still the most beautiful woman I've ever seen. I stand for a while, just staring, and then remember that I'm supposed to be bringing the coffee. I have to shake my head, just a little, to bring myself back to reality…

As I walk up to them, Emma moves to one side and I can see the other girl properly. My whole body stiffens. She's tall and slim, lightly tanned and she's wearing a short, white dress, with a narrow brown belt and matching ankle boots. Her hair is wild… I mean crazy wild. She's got a mane – there's no other word to describe it – a mane of untamed, wavy brown hair, with blonde streaks running through it and she's staring at me through light green eyes. Her lips are rosebud pink, open just a little and slightly pouting, or maybe that's just wishful thinking… But she can't be Megan. Matt wouldn't do this to me. He wouldn't put the greatest temptation of all time in my path, and then make her off-limits… He's my best friend.

"About time," Emma says and reaches for one of the coffees. "Megan…" She turns to the girl and I know with absolute certainty that I'm going to kill my best friend the next time I see him. "This is Luke Myers."

I hold out my free hand and she takes it in hers. Her fingers caress mine and my breath catches in my throat.

"Mr Myers," she whispers, and all my nerve endings shiver. Since when do I react like this to a woman?

"Call me Luke." Thank God, my voice worked… I was starting to wonder what was going on with me. "It's nice to meet you." *It's way more than nice.* "Would you like a coffee?" I ask her.

"Oh… if that's okay."

"Sure. Help yourself." She takes the one nearest to her and has a sip, then licks her lips… and I feel my cock throb at the sight of her tongue. Jeez, to think I was dumb enough to say I was looking forward to this trip.

Megan and Emma have gone to the ladies' room, so I dig out my phone and type a message to Matt.

— *Enjoy the last three weeks of your sorry life. I'm going to kill you for this when I get back.*

His reply comes through quickly.

— *I take it you've met Megan, then?*

— *Yes, you asshole.*

— *Just remember the rule, Luke.*

— *Yeah, yeah. I'll make you pay for this.*

— *Have a good trip ;)*

God… if he was here in front of me…

We board the flight and find our seats. Unlike the last time I flew trans-Atlantic, business class on this flight has standard wide seats, not pods and we've pre-booked the center three. Emma and Megan both opt for the aisles, so I sit between them. I settle down and glance across at Megan. Her hands are clasped in her lap, and my eyes drift down slightly to her thighs which are toned, tanned, soft. *Oh crap…* Not breaking Matt's rule is going to kill me. I think I'd like to go home now.

We were among the last to take our seats and the empties around us soon fill up. The doors are closed and we start to taxi.

Megan's hands twist, her fingers fidgeting. I move my gaze up to her face. She's staring straight ahead but she looks… I'm not sure what… concerned, confused? *No, jackass… that's fear.*

"Are you okay?" I ask.

She startles. "Um… yes, thanks." She doesn't look at me, just keeps staring straight ahead.

"What's wrong?" I whisper. Megan turns her head, her eyes meet mine and her mouth parts just a fraction. There's something other than fear in her eyes, but I'm too distracted by the panic on her face to think about that right now. "What is it?" I ask her.

"I… I've never flown before…" she murmurs.

"Oh. Well, don't worry about it. You'll be perfectly safe."

"Is it though? Safe, I mean?"

"Yeah. It's fine." The engine noise picks up. "Take off and landing are the worst bits… everything in between is a breeze." I don't mention turbulence… we might not hit any, and I don't want to scare her any more than she is already.

"So, the take off…"

"Will be any minute now."

"And what happens?" she whispers.

"Generally speaking, the plane leaves the ground," I reply. I turn in my seat. God, she's shaking. I have to do something. "Look at me," I tell her. She doesn't move. "Megan, look at me." She turns her head in my direction. "Okay, now don't think about anything else, except looking at me." I smile at her. She doesn't smile back, but she does keep her eyes fixed on mine. Now I'm close I can see hers are more of a dusky green with pale brown circles around the iris. They're beautiful; like her. I was going to divert her attention by asking her to tell me about herself, but she seems distracted enough at the moment, just looking at me.

The plane starts to move forward down the runway, picking up speed, and suddenly, her hand grasps my forearm, squeezing tight, her fingernails digging in. I still don't take my eyes from hers as the wheels leave the ground and the plane ascends at a sharp angle.

"Megan," I say a few minutes later. She doesn't register my voice. "Megan," I repeat, "look out the window."

She drags her eyes from mine and turns around. Through the window on the other side of the aisle the sky is clear blue, the ground has disappeared, and just beneath us is a layer of puffy white clouds.

She turns back to me. "We're above the clouds?" she says, her eyes wide with surprise.

"Yes."

"Already?"

"Yes." I nod my head.

"But that was so quick."

"I know. It's great, isn't it?"

She smiles. She's got a real sexy smile. I'm not sure I've ever seen a smile that sexy before… "I don't know that I'd go that far, but it wasn't as bad as I'd expected." She relaxes and I feel her fingernails retract from my arm and her hand move away. I wish she'd put it back. "Oh, I'm so sorry," she says, looking down at the semi-circular marks her nails have left in my skin. "I can't believe I did that to you." She looks so guilty, I can't help but smile.

"It's fine, don't worry," I say to her. She rubs her fingers gently over the marks, her eyes intent, and I focus on her face. A few loose strands of her wild hair are hanging down, obstructing my view and I long to nudge them back behind her ear, kiss and lick her neck, suck on her bottom lip… I shake my head. *Remember the damn rule, Luke.*

∞

Megan

"I really am sorry," I say, rubbing his skin.

"Honestly, don't worry about it." He pulls his arm away and turns back to face the front of the aircraft. "Are you okay now?" he asks.

"Yes, thanks."

He undoes his seatbelt and I do the same. I feel terrible for sticking my nails into his arm like that. I've left really deep marks and I know it must have hurt, but he didn't flinch. Can it be true that the gorgeous man I was admiring at the airport is Luke Myers, that I'm now sitting next to him, and that I get to spend the next three weeks with him? Just looking at him makes me tingle deep inside. It's not a feeling I've ever experienced before and, if I'm being honest, I like it.

His eyes are the lightest shade of blue you can imagine, his dark blond hair is messy and spiked, and he's got stubble… which I'd really like to run my fingers over. I have no idea where these thoughts are coming from, and they've got to stop. It's not like anything can happen between us. Even if he did find me attractive, which is unlikely, considering that every woman he meets must throw herself at him, I still couldn't have anything to do with him – for both our sakes. My dad made it clear when I left home for college that his rule still applied: if any man touched me, he'd pay – and so would I. And I know what that means. He broke the jaw of the only boy who kissed me in high school… I don't even want to think what he'd do if a man ever…

Still, Luke's too gorgeous not to at least look at. And looking never hurt anyone, did it?

The flight attendant approaches. Tall, with rounded breasts and hips, red-headed, red lipped and pouting, she's essentially sex on legs. She bypasses the seats in front of ours and comes straight to us, but then leans over me and asks if Luke would like anything from the bar… Excuse me? I'm over twenty-one. Maybe I'd like a drink too, Hot-lips. Actually, I wouldn't, but that's not the point.

He looks at her for a full minute, maybe even longer, then pulls his eyes away from her and turns to me. I guess he finds her attractive. I don't blame him – she is beautiful, and I wish, for a moment, he could think the same about me. *Don't go there.*

"Would you like a drink, Megan?" he asks.

"Um," I hesitate. I hadn't expected him to ask me. "Just a mineral water, please." Then he turns to Emma and nudges her. She's got her earphones in and she removes them.

"Drink?" he says to her.

"No thanks," she replies.

"Just two mineral waters then. Thanks." He barely looks back at the flight attendant as he gives her our order, and she hovers for a moment longer. He twists in his seat and leans forward and slightly across me so I can't help but watch him. His eyes trace slowly up her body, pausing – seemingly deliberately – at her breasts, taking in her curves, then moving on up until he gets to her face. "Yes?" he says.

"Will there be anything else, *sir?*" she purrs. Her voice has dropped a note and, even without looking at her, I know exactly what she's offering him.

"No," Luke says flatly. "Absolutely nothing at all, but thanks for the offer." He turns back to face the front and a tiny part of me feels sorry for the redhead… but only a tiny part. The rest of me is pleased he turned her down. I wonder why?

We're a couple of hours into the flight when Luke excuses himself, and goes to the men's room. After a little while, Emma leans over his seat toward me.

"Are you okay now?" she asks.

"Yes, thanks. I've never flown before and I feel like such a wimp for behaving like that."

"Oh, I don't know. It can be daunting if you've never done it before."

Like most things, I guess.

"Well, thanks to Luke, I'm fine. He was very kind."

"Yeah, he can be."

I sense she doesn't entirely like him and raise an eyebrow at her remark.

"Don't get me wrong," she continues, "Luke's a nice guy; he's fiercely loyal to Matt – that's our boss – but…"

"But what?"

"Yeah, but what, Emma?" Luke's voice interrupts our conversation and I'm frustrated, not knowing what she was about to say.

He sits back down between us and turns to me. "She can't help it, you know," he says, smiling at me. "She might be happily married, but I have this effect on her; I fill her every waking thought."

"Only in your dreams, Myers," Emma replies.

He smiles, shrugs and lays his head back on the seat.

Charles de Gaulle Airport is busy, but then it's just after eight in the morning, local time, and I'm really pleased that we flew business class, because I slept for a lot of the journey, so I don't feel as bad as I thought I would.

Our bags seem to take forever to arrive, but eventually they do and after we've finally cleared immigration, we're outside, where a man is standing next to a dark blue MPV. He passes the keys to Luke, saying something to him in French. Luke replies, fluently it would seem; they laugh, say something else, Luke nods and the man puts our bags in the trunk. Luke gets behind the wheel, Emma gets in next to him and I climb in the back. He starts the car, puts it in drive, and we take off into the traffic toward Paris.

For the first part of the journey, we're on a freeway. There's not a lot to see; in fact, apart from the signs being in French, we could be anywhere. After a while, though, buildings start to appear and we leave the freeway and join a smaller, much busier road, which is terrifying. Cars are darting everywhere, taking exits or entering the road, but Luke just seems to take it in his stride.

"Is this the Périphérique?" Emma asks.

"Yeah… It's a little crazy, but at least it's moving. I've sat on here for hours before now," Luke replies, keeping his eyes on the road.

"This is only a *little* crazy?" I say.

"You okay?" He quickly looks at me in the rear-view mirror, not taking his eyes from the road for long.

I nod my head just as our eyes lock for a moment.

"We're nearly there," he says. "We come off at the next exit."

"Thank goodness for that."

"Do you always stay in this hotel?" Emma asks.

"Yeah. It's a chain the company uses. They have one in London, one here, one in Milan. We use them when we come over for the shows and other meetings, if necessary. And we use the one in Boston to put up guests who come to see us."

This explains how he knows his way around so easily. He takes the next exit and follows the road.

"Only about ten minutes now," he says over his shoulder, clearly for my benefit.

It seems to take less time than that before he pulls up outside an imposing white building, with a large arched doorway. A man in uniform steps forward and opens the car door to let me out. I stand on the sidewalk and wait for Luke and Emma; we don't bring the bags, but go straight inside and I stop, and gasp – out loud, I think.

Luke turns to me.

"Is something wrong?" he asks.

I shake my head, trying to take in the magnificence surrounding me. The floor is a mosaic of different colored marbles, in the middle of which there is a large, modern sculpture. It's kind of abstract, and I'm not sure what it's supposed to represent, but I like it. Around the edges of the room are ornate tables, topped with fresh flowers, and at the end is a long mahogany reception desk, with three women standing behind it. They're all blonde, all beautiful, all perfectly made-up and wearing matching pale blue blouses. Luke leans in to me just a little. "Close your mouth," he whispers, and I do, turning to him. He's smiling down at me and I feel his hand in the small of my back, guiding me forward. "C'mon," he says. "Let's get checked in." Emma has moved to one side and is staring at a painting on the wall.

"You coming?" Luke calls to her.

"Hmmm," she says and joins us. "That's an original," she whispers. "An original Rousseau."

"Yeah, I know," he says. "Not my thing, but—"

"Philistine."

"No," he tells her. "I just know what I like." He looks at me. "And what I don't." I wonder for a moment into which of those categories I fall.

Chapter Three

Luke

I've showered, I've changed, I've tried lying on the really comfortable bed – because I know they have great beds in these hotels – I've paced the floor, I've stood out on the balcony… Nothing's working. I can't get the image of her out of my head, or the fact that she's just across the hallway. I can't stop thinking about how good it felt to touch her, even though there was a layer of cotton between my fingers and her back. Her eyes, mouth, legs, smile – they're haunting me. I wish I could just go across to her room, knock on the door, kiss those perfect lips, walk her backwards to the bed, lay her down and take her… hard… until she's screaming my name. But I can't… can I? *Can I? No, Luke, you can't.*

Matt made the rule for a reason. I should know because I'm the goddamn reason. It's been in place ever since I joined the company, eighteen months after Matt started it. He'd be the first to admit that he broke it himself, but that was a one-off a few years ago, with a model who wasn't really working for us, not like Megan is anyway. Brooke turned out to be a psychopath, who tried to kill both Matt and Grace. So, the rule goes double now. No sex with the models.

A little tiny voice in the back of my head says I could easily get laid. That's never been a problem, and it seems it still isn't… All three of the women on the reception desk were looking at me like they'd happily oblige. You get to know 'the look'. The flight attendant had it too and

I could have just accepted her thinly veiled proposition on the aircraft... it wouldn't have been the first time. And even now, it would be very easy to go downstairs, decide which one of the receptionists I like the most and make some kind of arrangement for whenever she finishes work. I could go back to her place with her later, or we could keep it real simple and I could just bring her back up here to my room, strip her naked, throw her down on the bed and fuck her senseless all night. I think about it... for roughly thirty seconds – if that. I run my fingers through my still damp hair. For the first time since my first time, all those years, all those women ago, I don't want to... Well, I still *want* to, of course I do – I always do – but I don't want to with any of them. I don't want a willing blonde, or a pouting, obliging redhead. I want the one person I can't have. I want Megan.

The next three weeks are going to be hell.

There's a knocking on the door and I walk over to answer it, still running my hand through my hair. I open the door and my breath hitches in my throat. Again.

Standing there, glancing down the hallway, is Megan, wearing a white toweling hotel robe, her bare feet sinking slightly into the thick carpet.

"I'm so sorry," she says, turning and checking down the other end of the hallway. "Can you help me?"

"Sure," I manage to say, closing my gaping mouth in the process. "What's wrong?"

"I can't stand out here," she pleads. "Can you come to my room for a minute?"

I've died and gone to heaven. *No, you've died and gone to hell, you jerk... where you belong.*

She turns and leads the way back to her room. I grab the entry card from the bowl on the table just inside my door, put it in my pocket and follow her, closing my door behind me. Her room is similar to mine, but in a different color scheme. My room is all blues and white; Megan's is gold and cream. Her bag is on the bed, most of its contents scattered. She's messy. It makes me smile.

"I'm really sorry," she repeats. "I know I'm an idiot, but I can't figure out how the shower works."

I'm so tempted to offer to get in there with her, and show her…

"No problem," I say. The bathroom is off to my left and I go in. She follows me into the comparatively confined space. Her bathroom has a walk-in shower with water jets, as well as the overhead spray, which, if it's like mine will have a couple of functions.

I go in, my feet still bare, and demonstrate it to her.

"Water jets?" she says. "I've never had a shower with water jets before."

"They're… relaxing." She's right behind me and I can feel the heat from her body. This is about as far from relaxing as it gets.

"I'll take your word for it." She sounds dubious.

"You all set now?" I ask, turning to face her.

"Yes. Thanks for helping. It's all a bit new to me." She seems embarrassed.

"Well, you should always try new things," I say. "It's the only way to find out if you like them." My mouth is just an inch or two from hers; I could so easily lean forward and taste her. "I'll leave you to get on," I croak, my voice strained… bordering on strangled, and I leave.

"Thanks," she calls after me, as I close the door and cross the hallway. I open the door to my room, close it quickly and pull off my shirt, then strip off the rest of my clothes, leaving them in a trail on the floor behind me as I walk to the bathroom. Then I step back into the shower, turn it to cold and stand under it for a good ten minutes, my arms braced against the tiled wall. My cock won't go down; there's no chance of that, but it would be nice just to breathe normally again.

We've arranged to meet in the bar at seven. I get there a little early because I need a drink, and because I don't want Megan to be there on her own, if she's running ahead of time.

I'm sitting at a dark wood table, with four beige leather armchairs surrounding it, and a glass of white wine in front of me, when Alec arrives.

"Luke," he says, his voice cold. We've never hit it off, probably because he drinks too much, is anti-social and treats the models like they're an inconvenience, far beneath his consideration. He takes arrogance to a whole new level. He's never met either Emma or Megan... and I'm really not looking forward to this evening.

As usual, he's only just about bothered to dress appropriately. They have a dress code in this hotel, so Alec being Alec, he wears the required tie, but it's half way down his chest, and the top two buttons of his shirt are undone. He's only got to do this once on the whole goddamn trip – is it too much to ask? *Clearly*.

"Alec," I reply. "Nice of you to dress."

"There's no food on the planet that's worth getting dressed up to eat," he says.

It dawns on me that Megan might not have brought anything suitable to wear for a place like this. If no-one warned her, she probably wouldn't have realized we'd be staying in one of the most exclusive hotels in Paris... Suddenly my tie feels a little tighter.

Alec sits and, when the waiter comes over, orders a whiskey with ice. He's starting as he means to go on.

"What's she like then?" he asks.

"Who?" I know exactly who he's talking about.

"The model." He gives me a mocking smile.

"You mean Megan."

"Little Miss Megan." His tone matches his smile. "What's she like?"

"You'll see for yourself in a minute."

"Trouble, no doubt. They usually are the first time they work with me."

"If you could—" I stop talking. Emma and Megan have just walked through the large arched doorway. I think I've mentioned already that Megan is the most beautiful woman I've ever seen. Well, I was wrong... She's way, way beyond that. Her mane of hair has been tamed and put up, with just a few stray strands framing her perfect face, and now I can see her long neck, I want to kiss it even more. She's wearing just a little makeup, but the pale gloss on her lips makes them seem even fuller. And I needn't have worried about what she'd be wearing either. Her dress is one-shouldered, black and floor length, and at the sight of her in it, my mouth goes dry. The bodice is moulded to her, then it cinches in at her neat waist, and the flowing skirt has a split, coming to half-way up her thigh.

Alec looks at me, then turns to see what has grabbed my attention.

"Is that her?" he asks, turning back quickly.

"Yes," I reply.

"Not bad, I suppose," he says. "She looks fidgety, though."

Megan and Emma have arrived at the table and I stand. Alec doesn't.

Emma's wearing a dress. It's blue, maybe, with lace on it somewhere, I think, but I'm not really interested. She could be wearing just her underwear… hell, she could be wearing nothing at all. I couldn't care less. I can't take my eyes away from Megan, who's staring at my chest. I don't know why she's suddenly gone shy. Maybe Alec's making her nervous.

"Would you like to sit down, Megan?" Emma asks after the silence between us has stretched for a little too long.

"Sorry," I manage to say and stand to one side so they can sit. Megan is next to me, opposite Alec, and Emma is across from me. I make the introductions.

"It's nice to finally meet you," Emma says to Alec with as much sincerity as she can muster. His reputation precedes him.

"No, it isn't," he responds. "I know everyone thinks I'm a shit… They're right. But I get results."

Emma doesn't know how to reply, but luckily the waiter arrives.

Emma asks for a dry white wine, Megan a mineral water. Alec orders another whiskey. *Oh good.*

As it's warm, we're sitting on the roof terrace for dinner, with a magnificent view over Paris. Megan's face when they showed us out here to our table, was something I'll never forget. Her eyes widened, her lips parted in a soft gasp and she smiled. It was the kind of smile a man can only dream of inspiring. "It's beautiful," she breathed, as the waiter held her chair for her.

The sky is streaked in various shades of pink and orange as the sun sets behind us. The Eiffel Tower dominates the Paris skyline and I take in the view before me, seeing it properly for the first time, as she is.

The menus are on the table in front of us, a candle in a hurricane lamp lit in the centre and I wish she and I were here alone, and I could tell her how beautiful she is, how she belongs here in this setting; that Paris and candlelight and her are just perfect together. But I can't. I've never said anything like that to a woman before; I wouldn't know where to start. So I open the menu instead.

It's in French, obviously, and I glance at Megan, who's sitting next to me. She studies the words in front of her, then looks up at me, our eyes meeting. I raise an eyebrow, but I don't want to embarrass her by asking if she needs help.

"Don't tell me... you haven't a clue what it all means," Alec says, a smile crossing his lips. Megan flushes.

"And you're a genius, I suppose?" I reply.

"I can understand spoken French; I can speak it well enough to order from a goddamn menu; I can buy a drink. What more do I need?"

"I can think of a few things..." Emma whispers under her breath, loud enough for everyone to hear. I smirk. "Would you mind translating the menu, Luke? I don't understand all of it myself." I glance at Emma and she winks just quickly. I've always got on okay with her, but I don't think I've ever liked her as much I do right now.

"Sure," I reply and Alec lets out a deep sigh as I start reading through the items on the menu.

Once everyone has decided what they want, I call the waiter over and give our order, and ask him to bring a bottle of Meursault. Alec orders yet another whiskey, which is his third that I know of.

"So, what's the plan?" he asks.

Emma turns to him. "We're leaving at nine tomorrow morning," she says. "Our first destination is Vallon Pont D'Arc."

"And what's there?" he asks.

"It's a river, with a beach and a natural rock archway, forming a bridge."

"How long do you think it will take to get there?" I ask her.

"About seven hours."

"Seven hours?" Alec is stunned.

"Yes. It's in the south, just to the north of Nimes."

"Can't we fly there?" Alec asks.

"No. We've got an RV," Emma says patiently. "We'll need it on location for Megan to change in. It'll be useful."

"We're not expected to stay in it, are we?"

"No. We're booked into either hotels, or villas at each destination. The first one is a villa, about a half mile from the river. The RV is just for transport and on location."

"Well, I'm not traveling around the French countryside in an RV," he says.

"Somehow I thought you might say that," I tell him. "I got Grace to organize you a separate car, so you'll have your own vehicle." Actually, the way I put it to Grace was that I didn't really want Alec traveling in the RV with the rest of us, not for three weeks.

"What did she get me?" he asks.

"I've got no idea. Grace dealt with it. I think it's probably a standard rental car. If you want anything different, feel free to change it up, but it comes out of your budget, Alec, not ours."

He scowls at me, but I glare back. And he knows I'll win.

Megan has sat in silence throughout the whole of this conversation. As our first courses arrive, I lean over to her. "Are you okay with the arrangements?" I ask. She turns and smiles.

"Yes," she whispers. "It all sounds fine."

By the time we've finished our main courses, it's dark, and the Eiffel Tower is now lit up, and dazzling. It's so close you almost feel you could lean over the railing and touch it. Megan is staring at it, the lights reflected in her eyes.

"Who have you worked for in the past?" Alec asks her, his words now slurred. I should have seen this coming.

"Sorry?" she says, dragging her eyes from the view and turning to him.

He repeats the question and Megan looks down at her empty plate, moving her knife and fork slightly.

"Megan hasn't done any modeling work before," I say.

"For fuck's sake," Alec replies, loud enough that the people sitting either side of us turn to look. "This is going to be a hard enough shoot as it is. I don't have time for this shit."

"Then you'll make time," I say, my voice firm. "It's what Matt wants."

"Then Matt should have damn well run it by me first."

"Matt doesn't have to get your permission to do anything, Alec. Remember that."

He stares at me.

"Well, she'd better do as she's told," he huffs.

I'm past being fed up with him now. "Alec," I say quietly, so the other diners won't hear me, "are you still sober enough to remember telling us you understood spoken French?"

"Yeah. Of course I am."

"Eh bien, va donc te faire foutre et laissez-nous tranquilles," I tell him, my voice low, my eyes fixed on his.

I can see him thinking, translating in his head for a moment, then – to my surprise – he just stands and walks away.

Emma turns to me, her mouth open. "Wow. What on earth did you just say to him?" she asks.

"I told him to go away and leave us alone… except I didn't exactly use the words 'go' or 'away'." The corners of her mouth twitch up, and then she starts to laugh. I turn to Megan and she's giggling, her hand over her mouth and soon I join in.

Megan

It's ridiculous how much mess I've managed to make in just one day, although to be fair, some of that is from breakfast, which was delivered an hour ago. The croissants were perfect, light and fluffy, and the coffee was strong, which woke me up, fortunately. After my shower, I let my hair dry naturally while I gather all my things together, including the black dress I wore last night, that I left draped over the back of the cream sofa at the end of my bed. I'm so glad I brought it with me, and the plum colored one as well. They're not new, but they're smartest dresses I have. I talked it over with Erin and she agreed it would be foolish to come to Paris and not bring something a little stylish, just in case.

When Emma knocked on my door and I saw her in her beautiful blue dress, I was so relieved I'd made the effort. She was very kind, and complimented my outfit, although it was nowhere near as pretty as hers. Still, I felt a lot less self-conscious as we walked downstairs together. That was, until we reached the bar and I saw Luke, wearing a suit. I thought he looked good in jeans and a t-shirt – and he does – but in a suit, he's jaw-dropping. I know I was staring at the way his shirt fitted across his chest, but I couldn't help it.

The evening itself was horrible, except the food, the view, and Luke, who was kind and thoughtful. And he put Alec in his place perfectly, and once he'd gone, we had a much nicer time. I haven't laughed so much in ages; but then I guess I haven't had much to laugh about.

As for Alec, I really don't like him and I've got no idea how this modeling thing is going to work with him giving out the orders in the way he does. I don't respond well to men like that. They tend to make me even more introverted than I already am, which I imagine won't be helpful.

He's the most conceited man I've ever come across. I'm sure some women would find him attractive, but he's like the darkness to Luke's light. His long brown hair hits his collar at the back and flops across his forehead. He has brooding dark brown eyes, and an almost permanent scowl. I guess he's around forty, maybe a little older, but it's hard to tell with people who drink. And he drinks – a lot. And that's another thing that's never going to help where I'm concerned. I don't like men who drink to excess. A glass or two of wine is fine, but not hard liquor… I know the damage it can do, and not just to the person who's drinking it.

Now, as I wander around the hotel room, checking I've not left anything behind, I don't know how to tell Luke that I'm wary – well, scared – of Alec. But maybe I'll get the chance to talk to Emma during the journey to this river beach, and I can ask if she'll speak to Luke for me.

Downstairs, Luke is waiting in the lobby. There's no sign of Emma, or Alec.

"Hi," he says, as I walk over to him. He's back in jeans and a t-shirt today, and every woman in the place is staring. He seems oblivious, but he can't be. He must know the effect he has. "Did you sleep okay?" he asks.

"Yes, thanks."

"You'll be pleased to hear, Alec's already left," he smirks. "He went about an hour ago, so you won't need to see him again until we get there."

I smile up at him. "Am I that obvious?"

"Yes. But don't worry about it. I don't like him either."

I laugh.

"Now we just need Emma," he continues. "Why don't we go outside and get our things loaded up?" I nod my head and he leads the way toward the main entrance.

Parked right outside is a large RV, and standing alongside it is the man who handed the car over to Luke at the airport yesterday morning.

"Megan," he says. "This is Michel. He'll be our driver."

"Oh… You won't be driving then?"

"This thing?" He looks at the big home on wheels. "No. Besides, I can work in the back, or sleep, or…" He stops talking all of a sudden.

Michel steps forward.

"It is pleasure to meet you," he says in broken English, holding out his hand. I shake it and smile at him. He's probably a few years older than Luke, with dark, almost black hair, and a really kind smile, that reaches his deep brown eyes. He takes my suitcase and stows it in the RV. Luke deals with his own, then we stand for a few minutes, and Michel tells me that the weather is due to be hot, and that his wife is not happy. She's pregnant and feeling the heat.

"You're leaving her for three weeks when she's pregnant?" I say, surprised.

"Oh yes," he replies. "Sophie has two months still… And she very moody. I better off away from her. Much safer." He grins. "Non, sérieusement, she go stay with her mother in the south. She hate Paris when it hot."

"Yeah and what he's not telling you," Luke says, "is that one of the locations we're going to is close to his mother-in-law's place… and he'll be sneaking off there for a couple of days, won't you?" Luke nudges Michel, who shrugs. Luke translates his sentence into French and Michel laughs.

"Mais bien sûr." He winks at Luke.

"Where the hell is Emma?" Luke says, checking his watch. "We were meant to leave ten minutes ago." He takes his phone from his back pocket and finds her details, waiting for the call to connect. "Great… straight to voicemail."

"Do you think one of us…?" I say.

"I'll go," he replies. "You wait here with Michel."

He turns and strides back into the hotel and I stand awkwardly with Michel for a moment.

"Is this your first child?" I ask him slowly, so he'll understand.

"Oui," he replies, nodding his head. "We try for long time. Nearly give up, and then…" His smile becomes a grin and his eyes light up again.

I smile back at him. "Do you know if it's a boy, or a girl?" I ask. His excitement is infectious.

"A girl," he says and his face softens. "We call her Eve. It was the name of my mother." A shadow crosses his face and I don't like to ask the obvious question about his own mother. Instead, I'm about to ask where his mother-in-law lives, when I feel someone tap on my shoulder and I spin around, expecting to see either Luke or Emma. Instead, I'm greeted by one of the female receptionists, all blonde and perfect.

"Excuse me," she says in English. "Are you Mademoiselle Ford?"

"Yes," I reply.

"Monsieur Myers needs you to go upstairs to room 312."

"Emma's room?" I say. I look at Michel.

"Go," he says. "I wait."

I follow the receptionist back into the hotel and make my way to the elevators.

Once upstairs, I go straight to Emma's room and am surprised to find the door partially open. I peer inside.

"Hello?" I say, a little hesitant.

"Megan?" Luke calls. "Come in here, can you?" I push the door open a little further.

I don't know what I'd expected, but this wasn't it. Sat on the bed, wearing pale blue pajamas, is Emma. She's nestled in Luke's arms and he's cradling her, rocking her. He looks up at me, with an entreating, kind of helpless expression on his face. I stand still for a moment, not really knowing what to do; what he wants of me.

"There's been an accident," he says. "Emma's husband, Nate… He's a firefighter back home. There was a fire in an apartment block. I don't know the details, but he's in hospital." He tries to pull away from her, but she clings onto him, her shoulders shaking. "Can you take over here for a minute, while I make some arrangements."

"Of course," I say, feeling a little shocked at the news, and I walk across the room and stand in front of them. He pulls away from Emma, despite her reluctance to let him go, then he twists and holds her firmly by the shoulders, looking down at her.

"I'll get you home to him," he says, "I promise. Just sit with Megan for a few minutes." She nods her head, and he gets up. I take his place and put my arm around her shoulder. She sobs again, as I watch Luke walk to the window, and take out his phone. He scrolls back and forth on his screen then dials a number.

"Hi," he says. "I wonder if you can help me. I need to book a ticket on the Delta flight to Boston, leaving at three thirty this afternoon." He waits. "That's fine. No, I don't care if it's first class." He waits again. "No, it's one way." There's another pause. "The name on the ticket will be Emma Conway." Emma shifts on the bed and I take my eyes and mind away from Luke for a few minutes.

"I need to get dressed," she whispers.

"We'll do that in a minute," I murmur. "I'll help you."

"Wait a second," Luke says and gets his wallet from his back pocket. He pulls out a credit card and reads the number into the phone. "No, it's a personal card," he says. "It's in my name, Mr L. Myers… Okay, I'll hold." He turns and glances across at us, raising an eyebrow as though to ask if everything's okay. I nod my head. He replaces the credit card in his wallet. "Thanks," he says into the phone. "And the ticket will be at the desk? That's great. Thanks for your help." He ends the call, then checks his watch, muttering, "It's too early." It must be nearly ten by now, so I'm not sure what he means by that.

He comes back over to the bed. "We've got an hour – just over – to get Emma dressed and ready," he says. "She needs to be at the airport by twelve thirty."

"I can't…" she says. "I can't handle it… I mean, I don't even speak French… not very well…"

"It's okay," he says soothingly. "I'll come with you." He sits down on the other side of her. "I'll take you to the airport and check you in. And I'll call Matt and arrange to have someone meet you at Logan and take you to the hospital."

"But I don't even know which hospital, Luke. I forgot to ask," she wails.

"Em, don't worry. Matt will find out." She stares at him and nods her head. "Do you want to shower?" he asks.

"You'll feel better if you do," I say to her.

"Okay," she murmurs. Luke gets up again.

"I'll go downstairs and tell Michel what's going on," he says. As Emma starts toward the bathroom, he takes hold of my arm. "I'm sorry about this." He looks concerned. "Can you stay and help her?"

"Of course," I tell him.

"Thanks, Megan." He stares at me for a moment, then leaves the room, closing the door softly behind him.

Within an hour, Emma's showered and I've packed her bag. We're sitting on the bed again when Luke returns.

"All set?" he asks, once I've let him into the room.

"Yes," I reply. Emma doesn't really respond, or even seem to notice he's there. He motions with his head that I should join him by the window and we walk over there together.

"Michel has taken the RV away for the time being," he whispers. "We can't just leave it parked outside indefinitely. I'll call him when I'm on my way back from the airport and he'll come back and collect us. I'm really sorry, Megan... Will you be okay here while I take Emma to the airport?"

"Of course. I'll sit downstairs in the lounge and read."

"You could come with us, if you want?" he offers.

"No," I say, "I don't really know Emma. I think she'd be better off with just you; that way you can concentrate on looking after her, not be worrying about me."

"I'll still be——" He stops talking, coughs and runs his fingers through his hair. Instinctively, I reach out and put my hand on his arm.

"Are you okay?" I ask.

"Me?" he says, seeming surprised by my question. "Yeah, I'm good."

"You sure?"

"Yeah. We'll be very late getting to the villa tonight."

"That doesn't matter."

"I'd better call Alec," he says. He checks his watch again. "We should be going. Are you sure you'll be alright here?"

"Yes."

"I'll be back as soon as I can. I guess we'll be able to leave around two?"

"It'll be fine," I tell him.

It's just after one-thirty when Luke gets back. I've spent the whole time reading and the people at the hotel have been very kind and kept me supplied with coffee. Luke explained the situation before he left and they couldn't have done more to help.

Still, I'm very relieved when he walks through the door of the lounge. He's obviously tired, but he smiles when I look up from my Kindle.

"Hello," I say to him as he walks across and stands in front of me.

"Hi."

"How did it go?"

"She's okay now. She's checked in and I think she felt better knowing she's on her way home." He's clutching a folder. "She's left me with all her notes," he explains.

"Are we leaving now then?"

"Yes, Michel's waiting outside. You all set?"

"Yes." I grab my bag and put my Kindle inside. When I look back up, he's holding out his free hand and I take it, letting him pull me to my feet. We don't start walking straight away though. Instead he looks down at me, still holding my hand.

"Thanks for everything you did this morning," he says.

"But I didn't do anything," I reply. "I think you'll find that was all you."

"I didn't do anything much either," he says and we start to walk slowly out of the lounge, into the lobby.

"If that's your idea of not doing anything, then I'd love to really see you in action." I hear him stifle a laugh. "What?" I ask. "What's funny?"

"Nothing." I look up at his face and he's still struggling not to laugh.

"No, tell me." I want to know now. "What did I say?"

"Really, it's nothing, Megan." We get to the door and he holds it open for me. As I pass through, he pulls me back and leans in toward me. "Except, let's just say it's mutual."

What's mutual? What does that mean?

We've been on the road for nearly half an hour. The RV is really comfortable. Michel is up front by himself, driving us south, out of Paris. Above the cab is a double bed and at the back of the vehicle are two bunks. Behind me is the bathroom, with a small shower and opposite that is the tiny kitchen. The space where we're sitting converts into another bed at night, if required. Luke's spread out Emma's notes on the table between us and is looking at them. I'm holding my Kindle, pretending to read, but really, I'm just staring at him. I can't help it. He's too beautiful not to stare at.

He lets out a sigh, looking up from Emma's notes and checking his watch. "Okay," he mutters to himself. "It should be safe to call him now."

I've got no idea who or what he's talking about. He picks up his phone from the table, presses a few buttons and holds it to his ear. There's a delay and then he says, "Take your time, Matt."

Ah, it's his boss... and mine for the moment, I suppose. He doesn't talk to him like a boss, though.

"I know it is, but I could have called you four hours ago, so be grateful." He waits. "Hmm. I believe you. Look, I need to talk to you... No, this is serious. I've had to put Emma on a flight back to Boston." There's another pause. "Of course not. Just listen, will you? She got a call from Nate's boss. He's been in an accident." Again there's a delay. "I don't know. She was too upset to get the details. I'm sure the guy told her, but she wasn't listening... Well, you don't, do you? Anyway, I got her a ticket home and she'll be taking off in an hour or so." He waits again. "No, Matt, I took her to the damn airport myself. I checked her in… I spoke to them and asked if they'd keep an eye on her during the flight. Short of flying back with her, I don't—" He hesitates. "She made me leave, because I'd abandoned Megan at the hotel by herself. What was I supposed to do?" He looks out the window. "That's okay… don't worry about it," he says. "I'm really calling because you need to get someone to meet her at the airport… Yeah, I thought you would. She's on the Delta flight, landing at Logan at five-fifteen. I'll text you the flight number. The problem is, we don't know where Nate is. Emma didn't get the details of that either… Can you…?" He listens for a minute. "Good. I told her that's what you'd do."

I turn in my seat, putting my feet up and bending my knees. When I look back, Luke is staring at me. "No, Matt, I haven't. Goddammit, I know the rule." His voice is harsher than before. He waits a little longer this time, taking a few deep breaths. When he speaks again, his voice is calmer. "I did think of that myself, believe it or not, but I haven't asked her yet. Hang on." He lowers his phone. "I've got to ask you a question," he says to me. "We need to know if you'd like us to fly someone else out… another woman. We can find someone from the company, or it can be a friend of yours, if you prefer… so you've got someone here with you." I gaze at him; his eyes are an even softer blue than usual, their intensity is breathtaking, mesmerizing.

"No, I'm fine," I tell him, going with my instinct. He continues to stare at me just for a second, his lips quirking upwards, just a fraction, then he lifts his phone again.

"Did you hear that?" he says. "Right. Yes, I'll remember. Give it a rest, will you, Matt?" He sounds weary now. He shifts in his seat, running his fingertip along the edge of the table. "Okay," he says. "I need to speak to Grace later… I'll have to run through Emma's notes, so I know what I'm doing. I might need Grace to e-mail me her layouts too." Matt says something. "Tell her I'll call when we're settled at the villa; probably around five, your time… Yeah, I guess she could e-mail them across anyway. It can't hurt."

He leans forward, his elbows resting on the table, his face down. "Can you do me a favor?" he asks. "Can you get Grace to check in with Will for me? We argued a while ago; we didn't really get around to making up properly before I left. I just want to know he's okay." *Who's Will...?* Luke's clearly very attached to him. He seems upset about their argument... I wonder... I think about how awkward he seemed when he was comforting Emma; all the beautiful women who've been falling over themselves to get to him, and he's not gone after any of them... Might he be gay? It's possible, I suppose. It doesn't make him any less beautiful to look at, but it might just make my life a little easier. I can look, I can admire, but there's no danger of it going anywhere, or him having any expectations... Yeah, that really does sound much easier.

He's talking again and his shoulders drop. "Yeah, I know I could call him myself, Matt, but he'll just tell me he's fine. You know what he's like. He'll probably talk to Grace, though." He waits. "Thanks," he says. "Make sure you look after Emma when you pick her up. She's in a bad place..." He pauses, then smiles. "Sure. Yeah, I will. Bye, Matt." He hangs up the call and drops his phone on the table, leaning back and resting his head on the seat behind him.

With his eyes closed, he looks like he has the weight of the world on his shoulders. I wish I could do something to help... even if it's just holding his hand. But then he'd probably rather hold Will's hand than mine. Considering him being gay makes my life so much simpler, it's weird that I should feel quite so disappointed by that thought...

Chapter Four

Luke

I don't usually like to think too deeply. That's a lesson I learned a long time ago: if you don't think about things, eventually they take on less significance and after a while, you can even pretend you've forgotten them altogether. As a philosophy, that's always worked for me in the past, but obviously not this time, because over the last couple of hours, I've done nothing but think. I'm still not entirely certain about the outcome of my thoughts, and neither am I comfortable with them, but the fact that I've had some suggests I needed to. I think I needed to admit to myself that something's different this time – even if I don't know what it is yet.

On the way back to the hotel from the airport, I realized that I've shut down every single woman I've come into contact with since meeting Megan – including the one who checked in Emma's bag at the airport this morning, who kept leaning forward, revealing the top of a black lacy bra and her overflowing breasts, and then passed me a scrap of paper with her cell number written on it. I threw it in the trash on my way back to the cab. When would I normally have passed up a chance like that?

I've been feeling real weird about Megan since the moment we first met. Normally, when I find a woman attractive, assuming she's interested, I just make a move – or they do. I don't have much in the way of conversation with them; I don't want to know their background, or what they like and don't like. I just want to get them into bed – or at least get them undressed and bury myself inside them, as fast as possible. The bed isn't strictly necessary… come to that, neither is the undressing.

With Megan, it's completely different. I want to know more. I want to know everything. I can't say, 'I don't know when I've ever felt like this,' because I know I never have. Ever.

Matt's warned me off again. But this time it made me a little mad, and he knew it. He apologized. Don't get me wrong, nothing's changed since yesterday; I still want Megan, pretty much like I want to take my next breath. I know I'm still going to need a cold shower probably every twenty minutes, once we start this shoot. And I really want to get her naked, to see all of her, to feel her, touch her, taste her, and yeah, to bury myself deep inside her. But there's something different now; after spending some time with her, watching the way she reacted when she saw the Paris skyline, laughing with her after dinner, seeing her with Emma this morning, I know I'd also like to just to go for long walks with her, hold her hand, talk to her, and laugh with her, listen to her stories, and even tell her mine.

I look across the table at her. She's sitting with her back against the window, her feet on the seat, her knees bent, and she's reading her Kindle. I've been pretending to work since we stopped for a late lunch a couple of hours ago, but I keep wondering what she's reading, where she went to college, what she studied, what she wants to do next. I want to know how it is her eyes sparkle quite so much when she smiles, how her laugh can be so sexy, what that furrow above her nose would be like to kiss… and why I get this feeling in the pit of my stomach, kind of like I'm melting, whenever she looks at me. I shake my head.

Like I said, I'm still not entirely comfortable with my thoughts.

We're just outside Lyon and it's a little after six in the evening. It's dawned on me that, by the time we get to the villa, it'll probably be too late to eat out, or go shopping for food. According to Emma's notes, the village is small; there may not be anywhere open.

"Michel? Can you find us a supermarket?" I call to him in French.

"Okay," he replies.

"Did that mean 'supermarket'?" Megan looks up from her Kindle, lowers her feet and turns to face me.

"Yeah. We're going to need supplies. You can bet your life Alec will be sitting by the pool, and if he's been to buy anything, it will consist entirely of whiskey." I notice her wince. "What's wrong?" I say.

"It's nothing… But… well, he does drink a lot, doesn't he?"

"Yes." I move my hand across the table, toward her, part of me wishing she'd take hold of it like she did at the hotel. She doesn't. "Don't worry about him," I say.

She smiles at me and I melt, just a little bit more. I expect the melting feeling to bother me. It doesn't – and that bothers me.

"Did you say 'pool'?" Megan asks, looking concerned.

"Yeah. All the villas we're staying in have pools. Why? Is that a problem?" I can't think why it would be. I can't think of anything better than relaxing in the pool after a hot day, but…

"I didn't bring a swim suit."

I smile. "We can pick you something up, if you like," I tell her, although there's part of me wanting to tell her not to worry; she can go without as far as I'm concerned… *I didn't say I was a saint, just that I'm interested in more than her gorgeous body*. "The supermarket will sell them."

"Oh." She still looks worried, but she turns and looks out the window. She's frowning. There's that furrow above her nose again. Her fingers are fidgety, almost like she's counting something out… Oh, I get it. *Been there, done that.*

Before Matt gave me a break, I had to watch every cent, and even then they used to run out on me, especially when Will was in college and I wasn't earning much. Those were tough days. Without Matt, I don't know where we'd have ended up.

I want to tell her I'll pay, but I don't. I'll just deal with it in the supermarket. She can't argue there.

"The supermarket," Michel announces, turning the RV into a parking lot. It's a massive store and, once he's parked up, I open the door and jump out, then turn. Just like at the hotel, Megan takes my hand and I help her down, then I close the door. I don't release her and she doesn't try to let go of me. Michel comes around to our side and glances down at our joined hands, then up at me. I just look at him and he shrugs, then we start walking toward the entrance.

Inside, Michel disappears to use the men's room and to get a coffee. I grab a cart and, with Megan at my side, we set off. The store is split in half. To our left are the clothes, household goods, and electrical items and I tell her to go find whatever she wants.

"But…" she begins.

"Just find a swim suit," I tell her. "And anything else you forgot to bring."

"I can't," she says, and her voice catches. I move a little closer.

"Yeah, you can, Megan. I do get it. Don't worry about the money, okay? Call it a thank you for helping out this morning. I'll be back in a while."

I leave her there and move quickly around the store. I hate grocery shopping, but it's a necessary evil. I pick up enough for four, for a couple of days. I remember reading that there's a barbecue at this place, so I get some meat, some salad, bread, fruit and cheese – we're in France, after all – and cereals and milk for breakfast. It's not a banquet, but it'll do. Then I head for the wines and grab a few bottles, before making my way back to where I left Megan.

To my surprise, she's still not picked up anything, even though I've probably been gone for about twenty minutes, if not a little longer.

"What's wrong?" I ask her. "Isn't there anything you like?"

"It's not that," she says. "I can't understand the sizing." She holds up a bright blue bikini that makes me salivate. "I'm not sure this is right." I look at it. It's not right.

I grin at her. "I can help with that." She looks at me, her eyes full of confusion. "Remember me? The guy who works in… clothing…" I say, choosing my words carefully. I can't say the word 'lingerie' to her right now; it puts all kinds of images in my head. The reality will be there soon enough... I run my eyes slowly over her body, even though I don't really need to. She's etched in my memory already, but it's nice to have an excuse to look. Then I lean into her and lower my voice a little. "I'm guessing you're a size four?" Her mouth opens.

"How do you know that?" she asks.

"It's what I do." I smile down at her. "So, am I right?"

"Yes," she says.

"Okay, well in Europe, a size four is a thirty-four..." I have to know this stuff: the European buyers expect it. I start looking through the racks and find the same bright blue bikini in the right size. "There you go." I hand it to her, then find another, this time in yellow, and another, in black. I don't take the white one. It'd probably kill me to see her step out of the pool in that.

At the end of the aisle are some kimonos. I stroll along to take a look. They're nothing like as nice as the ones we produce, but a couple of them will be practical, and may just stop me from having a heart attack. I grab two and hand them to her: one matching the blue bikini; the other a white one with yellow flowers around the hem.

"There," I say. "Is that enough?"

"It's too much," she replies.

"Do you like them?" I ask. "I mean they're not designer labels, but they'll do for the next couple of weeks, won't they?"

"Do? They're lovely, Luke," she sighs. *Oh, Megan... They're nothing compared to what I'd like to give you.*

"Okay, let's go." I start to walk away, then realize she's not with me. I turn, and she's still standing there, looking after me. I walk backwards, dragging the cart, and come to a stop once I reach her.

"What?" I say. Why's she being so difficult? I've never been shopping with a woman and I think I'm starting to understand why now.

"I can't take them," she says.

I let go of the cart and turn to her. She's hugging the clothes to her chest, like a child and my instinct is to mirror her; to pull her into me and hold her tight. Instead, I put my hands on her shoulders. "Look at me," I say, and she does. "I want to buy you these, okay?"

"But…"

Without thinking, I put my finger on her lips. The sensation reverberates straight to my cock and I put my hand back on her shoulder again. It's slightly safer there. "I couldn't have managed this morning without you," I say. "So, let me buy you these as a thank you."

"You don't have to thank me," she replies.

"Well, I want to. So let me." I stare at her. "Please," I add when she still doesn't react.

"Okay," she says and I let her go – reluctantly.

"Good. Can we go now?" I turn back to the cart.

She pauses and then laughs for a moment, and we start walking to the front of the store.

"Thank you," she whispers, leaning into me.

"You're welcome." I lean back into her and let my head rest on hers, just for a second.

It's nearly nine by the time we get to the villa.

Michel pulls the RV up outside and we all climb out, stretching our tired bodies. It's still just about daylight outside and, while Michel unloads the bags, I open the front door, switching on the light on the way in. Megan follows me into the spacious villa and we look around. It's essentially one big room, with the kitchen area on the far side, a large table and chairs, and an L-shaped couch. The left hand wall is made of glass panels, and overlooks the pool. I can see Alec is out there, lying on a sun bed, with a bottle of whiskey on the ground beside him. For the time being, we ignore him. To our right are two doors, and there's a set of stairs ahead of us. The two doors are to a bedroom and bathroom. Megan and I go upstairs to find three further bedrooms, two of which have their own bathrooms. Alec seems to have set himself up in one of these, so I suggest to Megan that she takes the other – it's for my benefit as much as hers. She won't have to wander around the villa semi-naked. Michel will take the downstairs bedroom, leaving me with the one next to Megan's.

Michel has brought in all the bags and, once we've put them in the respective rooms, we unpack the shopping and put everything away.

"I bought some steaks for tonight," I tell Megan. "I was going to barbecue them, but it'll take too long to heat up."

"We can just cook in here, can't we?" she says.

"Yeah. If I do that, can you make a salad?"

"Of course." She grabs a few ingredients from the refrigerator and starts chopping. She seems quite contented working in the small kitchen. Neither of us has mentioned Alec yet. I pull out the four steaks, heat the pan on the stove and add some butter, oil and garlic. While it's heating, I go to the glass door and open it.

"Do you want to have something to eat with us?" I ask him.

"What are you having?" he replies.

"Steak, salad, bread, cheese."

"Okay." That's a shame.

"Ten minutes," I tell him and close the door again.

When I get back to the kitchen, I notice that Megan isn't quite as happy. I guess she overheard my conversation with Alec. "Sorry," I say to her, as I add the first of the steaks to the pan. It sizzles and I turn down the heat.

"It's fine. I can't avoid him forever, can I?"

"You mustn't worry about him."

"That's easy for you to say," she says. "I'm the one who's got to work with him."

"I will be there, Megan." I turn to face her. "You won't be alone. You know that, don't you?"

She nods her head and I get the feeling that she could easily cry… I've never handled emotional women very well – this morning's episode with Emma was evidence of that – but every instinct I have is telling me to hold her… This is going beyond weird now.

"The salad looks good," I say, changing the subject.

"Thanks."

Michel comes in from the RV. "Dinner smell good." He sniffs the air.

"That's because there's garlic in it."

The steak is good, as is the salad. Alec doesn't say much, thank God. When we've all finished, Megan fetches the cheese for us to have with the remainder of the bread.

"I went to take a look at the location earlier," Alec says. I'm surprised he bothered. "You can walk there from here."

"Well, we could, if we didn't need the RV for Megan to change in." He ignores me.

"The light's very strong. I got there about three, and it was still too much. I think we need to try getting there really early in the morning; then if we don't get everything we need, we can finish off late in the afternoon."

"Okay. Well, I guess we can kick our heels at the lake, or come back here during the day, as it's so close. What time will we need to leave here?"

"Six."

"Six?" Megan asks.

"You got a problem with that?" he says, taking another swig of whiskey. He's drunk. Or at least too drunk to be civil.

"No," she says quietly, almost contracting in on herself.

"I think we should finish up, and get to bed." I want him away from her. Now.

"I'm going back outside," Alec announces and, getting to his feet, he staggers to the door.

"I'll clear the dishes," Megan says.

"I help." Michel gets up.

I've still got to call Grace. Once the table's cleared, I put my laptop out and open it, starting it up and going straight to my mail. Grace has sent me through her layouts as an attachment. I pick up my phone and call her.

"Hi," she says, answering after the second ring.

"Hi."

It's ten thirty here, so four thirty there.

"Matt's gone to the airport to collect Emma. We found out that Nathan's in Mass General, so he's going to take her straight there and I'm meeting them later."

"Okay. Can you let me know how he's doing?" I ask her about the designs and we talk through everything. "I'm worried I'll screw this up," I tell her. "I'm no designer."

"You'll be fine, Luke. There's nothing for you to worry about. Paul gave Alec a full briefing. He knows what to do. And follow Emma's notes and my drawings if you think he's going off on a tangent." He can do that sometimes. "If you're uncertain about anything, call me."

"I'm sure you'll appreciate that at midnight…"

"Midnight?"

"Yeah… We're leaving here at six tomorrow."

"Oh, for the light, I suppose."

"Yeah."

There's a moment's hesitation before she speaks again. "Are you okay, Luke?" she asks.

"I'm fine."

"Really? You don't sound fine."

"I've got a lot on my mind." I think I'd like to talk to her about Megan; explain some of it, ask her why I'm feeling like this, maybe get her perspective. I know Grace is a good listener; she's been great with Will, but if I told her how I'm feeling about Megan, she'd tell Matt and he'd probably fly over here and castrate me… then fire me. I'm acutely aware of Megan approaching. She stands near the table and I motion that she can sit if she wants. She takes the seat opposite mine and I hold her gaze. Considering what's going through my mind as I'm looking at her… yeah, Matt would definitely castrate me. "Have you been able to get hold of Will?" I ask Grace, partly because it's a welcome distraction from thinking about all the things I want to do to Megan, right here on this table, but also because I want to know.

"Yes. He's fine. I told him you were worried." Well, I guess she wasn't lying. "He said to tell you he's sorry for interfering." I smile. I wish he'd said that to me, not her. "I'm not sure what that meant, but he said you'd understand."

"He didn't interfere – not really. He just told me a few home truths. In a way I'm glad he did. They needed telling." She doesn't reply. "If you speak to him again, tell him I'm sorry too, can you?"

"You could speak to him yourself, Luke."

"Will and I have never been very good at that." Well, not for a long time, anyway.

"Okay. I'll tell him."

"Thanks, Grace."

We finish the call and I close down the laptop. When I look up, Megan is still staring at me.

"You'd better get some sleep," I say to her. "We've got an early start."

"I know." She's hesitating, like she wants to say something, but she doesn't. She gets up, then pushes the chair back under the table.

"Goodnight, Megan," I say as she starts walking away.

"Goodnight," she murmurs. I turn, but she's got her back to me. Her head's bowed and I see her lift her hand to her face. If I didn't know better, I'd think she was wiping away a tear... but that doesn't make sense. Why would she be crying?

Megan

I'm so glad I didn't actually cry in front of him. I did cry myself to sleep, but he'll never know that.

Yesterday was a very emotional day, I guess. Between the news of Emma's husband, the delay, the journey, the scene in the supermarket, getting here late and tired, Alec being a jerk – again... it was all a bit too much. And on top of all that, I'm even more convinced now that Luke is gay. He spoke so fondly of Will on the phone last night. I mean, it doesn't bother me if he is gay... obviously. Being gay isn't a problem. And really, it should be good news, because it makes my life much less complicated. In which case, why am I so upset? Why did that thought make me cry? It's ludicrous.

We arrive at the lake just after six-fifteen. The river is stunningly beautiful. Set in a low valley, the shallow meandering water is a blue-green, with a white shingle beach. To one end of this stretch, is the huge natural arch made of rock, forming the bridge between this side of the river and the other. The light is amazing, almost ethereal and Alec wants to get started as quickly as possible. He's already decided on the best locations and angles, so all I need to do is get changed. He runs me through what he expects while I'm still dressed, pulling me and pushing me around, making sure I know the right positions. There will be four shots required today, mainly on the beach, or just in the water. As we walk back toward the RV he tells me he'll need me to change quickly, so the light doesn't alter too much.

Luke comes out of the RV and walks over to us. He's wearing gray shorts and a white t-shirt, with canvas deck shoes. He still looks good... he has great legs. I don't want to think about that. There's no point in thinking about what you can't have... But then I couldn't have him even if he was straight, so why am I worrying about it? Besides, I need to concentrate on getting the job done and not annoying Alec. I really don't think I could handle any more of his comments today... and the last thing I need is to cry in front of him. He'd never let me forget it.

"I've had a text from Matt," Luke says to both of us. "He sent it last night. Nate's got a back injury and concussion."

"Will he be okay?" I ask.

"They're hopeful. It's early days..." He pauses for a minute. "I've laid out all the garments on the bottom bunk," he says to me. "And there's a robe for you to wear when you come back out." He swallows. "Then I'll take it off you at the last minute, when Alec's ready." He turns to Alec. "What's up first?"

"We're doing Smokey Quartz today, aren't we?" he asks.

Luke nods his head. It seems like an odd name for sportswear, but what do I know?

Alec thinks for a moment. "We'll start with the bra and thong," he says.

What the hell? I turn. "I'm sorry... What?" I say, my voice quite loud.

"The bra and thong," he repeats, enunciating each word like I'm hard of hearing.

"I heard what you said... I just..." I instinctively fold my arms across my chest.

Luke comes and stands in front of me.

"What's the matter?" he asks, his face filled with concern.

"That's... that's not sportswear," I say.

"No." He sounds confused. "Were you expecting to be modeling sportswear?"

"Yes, that's what they told me."

His light blue eyes darken and I pull away from him. "Hey," he says. "It's not your fault. Come with me." He holds out his hand and waits for me to take it. I feel like he's safe to be around, so I put my hand in his, letting him lead me toward the RV.

"Can we hurry up, for fuck's sake," Alec shouts.

"Shut up, Alec," Luke yells over his shoulder.

Once we're inside, Luke closes the door, then turns to face me. We're standing just a few feet apart.

"I'm sorry," he says. "The agency were told."

"But I'd never have taken the job if I'd known."

"I wasn't involved, but I'm guessing Matt chose you and they didn't want to risk losing the fee by letting you know what you'd be modeling." He takes a step back, running his fingers through his hair. "I don't know what we're going to do," he says. "Everything's set up."

I sit down at the table. I can see his predicament, but how can I do this? It's not so much that I mind for myself – it's not that different to wearing a bikini, not really – but if my dad ever found out...

"What are we talking about?" I ask him. "Is this every-day underwear, like you see in catalogues?"

"Um... no. Let me show you."

He goes to the back of the vehicle and returns a few moments later, carrying a bra. He places it on the table in front of me. It's beautiful, dark gray fishnet with light gray flowers around the top of the cups, and in the center of each flower is a red crystal. I touch the fabric and can't help but gasp, just slightly. It's the softest thing I've ever felt.

"Can I ask how much this costs?" I ask. It'll give me a clue.

"Sure. It retails at seven hundred and fifty dollars."

I choke. "Seriously? Just for the bra?"

"Yeah."

Okay, so there's absolutely no chance of my dad ever coming across this kind of lingerie. Ever. And I really need the money from this job... If I go to visit him next month with nothing, it won't be pretty. He'll want to know what I've been doing since leaving college... How bad can this be? I think of the bikinis Luke bought me yesterday. They had less fabric to them than this bra... And I wouldn't have worried about wearing those in front of him.

What's the matter with me? Why am I even concerned about what he'll think? He's more interested in the product than what's inside it.

"Okay, I'll do it," I whisper.

He sits opposite me. "Are you sure?" he says. "If you don't want to..."

I look up at him and find myself staring into his dazzling eyes. "W-what? What can you do?" I stammer.

"Well, nothing to be honest," he shrugs, "but equally, I can't make you do this either."

"You're not *making* me."

He reaches across the table and captures my shaking hands. "Megan. Don't do this if you feel uncomfortable about it."

"It's fine." I swallow hard. It is fine. He'll be oblivious to my near nudity; Alec's only interested in the angle, the lighting, the shot; Michel's gone for a walk. There's no-one else here. What does it matter? What does any of it matter? I pull my hands back and put them in my lap. I can feel the tears stinging behind my eyes again and I wish he'd just go away.

As though he's read my mind, he gets to his feet. "I'll let you get changed," he mutters and, without another word, he leaves quickly, closing the door behind him.

I go to the back of the RV, taking the bra with me and, blinking back my tears, I remove my own clothes.

I find the thong and put it on, with the bra. They're really comfortable. I'm just adjusting the straps when I hear Luke's voice and I jump out of my skin, flipping around. Then I realize he's outside, standing by the window and I can hear everything he's saying.

"I don't care if it is nearly one o'clock in the fucking morning, Matt," he says. "The agency didn't brief Megan properly." There's a pause in his conversation. "Well, they didn't tell her it was a lingerie shoot for one thing; they told her it was sportswear." He waits again. "No, of course I'm not making it up… why the fuck would I make this shit up?" I hold my breath. "It's not fair on her and it's unprofessional," he continues. "I've had nothing to do with organizing this trip… that's been down to you, Grace, Emma and Paul. But I'm the one dealing with the fall-out of this fuck-up, and I'll be the one carrying the can if it all goes wrong." I listen, still not breathing properly. "Of course she's fucking upset." He noticed? "I don't blame her… This isn't what she expected." He goes quiet again, just for a moment. "Oh, really?" he says, even louder than before, "I should calm down, should I? Well, how can I put this?" he snaps. "If you want me to come back to work – ever – the very least you'll do is to guarantee me, right now, that we'll never use that agency again." There's a long silence and I wonder if he's walked away. I let out a long breath, then he speaks again: "Save it. I'm not interested. Yes, I've dealt with it. How? How do you think…? No. I. Didn't. Quit busting my balls every time we speak, will you? You're making my life fucking impossible at the moment. I'm not doing a shoot ever again, Matt. Not for anyone… not even you." I hear him sigh and then footsteps as he walks away.

My mouth has gone dry. He's mad… really mad. And clearly hating being here. I guess he'd rather be at home with Will, sorting out their problems. I'm aware that time's moving on and the light will be getting stronger, and Alec more impatient.

I pull the robe on, tie it around my waist, put my sandals on my feet and open the door. Luke's waiting just outside and comes over to me.

"Are you okay?" he asks, his voice soft again. It's like his phone call never took place.

I nod my head. I'm not sure my own voice will work.

He takes my hand and leads me over to Alec, who turns as we approach.

"About time," he says and I hear Luke let out a sigh. Alec takes my arm and pulls me across the beach to the shoreline. The way he drags me around reminds me so much of my dad, it makes me want to curl up… or run away. I can't do either, so I let him do whatever he wants in the hope he'll go a little easier on me. "You stand just in the water for this one. You can keep your shoes on," he says. "I'll only be shooting you from mid-thigh up."

"But… they'll get wet," I murmur.

"Then take them off." I do and kick them away. "Now, walk out into the water, about three or four feet, so I can get the angle right with the arch behind you."

"Should the robe come off?" I say.

"No," Luke replies quickly. "Leave that till the last minute." He walks into the water, in his shoes and stands just behind Alec, who's set up his tripod in the shallows.

"Just a little more to your left," Alec tells me. I move. "And turn toward the RV a fraction." I adjust my head. "Not just your head, woman, your whole body." I wince at his tone, but do as he says. "Better." He pauses for a moment. "Okay, take the robe off and throw it to Luke, then put your hands on your hips and lean forward just a little. Myers… don't move – you'll disturb the water too much." I untie the robe, let it drop from my shoulders and catch it just before it hits the water. Then I screw it up and throw it to Luke, who's been studying the image on the camera screen. As I thought… he's more interested in the end product than me. He remains still and I readjust my position, hands on hips, leaning forward.

"Oh, for fuck's sake," Alec says, standing back from the tripod and looking to the sky. "I knew we were dealing with an amateur, but this is ridiculous."

I change my position again, trying to work out what it is I'm doing wrong. I'm sure this is what he wanted. I look at Alec, then at Luke, who's now glaring at Alec.

"I can see her fucking bush, man," Alec says to Luke. "Look, it's as clear as day." He points to me.

I bring my hands down to cover myself. I've never felt so crushed, so humiliated, in my whole life.

"Alec, you son-of-a-bitch," Luke says.

"What? I can't shoot that…"

"Shut the fuck up," Luke yells, facing up to him. I hate confrontation… I can feel the panic rising. I have to get out of here. Luke's still got the robe and he's busy arguing with Alec, so I run out of the water, grab my shoes and head straight back to the RV. I don't care that my ass is on display. Luke won't be interested and Alec will probably only criticize it anyway.

I sit at the table, with my head in my hands, still just wearing the bra and thong. Could today get any worse? *Probably, if I give it long enough.*

I change back into my own clothes, leaving the bra and thong on the bunk bed, then I open the door to the RV. It's only a short walk back to the villa; all I want to do is get back there without having to talk to anyone.

Luke and Alec aren't standing in the water any longer; they're walking up the beach toward me, but they're engrossed in a heated conversation. As I quietly close the door, I notice Alec jab Luke in the chest, and then he storms off along the beach. I take my chance and start walking quickly back toward the villa.

It doesn't take long and, once inside, I head straight for my room, and sit down on the bed.

If I'd known I'd be modeling lingerie, I'd have shaved – or even gone and got a wax. Well, that's not strictly true; I'd never have accepted the job in the first place.

I've never thought about being bare down there before, but how hard can it be? And if they can't take the photographs any other way… well, I guess I'll need to perfect my shaving skills.

I undress – again – and am about to head into the adjoining shower, when I hear the door bang closed downstairs. *Oh God, don't let it be Alec, come to taunt me again, or – worse still – give me instructions on how he wants me to be shaved.* Loud footsteps sound on the stairs, like whoever it is is taking them two at a time, and then there's a knocking at my door.

"Megan?" It's Luke.

"Yes?"

"Are you alright?" He sounds a little out of breath. *Did he run back here?*

"I'm fine," I tell him, feeling anything but fine.

"Look, I'm sorry... I'm really sorry about that," he says.

"It's okay." *Well, it isn't, but...*

"Can I do anything?" he asks.

"No, thanks."

I just want to get this over with, so I go into the bathroom and turn on the shower, giving him a hint to leave me alone.

Shaving takes forever – much longer than I would have thought, for such a small area. But I have to admit, I think I did a good job. I check it out using a hand mirror, and I stand in front of the full-length mirror too and I still can't see any places I've missed, certainly none that the camera will pick up from the distance Alec's shooting.

Once I'm dried off, and dressed again, I go downstairs. The villa is deserted. I go and look out by the pool, but there's no sign of Luke anywhere. Coming back inside, I notice a folded piece of paper, with my name written on it, propped up against an empty wine bottle on the table. I unfold it and read:

'Sorry again, for everything, Megan. Please forgive me. See you back at the lake. L.'

You see, it's things like that that make me wish he wasn't... *Oh, what's the point in wishing.*

I take a slow wander back to the lake. It's getting warmer now, and there's hardly any breeze. I'm trying very hard not to even think about

Luke; but that's nearly impossible, when he fills pretty much every space in my head.

When I get back, I find Michel sitting on a deckchair by the RV. He stands as I approach.

"Where is everyone?" I ask.

"Alec, he go away... Luke swims." He points to the lake and I look out. I can see Luke swimming, freestyle, cutting strokes through the water, keeping up quite a pace. He's perfect, utterly perfect. I tear my eyes away from his muscular shoulders and arms and look around the beach. There are a few other people here now; young families mainly.

"Alec say we wait till later for..." Michel struggles for the word, so makes the gesture of taking a photograph.

"Oh, okay," I reply. He steps to one side and offers me his chair. I shake my head. "I'd better not," I say, pointing at the sky. "Alec would be cross if I caught the sun."

Michel looks at me, a little confused, and I mime being burned by the sun.

"Ahh," he says and, raises a finger. "Sit, sit," he says. I wonder if he understood me, and take the seat anyway. It's not that hot yet. Then behind and above me, I become aware of an awning being lowered along the whole side of the RV. It provides me with the perfect shade and, as Michel re-appears, I smile up at him.

"Thank you," I say. I really want to cry, but I don't... or rather, I can't. Not yet.

Chapter Five

Luke

Alec's behavior this morning was juvenile. There were better ways of dealing with the situation than yelling at her.

But then I could have handled it better too. I should have taken care of her, put her first, not yelled at Alec and left Megan to fend for herself. Discovering she wasn't in the RV and had disappeared really scared me. For a moment, I panicked, thinking she'd just wandered off, upset by Alec's remarks and my reaction, but then the logical part of my brain kicked in and I realized she'd probably just gone back to the villa, so I ran after her… and I mean *ran*.

I get that she was embarrassed; I get that she turned the shower on to dismiss me – she didn't want to talk and that was fair enough. It seemed unwise to hang around and wait for her, so I came back here to the lake and went for a swim to calm down. I saw her get back and talk to Michel for a while, but she's hardly said two words to me, although I can feel her watching me sometimes, like when I walked up the beach after my swim. It's weird; it's like she's interested, but she doesn't want to be. Like there's something there, but she's suppressing it.

I've sat next to her under the awning all afternoon, pretending to work, watching her, trying – and failing – to make sense of her.

Matt sent me a text message this afternoon, apologizing, telling me he's spoken to the agency and we won't be using them again. He made light of my threat to not to come back to work, but I'm too mad to reply at the moment. I know the situation's not his fault, but I've got to be mad at someone. And, besides, his knack of assuming the worst about me where Megan is concerned is really starting to grate. Yeah, I want her... but it's different this time. I'm not talking about a meaningless fuck here. I don't know for sure what I am talking about, but there's nothing meaningless about it.

The light's starting to fade a little, the beach has cleared and Alec has returned.

As soon as he does, Megan gets up, goes over to him and whispers in his ear. He places his hand in the small of her back, nods his head, smiles and says something back to her. I've got no idea what that's about, and I don't like the intimacy his gestures imply. It stirs something inside me I've never felt before. It's not a good feeling, whatever it is.

"Okay," Alec announces, and I snap out of my thoughts. "Let's get this done."

Megan comes back and goes into the RV, not looking in my direction at all. I'm still staring at the door she's just closed when Michel turns to me.

"I go back to villa," he says. "I..."

"Speak French, Michel," I tell him. "It's easier."

He explains his idea that he'll walk back to the villa and get the evening meal ready, so we can eat when we get back.

"Good idea," I say and he leaves me with the keys to the RV, then wanders off and I wait while Alec sets up again. It doesn't take long for Megan to re-appear, wearing the robe. I offer her my hand as she steps down onto the pebbles. She looks me in the eye and I smile at her. She smiles back, but for the first time, it doesn't touch her eyes. There's no sparkle. She's had a horrible day and a lot of that is my fault, and I'd give anything to put that sparkle back.

I walk alongside her down to the shoreline and we repeat our actions from this morning, with her walking out into the water a few feet. I stand near to Alec, out of shot, getting wet shoes again.

"Right, Megan," Alec says, "after you give Luke the robe, put your hands on your hips—"

"Yes, and lean forward," she says quietly. "I remember."

I smile to myself. I'm relieved to see she hasn't let him get to her – at least not too much – and whatever they were whispering about, there's clearly no friendliness between them. The thought makes me feel better than I would have expected.

"Turn your body," Alec barks and she does as he says. "And try smiling. No-one wants a lingerie model with a fucking scowl on their face."

That's too much. "Knock if off, Alec," I say to him.

I hear Megan sigh. I glance up at her, but she's staring down at the water between us.

"Okay," Alec says at last, ignoring me. "Lose the robe. Don't move, Myers." I want to yell at him that I know what to do, but there's already enough tension in the air.

I stay still while Megan unties the robe. The lowering sun gives her exposed shoulders an exquisite glow, like a thin layer of gold dust. As she lets the robe fall and gathers it in her hands, I have to look away, although I still manage to catch it when she throws it to me.

"That's much better," Alec says, grinning. "Wasn't so hard, was it?" I glance at him. He's taking photographs already. What does he mean? "Okay, run your hands through your hair… pulling it up behind your head… that's it," he says. "What did you go for? A full Brazilian? Holly—"

"None of your business, Alec," Megan says, and he laughs… and realization dawns. She didn't shower to dismiss me – well, not entirely – she showered so she could shave… I lower the robe to cover my groin, because I'm instantly hard just thinking about her naked pussy.

"Now. I want you to turn around, slowly," he says, standing up straight and looking at her. "Don't disturb the water too much." So far, I've deliberately averted my eyes… This morning, I pretended to look at the camera screen over Alec's shoulder, even though the glare of the sun actually made that impossible… I couldn't see a damned thing, but

I figured it was easier than torturing myself by looking at Megan wearing almost nothing. I've tried being sensible; I've tried doing the 'right' thing, but dammit, I have to look. I watch her every move, taking in her pert breasts, encased in the gray fishnet fabric. Even from here, I can see her dark nipples harden in the slight breeze. Then, as she turns, her ass comes into view, framed to perfection by the thong, and my cock strains so much, it hurts.

"Okay," Alec tells her, checking the screen again, "I need you to look over your shoulder at me, like you want me to take you to bed and—"

"I can't do that," Megan interrupts.

"Try."

"Well, I can't… because I don't want you to take me to bed, Alec – not ever."

I laugh out loud, and she glances at me, a slight smile forming on her lips. The look in her eyes is like nothing I've ever seen before.

"That's it," Alec says. "That's the exact expression I want. Now hold it, and look at the camera." She does and Alec starts taking pictures again. Her eyes remain fixed on the lens, her gaze not quite as intense as when she was staring at me a moment ago. That look she just gave me was something else, but… Wait a second… If that's the look he was asking for, does that mean she wants me to take her to bed? If so, it wasn't the sort of look I usually get… I'm used to seeing 'fuck me now' looks. I'm used to acting on them. But the look on Megan's face was different.

"We're done," Alec announces, interrupting my confused thoughts. "Change into the top, but keep the thong on."

I go across to Megan and hand her the robe. She keeps her head down as she re-ties it. Oh, this is great. Now she won't look at me at all? How am I supposed to work anything out? She's barely spoken to me all day, she gives me a look that's got me hot, hard, horny, and more than a little confused, and now she won't make eye contact…

She starts off up the beach, but I follow a couple of paces behind. She doesn't know it yet, but she's going to need help. When she reaches the RV, she steps inside and closes the door. I stand outside, kicking my feet in the pebbles, trying to work out what it is she wants – and whether I can do anything about it.

"Hurry up," Alec calls after a few minutes.

The door opens again. Megan's standing on the threshold wearing the robe, but she doesn't step out. I've anticipated this.

"Can you… come in here, please?" she asks, her voice really quiet. She's staring at my chest again, just like at the hotel.

"Sure." I step inside the RV, but leave the door open – I assume it will make her feel safer. She looks at me, then at the open door, and I'm almost certain her shoulders drop just a fraction. Would she prefer it closed? She only has to ask.

"I need your help," she mutters.

"You need me to tie that up, don't you?" I say. I know the garment she has on. There's a bow in the back.

"Yes, please," she replies and turns around, then undoes the robe, letting it fall to her waist. I swallow hard, then take one of the silky ties in each hand, and do them in a bow. I long… no, I ache to trail my tongue across her shoulders and her neck; to run my fingers over her soft skin. But once the bow is done, I lift the robe back onto her shoulders.

"You're all set," I tell her. She turns to face me, her head still bowed, but as she moves to the door, just for a moment, I think I see tears in her eyes. What the hell is going on here?

There are two more changes of lingerie in this range, and the shoot is finished fairly quickly. Once we're done, while Megan gets back into her own clothes in the RV, Alec tells me he's going to walk into the village, and eat there.

He wanders off and I start packing everything away.

By the time Megan comes out, we're ready to leave.

"You can ride up front with me, if you like," I say to her.

She just nods her head and goes around to the other side of the unit. I jump into the driver's seat and she hops up next to me, closing her door. As I start the engine, I turn to her.

"Is everything alright?" I ask.

"Yes," she replies, which is annoying when it so clearly isn't.

The drive home was awkwardly silent, but thankfully short and, when we got back here, Michel had already prepared our evening meal. He'd barbecued some chicken, and made a caesar salad with it, since he didn't know when we'd be back. We sat out on the deck and ate, then cleared away together.

Michel's now gone to his room to phone his wife and I've come back out here, with my laptop in front of me, working out tomorrow's schedule. We don't have to leave too early; we've only got a four hour journey to Antibes, where we're booked into an exclusive hotel with a private beach – it's the private beach we really need for Alec to get the shots he requires. According to the drawings, with the right angle, the shots should feature Megan in the foreground, nestled by the rocks, with the town – out of focus – behind her. This is going to be the most difficult of all the shoots we have, because of the number of people around. But the hotel have said they'll let us have a section of beach to ourselves. I've already thought of another possible problem though, which is that Alec will want to work quickly, and will probably insist that Megan changes on the beach, but she'll want to walk back to the hotel between shots, for some privacy. It's only a few yards, but Alec will claim it's a waste of time. I can hear the arguments in my head already. I'll back Megan, but it's bound to create a tense atmosphere again.

I've turned on the outside lights, which include those around the pool, and I'm still looking at the drawings Grace sent through, when I hear the door open behind me and I know, without turning, that it's Megan. I'm not sure if it's her scent – although I don't know if she actually wears any – or if it's a sense of her being there. I just seem to know it's her.

She walks across the deck, depositing a towel on the chair at the other end of the table and, without saying a word, goes to the pool. I feel myself harden, and I'm finding it difficult to swallow. She's wearing the yellow bikini and she looks mouthwatering. It's essentially four small triangles of material, held together by strings. The temptation to go over and untie them is almost too much and, as she turns to lower herself into the pool, I avert my eyes, staring at my computer screen.

I need a distraction. I'm still not in the mood for talking to Matt. Apart from anything else, even if he takes the hint from this morning and doesn't question me about Megan, I know he'll ask how many women I've had since I've been here, and I'll either have to lie, which feels wrong when she's just a few feet away, or tell him the truth about how I feel, and then be read the rule book – again. I pick up my phone and text Will, which is unheard of for me.

— *What you up to? L.*

He replies instantly.

— *Can't tell you. Working. Will.*

Will's very secretive about his work for the government. I've got no idea what he really does most of the time. I know he's a bit of a genius, though.

A second message arrives almost straight away:

— *Is everything okay?*

I don't know what to say… Do I lie and say 'yes', or do I tell him the truth? I go for the truth.

— *Not really.*

— *What's wrong?*

— *It's just work stuff.*

— *No it isn't.*

I smile to myself. He knows me too well. I'm trying to think up a reply and watching Megan's long delicate arms skimming through the water at the same time, when my phone rings. It's Will. I answer immediately.

"Hey," he says. "Talk to me."

"You didn't have to call."

"You messaged me. I don't even remember the last time you messaged me. So, something's wrong… and it's got nothing to do with work, because if it was work, you'd call Matt… Talk to me."

I take a deep breath. "It's the model."

"Oh, Luke, you haven't…" I can hear the disappointment in his voice.

"No. I haven't. That's the problem."

"Oh… So she doesn't want to?"

"No. That's not it."

"Then I don't understand. If she wants to… and you want to… what's stopping you?"

"There's Matt's rule for a start."

"Since when have rules gotten in your way?" He has a point, but I know that's not the only thing stopping me.

"That's not all of it," I tell him.

"Okay."

I study Megan, and lower my voice to be sure she won't hear. "She's amazing," I say.

"Is she there?"

"She's swimming."

"And you're watching?" he asks.

"Yes. How do you know that? Have you got one of your goddamn spy cameras on me?"

"No. You lowered your voice, so she had to be nearby."

"Oh."

"So… she's amazing… and?"

"I think she's interested, but it's like she's holding back."

"And you?"

"And I'm holding back too," I say, honestly.

"Why?" he asks. "That's not like you." I know he'll have been surprised by my answer, but it doesn't show in his voice. All I hear is concern.

"Because… because I feel differently about her."

"In what way?" he asks.

"Well, I guess the fact that I feel anything for her is different. And… more importantly, I don't know what to do about it."

"Wow," he says.

"What does 'wow' mean?"

"Just that maybe she's a bit special."

"She's that… and more. I told you, she's amazing… but…"

"But what?"

"I'm stuck. I mean, what do I do? This isn't a position I've been in before, is it?"

"And you're asking me?" Although we live in the same house, Will's personal life is something I know almost nothing about. I'm sure he must have had sex a few times… but he keeps himself to himself. He talks to me when he needs to, and I respect that. I don't pry.

"No, not really," I reply. "It's just good to say it all out loud."

"I'm no expert, but I'd say you should probably go with your instincts."

"Even if my instincts are telling me to break Matt's rule?"

"Luke, I think Matt made that rule to stop you from having your usual casual affairs with the models, because if he needs to keep using them for future projects, it would make it awkward for everyone, if you'd slept with them. People can change though… even you. He gets that. I don't think he'd apply the rule if you're serious about this girl. That wouldn't be fair really, would it? He wouldn't want you to be miserable. But of course, that only applies if you're actually serious, Luke… If you're going to mess with her, then…"

"I'm not." I've got no intention of messing with her.

While he's been talking – and making sense – Megan has climbed out of the pool. Her bikini is glued to her and there are droplets of water trickling down her body. I want to lick them from her soft skin.

"Thanks, Will," I say. "That's really helped a lot."

"Your voice just changed… She's out of the pool, isn't she?" he asks and I can hear the smile on his lips.

"You got it," I say, smiling myself, as Megan approaches.

"I'll let you go," he replies. "Just remember, Luke… only do this if you're serious. Otherwise, leave her alone. Apart from the damage you could do to her, you don't want to screw things up with Matt." He's right – about all of it.

"Okay," I say, because I can't say anything else in case Megan hears. "Thanks again. Is everything alright with you?"

"Sure." I'm not certain I believe him, but I let it go. He probably won't tell me anyway. "Grace has invited me over for dinner tomorrow." I'm watching Megan walking slowly toward the deck, wringing the water from the ends of her hair with her hands, then running her fingers through it.

"That's good. You have a great time without me, Will – I don't mind. You can make it up to me when I get home. I'll let you cook dinner for a week."

He laughs. "Oh, yeah, it must be awful for you, sitting by a pool in the south of France."

"How do you know I'm in the south of France?"

"That would be telling." He's laughing as he hangs up.

I'm still smiling as I disconnect the call.

Megan picks up her towel and starts to rub herself down.

She looks across at me from her end of the table. The lights are shining off her damp skin, giving it a luminous sheen. "Was that Will?" she asks. She must have overheard the end of our conversation.

"Yes," I reply, grateful that she's actually strung a sentence together and aimed it at me.

She's running the towel across her flat stomach and I'm struggling to keep my eyes fixed on her face. I take a sip of my wine just to divert my attention. "So, how long have you two been together?" she asks, and I choke. *Did she just ask what I think she just asked?* I manage to swallow the wine, but I can't stop coughing for a full minute.

"I'm sorry," she says, once I've calmed down. "I didn't mean to embarrass you. But it's nothing to be ashamed of."

"Um… I'm not. Or I wouldn't be, but…" I get up and start walking to her. "Can I just get one thing clear? Are you… are you asking if Will and I are an item?" I come to a stop right in front of her.

"Well, yes. I'm sorry," she says, going to turn away from me. "It's none of my business."

I reach out and grab her hand, pulling her back. "He's my brother, Megan."

69

Her eyes widen and her mouth opens. I can see her tongue – it's like she's trying to form words, but can't quite manage it. Then she bites her bottom lip for a moment, before whispering, "You mean you're not…?"

"Gay? No, I'm not." I take a step closer to her, still holding her hand. Our bodies are just a few inches apart. "I'm straight… I'm very straight." I wish she'd just look down, so she could see how damn straight I am… how turned on she's got me.

She's studying my face, in detail, like she's seeing it – seeing me – for the first time. She focuses on my lips for a while, but eventually her eyes lock with mine. "Then why…?" she whispers, and I lean in a little closer. "I mean, I don't—"

"Luke!" Alec calls from the doorway. "There you are!" Megan jumps away from me and I release her hand just as Alec tumbles out the door, and stops himself from falling by catching hold of the back of a chair.

Megan takes one look at him and runs back into the villa, her towel clutched to her chest.

I take one look at him and wonder if killing him could be classed as justifiable homicide.

Megan

I seem to be finding new and spectacular ways of humiliating myself on this trip.

He's not gay… he's evidently 'very straight', whatever that means. Well, it means he's straight, obviously.

Part of me wishes I'd been able to ask why it is, if he's not gay, that he's been keeping a definite distance between us… And another part is glad Alec interrupted and I couldn't ask my question, because now I realize how self-obsessed that would have made me sound. I mean, he doesn't have to be interested in me, does he?

Except… sometimes he does seem interested. He's held my hand several times now, bought me swimwear, been really kind to me. And just occasionally, I catch a look in his eyes, but then it disappears before I even have time to interpret it. Then there was the way he seemed to be studying my body at the river this afternoon, which was weird, considering how much he'd avoided looking at me until then; there was the expression on his face when he said 'very straight' just now, the way he leaned in like he wanted to kiss me… Maybe I'm reading too much into little things that don't matter. Maybe if I had any experience with men, I'd understand, but I don't… and I'm lost.

He's just come upstairs to bed. He stops outside my bedroom door. I turned the light off about twenty minutes ago, so I guess he thinks I'm asleep. He hasn't moved away from the door yet and I'm tempted to call out to him; ask him to come in, so we can talk. But what would I say?

And what would be the point? I like him far too much to let anything happen between us. My dad would literally kill him, and I'm certainly not going to be responsible for that.

Knowing he's not gay changes nothing, not really… except, it also changes everything.

We're ready to leave by ten-thirty.

Alec has gone on ahead, thank goodness. I really hope he has a hangover; he deserves one.

Michel packs up the RV with our things and I go around checking we haven't left anything behind. Luke is just sending out a text message to someone and he looks up from his phone as I come into the main room from the downstairs bathroom.

"I'm sorry about last night," he says, putting his phone in his back pocket. "Alec's interruption was… unfortunate timing."

"It's fine," I tell him, trying to sound more upbeat than I feel. I decided, during a fairly sleepless night, to go for being friends, on the basis that it's really all I have to offer. "I'm sorry for jumping to conclusions," I add.

He moves a little closer and I feel that tingly fluttering in my stomach again. This isn't a very good start for my 'friendship' pact. "Don't apologize," he says. His eyes are piercing mine. I suppose I should look away, but I can't. "Megan, we need to talk," he continues.

"Do we?" I'm still trying to sound bright and breezy. I hope it's working – if it isn't I'm probably just coming across as slightly insane.

"Well, yeah." He sounds perplexed. "I thought… last night… I mean, didn't you…?"

I can't let him think there can be anything between us, other than friendship – and a temporary friendship at that – for his sake even more than mine. "I think I might have misled you, Luke," I tell him. "Whatever impression I've given you, I'm sorry. I can't––"

Michel comes in through the front door. "We ready?" he says, looking from me to Luke.

Luke stares at me for a moment. "Yeah, I guess so," he says and turns away.

The journey south has been silent so far. I think he's disappointed – or angry, or confused… or maybe a little of all three. I can't blame him for any of those sentiments.

What can I do though? I can't help being attracted to him, and I know I shouldn't have shut him down like I did – it was unkind. But I can't get involved either… Oh, why does everything have to be so confusing, so difficult?

He hasn't looked up for nearly an hour. I should know; I haven't stopped staring at him.

I'm not sure I can carry on like this. We've still got over two hours of journey ahead of us and then we have to work together.

"Can we talk?" I say to him. He slams down the lid of his laptop.

"Oh, so now you wanna talk?" Wow… He's definitely angry.

"Not if you're going to speak to me like that, no."

He takes a deep breath, looks out the window for a minute, then turns back. "Sorry," he says, and waits.

I put my hands on the table in front of me. "No, I'm sorry," I say. He raises an eyebrow, like he doesn't understand. "I meant what I said about misleading you, but I shouldn't have just shut you down. I should have—"

"It's fine. I wanted to talk; you didn't. I guess we won't be talking."

"Luke... don't be like that."

"Like what?"

"You're different."

"You mean you preferred me when you thought I was gay?"

"No." I stare at him, but he's changed. His eyes are icy blue now and I can't see a way into them. "Just forget it," I say and I get up and move into the cab, strapping myself into the seat next to Michel. He doesn't make any comment about my arrival, and I stare straight ahead, through the windshield, wishing today had never even begun.

We arrive just before three o'clock.

The hotel is amazing. It's right on the beach with views across the deep blue water to the old port, with its battlements and ancient fortifications. It's a beautiful scene, but I can't really take it in. Michel hands me my bag and I follow Luke into the hotel. He checks us in, and declines any help with our luggage. We've got rooms next door to each other... *Great.* Alec is already here, but nowhere to be seen. Michel is following on behind, once he's parked the RV at the back of the hotel.

We ride up in the elevator together in continued silence, neither looking at the other and, when we get to my room, which is first, he hands me my entry card, then goes on to his own room, not waiting to see me inside. I hear his door slam shut before I've even opened mine.

Once I've let myself in, I know I should be blown away by the room. I know it's magnificent, but I can't focus. I manage to go out onto the balcony for some fresh air before the tears start to fall... and then they don't stop.

I've ordered dinner in my room for seven, but I haven't bothered to tell Luke. I'm sure he'll be eating with Michel and Alec anyway. They won't miss me.

At just before seven, there's a knock at my door. I open it, expecting to see someone from the hotel with my meal. Instead, Luke's standing there, wearing a cream linen suit, and a white shirt, but no tie. *Still gorgeous, dammit.*

I know my eyes are red and puffy from crying, my hair's a mess, and I haven't changed from the journey. I'm wearing my cut-off denim shorts and a white camisole top – hardly suitable for going out to dinner, but okay for sitting in my room feeling sorry for myself, which is all I've got planned for this evening. His eyes wander down my body, and back up again, resting on my face, but he doesn't utter a word.

"I'm not coming down to dinner," I say eventually, by way of explanation.

"Why?" he asks. His voice is much softer now, his eyes much warmer; more like the Luke I know… and like… a lot. "You've got to eat."

"I've ordered room service."

He stares at me again. He's studying my face more closely now. His brow is furrowed.

"Okay," he says.

I try to close the door, but I can't. Something's blocking it. I open it again to check what the obstruction is, and find his arm raised against it.

"What do you want?" I say to him. He lowers his arm and takes a step forward.

"I was being stupid, and juvenile," he replies, looking down into my eyes. "I'm sorry I upset you, Megan." He walks away. And now I'm crying again.

I think Alec might kill me.

I look awful. I've hardly slept; I've got bags under my eyes from crying so much and I'm running late. I skip breakfast and go straight to the lobby.

Luke's waiting, but there's no sign of Alec.

"Hi," he says.

"Hello."

"About yesterday…" he starts, and I'm uncertain where he's going to go with this. I'm so done with humiliating myself.

"It doesn't matter. Can we just forget about it?"

"No, Megan. I can't forget about it… I don't want to."

"What does that mean?"

"It means… I want you to have dinner with me tonight."

"Won't we be doing that anyway?"

"Not if last night's anything to go by, no… And I don't mean with the others. I mean just you and me – away from here, away from everyone else."

"Why, Luke?" I ask.

"Do I need a reason?"

"Yes." *Of course you do.*

"Okay." He pauses for a moment. "Because I can't stop thinking about you… is that enough of a reason?" My mind has just emptied completely. I can see he's still looking at me… it's a look that goes on, and on… and on, like he's seeing right into my soul. He moves closer and leans in, a slight smile on his lips. "Megan," he whispers.

I choke, coming back to reality. "Sorry… What, um…?"

"You stopped breathing." He's smiling.

"I know," I say.

"Well don't. I like you breathing."

"You… You do?"

He laughs. "Yes, of course I do. So… Have dinner with me?"

"What the hell is keeping you two?" Alec calls from the main door.

Luke turns. "Wait a minute," he snaps, turning to Alec, then looks back at me. "Well?" he asks.

"We should go."

"Not until you give me an answer."

"Okay… Um… Yes?"

"Good." He smiles, then takes my hand. "Let's go."

Chapter Six

Luke

I've been a complete asshole. I'm not used to talking; I'm not used to explaining myself or my actions. That's one of the reasons I always stuck to experienced women who knew the score and who wanted the same thing as me. I never had to do any of this emotional crap in the past... not once. It's damned hard. Why does no-one tell you this?

I would have been quite happy to talk to her at the villa, explain how I feel – or at least try to – listen to her and see if she feels the same, then try and work out what we wanted to do... but no, she went all weird on me, pretending it was a misunderstanding. That was bullshit and she knew it, but I was surprised by how much it hurt. It hurt a lot.

So, like the petulant three year old that I am, I did the same back to her – twice. Point scoring on the journey down here and then shutting her out at the hotel when we arrived... What was I trying to prove? What a man I am?

I didn't feel like much of a man when she opened the door a couple of hours later and I saw she'd been crying. And I knew she'd been crying because of me; that much was obvious. All my plans to take her to dinner somewhere quiet and talk things through went out the window, and all I could do was apologize, because I owed her that – I owed her a lot more besides.

I didn't go to dinner in the end. I went for a walk along the beach for an hour or so... and then I sat on the terrace until around five in the morning. It took me that long to work out that I don't care about what's happened in the past; I don't care that this isn't how I usually operate; I don't care about the fact that I'm so far out of my depth, I'm drowning. And I sure as hell don't care about Matt's rule... not any more. There's only one thing I care about, and that's Megan. Once I'd worked that out, it all fell into place and nothing else mattered. Well, nothing else except getting her to agree to have dinner with me, so we can actually talk without being interrupted again.

When she appeared this morning, she still looked puffy-eyed, which won't please Alec one bit, but she has agreed to have dinner tonight – so, providing I can get her to talk, maybe I can work out what it is she wants. I know what I want now. I want to be with her... and I want more than just a night. One night with her will never be enough. I'm not sure one lifetime will be either. And that's what I mean about it all falling into place. I worked out last night that I want to try at forever, and I can't help smiling whenever I think about it. God, I really hope she wants the same thing, or at least something similar, that we can work on... together.

I've gotta say, her reaction when I told her I can't stop thinking about her was unexpected. I'd thought she might be a little surprised. I hadn't anticipated she'd temporarily stop breathing – or that I'd need to remind her to start again. She was flustered. That was kinda cute... kinda sexy... and kinda promising.

Alec's impatient, so we're hurrying down to where he's waiting at the end of the pathway. As promised, the hotel have cordoned off a section of beach for us to use, although it's very windy and there's hardly a soul out here anyway.

"Is this wind going to be a problem?" I ask Alec.

"No, far from it. It'll make the waves dramatic."

"What about Megan's hair?"

"Put it up," he says, as if it's obvious, then turns to her. "We can have a little bit of it flying loose, but if we let the whole lot go, you'll be invisible."

"It takes about half an hour to put up properly," she says.

"I don't have half an hour,"

"Then it won't be done properly."

"For fuck's sake."

"Lay off her," I say to him. "You want her hair up, let her do it." I turn to Megan. "Go on," I say. "You go back and do your hair. I'll bring the first items to your room for you to change into."

"And hurry up!" Alec barks.

Her head drops and she mumbles, "Okay," before she leaves. I hate the way she lets him get under her skin so easily.

Alec has already forgotten the conversation and has moved down onto the beach. He wants to photograph Megan on the rocks, with the waves coming up behind her. Looking at the setup, this could be a little dangerous. She could easily slip.

I go over to him. "Does she have to be on the rocks?" I ask.

"Yes." He doesn't bother to turn to me.

"But with the wind and the waves, she could slip."

"Then she'll slip."

"Are you always such an asshole?" *I thought that was my specialty.*

"Yes. You're in the way." He pushes me to one side, then turns back. "I want her in the camisole and briefs first." I'm being dismissed. I go back to the hotel and up to my room, where I go through the small case of samples and find the bag containing the Amethyst range.

The one good thing about this shoot – being as it's the most public one we'll be doing – is that this range doesn't feature anything too revealing.

I take out the camisole and briefs. They're silk-satin, with lace detailing and a very deep purple. I take them along the hallway and knock on Megan's door.

"Come in," she calls. I open the door and step inside. Once again, her bed is covered with what looks to be the entire contents of her suitcase. She's sitting at the dressing table, twisting strands of hair into curls at the back of her head. It looks complicated, but beautiful.

"I brought you these," I say.

"What are they?" she asks.

"Just the first two garments."

"I gathered that… I meant specifically."

"Oh, sorry. It's a camisole and some briefs."

"Okay."

I'm standing behind her, watching as she continues to arrange her hair. She looks at me in the mirror. "Was there something else?" she asks. I realize I'm staring.

"No, sorry. I'll leave these on the bed, shall I?"

"Yes, thank you."

"And I'll wait for you outside?"

"Okay." She's smiling at me. I smile back. It's a nice moment.

I've been waiting outside her door for about ten minutes by the time she comes out. She's wearing the same robe as yesterday and her hair's up now, just like it was when we had dinner in Paris, with a few loose strands framing her face.

"Ready?" I ask.

"As I'll ever be." We start walking to the elevator.

"You're not entirely comfortable with this, are you?" I ask as the doors open and she steps inside.

She shrugs. "It's okay."

"Really?" I press the button for the lobby and the doors close.

"I suppose it could be worse," she says.

"What do you mean?" My imagination's working overtime.

She's staring at the floor, while I'm looking at her reflection in the mirrored wall. "If you weren't here…" she whispers and I swear to God, my heart just did a somersault. I turn and, reaching down, I place my finger under her chin and lift her face to mine. I step a little closer, just as the lift doors open. She pulls back, and I let her. She might like having me here, but there's an instinct that tells me she'd run a mile if I tried anything at the moment. She's still holding back, even if I'm not… well, I'm not anymore.

We walk toward the entrance and, as I hold open the door for her, I lean forward, just slightly. "I'm here, Megan," I say quietly. "I'm not going anywhere."

"About damn time," Alec yells as we approach him.

Neither of us reply, but we walk over to him. He takes Megan by the arm, pulling her. He points to the middle of the group of rocks. "I need you in the centre," he says.

"You want me to climb over there… wearing this?" She indicates the robe. I'm inclined to agree with her.

"Yes. You see the rock that's a little lower than the rest. Stand on that one."

She looks at him and her shoulders drop once more. She puts her foot up on the first rock and I step forward, climbing up ahead of her and taking her hand to pull her up. As we start to make our way across the rocks, the wind catches the robe and blows it open. She lets go of me to pull it closed again and loses her footing. She starts to tumble and I turn and grab her around the waist. We fall together, but I twist to ensure I take the brunt of the impact, the rocks grazing my leg as I go down. Megan lands in my lap and she sits, breathing heavily for a moment.

"Can you two quit fooling around and get on with it," Alec shouts; and suddenly she's embarrassed and pushes away from me.

"Your leg," she says as she stands and notices the blood.

"It's nothing."

"But you're bleeding."

"I'm okay," I say. "More to the point, are you?"

"Yes." She nods.

"Today would be nice," Alec interrupts again and Megan moves into position on the lower rock. "At last," Alec says. "Now, lose the robe." She undoes it and hands it to me. The wind catches the few loose strands of her hair and they swirl around her face; the waves are crashing up behind us. I can see why it would make for a great photograph. "Get out of the damn shot, Myers."

I move away, back off the rocks and down to where Alec's standing.

"Good," Alec says. "Now twist slightly and stick your left hip out toward me… that's it. Give me that hot look you gave me yesterday… Great." He starts taking photographs and and, after a minute or two, he stops again. "Okay, now, with your right hand, lift the camisole." Megan's mouth drops open. "Don't sweat it," he says, "just lift it a couple of inches, and hold it in place with your hand on your hip." Very tentatively, she raises the front of the camisole top, to reveal the briefs beneath and a few inches of tanned, toned stomach. Again, Alec takes a few photographs. "Okay," he says, "now you need to turn around." Carefully, Megan turns so her back is toward the camera. "And just stick your ass out toward me a little. Lean forward a fraction and look back at me over your shoulder… That's it." He takes the final few shots. "Okay, that's it… Go get changed into the next outfit."

"Stay where you are, Megan," I call to her. "I'll come get you."

I clamber up over the rocks carrying the robe, then hand it to her and she pulls it on, tying it tight and we make our way back down again.

"What do you want her in next?" I ask Alec as we pass him.

He checks his notes. "The thong and slip," he says, looking at Megan. "And hurry it up. I don't know why you can't change out here, instead of wasting time going backwards and forwards."

He never ceases to disappoint. "Maybe because it's more private," I say.

"So what? It's a waste of time."

"You're being well paid for your time, Alec, so stop complaining."

We continue up the beach and into the hotel. Once we're in the elevator, I turn to her. "Can you come to my room for a minute?" I ask.

"Why?" She looks wary.

"Because I can give you the next outfit and then you can go back to your room and get changed, while I clean up my leg."

I hear her sigh of relief, and I'm more than a little confused. She likes having me here, she said so; and she even seems attracted to me, yet she doesn't like the thought of being in my room? What does she think I'm gonna do? Doesn't she trust me at all?

"Why don't you give me all the outfits – it'll save you coming back inside with me each time."

And now she doesn't want me walking her in and out? Why not?

Back on the beach, with my leg cleaned up, Alec explains that this time, he wants Megan to stand against the lower rocks, not climb up onto them. *That's a relief.*

She takes off the robe and hands it to me, then backs herself against a large pale gray rock. Alec kneels down on the sand, to get the angle he wants. "Lean back," he says, "and move your legs apart just a little. And put your hands up into your hair like you did yesterday... Now, tip your head back... Perfect." I glance around and the relief I felt that she wasn't having to clamber on the rocks is short-lived. The beach itself might be private, but anyone walking in and out of the hotel can see everything we're doing.

I don't know how Megan feels, but I'm hating every second of this. She's too exposed; I don't like it. I want to see her body, but I want it for myself, not for Alec and anyone else who happens to be passing. He takes his shots. "Okay," he says. "Now, turn around and hold onto the rock with your hands. Damn. We need to hitch the slip up a little so I can see the thong... Myers!" I hesitate then walk forward to Megan, standing behind her.

"I'm sorry about this," I murmur as I pull the slip up just enough to reveal her ass and the thong. She doesn't react at all. And neither do I. I'm not even vaguely hard – this isn't turning me on in the slightest. I don't want her displayed in public like this. I want to stand here and shield her from their view.

"Get out of the way," Alec barks at me and I move reluctantly. "Okay, Megan, look at me over your shoulder. Good." He takes his pictures. "Right, we're done for that one... Now it's the basque." Megan nods, as she pulls on the robe and heads back to the hotel. I don't go with her. She said she doesn't want me. I don't need telling twice.

Megan

This shoot has been more humiliating than the last one; probably because there are people around and, although the beach is private, anyone on the pathway into the hotel has a good view of what's going on... and a good view of me. Although it's fairly quiet still, I'm finding it embarrassing.

Oddly, I think Luke's found it difficult too this time. He's been much more protective than he was at the river. The thing is, since this morning, since he told me he can't stop thinking about me, and since I told him I like having him here, I feel even more awkward around him. It dawned on me that I'm leading him on, when I know perfectly well nothing can come of it. It's wrong of me.

But when I said I didn't need his help going back and forth to the room to change, he looked so hurt, I felt even worse... It doesn't matter what I do, I can't seem to win, really.

At least we're on the last shot now. The basque was okay, but I felt a little more exposed in it than I had in the previous two outfits, and now I've just had to come inside to change back into the original camisole, but with the thong this time. The point of this shot is to show the matching kimono, but if I put it on, I won't get the robe over the top, and the kimono has lace panels at the back, which won't hide anything, so I'm wearing the robe and carrying the kimono back outside.

As I walk down the pathway, it's nearing lunchtime and there are a few people sitting on the terrace overlooking the private beach. This is getting less and less secluded, and I'm very uncomfortable about it now. It was bad enough early this morning, but now...

I stop in my tracks. I can hear raised voices coming from our section of the beach.

"It's none of your damn business, Alec." That's Luke. What on earth's wrong now?

"Just answer the question…" It almost sounds like Alec's sneering. He's got that tone to his voice.

"No."

"Are you fucking Megan, or not?"

"I'm not answering that." *Why not? He isn't… He could just say 'no'.*

"Well, you won't mind if I give it a shot, then." *Over my dead body.* I hear a thudding sound, and a pause, then, "Shit. That fucking hurt, Myers." It's Alec again.

"Don't even think about going near Megan. In fact, other than doing your job, don't even look at her."

"Why the fuck did you hit me?"

"I barely touched you."

"Barely touched me? I think you broke my jaw."

"Oh, stop whining. You're still conscious, aren't you? And I didn't break your jaw either… you can still talk, unfortunately. Now, get up, shut up, and get on with the goddamn shoot."

I round the corner and see Alec climbing to his feet and Luke walking away from him in my direction. He stops when he notices me, looking anxious.

"Megan… I didn't see…" He must think I witnessed the scene.

"Sorry I took so long," I say.

"Have you only just got here?" he asks.

"Yes. Why? Did I miss something?"

"No. No, it's fine. I think Alec's ready for you now."

Alec turns, rubbing his jaw.

"Something wrong?" I say to him, trying not to smirk.

"No," he says.

"Well, that's alright then." I look across at Luke and he's hiding a smile.

With a wary glance at the people on the terrace, I start toward Alec.

"Wait a minute," Luke calls from behind me.

"What's wrong?" Alec says.

"We're stopping for now."

"What the f—"

"I said, we're stopping. This shoot was a stupid idea in the first place, but we're not carrying on with an audience."

"What does it matter?"

Luke glares at him. "We'll break for lunch," he says, "and meet back here at three."

"For Christ's sake," Alec splutters.

"Got plans for this afternoon?" Luke walks toward him. "Cancel them."

Alec doesn't say another word, but starts packing away his gear.

Luke comes back to me. "I'll get the management to clear the terrace before three," he says. "This is bad enough without that lot." He motions to the gathering crowd, who seem fascinated by our set-up.

"And if they won't clear the terrace?"

"Don't worry. They will."

Sure enough, by three o'clock, the terrace and the whole surrounding area have been cleared. I don't know how Luke did it, but I'm glad he did. It's much less embarrassing modeling the clothes when I know it's just him and Alec who can see me.

We get the final pictures done by four-thirty and, moaning loudly, Alec packs away again and leaves. Luke and I walk together back to the hotel.

"Are we still okay for dinner?" he asks as we get into the elevator.

"Yes, why?" I wonder if he's having second thoughts.

"It's just, you've been a little distant today. I... well, I thought we were past that." He looks shy all of a sudden.

How can I explain that I'm worried about what he expects from me – especially after hearing his argument with Alec. I have nothing to offer... nothing at all. The elevator arrives at our floor and we step out and start walking down the hallway. "It's just been an uncomfortable day," I tell him. It's not what's troubling me, but it is true – it has been a horrible day. I've hated it. "I didn't enjoy it at all. It was much easier at the river."

"I know," he says. "This shoot was always going to be a problem, but I didn't realize there would be this many people here. I'm sorry."

"It's not your fault."

We arrive at my door. "I should have done something earlier," he says.

"It really isn't your fault," I repeat.

I start to open my door, but he puts his hand on mine. "I'll call for you at seven-thirty," he says, then turns and walks away.

The restaurant is lovely. The lighting is dim – all candles, and fairy lights. It's right on the seafront and serves mainly fish, which is good, because I'm not very hungry; I'm very nervous.

Luke looks fantastic in navy blue linen pants and a white short-sleeved linen shirt. I decided to wear a dress, but not a really, really smart one. I think it was a good choice. It's deep red, off the shoulder, mid-thigh length, with embroidered flowers around the hem. I've taken my hair down again, so it's falling loose around my shoulders and down my back.

We make small talk all through the meal. We start off talking about his previous trips to Europe, what he's seen, how often he's been, his favorite places. He asks about college, what I majored in; my plans. I tell him how much I loved studying history, and that I've been looking for a job – without success. I ask about where he went to college and he tells me that's where he met Matt and how they've been friends ever since.

Being alone with him like this makes me realize how easy he is to talk to, although that doesn't mean I'm going to tell him everything. I heard how he reacted to Alec. If I tell him about my dad, he's going to want to try and make it right, and I can't let him do that. My dad's too controlling… too dangerous… and far too violent.

While the waiter clears the plates, I stare out to sea; the almost disappearing sun is casting glistening shadows on the calm, still water.

"I think we need to talk," Luke says all of a sudden.

"We are talking, aren't we?"

"I meant about us, Megan." I've been dreading this all evening. "We keep getting interrupted," he continues.

"Well, I owe you an apology." It may be embarrassing, but it avoids talking about anything else.

"What for?"

"That mix up with your brother... I can't believe I thought..."

"That I was gay?" He smiles and leans forward. "Neither can I."

"It's just..."

"What? What on earth made you think I might be?"

"Well, there have been quite a lot of women throwing themselves at you, for one thing."

"Does that happen to a lot of gay guys then?" That smile is still dancing on his lips, teasing me.

"Well, no – I mean, I don't know – but surely straight guys tend to respond, don't they?"

"Oh, I see. Well, yes they do... if they're interested. But I wasn't. I mean, I'm not."

I can't tell him that the other reason for my assumption was his lack of attention to me; it makes me sound so conceited, so I say, "Also, I think it was the way you spoke about Will and to him. You were so... affectionate.."

"Well, he is my little brother."

"And I know people with siblings, who positively hate each other."

"We're not like that," he replies.

"You seem to feel... I don't know... responsible for him?"

"Well, yeah. I love him, so of course I do."

I don't have an answer to that. It's such a beautiful thing to say, it doesn't need any more words.

"Besides," he adds, "Will's faced a lot in his life. He's needed my help."

"Why?" I ask, then realize I'm intruding. "I'm sorry," I say quickly. "It's none of my business... you don't have to tell me if you don't want to."

He pauses, looks out to sea for a minute, then turns back. "No, I do want to," he says and I wait. "Our mom died," he begins suddenly, like he wants to get it over with.

"Oh, Luke… I'm so sorry."

"Don't." He holds up a hand. "Please, don't. It… it was awful." *Well, it would be.* "Will was twelve when it happened." He takes a large sip of wine, leaning his elbows on the table, and his chin on his clasped hands. It's like he's gone somewhere else, somewhere very far away. "She… she was naked, in the bath." *Oh, God, no…* "I can still remember the water… it was red."

I can't get my hand across my mouth quickly enough to stop the gasp escaping. The sound brings him back to the present, and he stares at me.

"Are you okay?" he asks.

"Me?" *He's asking about me?* "Sure," I just about manage to say.

"It was Will who found her." He drifts away again. "I was walking home from school and I could hear a howling noise, like a wild animal – a terrified wild animal. I heard it right from the end of the street. I knew instantly it was him and I knew something was really wrong. I ran home, and through the house and I found him, kneeling by the bath, screaming at her to wake up."

I reach across and pull his hands down onto the table, holding them in mine. I need the contact, even if he doesn't… and I think he does.

"I dragged him out of there and shut the door."

"How old were you?" I ask.

His eyes meet mine for a moment. "I was fifteen," he says, then he looks away into the distance again. "I sat with him on the floor for ages, until he stopped howling. Then I took him to his room, and stayed with him until he went to sleep… After that, I went back into the bathroom. She'd used a razor blade…" His voice cracks for the first time. "It was lying on the floor where she'd dropped it." He releases one of his hands, takes another gulp of wine and then puts his hand back in mine again. "I knew I had to call someone… so I called the cops. They came quite quickly. They were kind… sympathetic. They took over, which was good, because I didn't know what to do. Once she... Once her body had been taken away and they'd done everything they needed to do, this cop – John was his name... he told me to call him John – he cleaned the bathroom. He got rid of everything." He looks at me. "That was good of him. I couldn't have faced doing it – and I couldn't have left it like it was for Will to see." I nod my head. He sighs. "They called my dad." It's the first time he's mentioned his father. I'd assumed he wasn't in the picture... "He took a while to come home from whatever hole he was in, but John stayed with me until he did."

I'm struggling to take this in and I let out a loud sigh.

"Did you want dessert, or coffee?" he asks, like everything's perfectly normal.

"Er... no. No, thanks."

"I'll get the check, shall I?"

"Okay."

He waves his hand to attract the waiter, and he brings the check. Without looking at it, Luke hands over his credit card and, after he's paid, we get up to go.

"We can walk back along the beach, if you want?" he says.

I nod my head and he takes my hand, leading me down the steps at the side of the restaurant, onto the stretch of sand. The sun has set, but all the restaurants and hotels along the beachfront are lit up, and it's bright enough to see by. We walk slowly along the shore, holding hands.

"Is Will okay now?" I ask, because I want to know.

"Mostly," Luke replies "But he didn't speak for a long time after it happened."

"Not at all?"

"No." He looks up to the sky. "I guess it was about eighteen months before he said anything. And when he did, it was weird... He just asked me what I was making for dinner, like nothing had happened in between."

I don't say anything, but take on board that, at sixteen, maybe seventeen, Luke was making dinner for his younger brother. Where the hell was their dad? *Drunk, or high... like mine, maybe?*

"For ages, all he talked about was mundane stuff: schoolwork, food, music, TV shows."

"He talked about your mom eventually though, right?"

"Not for years. Not until… not until he came to live with me. And that was only because I made him do it."

I stop and turn to face him.

He takes another deep breath. "I left home to go to college," he says. "That was a tough decision. I needed to go – for myself, for my future. But leaving was hard, for both of us. He'd gotten used to me being around." He pauses, then sighs. "I'd slept on his bedroom floor for the three years since it happened," he says. "He still had nightmares every night… it was easier if I was right there. In the end, he talked me into going; said he'd be fine. So, I left. I met Matt and, within a couple of weeks, we'd moved into an apartment." He thinks for a moment. "I guess it was about six weeks later, I got a call in the middle of the night from Will, begging me to come fetch him. I told him to wait and I'd get there. Matt had a car, so we jumped in it and drove to my dad's house. Will was sitting on the front step, his bags packed. We loaded him up and drove back. He slept on our couch for four years." We start walking again.

"How old was he then?"

"Fifteen."

"What about school?"

"I got him a place in a local school; made sure he went every day. He was a bright kid… he didn't take a lot of persuading. But he struggled with social skills… making friends, sometimes just basic communication. And that was when I made him get some help. He still wasn't talking to me about anything important, but he did speak to the therapist. It really helped. He's so much better than he was. I mean, he's still quiet with other people, but he does talk to them. And he comes to me when he needs to. I never push him, but he knows I'm there for him… not that I know what to say most of the time…"

"How did you cope?"

"Financially?" *No, that wasn't what I meant.* "It was tough… That's why I get not having money," he adds. "We really struggled. I worked a couple of jobs to put food on the table and keep a roof over our heads."

"But you're okay now?"

"Sure, but that's thanks to Matt, not me. He's an amazing guy. He started his company straight out of college, and gave me a job as soon as he could, which was around eighteen months later. Then a few years after that, he made me a partner and gave me a share of the business."

"He must have had a reason to do that... Even nice people don't just *give* away a part of their business."

"Well, you'd have to ask him why." *No, I wouldn't. I really wouldn't.*

"And Will?" I ask.

"He aced college, and he works for the government now – I don't have a clue what he does though. He always uses that old 'If I told you, I'd have to kill you' line. We share a house in the center of Boston... well it's a prison, really."

"A prison?"

"I'm kidding. There's a massive security gate and cameras everywhere. Some people find it intimidating, and weird, but Will likes his set up."

We're back at the hotel, standing by the steps up to the entrance. He suddenly seems drained.

"I'm sorry," he says. "I feel as though I've talked about nothing but myself all evening. That wasn't what I intended at all."

I hesitate for a moment, because I need to tell him something and I don't want to make a mistake. "I think you undervalue yourself," I say, eventually finding the right words. "You give the credit to everyone else, but you've done so much in your life. You made yourself, Luke – no-one else did that." He looks down at the ground.

"If you really knew me, you'd know I've achieved nothing... that the end product isn't anything to be proud of," he murmurs

"You've practically raised your brother by yourself; you put him through college; you've become a successful businessman." I pause again. "All you've talked about is other people... not yourself. When I asked how you coped, I didn't mean financially, I meant how did *you* cope with losing your mom like that, having to deal with everything, helping Will and having to put your own feelings aside for his sake? You didn't even think about that, did you? You're so focused on Will, you've forgotten about yourself. Whatever negative thoughts you're hanging on to, you need to drop them, because you're worth more than that…" I can feel tears welling. I have to go before they start to fall. I lean up and kiss him on the cheek. "I wish you could see the man I'm seeing, Luke… Thank you," I mutter, "for a lovely evening. And for letting me see the real you…" My voice cracks and I turn and run up the blurring steps into the hotel.

Chapter Seven

Luke

I stand, watching her run into the hotel, torn between going after her to make sure she's alright, and sitting down on the steps to work out what just happened.

I choose to sit. I'm not sure I'd be of much use to her right now. I've got too many questions running around in my head… my confused, muddled head.

I never speak about my past. Matt only knows because he was there when Will moved in with us. Will used to have nightmares and wake up screaming, so I had to explain to Matt; it was only fair. He wanted to help, and he did. He and I used to talk for hours – sometimes all night – and, on a more practical level, he paid for Will's therapy. Will needed it; I couldn't afford it, so Matt stepped in… but that's Matt for you.

Even so, Matt doesn't know it all – and neither does Megan. I've only touched the surface with what I've told Megan this evening and, with Matt, I left out one thing. The thing Will hates talking about the most; he feels it diminishes our relationship. I tell him that's bullshit, but we keep it between ourselves… Well, ourselves and my dad, of course.

Megan was really easy to talk to though, even if that wasn't the conversation I'd planned to have with her. At the very least, I'd wanted to ask if she'd let me take her out – and I don't just mean while we're here, but when we get back to the States as well. I've never dated a woman in my life, but I want to date her. I wanted to ask if I could get to know her better... I probably wouldn't have mentioned how much I want her in my bed, but I was going to ask her to try being with me. Being mine can follow later – when she's ready. I'll wait for as long as she needs... and that's another first for me... a big one.

I wish she hadn't made that final speech, though. I mean, sure, it's nice that she thinks about me that way, but, like I said, she doesn't know the real me. She only *thinks* she saw me... She doesn't know anything about the guy who's spent the last thirteen years sleeping around, making an art form out of not getting involved. I know why I lived that life; I've always known... I've never wanted to let anyone get close enough to hurt me, because then they can abandon me... Once in a lifetime is enough for that. I've sometimes wondered if I'd have turned out differently if my mom hadn't done what she did; but then I've never been a great one for what ifs. They don't get you anywhere.

So, I'm back to those questions that are running around my head... Am I worried that if I get involved with Megan, I might get hurt? Sure. I'm terrified. I know now how easily she could rip my heart out. Do I think she will? God, I hope not. And is that fear going to stop me? Not a chance.

For the first time in my life, I really want to take the risk.

Today, we're leaving for Grasse – our next destination and the one I've been looking forward to the most. I'm sure Michel has too, since this is where he'll leave us for a couple of days, to go stay with his wife at a place called Valbonne. This time, we're staying in a château. It's got seven bedrooms, all en-suite, an indoor pool, extensive grounds – for the photography – and a housekeeper, who'll cook for us. It's the most luxurious of the places we're staying in and, with Michel gone and Alec mostly drunk, I'm hoping Megan and I will get to spend some time together. Who knows? I might even be able to say all the things I wanted to say at dinner last night.

We spend the morning at the hotel and leave just after lunch. Alec's gone on ahead. It's only an hour's journey and Megan sits opposite me at the table in the RV, as usual. She's quiet again, but I need to ask her something.

"Megan," I say. She looks up from her Kindle. God, she's got such beautiful eyes.

"Yes?"

"I have a favor to ask."

"Okay."

"It's about last night… those things I told you." She nods her head. "I know I can trust you, but… well, there's no-one else who knows all that except Will, and Matt. Can you…?"

"Keep it to myself?" she asks, turning in her seat to face me. "Of course." She reaches her hand across the table. I take it in mine.

"I know I didn't really need to ask," I say.

"No, you didn't, but it's fine."

My phone buzzes, announcing a text message. It's from Will. I smile as I read it.

— *How's it going? Will*

I quickly type out a one word answer:

— *Progressing.*

His reply is instant.

— *Good. Take care, Luke. W.*

He knows this is a big deal for me. But I think he's also reminding me to take care of Megan, as well as myself. Unlike Megan, he does know the real me. He knows what a selfish asshole I usually am. I stare at the screen for a while, acknowledging the thought, and the fact that, when I'm with her, I don't want to be that guy anymore.

"Is everything okay?" Megan asks.

"Yeah. Sorry – that was Will."

"Is he alright?" she asks.

"He's fine."

"Good." The soulful look in her eyes tells me she means it.

The château is everything I thought it would be – and more. It's perched at the top of terraced gardens, surrounded by palm trees and approached via a long, winding driveway. When the property itself comes into view, Megan gasps – and I don't blame her. There's a tower at one end, and the windows at the front overlook the wide expanse of valley below. The bedrooms upstairs all open onto a balcony which wraps around the whole upper floor and there are formal gardens, surrounded by stone balustrades to the front and side.

Michel parks up the RV and we jump out. Megan stands for a moment and I lean toward her.

"You're doing it again," I whisper.

She turns to me, her eyes sparkling. "What?"

"You need to close your mouth," I smile down at her, "and breathe."

"But… look at it."

"I know." I can't help but grin. "Come on." I take her hand and lead her to the door, which opens as we approach. We're greeted by a smiling, plump woman, of probably about fifty, wearing a black skirt and white blouse, who introduces herself as Carine – the housekeeper.

She shows us into the property.

I ask if Alec has arrived and she says he came by earlier, left his things and went out again.

Michel drops off our bags; we say goodbye and he heads off again to visit his wife. We won't be needing the RV while we're here: all the photographs will be shot in the gardens, and maybe some indoors, if Alec chooses. This is much better… No onlookers.

Carine shows us upstairs to our rooms, telling us that she'll call us when dinner is ready. Mine and Megan's rooms are next door to each other, both with doors out onto the shared balcony. I throw my bag onto the bed and go straight out there to look at the view.

"This is amazing." Megan's voice startles me. She's standing by the stone parapet and I go over to her.

"Isn't it?" I take a chance and put my arm around her. She looks up into my face, but doesn't pull away. Instead she leans into me, and goes back to gazing out across the valley, across the orange rooftops of the villages and lush green trees to the hazy hills beyond. But the view doesn't mean a thing anymore, because she's in my arms, she didn't pull away from me, and she feels good… really good.

"It's breathtaking," she whispers.

"Hmm," I murmur into her hair, "you are."

She twists, looking up to me again. I run my finger down her cheek, then clasp her chin and turn her around to face me. "Megan," I whisper, "I really want to kiss you." I wait. She closes her eyes and leans up toward me. It's an invitation I can't refuse. I lower my mouth to hers and kiss her gently on the lips. She moans softly, opening her mouth to the touch of my tongue and I explore her, just a little, discovering her softness. She tastes sweet, like honey. Apart from my hand on her chin, and my lips on hers, neither of us touches the other, but it's the sexiest, most arousing kiss I've ever had. I pull back eventually and gaze down at her. She's staring at my chest.

"Hey," I say. "Look at me."

She raises her eyes and I immediately wish she hadn't. They're filled with tears. Normally, I'd back off... but weirdly, I move closer to her.

"Hey... what's wrong?" I ask, pulling her into my arms.

"I'm sorry, Luke," she says. "I should never have let that happen." *What the hell?*

An awful idea occurs to me for the first time – although why I've never thought about it before now, I don't know. She's so beautiful, it would make perfect sense... "Y—you don't have a boyfriend back home, do you?" I ask, dreading her reply.

"No," she says, shaking her head.

"Or a husband?" *Please say no.*

She gives off a half-laugh. "No, I don't have a husband either." Her voice is so filled with sorrow, I guess maybe some guy broke her heart.

I pull her closer. She's stiff in my arms, but I place my mouth next to her ear. "Just let me in, baby," I whisper. "I promise—"

"You don't have to promise me anything," she interrupts. "I can't let you in – well, not in the long term. It's not possible." She pulls back, but I don't let her go.

"Why not?" This isn't making any sense at all.

"I can't tell you that."

"Wait a minute... You're telling me you can't get involved with me – and you're not going to even tell me why?"

She nods her head.

"But that's——"

"I know it is," she interrupts again. "I know it's completely unfair and unreasonable of me. But that's why I shouldn't have let you kiss me."

"This isn't just about a kiss, Megan." She looks at me, her head tilted to one side. "I want more than that… I want us to be together. I want something a lot more permanent than a kiss. I——"

"And that's the whole point," she sobs. "I can't… I can't do that."

"So, you don't want to be with me?"

As the first tear falls onto her cheek, I wipe it away with my thumb. It's like an instinct. "You know I do," she whispers. "But… I can't. I'm sorry. You want something permanent, and I can't do that."

And finally, I begin to see the light, although I really don't like it. I don't like it one bit. "Then what you're saying is, you *do* want us to be together and we *can* be together, but if we do, it's not long term… Once we get home, it's over. Is that it? Is that what you're saying? This is all we get?"

She's real still, real quiet.

"I don't know if I can do that, Megan. I'm not…"

"Then we'd better just forget about it," she says. She pulls away from me and this time, I let her go.

She's gone back into her room and closed the doors and I'm still on the balcony, wondering what just happened… and what the hell I'm going to do about it, because I have to be able to do something, don't I?

I stand for ages, trying to think things through.

Kissing isn't something that's really interested me in the past – it's just been a means to an end… a precursor. I've never kissed a woman before just for the sake of it… but that kiss with Megan was something else. She felt so good, even though I wasn't really touching her. I'd never have thought that something as simple as a kiss could feel like that; could make *me* feel like that.

I'm so damn confused. She doesn't seem the type to have casual sex. On the contrary, she seems exactly the opposite. I should know… I'm the goddamn expert. The irony of this situation isn't lost on me. Having spent years avoiding commitment, the moment when I'm happy to pursue it, the woman I want to be with is just looking for something casual. I wonder if this is what they call Karma… All my past misdemeanors catching up with me? If so, Karma's a bitch.

The question is: what to do about it? The way I look at it, either way I'm screwed.

I could do things her way… and risk getting hurt, but at least I'll have had some time with her, even if it is too brief… Can I do that though? Can I have her now and walk away when we get back home, like none of it happened? I shake my head, because I just don't know.

I wander back into my bedroom and lie down on the bed.

Should I do it my way? Should I walk now? Can I go through life knowing I had the chance to be with her, even if it was just for a while, and that I didn't take it? Can I live with never kissing her again, never knowing her, never discovering her secrets? I close my eyes and think, just for a second or two.

No. No, I can't. I can't do that.

If doing it her way is the only chance I have to be with her, then I'll do it.

And I'll just have to walk away at the end… and hope to keep my heart intact.

Some hope.

Megan

I can't even cry anymore. It's getting dark; it'll be time for dinner soon and I'll have to sit across the table from him, and pretend that the kiss never happened; that I didn't make a fool of myself – again.

Was it wrong of me to let him think I'm the type of woman who has casual sex? That's not who I am at all. But when he asked the question, I couldn't say 'no'. I couldn't deny that, if a brief affair is all we could have, then I'd take it. I'd take it with both hands and be grateful, because I love him. I really do love him... and I'd rather have whatever time I can with him now and deal with the pain of saying goodbye, than have a lifetime of regret, filled with 'what ifs', and 'if onlys'.

Still, he said he couldn't do it... At least one of us was being sensible.

I recall the pained look on Luke's face when I told him I shouldn't have let him kiss me. The regret he saw in my eyes wasn't about the kiss... not really. It was for what we can't have... what I can never have. I can't risk us getting involved and my dad finding out. He'd kill Luke... and probably me as well. It's what he's always threatened... and with his track record, I believe him. I've spent a lifetime... well, nearly a lifetime, living in fear of that man... it's a hard habit to break. Your parents are meant to be the ones you trust most... the ones you turn to when you're in trouble and you need help. Mine turned out to be the opposite. Still, I don't want to think about that now. I'd rather think about Luke than that... and that's saying something.

For the first time in my life, I know what it feels like to be wanted. I saw that in his eyes, just before I hurt him; just before I told him we couldn't be together like he wants. But now I've seen that, I want more. I want him. Even if it can only be for now and not forever. Admittedly, if he and I walk away from each other once we get home, and agree never to contact each other again, the chances of my dad finding out are about the same as they are of him finding out about this photo shoot, so we'd probably be alright. It might be worth the risk, but... well, it's not going to happen now, so there's no point in thinking about it. Luke can't do it, no matter how much I want to... And I really do want to.

I hear Carine calling us for dinner. I haven't changed out of the white sundress I've been wearing all day. I'm a mess... I quickly splash my face with cold water, but as I look at my reflection in the mirror, I wonder... what does it matter if I'm a mess? Does anything really matter anymore?

I make my way downstairs and Carine directs me to the sunroom, where she's laid the table for two. Alec hasn't come back, so it's just Luke and I. This could have been so different, if only... *Oh God. The if onlys have started already.*

I stand alone... very alone. For the first time since we got here, I just want to go home.

"Hi." His voice sends shivers down my spine.

I turn and he's right behind me. He looks down, straight into my eyes, and I know I've stopped breathing – again. Carine comes in from the kitchen.

"Sit, sit," she says and we do, opposite each other, and she lays out plates of goat's cheese salad in front of us, and opens a bottle of wine.

"Can we have some mineral water for Megan, please?" Luke asks her.

"Certainly," she says and goes away again, returning quickly with a bottle of sparkling water. She pours some into my glass.

"Bon appetit," she says and leaves us alone.

We eat. I'm sure the food is lovely, but I can't taste anything at all. I don't look up through the whole of the course, and Luke doesn't say a word. I wonder if we can get through a whole meal like this. Can we get through the rest of the trip like this?

Carine comes in and clears the dishes, then re-appears, with a two plates of chicken in a creamy mushroom sauce, with crispy potatoes and green beans. She leaves again, muttering to herself in French. The smell is delicious… and I feel sick. Once she's gone, Luke picks up his knife and fork, he pauses for a moment, then he lays them down again and looks at me.

"I can't keep this up any longer," he says. "I've gone over and over it in my head… If we do this, Megan… if we get together, do you really want to say goodbye when we get home?" he asks. *I have no choice.*

I nod my head. I may as well tell him… "It's not something I have a choice in, Luke."

"And you won't tell me why?"

"I can't." *You'll only try and make it right… and you can't.*

He sits back in his chair and sighs deeply. "Okay. We'll do it your way," he says.

"Sorry?" *What's he saying?*

"If that's the only way I can have you, then so be it. We'll say goodbye at the end." He looks really sad.

"No, Luke. That's not what you want." *It's not what I want either,* I'm screaming inside. "You want a relationship – something more permanent. That's what you said."

"Yeah, I do."

"And when we get home?"

"If you still want us to go our separate ways, I'll respect that. I'll walk away."

"Really?" *Will he? Or does he think I'll change my mind?*

"Yes, really." He sounds sincere. "I never go back on my word, Megan. And you have my word. Don't get me wrong, I'm gonna do everything in my power while we're here to persuade you that we can make this work, but when we get back to Boston, if you still want nothing more to do with me, I'll walk away and I'll stay away. You won't hear from me again. I promise." He means it. He really means it. He's looking at me, like he's waiting for an answer… which I suppose he is.

I know that saying goodbye, when it happens, is going to break me. But I can't go back now. I've had a glimpse of what I could have with him and there's no going back.

I close my eyes, just for second. When I open them, he's still staring at me. "Okay," I whisper.

His eyes widen, just a fraction, then he gets up, his chair scraping against the tiled floor, and he's next to me, pulling me to my feet and into his arms.

"You want this?" he says. I nod my head and his lips are on mine, crushing them. His tongue is in my mouth, claiming me. This is much more... much, much more than the kiss we shared earlier. There's a heat, a need that wasn't there before. His hands are in my hair, his feet either side of mine and I can feel his erection pressing into my hip. I suck in a breath and he pushes his tongue deeper into my mouth. He breaks the kiss, breathless. "Sure?" he asks, looking into my eyes.

"Yes," I breathe.

He leans down and picks me up... and I'm in his strong arms. I wrap my own around his neck and he carries me to the stairs.

"Wait a minute!" I say, just before he starts to climb.

"What?" he asks.

"What about dinner?"

"You want to eat? Now?"

"Well, no, but Carine went to a lot of trouble. It feels wrong to just leave it."

He laughs, looking down at me. "Did you hear her muttering to herself?" I nod my head. "She was questioning why I didn't just take you to bed, being as that was what we both so obviously wanted."

"Oh..."

"So, can we carry on now?" he says.

"Yes." He doesn't take his eyes from mine as he climbs, or when he opens the door to his room, and we go inside. He doesn't turn on the light; the sun's last rays cast a pale golden glow across the room and he gently lays me down on the bed, then pulls off his shirt, over his head, and drops it on the floor. His chest is solid muscle and he moves toward me, his smoldering eyes still fixed on mine.

He climbs up over me, and kisses me again, just briefly, before moving back down, his lips touching briefly over my neck, my shoulders

103

and my breasts, through the thin cotton of my dress. I gasp at the contact. He continues downward, raising the skirt of my dress to reveal my white cotton panties. I close my eyes and surrender myself to him.

Chapter Eight

Luke

Iknew she'd look good… I knew she'd look incredible. But she's beyond anything I could have imagined. She's perfect. She's lying on my bed. She wants me. All I have to do is forget that this can't be forever. *Yeah, right… that'll be real easy.*

I raise the skirt of her dress. She's wearing cotton panties. They're cute… not sexy, but cute.

"I want you naked," I say to her. Her eyes pop open and I pull her up and stand her on her feet, then slowly undo the zipper on her dress and lift it over her head. She's not wearing a bra and her breasts are revealed, her nipples hard, like pebbles. I lean down and take one in my mouth, sucking hard, and she heaves in a gasp of air between her teeth. Then I kiss my way downward, kneeling as I go, until I reach her panties. Hooking my thumbs in either side, I pull them down her legs and she steps out of them, kicking off her shoes. She's standing before me, beautifully naked. I can smell her arousal. I can even see it. She's shaved and slick… I sit on the floor, and move her so she's standing astride and above me, her legs wide apart. There's something wanton about having her revealed to me like this and I run my tongue along her folds, using my fingers to part her wider still, opening up her gorgeous pussy. She squeals as I lick her clitoris, swirling over and over, around it, stimulating her. I start to suck and nip at her gently with my teeth, alternating between soft and rasping motions. Her breathing soon becomes labored and heavy. Christ, she's responsive… She's close already, and I want to feel her come apart on my tongue… And even as I'm thinking it, she explodes. She screams and her legs start to buckle. I hold her up, while she rides out her orgasm, letting her calm.

I sit back, resting on my hands and look up at her. Her eyes are still closed, her mouth parted, smiling that sexy smile of hers. That's a look a man would die for.

I move back from between her legs, then stand and, in one move, I'm out of my pants and trunks, then I lift her onto the bed, spreading her legs wide apart with my own, and kneeling between them.

"You still sure?" I say, giving her one last chance to change her mind. *Please don't.*

She nods her head, then closes her eyes again.

I rub the head of my cock along her soaking entrance and then push into her. Man, she's really tight… I mean, unbelievably tight. I stop for a second, then try again, pushing a little further… then… *What. The. Fuck.*

I pull out of her – not that I was ever really in her – and kneel back.

"What?" she says, her eyes open again. "What's wrong?"

I look down at her, my mind racing. "You're… You're a virgin?"

"Well… yes."

"And when were you thinking of telling me this? Clearly not at all."

She sits up. Her arms folded across her chest. She looks embarrassed. "I wasn't aware *telling* you was necessary. I thought it would become obvious."

"Well, yeah… It just did."

"And this is a problem?" *No shit, Sherlock.*

"Yeah, it's a problem." Isn't that obvious? "I can't do this… *We* can't do this…"

I get up, running my fingers through my hair. She scrambles off the bed, comes around and grabs her clothes and, without saying a word, runs from the room. I hear a sob just as the door closes.

"Megan! Wait!" I call after her, but she's gone.

I flop down onto the edge of the bed. How could she even think of doing this? How could she think it's okay to have casual sex when she's still a virgin? Does she really want me to be her first, and then to just forget about me? Doesn't she realize what a big deal this is? I should know. I've never had a virgin before – not once – for the very simple reason that I know it's a big deal… and not one I've wanted to handle.

I thought she'd had some experience at least, or I'd have gone about that totally differently. I'd have taken a lot longer… I'd have been a lot gentler. I feel like such a jerk. But I didn't know, because she didn't damn well tell me.

I close my eyes and think back over what I've just done with her. Yeah, I could have done that very differently. I could have taken it more slowly, been more considerate, more tender… But she tasted sensational; she felt amazing. I wonder, briefly, if that was her first orgasm. Surely not… She's twenty-two. Some guy, at some time, must have made her come – or she might do it herself. I like the second thought… I find I'm not so keen on the first one.

She was crying when she ran out of here. Of course she was. I stopped what I was doing, but I didn't really tell her why – not properly – and I think I probably came across as a bit angry. I'm not… I'm not angry at all. I'm confused. I get to my feet and pull on my pants. I need to talk to her.

I knock on her door. There's no reply, so I knock again – louder, then louder still until she yells, "Go away!" Not ideal, but at least I know she's in there.

"Let me in," I call through the door.

"No."

I think for a minute, then go back into my room, out onto the balcony and enter her room through the unlocked glass doors. She's lying on the bed, still naked, her dress clasped in her hand.

"Megan," I say. She starts and sits up, clutching the dress to her, trying to cover herself. "I'm sorry."

"Go away," she says.

"No. Not until I've explained."

"Explained what? How you don't want me? I think I've been humiliated enough for one night, thanks."

I walk across and sit on the end of the bed, giving her space.

"No," I say. "I want to explain that I do want you. I want you so much. But… but why didn't you tell me you're still a virgin?"

"Why does it matter?"

"Sorry?" Did she really just say that?

"Why does it matter to you so much that I didn't tell you?"

Oh, I see. "Because I'm not sure I'd have agreed to your… your terms, if I'd known. It's a big deal, Megan. You shouldn't throw it away on a casual affair."

"It's *my* virginity, we're talking about – not yours. What I decide to do with it is up to me."

I move closer to her. Can't she see what I'm getting at here? "Yeah, Megan, but given what you've asked for, given you don't want a long-term relationship with me, some of that decision is mine, isn't it? Don't I have a right to choose too? I might not like the idea of taking your virginity and just walking away from you… it makes a difference. It's a big responsibility."

She slumps, all the fight gone from her. "I'm *not* your responsibility, Luke."

And then it hits me… That's exactly what she is. That's exactly what I want her to be. Because that's what happens when you love someone. And I do love her. *Shit*… I really do love her. I reach for her and pull her into my arms, covering her mouth with mine and she melts into me. She wants this just as much as I do… I know she does. And if we both want it so much, we can make it work, can't we?

I break the kiss and look down at her. "You *are* my responsibility," I whisper and she nods, like she's accepting my words… accepting me. She lies back down on the bed, moving the dress to one side and revealing her body. Despite the temptation to lower my eyes, I keep looking at her face. She's staring at me.

"You still want…?" I ask, unable to finish the sentence.

"You." She does it for me.

I stand and take off my pants, and lie down next to her.

"Sure?" I ask. I have to be certain – even more so than before.

She nods her head.

Leaning up on one elbow, I trace my way down her body with the tips of my fingers, pausing at each breast, to circle her nipples, and gently pinch them between my forefinger and thumb. She tips her head back and raises her hips.

"Slow," I whisper, leaning down and swirling my tongue across each extended nipple, while my fingers move down, to her smooth, wet pussy.

She parts her legs and I rub her clitoris, with soft, slow motions, over and over, until she's arching her back and writhing next to me.

"Please, Luke," she whispers. "Please…"

"Hush, baby," I say and I kneel between her legs. She's staring up at me as I rub the head of my cock against her, right at her entrance. She's tight. I'm gonna stretch her… and it's gonna hurt. I have to go slow, even though every fiber in my body is begging me to take her. I push in, just a little and she gasps. "Just relax, baby," I murmur. I hold where I am for a while, then push again, and again, a little harder this time. She cries out. I hate that I've hurt her and I still, leaning down to hold her for a minute while she gets used to the sensation. "You okay?" I ask.

"I think so," she says.

I raise myself up again. She's looking into my eyes. "I'm gonna move," I tell her. "Stop me if it hurts." I push a little further inside her. She doesn't flinch or stop me, so I keep going, inch by inch, until she's taken my whole length. She's so tight, I just want to stay here forever, clamped deep inside her.

But I have to move… I need to, more than anything. I pull out, then push in again, slowly. I hear her breath catch, but she's smiling, her eyes closed. I stop again, deep inside her, and just watch, absorbing the moment, letting it imprint on my brain, because whatever happens, I know I'll never have this time again. She opens her eyes, locking them with mine and I swallow down my emotions and start to move again, building a steady rhythm. She raises her hips, meeting me, matching me. Tiny moans escape her lips and I lean down and kiss her, capturing the sounds she makes, storing them away too. Her hands come up my arms, resting on my biceps for a while before moving up and around my neck, and I start to move faster, deeper… just a little harder.

She groans into my mouth, then breaks the kiss, throws her head back and screams my name, as she climaxes again. And that's it for me… I choke back the lump in my throat and plunge deep into her, filling her for what feels like forever. And now I know for sure it's going to kill me if I really have to walk away from her.

Megan

How am I ever going to give him up?

He's still lying on top of me and I never want him to move. Ever. If we could just stay here, joined like this, forever…

He lifts his head and stares down at me. There's a new, intense look in his eyes that wasn't there before and I wonder if he sees the same thing in mine.

"You okay?" he whispers, his voice rasping.

I nod my head. My voice won't work yet. Without pulling out of me, he turns us onto our sides, facing each other, our legs entwined.

He leans in and kisses my neck, along my jawline and up to my ear. "Thank you," he whispers.

"What for?" I manage to mutter.

He leans back. "You need to ask?" I stare at him. "Letting me make love to you," he explains. "Letting me be your first."

"It was my pleasure." I can't help but smile.

He smiles back. "I noticed." I can feel my face reddening and I look down a little. "Don't be embarrassed," he says. "You looked beautiful when you came." He hesitates for moment. "Was that your first?"

"Um… I thought we established that already?"

He smirks. "No. I meant your first orgasm."

"No." A shadow crosses his eyes. "It was my second. I had my first in your room earlier… remember?"

He smiles. "You mean, you've never done anything before tonight?" I shake my head, and look down, embarrassed again. "Will you stop doing that," he says, putting his finger under my chin and raising my face to his. "I have no idea how someone as stunning as you got to be twenty-two and untouched…" And I'm not going to tell him either, because then I'd have to give away the reason we can't be together when we get home. "But I'm glad you did," he continues, a broad grin spreading across his lips. "It means everything about you is mine."

"Not entirely," I say.

He raises an eyebrow, looking inquisitive.

"I have been kissed… once."

"Just once?" He's surprised. *You wouldn't be, if you knew.* "We won't count that then," he says, and leans down to take my mouth again.

As our tongues start to twist and dance, I can feel him growing hard inside me and he begins to rock back and forth, grinding his hips into mine. It's gentle, slow, and so tender… and I know I'm lost to him… forever.

I think we must have both slept for a while. When I wake up, I'm cold and I curl into him.

"What's wrong?" he murmurs.

"I'm cold,"

"I'll shut the doors." He climbs out of bed and goes over to the doors, pulling them closed. When he returns, he stands by the bed for a moment, looking down at me. "God, you're beautiful," he says, then gets back in, pulling me across and covering us both with the comforter. I rest my head on his chest and he puts his arms around me, and we doze.

When I wake again, it's just after dawn and he's on his side, staring at me.

He looks really worried. "What?" I say. "What's happened?"

"I'm sorry," he says. "I really, really screwed up last night."

I've been wondering how long it would take him to regret what we've done – I thought it might be a few days, rather than a few hours, but I knew this moment would come eventually. This isn't what he wants… He's obviously not a short-term fling person any more than I am. And now he's had time to think it through, he's realized he can't go on with it.

"I understand," I tell him. "I knew it was too good to be true—"

"What are you talking about?" he says, raising himself up on one elbow.

"I knew you'd regret your decision. This isn't what you wanted at all, is it?"

"Of course it is. You're just what I want. More to the point, I think you're just what I need."

"No… I mean the whole relationship thing. Short term clearly isn't your style…"

"Megan, I've spent my whole life avoiding commitment. None of the women I've been with in the past has ever made me want to have a relationship with them. Having one with you was going to be… well… new."

What? How can that be? "But…"

"You're different. You make me want to try and be a better man…"

Now I feel even worse. "So I'd have been *your* first?"

He smiles. "Yeah… Ironic, isn't it?"

I feel so selfish, I can't even look at him. He runs his finger down my cheek and I shudder at his touch. "Hey, it was my choice." He turns my face to his. "I could've walked away. I chose not to. You didn't force me into this."

"You don't regret it?"

"No. I'll never regret it." He's still smiling. "Best decision I ever made… whatever happens in the future."

My eyes are filling with tears, and I reach up and pull him down into a kiss. He starts to delve into my mouth with his tongue, his hands finding my breasts and I arch my back off the bed. I want him again.

"Wait!" he says, breaking away. "You manage to make me forget everything… and I mean *everything*." I look up at him, feeling a little deprived without his lips, his touch, the anticipation of what he can do to me.

"What are you talking about?"

"That's what I was trying to tell you before you distracted me… I screwed up last night. I really screwed up… I forgot to use a condom."

My mouth falls open. I can't help it. "Oh." It's all I can manage to say.

"I'm sorry," he says, adding, "I'm clean – I promise. I had a medical not long before I came over here. And I'm always careful… except when I'm with you, it seems… "

We both know I'll be clean. Neither of us needs to even go there… "But… but…" I can't get the words out.

"But you're not on birth control?" He does it for me.

I shake my head. *Why would I be?* He closes his eyes, just for a second.

"I'm sorry, Megan," he repeats, opening them again.

"It's as much my fault as yours…"

"No it isn't. I told you last night – you're my responsibility." He moves on top of me and I instinctively part my legs so he can nestle between them, resting against me. He raises himself up on his elbows.

"I'm sure the dates are wrong," I tell him. I can't remember if they are or not. I've never been very regular anyway, but I don't want him to feel obligated. I should have thought about it too.

"Okay," he replies. "But if they're not…"

"Well then, we'll—"

"The agreement's off, Megan." *No, it can't be.* "I mean it," he says firmly. "I won't walk away from you, not if you're carrying my child. I don't care what promises I made last night… if you're pregnant, the deal's off."

And just for a second, I hope that I am.

"For Christ's sake, Megan, will you stop staring out the window and look at the camera." Alec's voice penetrates my thoughts. He doesn't realize I'm looking at Luke, who's talking on the phone, and standing just outside the window. He's got his back to me, but even from that angle, he's still beautiful. "About time," he says as I turn to face him. We're in the room which Carine calls the 'Salon', which has floor-to-ceiling windows running along two walls, so it's almost like being outside, and I'm leaning up against a black, shiny grand piano, partially covered with a white jacquard cloth.

"Okay. Take off the robe and just throw it over here, being as Myers has decided he's got someone more interesting to talk to." The thought makes me shiver. What if it's another woman? I glance back at Luke. He made no secret of having been with other women... women he didn't want to have relationships with... maybe he's talking to one of them... No. He wouldn't do that. Would he? He says sweet, romantic things to me... he makes me feel special, but I don't really know him. Oh, God...

I undo the robe, shrug it off and throw it across to where Alec is standing. I'm wearing a black lace underwired bra with scalloped edging, studded with crystals, a matching thong and garter belt, with black lace-topped stockings and high heeled shoes.

I hear a sharp intake of breath and look up. Luke has come in through the patio doors and is staring at me, a slight smile on his lips. I wonder again who he was talking to.

"Put your right hand on the piano," Alec says. "And with your left hand, make like you're going to tuck your hair behind your ear... that's it. Now, look at the floor about two feet in front of where you're standing. Great. Hold that." He starts taking pictures.

I can feel Luke's eyes boring into me. I want him... I want to feel him inside me... I need the reassurance of his words, his touch, his kisses.

"Okay," Alec says, snapping me back to the present. "Put your hands on your hips and push your tits toward me." I let out a sigh. "Just do it, Princess." I do as he asks. "Good," he says, and I hear the camera shutter clicking again.

"Turn around," he orders me. I do, although I miss the view of Luke. "Now, lean over the piano, just a little. I still need to see the back of the bra, not just your ass." *Thank God for that.*

I lean. "Move your legs just a little further apart... That's it." He takes a few more shots. "Okay," he says. "We'll take the next ones outside by the parapet."

"What do you want Megan to change into?" Luke asks picking up the robe and handing it to me. I shrug it on, tying it loosely.

"The corset, I think. Keep the thong on, though."

"I'll have to help you," Luke says. "Unless you'd rather I asked Carine...?"

I glance up at him... *You're kidding, right?* He gives me a wink behind Alec's back.

"No. It'll be fine," I say, trying to hide a smile. "You can just do me up."

"I'll get set up outside," Alec calls as we both leave the room.

Once the door's shut, Luke takes my hand. "C'mon," he says and we run up the stairs together.

He slams my bedroom door behind us and pushes me back against it, pulling the robe off and letting it fall to the floor. He moves closer, his body holding me in place, his lips hard on mine as his hands roam over my sensitized, heated skin.

"You're too much," he says, leaning back.

"I need to get changed," I pant, my earlier fears forgotten already. How can I be so breathless, so quickly?

"Really?"

"What?"

"You're standing there, looking like that, and you want to just get changed?"

"Well, yes... into a corset." I smile at him.

"Oh... well, if you put it like that." He grins and reaches behind me to undo the bra. He lets it fall to the floor, kicking it aside, and bends to take one of my nipples in his mouth, sucking it, then taking it between his teeth. The sensation sends a shivering tingle straight down between my legs.

"Um… Luke," I breathe. "How much is that bra worth?"

He straightens, looking at me. "A little under eight hundred dollars… Why?"

That's more than my share of the rent on our apartment. "Because you just dropped it on the floor, that's why…"

"I don't care." He returns to my breast, cupping it and sucking my nipple into his mouth. I let out a sigh and grasp his shoulders, hearing him chuckle.

"What's funny?" I say.

"I thought you were in a hurry to change?"

"You distracted me."

"You're very easily distracted."

"So are you."

He drops to his knees and undoes the garter belt, unfastening it from the black stockings, and rolling them slowly down my legs to pull them off. Then he kisses me at the apex of my thighs, and stands up again. "Stay there," he whispers, and walks over to the bed, returning with the corset. He wraps it around me, doing up the hook and eye fastenings down my front.

"Did I really need your help for this?" I ask.

He straightens. "Yeah… just give me a minute." He stands back, his eyes roaming over my body. "Turn," he says and I do. He tightens the lacing in the back, then he kneels again and I feel him run his hands over my ass. Instinctively, I move my feet back a little and bend forward just slightly, my hands resting on the door. He stands up behind me and leans over, his mouth next to my ear.

"I think you're ready," he murmurs and I feel myself deflate.

"Oh." I can't hide my disappointment as I turn to him.

He's grinning. "I meant ready for me." He takes my hand and leads me to the end of bed. "We don't have long," he says. He reaches into his pocket and pulls out a condom. "See? I remembered this time," he says, yanking his t-shirt over his head. He undoes his shorts and lets them fall to the floor. He's not wearing underwear and, standing naked before me, he makes me tremble with anticipation. Last night it was dark, and – if I'm honest – I was a little frightened of looking at him… but now… I can feel myself staring at his erection. He steps closer and my mouth opens slightly, my eyes fixated.

"Don't look so worried. We fit together, Megan," he says. "We fit together perfectly."

"I guess… but it's…" I gulp. "Are you sure?"

He laughs. "Yep," he says. "Want me to prove it?" I manage to move my eyes up to his face. How can I not want this beautiful man? I nod my head. He turns me toward the bed. "Bend over," he says. I do as he asks. It's a sleigh bed and I bend, grabbing the wooden footboard, then I feel him behind me, his arousal pressing against me. "Ready?" he asks.

"Yes," I whisper… although I'm not sure for what. I hear the tearing of a foil packet, then a pause.

He pulls the thong aside and enters me in one swift but gentle movement, until he's deep inside me. "This'll be quick," he says, holding still, "and fun. Just hold on to the bed." And, grabbing my hips tight, he starts to move, pushing into me harder and harder, until my heels lift off the floor with each deep thrust.

Holding onto me with his left hand, he brings his right around in front and starts to rub my clitoris with his fingers, making small circular motions. That fluttering starts up, and builds quickly, until I'm moaning loudly.

"Try…" he mutters, plunging hard into me. "Try not to…" He thrusts again. "Scream." *Really? And how on earth do I do that?* He drives into me one last time, and cries out loudly as he lets go. I clamp my muscles around him, and the pleasure overwhelms me, his name escaping my lips as quietly as I can manage, my gasps becoming a gentle whimper as I calm.

He pulls out of me and I stand up and turn into his arms. "I wasn't too rough, was I?" he asks, leaning back to look at my face.

"No. I enjoyed it," I tell him truthfully.

He grins. "Good… So did I." He kisses me gently.

"Um… you weren't exactly quiet, though. And you told *me* not to scream."

"I know. Sorry about that. I couldn't help it. I just don't want Alec to know about us."

"Neither do I. But what if he heard you?"

"I'll think of something." He kisses me again, then lets me go. "On which note, I guess we'd better get back down there." He goes into the bathroom and returns a couple of minutes later. The condom has gone, although he's still quite hard. I can't stop staring, even as I straighten myself out and run my fingers through my hair.

"Oh, that won't do," he says, coming to stand in front of me again. "That won't do at all."

"Why? What's wrong?"

"Your face."

"What's wrong with my face?"

"Absolutely nothing… it's perfect." He steps closer, resting his hands on my hips. "But your eyes give everything away."

"What do you mean?" I panic. Can he see how I feel about him? Can he tell just from looking at my eyes that I'm in love with him?

"You've got a satisfied, contented – frankly, just-fucked – look in your eyes… It kind of gives away what we've been doing."

Thank God for that. At least I'm not completely transparent then. "Don't worry. Alec will soon wipe any trace of happiness from my face."

"Then I'll have to try and put it back again later," he says, leaning down and kissing me. "I really kinda like that look on you."

Once we're dressed, we head back down the stairs, but at the bottom, I pull him back and he turns. Alec's earlier comment is still bothering me and my expression must give me away, because Luke moves closer – much closer.

"Something's wrong," he whispers. "Tell me."

"I need to ask you a question." I can't hide the nervousness in my voice.

"Then ask."

"I'm sorry…" I know I should try and trust him, but it's only going to play on mind if I don't find out… "Alec made a remark earlier about you having someone better to talk to than me… when you were on the phone. It got me thinking…"

"You want to know who I was talking to?"

He sounds so sincere and I know I'm being unreasonable. "No," I say. "It's fine. You don't have to tell me. Alec was just being Alec. I don't need—"

"It was Will," he says.

"But it must have been about four in the morning at home."

He places his hand on my cheek. I lean into it, closing my eyes. "He had to work all night; something's worrying at him and, although he can't tell me anything about it, he just needed someone to talk to. That's all."

"I'm sorry," I whisper, opening my eyes. "It's just… well, you said there had been other women…"

"Yeah, there have been. But they're in the past. They're not important."

I nod my head. I'm not giving him a future with me, so what right do I have to question him about his past?

His eyes are searching mine. "I'll never cheat on you. You know that, don't you? You have nothing – *nothing* – to fear."

Except trying to live without you when this is all over.

Chapter Nine

Luke

Without a doubt, these have been the best – and the worst – ten days of my life. Ever since that night at the château, when I first made love to Megan, I can't get enough of her; I can't keep my eyes or my hands off her. We've had to do a lot of sneaking around, which can be fun, and can add to the excitement, but can also be annoying, because I want us to just be together, be ourselves, not have to check where everyone else is first, and make sure that no-one can hear or see us. Each time we're together, it just seems to get better, but then, with every passing day, I'm reminded that our time is limited, that I've promised to walk away when we get home, and that I'm going to have to find a way to somehow live without her. And the more time we've spent together, the more I'm doubting I'll be able to do it. I'm still trying, and so far failing, to find a way to persuade her we can work this out.

Fortunately, she hasn't raised the subject of my past again. That morning, at the foot of the stairs in the château, I really thought she was going to ask me for details. I couldn't have lied to her, but telling her the truth would probably have finished us before we'd even got started. As it is, she seems to have accepted that I have a past, and I don't care about it. I don't. I only care about her, and the future I still desperately want to have with her… the future she keeps telling me can't happen.

Today is the last day of shooting. We're in Carcasonne, in south-west France, working in a field of glorious sunflowers.

Alec is taking the final set of pictures; it's late afternoon and the sun is waning, so he can get the light effect he wants and we've saved the best till last really. This is the Rose Gold design, which I know Matt particularly likes. Megan's wearing the bra, thong, garter belt, with stockings, and kimono. The fabric features two layers of lace, the one on top being silver, and the one beneath being antique gold. She's facing away from me right now, talking to Alec, and her hair is cascading down her back in ringlets. She's shimmering against the green and yellow sunflowers in the soft golden sunlight. And it's not just the underwear that's creating that effect. Megan's positively glowing. We made love twice this morning at the villa before coming out here, and then at lunchtime in the RV, I took her over the table, and I want her again already. It's never been like this with anyone else... this need in me, this want for her. How the hell am I ever going to let her go?

I wander back to the RV, pulling out my phone as I go, and connecting the call I need to make.

"Hi, Luke," Grace says, answering on the third ring. "How's everything going?"

"We're wrapping up tonight," I tell her, pacing up and down.

"That's great," she says. "You're finished early."

"Yeah. That's why I've called."

"Oh?"

"Yeah. Do you remember Matt said I could take some time and have a short vacation?"

"Yes," she replies.

"Well, I'm going to."

"Okay... but shouldn't you be telling him this?"

"I can, if you like. But I wanted your advice."

"Oh?" She's surprised.

"Yeah. I felt like going somewhere different. I thought about going to England, but I don't really want to stay in London... I've kind of done that over the last few years."

"Right…"

"So, where can you recommend?"

"That depends what you're looking for."

I can't tell her I want to go somewhere romantic, where I can spend a week trying to persuade Megan to let me stay in her life. "Somewhere quiet, nice scenery…" I run out of things to say.

"Well… you could go for the Lake District."

"We've spent a lot of time around water on this trip… I'm guessing there are lakes in the Lake District…?"

"Well, yes, but there are also mountains and hills. It's beautiful, Luke, really beautiful."

"Okay… I'm sold."

"Good. You'd have to get a flight to Manchester, I guess," she says. "You're in Carcasonne now, aren't you?"

"Yeah." I can hear her tapping on her keyboard. There's a pause.

"You can get a flight from Toulouse, to Manchester via Heathrow," she says. "Do you want me to book it for you?"

"No," I say quickly – maybe a little too quickly. I breathe and calm down. "Don't worry, I'll take care of it… So, where's a good place to stay?"

She goes quiet for a moment. "I used to go there with my parents for holidays. They liked the area around Keswick. And just so you know, that spelt K-e-s-w-i-c-k… You don't say the 'w'."

I laugh. "Thanks for the heads-up."

"There's a nice hotel not far from there… I can't remember the name… Hang on." Again I hear her tapping. "Yes… It's called the Lake Falls Hotel," she says. "It has spectacular views."

"Okay. I'll check it out."

"How's everything gone?" she asks.

"Not too bad," I tell her, trying to sound nonchalant. I can hardly tell her that I've met the woman I want to spend the rest of my life with, or that I've got just one week in the Lake District to convince her to agree to that.

"Not too bad?" she repeats. I'm worried by her tone – has Alec found out about us and filtered the information back to Matt? No... he'd have contacted me himself by now if he knew. "From what we've seen, it's been amazing," she continues. "Alec's sent back the images from the first two shoots. They're beautiful. Megan looks just stunning, Luke. You've all done such a good job. Matt's really pleased."

"Thanks," I say. "I can't really take any of the credit."

"I'm sure that's not true... not if Alec's reputation is anything to go by." I don't really want to talk about reputations, not when I'm trying to forget about mine. "Oh... Matt's just come in... did you want to talk to him?"

I can hardly say 'no', although we've not spoken since our argument about the agency, and I never did reply to his message.

"Sure," I say.

"Oh... just before I put him on, we've had an update from Emma. Nate's doing really well. They think he'll be allowed to go home in a few days."

"That's great news."

"It'll be a while before he can go back to work, but the doctors think he'll make a full recovery."

"How's Emma doing?"

"She's much better now she knows Nate's okay. Matt's given her indefinite paid leave so she can look after him."

"Good." I'm not even remotely surprised. It's exactly the kind of thing Matt would do.

"I'll put Matt on now," she says. "Enjoy your break."

"Thanks, Grace."

I wait a couple of seconds, then, "Hi." It's Matt. He sounds nervous. "You talking to me now?" he says.

"Sure."

"I'm sorry about what happened... I should've checked up that Megan knew what she was doing. I was aware it was her first time as a model, and I—"

"Matt, give it a rest, will you? It was an awkward situation and I'm sorry I took it out on you." It's true. I am sorry. "It wasn't your fault."

"The images we've seen so far are amazing, Luke," he says. We're both real good at letting things drop once we've cleared the air. Neither of us can hold a grudge.

"Wait until you see the ones we've done today. They're breathtaking." *Well, Megan is.*

"Did I hear Grace say you're taking a break?"

"Yeah. She's suggested the Lake District, so I'm gonna try and get a flight there tomorrow."

"Well, you've earned it." There's a pause. "How's it gone with Megan?" he asks.

"Fine." I try to sound normal.

"Good. And how many beautiful French women have you managed to seduce?"

In the background I hear Grace say, "Leave him alone, Matt."

"Sorry," he says. "It's none of my business."

"Have you seen much of Will lately?" I ask, just to change the subject. I've been keeping in touch with Will. I know exactly what he's been doing. "He's been working some long hours, but…"

"He came over last weekend, but we haven't seen him since. We'll check in with him on Friday and see if he wants to come by again."

"Thanks. I appreciate it." I look up. Megan's finished; she's walking toward me. Damn, she looks good. "I'd better go," I say. "It looks like Alec's finished for the day."

"Okay. We'll see you when you get back."

"Yeah."

"Have a good time," he says.

"Thanks."

We finish the call just as Megan walks past me on her way to the RV to get changed. She gives me a slow, sexy smile as she passes. "I'll need a hand," she says. "And you'll have to pack away these things."

"Sure."

I follow her into the RV and, as soon as I've closed the door, she turns, pulling me into a deep kiss. She winds her fingers into my hair, standing so close, I can feel the heat from her body along the length of mine. I pull back, just a little.

"I need to talk to you," I tell her.

"Okay." She keeps her fingers in my hair, her breasts hard against my chest.

"We're done here," I say. Her head drops. She knows the end of the job means going home, even if we've both avoided talking about it. "We can drive back to Paris tomorrow, I'll change our tickets and we can fly home, if that's what you really want. But we've still got a week before we're scheduled to go back. I'd rather we took the extra time… and I want us to spend it together." She looks up at me. "I want you to come to England with me."

"England?"

"Yes. I'll book the flights for tomorrow; find us a hotel, arrange a hire car, and we'll spend the week together… just the two of us. No work; no Alec; nothing to do except be together. What do you say?"

She closes her eyes for a moment or two; when she opens them again, they're glistening. "I can't think of anything I want more…"

I grin at her. "What? Nothing…?" I pull her hair to one side, and kiss her neck. "Nothing at all?" I whisper.

"Well…" she breathes, "maybe one or two things."

I work my way up to her ear. "Just one or two?" I murmur.

She gasps as I bite her earlobe. "Okay, more than one or two."

I straighten and lean back a little, looking down at her. "Then we can go?" She nods her head. "Good… Because, for the next seven days, you're mine." She lays her head on my chest and I hold her there.

We've both been real quiet all day. Alec left last night almost as soon as the shoot had finished. He wanted to drive back to Paris, and then fly straight home. That's his choice. I don't think either of us were sorry to see him go.

We said goodbye to Michel this morning when he dropped us at the airport. He's driving the RV back to Paris. We both wished him luck with the baby – and Megan gave him her e-mail so he can send photos.

I held Megan's hand during the take-offs and landings, but she was much less nervous this time around and we arrived at Manchester at just after two this afternoon, after a two hour lay-over at Heathrow. I picked up the rental car – a Range Rover – at the airport, and we're now on the M6 motorway, heading north, with the details of the hotel plugged into the SatNav.

I sense Megan watching me and I glance across at her.

"It's odd," she says, "having the steering wheel on that side, and driving on the wrong side of the road."

I laugh. "Don't let Grace hear you say that,"

"Why?"

"According to Grace, this is the right side of the road. It's the rest of us who've got it wrong. She gets quite protective of British customs."

"Well, I doubt I'll ever meet her, so…"

And there it is… Whatever the last ten days have meant to me; however much I want her in my life… She's still dead set on walking away.

Megan

The hotel is exactly how I would have imagined an English country hotel to be; but with more luxury. Luke has booked us into a suite, with a large king-sized bedroom, adjoining bathroom, a separate living room, with a small dining area, and a balcony which overlooks the lake and the mountains beyond. The staff are attentive and we're shown to our room by the deputy manager, who, according to his name tag is called Gary. Champagne, chocolates and flowers have been laid out on the coffee table by the slate gray sofa.

"Would you like to have afternoon tea brought up here?" Gary asks.

Luke looks at me. "Um… okay." I don't really know, but it sounds nice… and very English.

"Very good," Gary says and turns to leave. "I'll arrange it." He closes the door behind him.

I go over to the balcony doors and open them, stepping outside and leaning against the iron railing. I take in the view. In the foreground is a green field, leading down to the lake, beyond which are a series of peaks and fells, their slopes a multitude of colors: greens, sandy browns, grays and a deep, deep purple. I could wake up to this view every day and never tire of it. I feel Luke's presence behind me, even though he's not touching me.

"Beautiful, isn't it?" he says.

"Hmm." His arms come around my waist and he leans into me.

"I'm gonna be honest with you, Megan," he says. "I'm finding this real tough." I twist in his arms and turn to face him, gazing up into his eyes. He looks miserable.

"Oh, Luke," I mutter.

"Shhh." He kisses my forehead. "I promised I'd walk away… I know I did. And if that's what you still want, then I will… I'm just not finding the reality of that so easy to deal with."

"Neither am I." His eyes widen. "But I'm sorry. Nothing's changed," I add quickly, because I don't want to get his hopes up.

He sighs and deflates. "Okay." He brushes a stray hair away from my face. "The thing is… I don't want to spoil our last few days by focusing on how awful next Thursday is going to be. Even if we've only got seven days together, can we try and enjoy them? Can we make some amazing memories, if nothing else?"

"I'd like that," I tell him, because it's all we'll have… the memories, and the heartache of goodbye.

"I can't eat another thing," I say, leaning back on the sofa and patting my stomach. "I'm so full."

"I thought when he said tea, he meant the drink; not a full meal."

"The sandwiches were delicious… you ate a lot of them."

"Oh, come on… You ate all the cream cake."

"Okay, I guess I'm busted."

He smiles down at me. "They've left us with a menu for dinner, too."

"We're supposed to eat dinner as well?"

"We can eat late and I can order room service, if you like. It'll save changing. They've got a dress code here."

"Really?"

"Yeah. It's not suits and ties, but smart casual."

"Oh. I think we can manage that."

"So, up here or downstairs?"

I think for a moment. "Up here."

"I was hoping you'd say that." He throws the menu back on the table. "We'll look at it later." He leans over and pulls me into his arms, kissing me deeply.

Luke phones our dinner order through from the bed, while I lie curled up next to him. He's given me three orgasms in the last forty-five minutes… curling up is all I can manage.

"We've got an hour," he says hanging up the phone, then turning back to me.

"An hour…" I rest my head on his chest, but he flips me over onto my back.

"Yeah," he says, looking down at me.

"Luke… I'm…"

"I know," he says. "You're exhausted. I was going to suggest I run you a bath." I close my eyes, luxuriating in the prospect.

"That sounds lovely."

"Wait here," he says, kissing me gently. "I'll call you when it's ready."

I must have drifted off to sleep because the next thing I'm aware of is Luke kneeling on the bed, his lips on mine. "Wake up, sleepy." He's smiling. "Bath's ready." He's wearing a hotel robe and he stands up, holding out his hand. I take it in mine, letting him pull me to my feet and lead me into the bathroom, where a bath full of soft bubbles awaits.

I quickly tie up my hair, and he holds my hand as I climb in, then leaves for a moment, returning with a glass of red wine for himself and an ice-cold mineral water for me, from the mini-bar. He sits on the chair in the corner of the room and watches me as I lie back in the bath.

"You can join me, you know," I say to him. "I don't mind."

"I know. But if I do, I'll just want to make love to you again… and you're already exhausted. I'm quite happy watching you."

I close my eyes. "This is perfect, isn't it?" I say.

"It sure is." His voice has a far-away, melancholy tone, which I don't want to think about. I don't want to think about anything except this moment… this memory.

I feel a movement in the water and open my eyes again, half expecting to see he's changed his mind and is getting in with me. Instead, he's kneeling next to the bath, a washcloth in his hands, which are in the water beside me.

"Sit up," he says softly. I do, and he soaps up the cloth, rubbing it gently across my back in circular movements. He rinses it, then, moving the loose strands of my hair to one side, he drizzles water slowly down my back. "Lie back." He watches me recline, then takes the soap in his hands and lathers them, before washing my neck, shoulders and arms, and moving down, my breasts, taking his time over each one. He moves lower still, cupping the soap in his hand as he continues his movements across my stomach, and downward, between my legs, letting his fingers slide between my soft folds. I close my eyes, reveling in his touch. He moves back a little, picking up the washcloth again to clean off the suds from my shoulders, neck and breasts. Then he soaps up again. "Right leg," he murmurs, and I raise it up straight so he can wash it, holding my ankle with one hand while the other sweeps up and down the length of my leg, from foot to thigh. Eventually, he lets go and I allow my to leg fall slowly. "And the left," he says, and we repeat the process. Once I'm completely washed, he leans over and kisses me, his tongue gently twirling around mine.

129

He pulls away slowly and gets to his feet, fetching a towel from the rail and placing it on the shelf at the end of the bath. Then he holds out both hands to me. I take them and he pulls me to my feet, helping me from the bath. He turns me, so I'm facing away from him, then wraps me in the towel, his arms coming around me.

I can feel his breath on my neck. "That was one of the most erotic things I've ever done," he whispers in my ear. "Thank you." He releases me and I hear the bathroom door close behind him.

Today, I wake up to bright sunshine.

I turn to Luke, all sleepy. He's already awake and looking down at me.

"Hi," he says.

"Hello."

"You're beautiful."

"So are you."

He smiles.

"I've been thinking," he says. "The way I see it, we've got two choices… Either we can stay here and explore each other, or we can go out there…" He motions toward the balcony. "And see what the Lake District has to offer."

"That's a tough choice. But I suppose it does seem silly to come all the way here and not at least have a look."

"Good."

I'm not sure whether to feel disappointed – and it must show on my face.

"And that doesn't mean I don't want to explore you… every single inch of you," he says. "But I want memories of us being… well… normal. I want us to go for walks, find country pubs for lunch, taste new things, watch the sun set… hell, I'll even go shopping with you, if you like." He turns and looks out the window at the view. "I just need to do all of it with you," he whispers.

"Me too."

"Okay… shower, breakfast, and we'll hit the road."

Keswick is delightful. It has so many shops, selling everything from walking and climbing gear – which it seems is essential around here – to candy, gifts, antiques, jewelry, slate, clothes, books… the list is endless. There are bakers and tea rooms, hotels and coffee shops, and, in the centre, a slate and stone building with a square tower at one end. At the top of this is a clock, which only has one hand, and is dated '1814'. Curious, we go inside, where a leaflet informs us this is the 'Moot Hall', and that a building has stood on this site for nearly five hundred years. It currently houses the tourist information centre, and Luke picks up some walking maps.

"You're taking me walking?" I ask him as we leave with our bag of maps.

"Well, if we get properly kitted out, yes."

"Kitted out?"

"We'll need boots at least," he says. "Look around."

I do, and he's right. Pretty much everyone is wearing thick soled, deep treaded walking boots or shoes. My sandals feel inadequate.

"Come on," he says. "Let's go buy some boots."

The man in the shop was very helpful and we're now 'kitted out', as Luke put it. We've loaded everything in the back of the car and, on the advice of the man in the shop, we're headed toward Buttermere, which means driving back past the hotel. He said the lake there is easy to walk around and there's a pub we can visit for lunch. We have to drive along – or it is across, or even over – something called 'Honister Pass'. The man asked what kind of car we were driving and, when Luke said it was a Range Rover, he just nodded and said, "You'll be fine then."

I can understand why he asked now. The road is full of twists and turns, sharp gradients and sudden slopes. To either side are steep hills, and occasionally, as we round a bend, we're faced with a sheer drop. We pass a slate mine to our left and then turn a sharp right corner… and I feel a lump forming in my throat at the beauty before me. The view just opens up; the hills become more like mountains, the slopes stretching skyward, the road snaking through them into the distance. Boulders dot the green fells. A stream meanders alongside us and, as we twist and turn on our passage, we cross a stone bridge, the sparkling water flowing beneath us. Just beyond, there's a space to park.

"Please, can we stop," I say to Luke.

"Sure." He pulls the car over onto the gravel. "Are you okay?" I jump down from the car and try to take it in. He comes round and stands beside me. "Megan?"

"Look at it." I can feel tears welling in my eyes, although I couldn't explain them if anyone asked why they're there. "Luke, it's just magical."

"It is," he says, looking around us. "It's… majestic."

He's right. There is something noble, as well as beautiful, about these ancient hills and rocks. I move closer to him, placing my arms around his waist, and tucking my thumbs into the top of his jeans. "Thank you," I whisper.

"What for?"

"This… It's the perfect memory. If we don't do anything else while we're here, I'll always have this."

A pained expression crosses his face.

"I'm sorry, Luke," I say.

"Don't," he replies, putting his hands on my shoulders, resting his forehead on mine. "Don't be sorry."

"But I'm hurting you, and I don't want to."

"I still don't want you to be sorry. I'm not."

"Yes you are," I counter.

"No… I'm not sorry we're here. I'll never be sorry we came and saw this. I'll have this memory too. I can add it to all the other memories I've got of you, and I wouldn't change a single one of them…"

Chapter Ten

Luke

The first part of the walk around Buttermere takes us along the shore of the lake – sometimes literally right at its edge. We're lucky with the weather… the sky is a clear blue, the sun is warm and there's a light breeze. The lake is still enough to see the reflection of the fells that surround it.

"It's just so beautiful," Megan says, stopping to stare across the water to the hills beyond.

"Isn't it?" A puff of wind catches her hair and I pull it back from her face, then lean down and kiss her cheek.

We continue our stroll. It can't really be called a walk – it's so lazy and gentle.

At the far end, we have to leave the lake for a while to follow the path, but we rejoin it soon enough and are half-way along the opposite side when we come across a surprise tunnel, hewn into the rock. It's low… so low that we have to bend over to pass through, and it's dark in the middle. As we come back out into the bright sunshine, we continue along the path, which occasionally takes us up into wooded areas. Within one of these, I grab hold of Megan and pull her over to a tree, pushing her back against the bark, and kissing her hard. Our tongues clash and I lean into her, feeling her breasts heave against my chest.

"We… we need to get back… to the hotel," she mutters between kisses.

I can't help but laugh. "Why would that be?" I ask, pulling back and feigning innocence.

"Because I… I want you."

"You could have me here…"

She glances around. "Someone could come along the path… They'd see us."

"I'm sure we can find somewhere more secluded."

"Or we could just go back to the hotel."

"If that's what you want."

"It is… desperately." The last word comes out as a whisper.

"Well, in that case… let's go." I take her hand and pull her back to the path and, giggling, she walks alongside me back to the car.

The walk took nearly three hours, allowing for interludes and, back at the car, we remove our walking boots and replace them with our shoes, ready for the drive back.

"There's another way to get back to the hotel," I tell her, looking at the map while she fastens her sandals. "Or we can go back the way we came."

"Can we go back the same way?" she asks, her eyes alight. "I like our magical road."

"I was hoping you'd say that," I reply. "It's the most fun I've had in a car in ages." Even as I'm saying the words, I regret them, and hope she doesn't want details of the many other things I've done in cars in my checkered past, but she just raises an eyebrow and smirks at me and I can't help adding, "Still, I haven't had you in a car… yet."

"No… you seem to have had me just about everywhere else, though." She starts counting on her fingers: "Various showers, the RV, twice on the kitchen countertop at the villa in Provence, the bedroom floor at the hotel in Toulon…"

"Don't forget up against the wall there, too…"

"Hmm… I'm not likely to forget that… and then there was the pool…"

"Now that was good." We look at each other and I know we're both recalling the swimming pool in the villa at Carcasonne on the night we arrived there. It had steps at one end, which I sat on, while Megan rode me… It was another occasion when, in the heat of the moment, the condom was forgotten. I don't think either of us cared. "But right now, I'll settle for the hotel."

"Me too."

I don't want to spoil the moment by telling her that the place I want her most is the one place I'll probably never get to have her: my own bed, at home, in Boston.

We've decided on a more adventurous walk today. We're novices, so we're not going to attempt any of the higher hills or mountains, but we feel we could try something a little more challenging, so we've chosen a walk to Walla Crag. We've learned from the people at the hotel, as well as the man in the shop where we bought our walking boots, that it's advisable to follow maps, stick to pathways and be prepared. The weather can change real fast around here. So, with that in mind, we take our map and instructions, our new wet weather gear packed in a rucksack, and head off to park up at Great Wood.

From there, we follow the path above the road, but soon we leave the traffic behind and make our way into the forest. We haven't gone far before we hear the sound of gushing water. There's a stream alongside us, but it doesn't account for the noise we can hear, which only makes sense when we round the corner and see a waterfall cascading over the rocks, the milky white water spilling into a pool at the bottom.

We halt and Megan leans into me. "You've done it again," she says.

"What have I done?"

"Found a perfect memory." And as she speaks, the sun breaks through the branches overhead, forming a rainbow in the water's mist. She gasps and I turn to see tears in her eyes. I put my arm around her and pull her close just as a lone tear falls onto her cheek. I don't know whether she's crying because of the beautiful scene in front of us, or because we've only got five days left together. I do know I don't want her to cry alone.

We stop at a pub on the way back to the hotel and have an early dinner, then we find a place to park down by the lake, and we go for a walk along the shore.

The sun is waning in the sky, casting shadows of orange, pinks and purples on to the silky flat surface of the water.

We've only gone a few paces when I turn to Megan. "Are you warm enough?" It occurs to me that, as the sun is setting, it's turning a little chilly.

"Hmm." She nestles into me. "I've got you."

"Sure have."

"For now," she adds, then stops. "Sorry. That wasn't meant to come out."

I turn her toward me. "It doesn't have to end, Megan," I tell her. "It's obvious we neither of us want it to. Whatever the problem is at home, we can make this work."

The tears that were threatening earlier in the day overflow and cascade down her cheeks. "No," she says, her voice breaking. "No, we can't."

"Tell me what it is. What's stopping us being together?"

"No."

"Why not?"

"Because you'll want to do something about it… and there's nothing you can do."

"You don't know that."

"Yes… yes I do. Please, Luke. Don't make it any worse."

"How can it be any worse?" My voice is harsher than I intended and she pulls away a little "I'm sorry," I say immediately, softening my tone and pulling her back to me. "But how exactly can it get any worse than us not being together?"

"Trust me… it can."

Really? There's something worse than this? Worse than the prospect of a life without her? I wish I could understand. But then I'm starting to wonder if there's any point in wishes.

We don't talk on the way back to the hotel. I'm finding it hard to be a placid bystander in the destruction of our relationship, but I can't fight her. She's resolute… on Thursday we go home, and we go our separate ways.

Once back in our room, I stand her by the bed and, without saying a word, I undress us both, leaving our clothes in a pile on the floor, then I take her hand and lead her into the bathroom. I turn on the shower and we stand beneath it, in each others arms, letting the water pour over us. Maybe there's a part of me hoping it will heal us… Some hope.

When we're done, and I've dried us both, we go into the bedroom and lie on the bed. I'm on my back and Megan is lying with her head on my chest, a hand on my stomach. I'm hard, but then I'm always hard when she's around.

She twists and looks up at me. "Can I touch you?" she asks, as though she needs permission. She hasn't touched me yet, or shown any sign of wanting to. I haven't minded one bit.

"Of course, baby. You don't need to ask."

"It's just… there's an atmosphere…"

I pull her closer. "I know. That's my fault. I'm sorry."

She shakes her head. "No, it's not. This is my doing, Luke. I knew… I always knew we had no future."

"And I keep telling you… I don't regret any of it."

She looks into my eyes, like she's trying to see inside me. I don't mind letting her in, because I know all she'll find is the truth of my words. I don't regret it. If I had my time over, knowing the end result, I'd do it all again.

Even as she's watching me, I feel her hand move down my body and come to rest around my cock, her fingers gripping gently.

"I… I don't know what to do," she whispers.

I place my hand around hers and start to move them both together, stroking my length between us. She drags her eyes from mine and, together, we watch our hands entwined around me.

"Does it hurt if I squeeze?" she asks.

I chuckle. "Depends how hard you squeeze, baby."

She presses her fingers tighter around me and I let out a gasp.

"Sorry," she says, releasing her grip.

"No…" I say. "That was good."

"Oh." She smiles up at me and tightens her hold again. I let go of her and she continues to rub my cock, twisting her hand slightly every so often and squeezing the tip. I close my eyes, put my hands behind my head, and savor another moment… another memory.

After a little while she stills and I open my eyes, looking down at her. She's staring at me.

"What's wrong?" I ask her.

"Nothing… I just…"

"What?" Something's bothering her. She seems embarrassed… uncertain. "What is it, Megan."

"I want to… taste you." My cock twitches in her hand and she lets out a gasp, giving me a tentative smile.

"I think you can assume my cock is as pleased as I am about that idea." Something still isn't right, and it only takes me a moment to work it out. "You don't know how?" I ask. She shakes her head and I can't help but chuckle. "This isn't really something I can give instructions on," I say quietly, "being as I've never done it before."

She opens her mouth in surprise. "You mean, no-one's ever…?" Oh… I hate to disillusion her.

"No… I mean I've had it done to me, but I've never done it to anyone else."

"Well, I'm glad to hear that," she says. There's a pause. "So what do I do?" she asks.

"Whatever you want," I reply, grinning. "Do whatever feels good. Just as long as there are no teeth involved."

"So, I just take it in my mouth?" she asks.

"Yes." *Please…*

"And how much of it do I take?" She looks from my face to my cock, her eyes widening.

"As much as you feel comfortable with."

"And what if you…"

"What if I come?" She nods her head. "Your choice, baby."

"Whether you come or not?"

"I meant your choice whether you swallow. I think it's a certainty I'm gonna come…"

"And if I don't want to swallow? How will I know when to stop?"

"I'll give you a warning and you can get out of the line of fire."

She grins up at me. "Which would you prefer me to do?" she asks.

"Not my decision. That one's always down to you."

She hesitates for a moment, then leans closer and opens her mouth wide, taking the head of my cock and letting her lips close around me.

"Fuck, yeah…" I inhale through gritted teeth. She stops, holding me where I am and looks up at my face. Despite my reaction, I think she's uncertain whether she's doing it right, but the sight of my cock in her mouth and her eyes on mine is nearly enough to push me over the edge already. I smile and nod down at her to give her some reassurance and I think she smiles back; it's hard to tell when her mouth is clamped around me. Then she starts to move her head up and down, taking me deeper, until I'm hitting the back of her throat. Her hand is wrapped around me still, heightening the pleasure, her tongue circling around the tip and down the length of my shaft each time she takes me… over and over. I know I can't last…

"Megan," I hiss, "I can't hold back much longer. Stop now… unless you want me to…" She doesn't stop. Instead she takes me deeper. "Megan. I'm serious… I'm gonna come…" I give her one last warning, then raise my hips and ejaculate down her throat. I can feel the motion of her swallowing on my cock; it's almost painful, but in the most pleasurable way imaginable.

I can't breathe. I can't move. Literally, nothing works. She releases my cock and moves up to lie in my arms and I just about manage to pull her close, but that's my limit.

"How…?" I manage to say.

"How what?"

"How… how did you do that?"

She shrugs. "I don't know, but I wanted to. You said it was my choice, and it felt right…"

"It felt better than right." I kiss the top of her head.

"Was it okay then?"

"Okay doesn't really cover it." I manage to pull her further up my body, so we're facing each other. "Just do me one favor?"

She looks doubtful, but nods her head.

"Don't ever do that if I'm not lying down… or at least sitting."

"Why?"

"Because my legs don't work… I can't even feel them. I'd hate to end up wrecked on the floor."

"Okay. I'll remember… beds and chairs only in future." Her voice fades on the final word.

I hold her. "Thank you," I whisper. "That's something I'll never forget… ever." *Like everything else about her.*

Megan

It's already Tuesday. Which means we have to leave here tomorrow, to fly back to Paris for the flight to Boston early on Thursday morning.

We've decided to visit Grasmere, because it's a village, rather than a walk, and I think we both hoped there would be plenty here to distract us; to stop us dwelling on the inevitable.

It's a pretty place, with very few cars, so people tend to wander in the middle of the street. There are shops, lots of cafés, hotels, pubs and restaurants. And there's a really quaint little place which sells gingerbread. We stop off to buy some and come out with a bag of six pieces. Luke hands me one and I take a bite. It's got a really strong ginger taste, and is sweet... and delicious. And we walk along, finishing off the whole lot.

We visit Dove Cottage, which is where the poet William Wordsworth lived. Luke spends most of the time with his head bent down, as the ceilings are so low, and when we come out, he makes a point of stretching.

"It wasn't that bad," I tell him.

"You try walking around looking at the floor for forty-five minutes," he says. "Was there anything in there, apart from flagstones, floorboards and rugs?"

I laugh. "Yes... Do you know what amazes me?"

"How short they must have been?"

I laugh again. "No. That they had so many children in such a small house."

"And his sister lived here too?"

"Yes, and his wife's sister as well..."

"Cozy. I'm amazed they found the privacy to conceive the children in the first place."

"Luke!" I glance around at the people milling about us.

He grabs me around my waist and pulls me in close. I yelp and we attract even more stares.

"What?" he says, resting his hands on my hips. "I'm just telling it how it is. I don't know I'd want to live with Will any more, if we..." He stops speaking and closes his eyes. "Sorry," he says. "It just slipped out."

Suddenly we're both serious again, and it's like a dark cloud has crossed the brilliant sunny sky.

Back at the hotel, we have dinner and go upstairs to pack. We've got an early start. Our flight to Paris is at least direct, but it departs at eleven-thirty, which means leaving here at seven-thirty in the morning.

We move around the room in silence, even handing each other things to put into our cases, without saying a word. Luke finishes before me and stands for a while, watching, then says he's going to take a shower. I don't ask if I can join him, and he doesn't invite me. It's the beginning of the end, and we both know it.

I feel so torn. I know how much he's offering me; I know I should be snapping it up. I also know my father. I know, from years of bitter experience, exactly what he's capable of.

Even so, I have to tell Luke how much this has meant to me; how much he's meant to me. I go to the desk in the corner of the room and open the drawer. Inside, as I'd expected, is a small pile of headed writing paper, a few envelopes and a pen, with the name of the hotel stamped on the side. I sit, and without needing to think, I start to write.

We're staying at a hotel at Charles de Gaulle airport. We have to check in for our flight home at seven o'clock tomorrow morning. It's a very impersonal airport hotel, which seems somehow appropriate for the ending of our affair. Last night – our last night in paradise – for the first time since that night at the château, we didn't make love. Luke held me all night. I don't think either of us slept much; we just held onto each other.

Tonight, he does make love to me and he's more tender, more considered and slow, more gentle than he's ever been. The temptation to tell him I've fallen in love with him is so great, I have to bite my lip to stop myself.

He'll find out soon enough.

Chapter Eleven

Luke

I don't know why, but part of me is still hoping. Surely, she can't just end this, can she? When it comes down to it, when we get back to Boston, she won't be able to go through with it; she'll see we're meant to be together... She has to.

On the flight, all I've been able to think about is that I don't know how I'm going to live without her if she won't change her mind. Maybe that's why I'm still hopeful – because deep down, I think she feels the same. She's said all along that she doesn't want it to end either... so I have to trust that our love is strong enough to banish whatever demons are haunting her. I say 'our love' because I honestly believe she loves me too. She's never said anything, but there's something about the way she looks at me, that just makes me believe in us.

Of course, then I'll have to tell Matt. If Megan agrees to give it a try and she and I are going to have a chance, Matt has to know. We can't sneak around behind his back; it'd never work. Besides, if we're together, I'll want the whole damn world to know anyway. He'll go through the roof, but I don't care. There are more important things in life than rules.

It's just after lunch, local time, when we land at Logan.

I've got Will picking me up and Megan's friend Erin will be waiting for her. I don't want a scene in front of either of them, so while we're waiting for our bags, I pull her to one side.

"I'm going to say something," I tell her. "And I just want you to listen." She's looking up into my face, but her expression isn't giving anything away. She doesn't reply, so I take a deep breath. "I know we made an agreement—"

"Luke," she interrupts, "please don't do this."

"Just listen…" She nods her head once, but she's staring at my chest now. "I know we made an agreement," I repeat. "I know we said that if you still felt the same when we got back here, then I'd walk away, but I really don't want to do that. If we have to start from the beginning for some reason, then so be it. We can date for a while; go out to dinner, the movies… we don't have to sleep together, if that doesn't work for you. We can slow it all down; I'll play it however you want, Megan. I just don't want this to be all there is."

She sighs, deeply. "Please, Luke. I've told you over and over. It can't carry on." So, she hasn't changed her mind. I was wrong. She doesn't love me at all.

"Then will you at least tell me why?"

"No."

Seriously? "I know you told me you don't have a boyfriend, but is there someone else… or the hope of someone else?"

"No." She rests her hand on my chest and it burns a hole there. "I promise, there's no-one else."

I put my hand over hers. Despite the burn, she's freezing cold. "After everything we've had; everything we've done, you still want this to be over?"

"You make it sound easy," she whispers. "It's not… It's not easy for me either."

"Then don't do it… Don't end this."

"I have to!" She raises her voice a little, pulls her hand from under mine and looks up at me. The hurt in her eyes mirrors my own, but still it takes me by surprise. "Nothing's changed," she says.

A little voice somewhere in the back of my head says that at least Matt will never need to know and then I suddenly remember the whole point of his rule. Why didn't I think of it before? "But we have to see each other again," I begin to say, hope blossoming once more.

"No, Luke… how many times—"

"Wait, you didn't let me finish. You're contracted to do the shows in the fall. I always attend them to meet with the buyers. It's part of my job. We'll get to spend the best part of four weeks together in New York, London, Milan and Paris. I know it's a few months away, but we can wait for each other, can't we? And then we can at least—"

She closes her eyes and the look on her face is one of pure pain. "No. I can't…" she says.

"But you—"

"I can't, Luke. I can't do it."

"It's part of the contract. You have to do it." Did I really just say that? I'd never use the contract against her. I'd rip it to shreds, burn it and bury it before I'd use it against her.

"I can do the shows. I just can't see you."

Well thanks… that didn't hurt at all. I stare at her for a long moment. She doesn't flinch – in fact I'm not sure she even blinks. "Okay, have it your own way." Wow… Even I can hear the hardness in my voice, but I can't seem to stop myself. "I'll see if Matt can cover them for me. I can't make any promises, but I'll do my best… If it's not possible, I guess you'll just have to put up with seeing me. Can't guarantee I'll be on my own, though." What's wrong with me? Why would I say something as shitty as that? Being hurt is no excuse…

"Luke, please don't…"

"Don't what? Don't be a heartless son-of-a-bitch? I thought you knew – that's who I am." *Snap out of this, Luke… now. You're not that guy anymore. And you're hurting her…*

"No, you're not." She blinks and two tears fall down each of her cheeks. And that's all it takes… I grab her and pull her into my chest. "You're not," she sobs into me. "You're not."

"No… not with you. Never with you." I take a deep breath. "If I have to do the shows, I won't get in your way. I'll leave you alone. And I'll be by myself, I promise…" I kiss her forehead. "I'm sorry, baby… I'm sorry I said that. I didn't mean it." I hold her. I know I'll have to let her go, but for now, I hold her.

We make our way through to the arrivals area. I've already spotted Will and, although I didn't want a scene in front of him, or Megan's friend, I need to give her something.

"Wait," I say, pulling her back.

"Please, Luke. No more." She looks drained, like she's got nothing left.

"It's okay. It's not about that." I take my wallet from my back pocket, and pull out a business card. "Take this," I say offering it to her. She clasps it between her thumb and forefinger. The tears are welling up in her eyes again. I lean down and kiss her deeply one last time, then I hold her close, my mouth next to her ear. We haven't really talked about this since that morning at the château, but it needs to be said again. "If the dates were wrong… If you are pregnant, call me, Megan. I meant what I said. I won't walk away if you're carrying my child. The deal's off." I lean back and look down at her. "Tell me you agree." She stares up at me. "We can stand here all day if we have to… I've got nowhere else to be. I'm not letting you go until you agree." She nods her head. "Say it out loud."

"I agree," she whispers.

I sigh out my relief. "And even if you're not pregnant, if you're in trouble… or if you ever just need me for anything, then call me, text me, e-mail me, I don't care how you do it… just find me. I won't make myself invisible. I'll be here. I'll always be here…" We stand staring at each other. Tears are flowing freely down her cheeks now.

"I promised I'd be the one to walk away, didn't I?" I can hear the break in my own voice and I swallow it down.

"No. I'll do it," she whispers. "It's my fault."

"It's not your fault. And I gave you my word." I kiss her forehead. "Thank you," I whisper. "Thank you for letting me into your life… and for letting me be the man I always wanted to be," and I turn away; and without any warning, the pain cuts through me, cleaving me in two.

I don't look back. Will's staring at me, his head tilted to one side, confused.

"Luke? What's——?" he says, his eyes darting over my shoulder in Megan's direction. I don't want to know what he can see.

I hold up my hand to silence him. "Just get me the fuck out of here."

Megan

I'm aware of Erin's arms around me, as I feel myself falling and she stops me from actually hitting the floor.

"Megan?" she says. "What's happened, what's wrong?" I stare past her at his blurred back. He's walking away – out of my life – with another man, a dark haired man. They're not talking, just striding quickly out of the building. His head is down, his shoulders slumped. Only once the doors have closed and he's disappeared from sight do I turn my head.

"Megan?" Erin's looking at me. "Tell me," she says. "Tell me what's happened…"

"Oh, Erin," I sob, and she holds me.

"What's wrong?" she asks. "Who was that man?"

I shake my head. I don't want to talk about it. And, as if she can read my mind, she releases me, picks up my bag and just says, "Come on. I'll take you home."

It's odd being back in our tiny apartment after so long away. Nothing feels the same anymore. But it's not like anything here has changed, which I guess must mean I'm the thing that's different… Oh, but, of course I'm different; I've broken my own heart.

I know this is what I asked him for, but it's not what I wanted, any more than he did. I wanted what he was offering – a future. A future with him in it.

Erin's been great. She hasn't pressed me for information. In the few hours we've been home, she's not actually asked me anything at all about my trip. She knows that when I'm ready to talk, I will. I'm not sure I'll ever be ready to talk about Luke, though. Even thinking about him hurts – it hurts most of all in the place where my heart used to be.

She's made us an early dinner of spaghetti bolognese, so I can get to bed. I'm exhausted, and it's not just the jet-lag. I've never felt so drained.

"I'm not going to unpack tonight," I tell her once I've finished eating. "I'll do it tomorrow, and I'll sort out all my laundry while you're at work."

"Okay," she says. She hesitates. "Are you alright, Megs?"

"No."

"Wanna talk about it?"

"No."

"Okay. Let me know when you do."

"Thanks," I manage to say. Then I get up and go through to my room.

I throw my bag on the floor and lie down on the bed. Pinned on the wall next to me is my calendar, and I go to turn over the page so it reads 'July' instead of 'June'. Then it dawns on me... There's no letter 'P' marked anywhere in June. I flip back to May. There it is... a red – *how appropriate* – letter 'P' against May 28th. I've marked the first day of my period on the calendar this way for years. I look back through the year from January forward; there's one 'P' in each month, except June. So... I'm late. I take a deep breath and try not to panic. Today's only July 2nd. It's a few days, just a few days... And I'm notoriously irregular. *Yeah, except for the last five months, it seems, when I've actually been as regular as clockwork.* But I couldn't be that unlucky... could I?

Luke said he'd stand by me, and he gave me his card to contact him, but with the number of women who fall over themselves to get to him, it won't take him long to find someone else. I know he said he'd be alone if we had to do the shows together, but I'm fairly sure he meant just while we're away, working, he'll be professional… he wouldn't do anything to make me feel uncomfortable. He didn't mean he's not going to meet up with women at all… that would be unreasonable. It's not like we're together, so I can't expect him to stay single. No… He'll find someone, I know he will, and then the last thing he'll want or need is me turning up with a little reminder of our time together.

Still, if I am pregnant, I'll have to contact him. I can't take that away from him. It's his right to know and I owe him that; even if he has hooked up with someone else.

The thought of him with another woman, doing with her all the things he's done with me, makes we want to be sick, just like it did when he said it so harshly at the airport, and I run to the bathroom and sit on the edge of the bath for a while, my stomach churning, and images of him with someone else playing out in my head.

Eventually, the feeling passes, my stomach settles and I go back to bed.

I pick up the calendar again and turn over the page to July, noticing the circle around the nineteenth; the day I go to visit my dad for two weeks. *Great… Life just doesn't get any better.*

Chapter Twelve

Luke

Will didn't say a word on the ride home, which is just as well, since I had nothing to say back. I haven't slept all night, and I'm still incapable of speech.

I don't have to work today; Matt sent me a text telling me to take the extra day and go back into the office on Monday. Thank God for that. The thought of facing work, Matt and Grace, everyone wanting to know about the trip… I couldn't do it.

I haven't showered yet, even though it's gone ten-thirty. Will's working, and I'm just sitting in a pair of shorts, perched on the edge of my bed, staring at the wall. I wonder for a moment how long this will go on for… a week; a month; forever?

I sigh and grab my bag, unzipping it. I didn't unpack last night; I couldn't be bothered. I pull out my clothes and throw them on the bed. Tucked down the side is a white envelope. It has my name on the outside, so I open it, and the envelope drops from my fingers to the floor, as I see straight away who the letter inside is from.

'*Dear Luke,*' I read,

'*I can't say any of this to your face, because I know you'll try even harder to change my mind. Even so, there are things I need to tell you.*

I'm so sorry this has to end; I really am. Please believe me, it'll be as hard for me to say goodbye as it will be for you. And please trust me when I say that I have a very good reason for doing this. If I didn't, I couldn't even consider it.

I can't change my mind. I wish I could, but I can't. We can't keep seeing each other; and when we get home, we will go our separate ways. But I needed you to know that I'm grateful to you for everything; for everything you've given me, everything you've done for me, everything you've meant to me. I'll never ever forget you or what we've had together and there will never be anyone else for me.

I also couldn't let you go without telling you that I love you, Luke. I always will.

Please forgive me.

Megan.'

I read it through twice.

She loved me. No, she *loves* me.

I rest my elbows on my knees, clasping the letter in my hands, and I wonder whether it would have made a difference if I'd told her that I love her too; that I've loved her from the beginning, probably from the very first moment I saw her. I close my eyes and picture her, standing with Emma by the check-in desk. *Yeah… I think I knew, even then.*

Instinctively, I reach for my phone, which is on the nightstand. And it's only at that moment I realize I don't have any contact details for her. We were never really apart during the trip, so I didn't need to ask for them; and maybe she didn't offer them, so I couldn't get in touch when we got home.

I reach into my messenger bag for Emma's file, to see if there's any information in there, but the only details I can find are for the agency.

I'll call Matt and get him to find out. No… Grace would be a better option. I look up her details on my phone. Then I hesitate. What reason can I give for contacting Megan? I can't tell the truth, obviously. I could say I've accidentally brought home something belonging to her – except I've been in England, supposedly on my own for a week – she'd be bound to wonder why I haven't noticed – and, therefore, called – before now. Damn.

"Will!" I yell and, putting the letter on my bed, I stand and walk quickly out of my room, along the hallway, through the kitchen and up to his office door. It's shut. This means I should knock. I don't care. I barge in.

"What the—?" He flicks a couple of switches and all the screens on the facing wall go blank. "Luke," he says, "you know…"

"Yeah… I'm meant to knock."

He looks at me. "What's wrong?"

"How do I find out someone's cell number?"

"There's a directory…" The tone of his voice makes it sound like I'm being stupid.

"Okay."

"You just go online…" He turns to his desk and opens his personal laptop. He taps the keys a few times, then looks up at me. "What's the name?" he asks.

"Megan Ford," I tell him. He doesn't even blink, he just types in her name.

"Where does she live."

"Here, in Boston. I don't know the address."

Again he types. I walk around behind him in time to see a list of people's personal details appearing on the screen. They include addresses, dates of birth and all known phone numbers. There are two people called Megan Ford; three by the name of Meg Ford, and eleven who just use the initial 'M'. He scrolls through them faster than I can read.

"Slow down," I say to him.

"She's not listed here," he says.

"How the hell can you tell that?"

He stops scrolling and turns to me. "I'm guessing this is the girl at the airport? The model?" I nod my head. "She'd be about twenty-one or twenty-two?" I nod again. "Well, look," he says. "None of these people are under thirty." He goes back to scrolling up and down the screen, more slowly this time, and I see he's right. Looking at the dates of birth, the ages range from thirty-two, to sixty-seven.

"How can you read it all so fast, though?"

"It's part of what I do."

I feel deflated.

"But she had a phone," I tell him. "I saw it." I remember her belongings scattered on her bed.

"Maybe it's not registered to her in Boston. Where's she from originally?"

"I don't know." I never asked her that. I can't see a way forward now, not unless I can contact the agency on some pretext, but I expect they'd want to get in touch with Megan on my behalf, not give out her details... Besides, I doubt they'd even want to speak to me; Matt balled them out and we won't be using their services again. "Thanks for trying," I say. I leave his office and quietly close the door behind me.

I go back to my room, pick up the letter and read it again – three times. She's grateful to me. She gave me so much, she's changed my life completely... she's changed *me* completely... and *she's* grateful to *me*. I need to speak to her, to tell her...

"Here." I spin to face Will, who's standing just inside my room. He's holding out a piece of paper. "I'm not telling you how I got it; and if anyone asks, you didn't get it from me." He closes the door on his way out.

I look down at the letter in my right hand and the piece of notepaper in my left; both my hands are shaking. If I'm going to speak to her, I need to be a lot calmer than I am now. And I need to be absolutely certain about what I'm going to say.

I put both pages down carefully on the bed and head for the shower.

I've showered, dressed, paced my room, and re-read the letter at least a dozen more times. Now I'm standing by the window, with my phone in my still shaking hand. I dial the number carefully, hoping Will's got the right person. I know my number will come up as 'unknown' on her phone; and I know a lot of people reject unknown callers. I usually do. If she does, I'll just have to leave a message and hope she calls back. And keep calling her if she doesn't. I need to speak to her; I'm not giving up.

It connects and rings four times, then a fifth... I'm poised for her voicemail when, "Hello?" *God, it's her.*

"Hi," I say.

"Luke?" At least she recognized me.

"Yeah."

"What are you…?" she says. "I mean… how…?"

"I needed to talk to you." I bat aside her inevitable question about how I got her number.

"But we agreed," she says. "You said… You promised you'd stay away. You promised I'd never hear from you again." That's all completely true – pretty much word-for-word. I can't deny it.

"And then you wrote me a letter," I say, because it justifies breaking that promise – well, it does to me, anyway.

The silence stretches for a while until she says, "Yes," in a voice so quiet I can barely hear her.

"And you didn't expect me to respond at all?"

"No. I just wanted you to know."

"You write me a letter, telling me you love me, and I'm not supposed to do anything?" She doesn't reply. "Megan, can't you see it changes everything?"

"No. It changes nothing. We can't see each other again. And you can't call me."

"Are you serious?"

"Yes. You promised to stay away, Luke. Please…" I can hear the catch in her voice.

"If you really want me to stay away, why are you crying?"

"Because," she sobs.

"Please don't, baby." *It's breaking me.* "Please don't cry. I'm not there."

"I'm… I'm sorry," she says.

"Don't be."

"I have to go."

"No. Please," I beg her. "We need to talk…"

"I love you, Luke." She hangs up.

"I love you too." She's already gone.

I've never said 'I love you' to anyone in my life; and the first time I do, it's to a phone, with no-one on the end of it, a second after the woman I love has hung up in tears, vowing never to speak to me or see me again. I didn't think it was meant to be like this.

I notice it's getting dark outside. I've been in here all day, doing nothing. I don't care.

"Coffee," Will says, putting a cup down by the side of the bed. "Wanna talk?" he asks. I shake my head and he turns away, heading toward the door.

"She wrote me a letter," I say quietly. He stops and turns back, coming over to the bed and sitting down next to me. I pick it up and hand it to him.

"You want me to read it?" he asks. I nod my head. After a minute, he turns to me. "I don't understand," he says, and like the waterfall we stood beside on the climb up to Walla Crag, the words pour out of me.

I tell him the whole story; how I wanted Megan so much I ached for her, and I still do. How she could make a bad day bearable and a good day better. I tell him how, for the first time ever, it wasn't just about sex: I wanted so much more. I wanted to protect her, to care for her. I wanted to share my life with her. I tell him about the arrangement; that I don't understand why it has to be this way, but that she's made up her mind and I can't unmake it… even though I love her more than life and I'd give up everything I have to be with her.

"I've thought since the beginning that I didn't deserve her; that she was too damn good for me. I wondered if my past was catching up with me… I guess I was right."

"What do you mean?" he asks.

"Oh, come on, Will. Think about the way I've always treated women. I don't deserve someone like Megan."

"That's bullshit." Will's so quiet and placid, his tone grabs my attention. "Well it is," he says. "I may not have liked the way you lived before, but that was because I knew you were unhappy. You were always totally honest with the women you saw. You never brought any of them back here; you never gave them even the pretense of a relationship. They knew the score; and a lot of them approached you – not the other way around." He thinks for a minute. "I wonder if there's more to this…"

"Such as?"

"Well, it seems odd that Megan would insist on the arrangement you made, and then write that letter. And I saw her at the airport. She—"

"Don't," I say to him, holding up a hand. "Please don't tell me." And then, for some reason I don't understand, I change my mind. "What did you see?" I ask him.

"You wanna know?" I nod my head. "She collapsed." Fuck. I stand. I should be with her. "Her friend… she held her up," he says, "but the look on her face…"

"What about it? Tell me."

"She was devastated… like she'd lost everything. Sorry." He pauses then says, "We left at that point, so I don't know what happened next." I sit down again, my head in my hands.

"I should never have gone along with it…" I murmur.

"Why did you?"

"I thought I could convince her to stay with me… fucking idiot that I am." I turn and look at him. "Whatever's keeping us apart is more important… stronger than her love for me."

"And did she give you no clue about what it was?"

"No. She adamantly refused to."

"There has to be more to it… something behind it. You could try calling—"

"No," I tell him. "I couldn't. You didn't hear her on the phone earlier. I can't keep pushing her. You say she collapsed at the airport… God knows what she's like right now. I can't keep putting her through that pain over and over… I promised I'd stay away and I have to do that. It's what she wants."

"Does she? Are you sure?"

"She says she does. She acts like she does."

"And you?"

"I'll respect her wishes."

"That's not what I meant."

"I know."

I've got so much work to catch up on, getting through my first day back should be easy… except, once I'd cleared the backlog of mail and dealt with my messages, the work I've been doing all afternoon has involved going through the images from the trip with Grace and Matt.

We're in Grace's office, where she's got a large screen set up. While Megan and I were in the Lake District, Grace has been working on the designs for the new web pages, using the photographs from the shoot.

"I particularly like this one," she says, scrolling down the screen. A new layout comes into view. The photographs are of Megan by the grand piano at the château. They were taken the morning after we first made love; after I took her virginity. I close my eyes and recall changing her from this outfit into the corset, then taking her over the end of the bed, hard and fast.

"What do you think?" Matt's voice interrupts my thoughts.

"Yeah, looks good."

"And these," Grace says, scrolling again, to the photographs we took in the lavender fields in Provence. In these, Megan's wearing this season's bridal range. It's white, sheer and lacy with embossed flowers and pearls. The night after these were taken, we made love in the shower at the villa. I pinned her against the wall, kissing her gently, then lifted her up into my arms. She wrapped her legs around my waist as I entered her, taking her deep and slow. She screamed my name loudly that time – twice – before I exploded inside her.

I smile and nod at the appropriate points as Grace talks me through the rest of the designs, each one holding a memory of Megan. I recall various scenes, in bedrooms, baths, kitchens, pools, showers. And, in the ones before the château at Grasse, I can still remember the longing – the aching – to make love to her. I suppress the lump rising in my throat. I'm not going to deny that I long to be inside her; that I ache for her more than ever… but the thing I need more than anything is just to be with her, to hold her and never let her go, to know she's in my life, forever.

Finally, the screen fills with an image of Megan in the field of sunflowers at Carcasonne, on that last day.

"She's beautiful," Grace says. "She's glowing with something…" *Yeah… that would be love, for me. I know that now, because she wrote me a letter…*

"She was probably just glad to be at the end of the shoot, and looking forward to coming home," Matt says.

"No, there's more to it than that." Grace's voice is soft, inquiring.

"Well," he replies, "whatever it is, the photographs look amazing, don't they, Luke?"

I nod my head, but I'm not sure how much longer I can keep doing this… looking at images of Megan, reliving those perfect memories, day in, day out for the next few months, while we ramp up the promotions. She's going to be everywhere, on posters, adverts, packaging, the Internet. And knowing I'll never look into her eyes, hold her, touch her, be with her again… I really don't think I can do it. It's too much… it hurts too much.

Megan

Was the letter a mistake? I've spent the whole weekend wondering. At the time, it felt like the right thing to do; to be honest, to let him know how I felt – well, how I feel – but now I'm not so sure.

I've got no idea how he got hold of my phone number, but he has it now, which means he can contact me anytime he wants – although he hasn't done so since Friday, and it's now Wednesday. Maybe he won't. Maybe he'll leave me alone, like he said he would. That should make me feel better, shouldn't it? It's what I asked him to do so many times. So why do I feel like calling him, and telling him it was all a mistake, and asking if can he please come back? And why can't I stop crying?

The one and only good thing that's happened since I got back is that a job has come up. It's at the Boston Public Library, so not exactly what I was looking for, but I've applied for it anyway. The closing date for applications isn't for another two weeks, and interviews will start on August 4th, by which time I'll be back from my dad's... *Damn*. I'd been trying to forget that I'm going there soon.

I'm standing in the doorway of a strange bedroom. I've never seen the room before. It's very masculine, but it's not the dark wood furniture and neutral decor that's holding my attention, it's the woman spread-eagled naked on the enormous bed. Her legs are wide apart, her arms above her head. She's got really large breasts and rigid, dark pink nipples. Her long red hair is fanned out on the pillow and her painted lips are parted in a knowing smile... She's vaguely familiar, but I can't place her. Then I notice the red high-heeled shoes, the blue skirt, and jacket, all lying on the floor. Of course... she's the flight attendant. I glance around but the room is empty, apart from her... It's odd. I feel confused.

Then, from a door to my right, he appears. His hair is damp, presumably from the shower. He's also naked, his arousal more than obvious.

He looks down at her as he approaches the bed, and takes his erection in his hand. Her eyes widen and he climbs onto the bed, kneeling between her legs. Neither of them says a word.

Just as he leans forward, about to penetrate her, I hear a voice screaming through the silence, "Luke, No!" It's my own voice. He turns, looks at me, and waves his hand, like he's dismissing me.

"What?" he says, his voice cold, just like it was for those few minutes at the airport. "You thought I'd live like a monk, did you? You had your chance. You got what you wanted, Megan." He turns back to the woman and with one swift movement and a loud groan, he enters her. She moans and wraps her legs around him.

As he starts to move in and out of her, faster and faster, I hear myself screaming again…

"Megan!"

"Please, Luke. No…"

"Megan… wake up." I open my eyes. Erin is crouched beside the bed, looking at me. "You were screaming," she says. I burst into tears; long drawn-out sobs that wrack my whole body. Erin sits up on the bed and hugs me while I cry and cry. It was a dream, nothing more, but the images and his voice, they were so real.

"This is about the guy at the airport, isn't it?" she says once I eventually start to calm. I nod my head. "That was nearly two weeks ago. You need to talk about it, Megs." She's right, I do. So, I tell her everything… well, nearly everything.

"Are you sure you made the right decision?" she asks, when I'm finished. "All it seems to have done is make you both miserable." I look up at her. How does she know whether Luke's miserable, or not? "I saw his face, when he walked away from you," she explains. "I've never seen a man look so… well, broken."

"Don't say that."

"Sorry, Megs, but it's true. He did." I felt bad before, but now… "And you did all this because of your dad?" she asks.

"Yes."

"But what does it matter if he disapproves? I'm sure my parents wouldn't have approved of half my boyfriends – it hasn't stopped me seeing them, though."

She doesn't understand – because that's one of the things I didn't tell her – that it's a lot more than disapproval I'd be dealing with. I've never been able to tell her what my dad's really like, because I'm fairly certain she'd do everything she could to stop me from visiting him… including locking me in my room… and maybe calling the cops. And if I don't visit him at least two or three times a year, and send him money in between times, he'll turn up here… And she *really* doesn't want that… neither do I.

"You know how strict he is," I tell her; because that's what I've said in the past when she's wondered about my lack of boyfriends, or just friends in general, for that matter.

"Yeah, but you don't have to ruin your life over it. You're going there the day after tomorrow. Why don't you talk to him? Tell him you've met someone. Luke looked like a nice guy. You could introduce them to each other. Who knows? They might get along… I mean, what's the worst that can happen…?" *Um… Luke could end up dead, that's what.*

"I'll think about it," I say, to appease her.

"Good." She looks at the clock by my bed. "Now, it's four in the morning… and I need my sleep." She gets up. "Are sure you're okay?"

I nod my head. "Yes, thanks."

"Get some rest," she says.

Once she's gone, I turn over and think about the other thing I didn't tell her… I bought a pregnancy test yesterday and took it this morning, although I don't know why I bothered. I already knew what the result would be… I'm pregnant.

Chapter Thirteen

Luke

It's three weeks yesterday since we got back. Three weeks in which all I've done is get up, shower, come to work, try to keep busy, try to avoid looking at pictures of Megan, go home, eat something that Will's cooked and go to bed again. The last two days have been slightly different, because Will's been away. He's gone on an assignment. I don't know when he'll be back, and he's told me he can't contact me. He was worried about leaving me on my own, but I told him I'll be fine… Okay, I lied to him and said I'll be fine.

I'm sleeping – sometimes – but it's weird sleep. I've never been someone who dreams much, but I've dreamt almost every night in the last three weeks. Sometimes the dreams are good. We're together, Megan and I… We're somewhere nice, like the hotel in the Lake District, or the villa at Carcasonne, and we're making love. Those dreams are amazing… and difficult, but only because I wake up with a hard-on, and the urge to do something with it… and then I realize Megan isn't with me, and the urge goes, and I'm left feeling empty. Much worse though, are the dreams where she's leaving me. Oddly, they're not at the airport, where we actually parted. They're in places where we were happy, like on the drive through Borrowdale, or at the château. When I wake up from those, it feels like like even my good memories are being snatched away, because for a while, they're tainted.

And then, there's the worst one of all. I've only had it once – thank God – the night of my first day back at work. I woke Will with my screaming, but I didn't tell him about the dream. I couldn't... I couldn't tell him that I'd imagined Megan lying in a bath... a bath with red water... and a razor blade on the floor beside her.

I still can't stop thinking about it.

I think the thing that's surprised me the most is that I haven't minded not having sex for three weeks. I'm not sure I've ever gone that long before, well not since Will moved in with Matt and I when we were at college, and I had to be there for him and put my own life on hold for a while... but I haven't even thought about sleeping with someone else. Well... that's not strictly true. There was a night, in the second week, when I was feeling really low. I'd had a lot to drink, Will was working, and I wondered about going out and finding someone – anyone – just for sex... to have some physical contact. But then, after about a minute's thought, I realized that I didn't want to just have sex... I don't think I'll ever want that again... it's not enough. And it's not with Megan...

She's changed me. I'm a different person now. And, although it shocks the hell out of me to say this, I'm okay with that.

Today is Friday and, as much as I'm looking forward to getting away from the office, and the reminders of Megan that surround me here, I'm dreading a whole weekend by myself. It's been bad enough the last couple of evenings, but two whole days... by myself, without Will to keep me sane... I'm not sure I can do it.

This morning, I'm keeping busy preparing some sales figures. I don't really need to do this, but it's occupying my mind, and it's keeping me out of the marketing meeting that Matt's having in his office. There will be far too much of Megan in the room for me to handle. I'm also still trying to work out how I'm going to get Matt to cover the fashion shows in September. I've reached the conclusion that, if I can't be with Megan, then I can't do the shows. When we parted at the airport, I thought I could, but I was wrong. I've been putting off talking to Matt, but I can't for much longer. I know the only way around it is to tell him what happened. It's the right thing to do, really, but I'm not looking forward to it. I'm wondering about taking him out somewhere tomorrow or Sunday, just the two of us – somewhere away from work – and explaining the whole thing to him. I know he's going to be mad, and he'll argue that he can't be away from Grace, but maybe she can go too, and I'll stay behind and take care of things here. I hope, when he knows what happened, and how much I'm hurting, he'll understand…

I flip over the page on my desk and start entering the next row of figures onto my screen, when I hear a man's voice outside my office door. He's talking very loudly. Heather, my secretary, says something, and he yells back at her. I get up and go across to the door. Whoever he is, he needs to learn some manners. I pull open the door and everything stops. Heather's desk faces my office door and, standing, with their backs to me are a man and a woman. I have no idea who the man is, but I'd know the woman anywhere. I'd know her even if I was blindfolded.

"Megan?" I say. God it's so good to see her, although things definitely aren't right here…

The man spins and faces me. He's a little taller than Megan, but about three or four inches shorter than me. He's well-built, muscular, in good shape for his age, which I'd say is about forty-five. He's wearing jeans, a t-shirt and a leather jacket, his hair is steel-gray, matching his eyes. "So you're Luke Myers, are you?" Megan turns more slowly. She looks pale, tired. *Baby*. I take a step forward.

"Yes." I don't take my eyes from Megan as the man grabs her arm, pulling her closer to him. She goes, like a rag doll, like she has no control. "Let go of her," I tell him, clenching my fists.

He smirks, but doesn't reply.

"I said, let go of her." He takes a step toward me, dragging Megan with him. "Now."

"You gonna make me?" he hisses, a smirk on his face. Does he *want* me to hit him? He has no idea… I might wear a suit, and work in a nice office, but this isn't where I'm from. If I hit him, he won't be getting up again.

"Yes," I say quietly.

Out of the corner of my eye, I notice Matt standing close by. He must have heard the commotion and come out of his office, which is around the corner from mine. There are half a dozen other people standing around too, watching the spectacle. I guess this car crash is more exciting than the marketing meeting.

"What's going on here, Luke?" Matt asks.

"Good question," the man says, still staring at me. I'm thinking something similar myself, since I'm none the wiser.

"Let go of Megan and I'll talk to you," I say to him, ignoring Matt.

"I don't think you get to call the shots," he says, "not after what you've done."

What I've done? I turn to Megan again.

She opens her mouth, then closes it. Then she says, "Luke… this is my father, Martin Ford."

Her father? I feel my mouth dry and I know exactly why they're here.

Megan

Luke's eyes widen, and his skin pales.

"Your father?" he says eventually, not taking his eyes from mine. I can feel my dad's fingers digging into my arm; it's really starting to hurt now, but I don't want to show it. Luke's already tense and I don't want him to react any more.

"Yeah, I'm her father," my dad says, like he should get some kind of prize for it. "And I want to know what you're going to do."

"What about?" Luke asks, still looking at me. He knows… I can tell he does. And he's wondering why I haven't told him myself. *Because I didn't get the chance, Luke*.

"You know what about."

"Let's go into my office," Luke says, relaxing and stepping back to let us into his room. His eyes drop to the floor. He doesn't want to look at me any more.

"Why? Don't want your snooty friends hearing what you did to my little girl?" *Little girl? Since when?*

"Dad, don't…" I whisper.

"Shut up," he barks, tightening his grip on me. I wince and Luke makes a move back toward us, his fists clenched again.

"Sir." A man steps forward. He spoke a moment ago, asking Luke what was going on. I don't know who he is, but he's got an air of authority about him. "I think it would be better for everyone – especially your daughter – if you were to both step into Mr Myers' office."

My dad looks up at this man, who's huge – even taller than Luke, by a couple of inches – and backs down, just a little. "Okay," he says, and we step past Luke into his office. As I pass him, the heat from his body radiates fleetingly into mine and I know if I were to look at him, I'd forget all my resolutions to keep my distance, to protect him. I'd be drawn to him, like a magnet.

His office is large, with a big desk in front of floor-to-ceiling windows that overlook the city. In the corner, is an L-shaped leather sofa with a coffee table in front.

"Have a seat," Luke says and my father drags me across to the desk, not the sofa, where Luke had directed us. *This is a business meeting, Luke*.

We sit in the two chairs facing his desk and, within a few seconds, he's opposite us, in his own seat. The other man – the taller one – also appears. He stands to one side, leaning against the wall, his legs crossed at the ankles, his arms folded. Luke looks across at him just briefly and raises an eyebrow. The other man mirrors his expression. Neither of them smiles and then they both turn back to us.

"Can I get you anything… coffee——?" Luke asks.

"No," my father interrupts.

"Megan… would you like anything?" Luke turns to me. I shake my head, still not looking at his face. I'm staring out the window, at a cloud in the sky above his head. There's nothing remarkable about it: it's just a regular cloud, but I need something to distract me.

After a short pause, Luke finally breaks the silence.

"What can I do for you, sir," he says to my father. I'm trembling. I know what my dad is capable of; the only question is, how far will he go?

"I think you've done enough already," he says.

"You implied that outside," Luke says. "Would you like to be more specific." He's being very polite, but I sense it's restrained… Like he could explode at any minute. *Please don't.*

"Sure," my dad says, his voice filled with sarcasm. "I can be specific. She's pregnant. It's yours. What are you going to do about it?"

Luke gets up and comes around the desk, leaning back on it, right in front of me. "Is this true?" he asks. His voice is so soft, I'm transported back to France… to England… to all our happy places.

"You calling me a liar?" my dad blurts out.

"No, sir."

"Trying to wriggle out of it then? Trying to suggest it's not yours?"

"No." Luke raises his voice a little. *Please, Luke, don't do that.* "I just want to hear it from Meg——"

"You don't need to," my father interrupts again. "I can tell you everything you need to know. I had my suspicions the slut had been up to something as soon as she got home for her visit. There was something different about her – something in her eyes that wasn't there before. Anyways, she started throwing up the next morning… and then I knew. So, I took her to the doctors. They didn't like me staying in the room, but I insisted; I didn't want her lying to me about the result… but it seems it wasn't news to her. The slut already knew——"

"Mr Ford." Luke's raised voice cuts through everything, like a sharp blade.

"What?"

"That's twice you've called Megan a slut. Don't do it again."

"Why not? She is."

"No. She isn't."

"Slept with you, didn't she?"

"And that makes her a slut?"

"Yep." *It's pointless, Luke.* "She already knew she was pregnant since before she came to stay with me," my dad continues, like the interruption never happened. "But she refused to tell me who the father was to start with…" I know they're all watching me. I can feel it, even though I'm still staring at the cloud. "Took me a day or two, but I got it out of her…"

"How?" Luke pushes himself off the desk and stands in front of my dad. He stands as well, and then the other man takes a step forward.

"Found your card in her stuff. She tried to make out you were just a business acquaintance, but I knew that was bullshit. I wasn't falling for that."

My eyes move away from the cloud just for a second. They find Luke's automatically and are met with such hurt, such pain, and a hardness I've never seen before. *Please forgive me. Please, Luke. I was going to tell you…*

Even as I'm thinking that, his expression softens again. Maybe he does understand.

Chapter Fourteen

Luke

I don't understand why she didn't tell me. We agreed she would... We had a deal, so why didn't she come to me? And how could she deny me to her father? 'Just a business acquaintance'? I need to know the truth. I need to hear it from her. I need her to tell me why she did all that; what it all means. And, dammit, more than anything, I just need her.

I move back to where I was, leaning up against my desk, looking down at her. At least she's stopped studying the damn sky for a moment. She's focused on her hands now... they're clasped in her lap. Shaking.

"Megan," I say, keeping my voice low and soft.

"She's got nothing to say to you," her dad interrupts. He's good at that.

I ignore him. "Megan." I try again, but she's not going to look up. *Okay, baby, have it your way.* I step forward and crouch in front of her, lowering my voice further still, so it's little more than a whisper. I don't relish having this conversation in front of Matt – or her father. This should be something we're talking about alone, just the two of us. "I gave you my card so you could call me. You had my number. Why didn't you get in touch? I told you... I told you I wouldn't walk away." She keeps her head down. I wait.

"I don't know what you're whisperin' about, but I told you," her dad says, "she's got nothing to say to you."

I take a deep breath and wait another minute. She still doesn't move. "Megan?" I say, a little louder. "What do you want from me?" She shrugs her shoulders.

"She doesn't want anything from you, except that you take responsibility for what you did to her."

It's like he thinks I forced her to have sex with me.

"You're making it sound sordid," I say to him.

"It was."

"It wasn't. You don't know anything about what happened between us."

"I know enough."

What the hell has she told him?

"No you don't," I tell him.

"I know you got my little girl pregnant." Now he's making it sound like she's a child… like I'm some kind of deviant.

"Yeah, and I'm not denying my responsibility. I'm not saying I'll walk away from her." I look back to Megan. "I never did say that, did I?" I say to her. "I told you I'd be there for you."

"You mean you knew?" Her father leaps forward, standing over me. I think I'm supposed to feel threatened. "You knew she was pregnant?"

"No, not at the time, not for sure. But I told Megan that if she was, she should call me…"

"Except she doesn't want you anymore. *That's* why she didn't contact you." I can feel all the air being sucked out of my lungs.

"Is that true?" I ask her. She looks at me… There's something in her eyes, but it's gone before I can identify it. She doesn't reply.

She doesn't need to. I get the message.

I stand and move back around my desk, glancing briefly at Matt as I pass him. He's glaring at me, his eyes dark as thunder. I don't care. I glare back at him.

I sit down again.

"What do you want, Mr Ford?" I ask Megan's father, my voice cold, like ice. Megan looks up sharply, her mouth opening, just a little. She shakes her head, looking bewildered, lost. *Yeah, baby, this is me. This is the real me – or at least the me who existed before you came along and made my life fucking perfect for a while.*

"Like I said, she wants nothing to do with you. I'm just here to stand up for her, to make sure she gets what she's owed. You need to do the right thing. Kids ain't cheap," he says, leaning over my desk toward me.

"So, you want money, do you? That's why you're here?" I don't take my eyes from Megan. *Tell me that's not true...* She doesn't move a muscle.

"Of course she wants money. There's gonna be expenses, medical bills..."

"Okay. I get it." I don't say another word. I open the top drawer of my desk, reach in and pull out my personal check book. "Who do you want this made out to?" I ask.

"Cash," he says.

I do as he asks, tear out the check and hand it to him. He snatches it and looks down, whistling between his teeth.

"C'mon," he looks at Megan. "You got what you wanted." He pockets the check and grabs her by the arm. She lets him pull her to her feet.

"Mr Ford," I say, standing. "Let go of Megan's arm."

He reaches behind him, like he's tucking his shirt into his pants. "Leave it, Luke," she says. It's the first time she's spoken since they came into my office and there's a note of panic in her voice. "Please, just leave it."

"No, Megan. I'll never leave it, not where you're concerned. You know that. I told you... you're my responsibility, and now you're pregnant, with my child—"

"She ain't your responsibility," says her father. "And, if you know what's good for you, you will leave it..." There's a menacing tone to his voice, but I'm not even remotely scared of him.

"Please, Luke," Megan says, imploring me through tear-filled eyes. "Please, just do what he says."

"So, you really don't want me?"

171

She doesn't reply, but shakes her head slowly, tears now falling down her cheeks.

I thought I couldn't hurt any more… I was so fucking wrong.

Megan

There's a small part of me wishing Luke would follow, chase after me, rescue me from whatever else my dad's got planned, because I can't fight him. But he doesn't. The door to his office remains firmly closed. I keep my eyes fixed on it while we wait for the elevator, which seems to be taking forever, willing it to open and for him to come out. But he doesn't. Why would he? I just rejected him… again. I had to.

I can feel people staring at us. I'm not surprised. I think we've created quite a scene, which is something else for Luke to hate me for.

Finally, after what feels like a lifetime, the elevator doors open and a woman steps out. She's slightly shorter than me, with brown shoulder-length curly hair. She's beautiful. "Megan?" she says. That's odd. I don't know her.

I'm confused.

"I'm Grace," she explains. "Matt's wife."

Oh. Now I can hear her British accent… it's soft, quiet. Her eyes are kind and I think I could talk to her… I think I could ask her to tell Luke I need him; to beg him to find me and help me… if only…

"Are you here to see Matt?" she asks. "Is this about the shows?" My dad's grip tightens on my arm and I shake my head. "Can I help with anything?"

I shake my head again.

"Is everything alright? You look pale." How would she know that? I might always look this way. Oh, I suppose she's seen all the photographs. That's how she knows who I am… and what I look like on a good day, when I'm with Luke.

"We haven't got time for this, lady," my dad says and pushes me into the elevator, pressing the button for the lobby.

"Megan, can I—?" Grace looks from my dad to me.

"I'm sorry. I'm so sorry," I mutter, as the doors close. I wonder if she'll realize I want her to pass that on to Luke. *No, of course she won't.*

"Who the hell's Matt?" my dad asks, leaning in closer. "Another guy you've fucked?"

"No." My voice is flat. I can't even feel outraged any more. "He owns the company."

"Oh... That's a shame. Now you've found your natural talent, if you'd had him instead of this Myers guy, we might have gotten even more – especially as he's married. Still..." He pats the pocket where he put Luke's check. "... this will do for now."

"For now?" I turn to him.

The doors open and he puts his finger to his lips, telling me to be quiet. I do as I'm told.

Once we're outside, he keeps his grip on my arm and drags me away from the building.

"Where are we going now?" I ask, trying to keep pace with his long strides.

"The bank. Where d'ya think? I need to cash this check. Then I can pay off Marco... And we can get rid of your little problem too."

"Get rid of...?"

He stops in his tracks, dragging me to a halt too.

"Yeah... God, you're as dumb as your mother. You didn't think you were gonna get to keep it, did you?"

"But you told Luke there'd be medical expenses..."

"And there will be – for your abortion." I want to be sick – and it's got nothing to do with being pregnant. "And then I'll go visit him again... on my own this time."

"No!" I shout. "You stay away from him!"

"Keep your voice down," he hisses. "I'm not going to hurt him... not yet." He takes the check from his pocket and looks at it. I can't see what it says, but he's wearing a broad grin and his eyes are wide, so I assume the amount is quite large. "You might have turned out to be a slut, just like your mother, but at least you had the good sense to get knocked up by a rich guy," he says. "I'll go pay him another visit in a few weeks and tell him you need more money."

"And how's that going to work, if I've had an abortion?"

"You're not listening. I said *I'll* go visit him. I didn't say nothing about you being there… He won't know anything about the abortion."

"I have his number… I can easily contact him."

He laughs, and a shiver runs down my back. "No you won't." He leans into me. "You make any attempt to even try and contact him, I'll deal with him." He looks at me. I know what he means. "And just to make sure, you better give me your phone." I shake my head. "Give me your fucking phone, Megan." He squeezes my arm tighter and I yelp in pain.

"Excuse me, are you okay?" The voice belongs to a young man, wearing a suit, probably in his mid-twenties, who must have heard me cry out. He's standing beside me. "Is this guy bothering you?"

"Fuck off," my dad says to him.

"I was talking to the lady," the man replies.

"It's fine," I tell him. "Thanks…"

"It doesn't look fine."

My dad glances around really quickly, then reaches behind him and pulls out the automatic that I've known was tucked in his waistband all along. "It's fucking fine," he says, pointing it at the young man. "Now move along, sonny."

The man looks at me, then down at the gun and backs away, his hands raised slightly. As he moves down the street, I see him take his phone from his jacket pocket. *Please, please be calling the police.*

"We need to get out of here," my dad says, replacing the gun behind his back. "The good samaritan is calling for help."

He drags me further along the street, then around a corner. "Your phone, Megan." He holds out his hand. I reach into my bag and take it out, handing it to him. He drops it onto the floor and, barely breaking his stride, treads on it, crushing it into little pieces. "I've got his business card," he says. "And I know you now know where he works, but believe me…" He stops. We're outside the bank now. "Believe me, you even try to contact him, you'll never see life in those pretty blue eyes of his again."

Chapter Fifteen

Luke

Even as the door is closing, I know I should go after her. Her father's not normal. Even by my father's standards, he's not normal, and that's saying something.

"How many times, Luke?" Matt says, cutting in on my thoughts. "How many goddamn times?" He's still standing by the wall.

"What?" I turn on him. "What, Matt? Is this about your rule… your precious fucking rule?"

"Yeah… which is there for a reason. Namely you. Namely so you don't bang the models, mess with their heads, their lives, and my business. Jeez, you've really surpassed yourself this time. Not only did you screw her and, from the looks of things, screw with her head *and* her life… you got her *pregnant?* What the fuck is wrong with you? How hard is it to exercise a little goddamn control?" He's mad… but so am I. I'm real mad.

"I don't know, Matt… You tell me. You showed precious little control when you broke the rule first, if you remember. Only you managed it with a psychopath, a bone fide batshit crazy psychopath, who terrorized Grace and could have killed you both, and who ended up dead on your kitchen table… So look in the mirror before you start throwing accusations around." That hurt him. I can see it in his eyes… It was a terrible time for him and Grace. I know the guilt still lingers, and a huge part of me wants to take it back. No, all of me does.

"Matt… I'm—" I start to apologize.

"Brooke *wasn't* a model—" he growls. Whoa… He's still mad. Well, okay then…

"Like hell she wasn't."

"She wasn't one of *our* models." He yells. "And she sure as shit wasn't our first solo model, who we're relying on for the next three months… who's now pregnant, Luke… with *your* child." He runs his fingers through his hair. "You do know how *not* to get a woman pregnant, don't you?"

"Fuck off, Matt." To listen to him, anyone would think I screwed the models and got them pregnant all the time.

"Why can't you think with something other than your dick, just for once in your life?"

"Why can't *you* think about something other than your fucking company?"

As I'm talking, I move forward, so I'm just inches from him. For the first time in the thirteen years I've known him, I really want to hit him. I raise my clenched fist. So does he.

"Stop it. Stop it, both of you." I freeze at the sound of Grace's voice. I turn, as does Matt, and I drop my arm back down by my side. She's standing just inside the closed door. I don't know how long she's been there, but there are tears in her eyes.

Matt pushes me out of the way and I let him.

"Grace," he says, going to her. "I'm sorry." He pulls her into his arms and I want to yell at him that I had that… I had what he's got. For about five minutes, I had it perfect, just like him. "What are you doing here? Is something wrong?" he asks her and he takes her across to the couch and sits her down, kneeling in front of her. I walk back to my desk and slump into my chair.

"Clearly. Between you two there is," Grace says. "Heather called me and told me there was a commotion – some man was here – but I was with Paul, so it's taken me a while to get here." She looks up at him. "And you're apologizing to the wrong person, Matt," she says.

"You want me to apologize to *him?*" He nods his head in my direction. "You do realize what he's done, don't you? You do know that Megan's pregnant, thanks to him?"

"I gathered that, and so did half the building, the way you two were shouting at each other."

I rest my head in my hands, staring down at my desk. How can this be happening? She's pregnant. Why didn't she come to me…?

"He needs shouting at. Someone's got to get through to him."

Matt's voice is closer again. I look up. He's walked back across the room and is standing behind the chair Megan was sitting in just a few minutes ago, his hands resting on the back.

"Fine… go ahead," I say to him. "Yell all you like."

"Why, Luke? Why did you have to go and ruin everything?"

And that's it… That's all it takes for me to lose it. "Ruin everything?" I shout at him. "You think I've ruined everything? Try being in my shoes. See how ruined feels… I didn't do this on purpose. I fell in love, for fuck's sake. For the first time in my life, I met the perfect woman, and I fell in love with her. And she loved me… and for a little over two weeks, I had it perfect… just like you and Grace. Well, it was nearly perfect. There was one small problem… Megan made it very clear right from the start that it couldn't last. I wanted forever; I told her that, but she told me that we could only have our time in Europe, and once we got back here, we had to go our separate ways. I don't know why. I never found that out. It didn't matter what I said or did, she was adamant, and since we got back, I've done my best to respect her wishes." I look up at him. There's something in his face. To me it looks like doubt… uncertainty. "You don't believe me, do you? You'd rather listen to the shit her father was coming out with, because it fits your image of me. I'm just the unreliable fuck-up, always letting you down, aren't I? Well, to start with, despite what her father said, I didn't force her to sleep with me. You know me. I may be an asshole, but I've never forced any woman. Ever." He looks down at the chair in front of him.

"Luke—" he says.

"Just wait a second," I interrupt and I pull my wallet from my jacket pocket and take out Megan's letter. It's been folded away in there since the day after I phoned her. I like knowing it's close to me. I stand up and unfold it, glancing down at the words I know by heart as I walk around the table and slam the page into his chest. "Read that," I say to him, holding it there until he moves his hands up and takes it from me. "It's the letter she wrote me on our last day in England. Read it. She says she loves me. Hell, she even says she's *grateful* to me… They're not the words of a woman who was being forced into anything… except giving up the relationship that she wanted just as much as I did…" He's holding the letter in his hands, staring at me. "I was going to tell you about her when we got back. I was going to tell you and to hell with the consequences, because she matters to me more than anything. But when we got to the airport, I couldn't change her mind about ending it. She made me walk away and leave her there, because I'd promised that's what I'd do… It damn near broke me. She was my fucking redemption, and I had to walk away from her…" He still doesn't say anything. We just stare at each other. I take a deep breath, and let it out slowly. I suddenly feel calmer, and kind of cleansed… and I know what I have to do. It's the only thing I can do to keep what's left of my sanity. "I'm sorry," I say quietly, looking down at the floor. "I'm sorry for breaking your rule, and fucking up your business. I get that this is gonna cause you problems and I think it's best for everyone if I quit. You can have my shares back too; you don't need to pay me anything for them. You gave them to me… I'm giving them back. I'll come in over the weekend sometime, if that's okay, and get my things… Oh, and I'm due to meet with Frank Watson for breakfast on Monday. You'll have to take that…"

"Luke, please…" I glance up at him. His expression has changed. I see a mirror of my own sadness in his eyes. "I'm sorry," he says. "I had no idea…"

I shrug. "I don't blame you. I deserve everything you said."

"No you don't. I overreacted. I was wrong. I should've listened to you first. You were right; I was just thinking about the business… It never even occurred to me…"

"What? That I'd fall in love?" He doesn't reply, but he stares at me and I can tell he feels awful. I don't want that. "Let's face it, Matt, it wouldn't have occurred to anyone, not with my history…"

"Even so, I should have listened."

"Why? We both know what I was like. It was a natural assumption to make." I manage a half-laugh. "I thought really long and hard myself before starting anything with Megan – because of my past. I knew your rule was set up mainly for me and I thought she deserved better than a guy who needed something like that in his life. In the end it was Will of all people who convinced me I should give it a try. Just talking to him made me think I could change, and he said he didn't think you'd apply the rule if I was serious about Megan, because that wouldn't be fair."

"Will's right," he says. "I just didn't know how you felt about her."

"I know… you thought I was screwing around, as usual… Not this time…" My voice fades for a moment. "But in the end, what does it matter? We're still here, aren't we? We're in the same place. I've still lost them both, *and* I've messed up your business. I'm sorry." I look down and realize he's still holding Megan's letter. "You can read it if you want, if you need proof."

"I don't need to. I believe you." He hands it back to me.

I fold it up and put it back in my wallet. "I'm gonna go home now," I say, starting toward the door. "I'll hang onto my keys until Monday, just so I can—"

"Luke…" Grace says. She's sitting curled in the corner of the couch, tears pouring down her cheeks. I glance back at Matt.

"You're needed," I say to him, but for the first time ever, he doesn't go to her.

"No. You are," Grace says.

"Not my department," I tell her. "I'm not good with crying women, I never have been… well, except Megan."

"You can't leave," Matt says, still standing at my desk.

"I have to."

"Why?" Grace asks. "Matt's admitted he was wrong. You don't bear grudges, I know you don't."

"It's got nothing to do with that…" I feel my shoulders slump. "I can't stay… You've designed her into everything, Grace. She's everywhere I look. Do you have any idea how hard it's been these last three weeks? Every single picture has a memory of her; a memory of us, of our time together… Every damn one of them."

She nods her head. She gets it. "Sorry," she whispers.

"It's not your fault. I just can't do this anymore… It's too hard."

"But you can't leave," Matt repeats. "I'll find you another job to do."

"Thanks," I say. "What did you have in mind? Whatever it is, I'll be reminded of her. I helped her get changed for the shoots. Even seeing or handling the garments reminds me of how she looked and felt in them. I can't do it, Matt." I need to get out of here before I break down completely in front of Grace. I take another step closer to the door.

"Okay," he says. "Then I'll find you something that's just to do with the sportswear side of the business… completely away from Amulet. I'll create a position for you, if I have to." He comes and stands in front of me. "Whatever you think of yourself, Luke, you're not a fuck-up… and you've never let me down. Never… Please, don't do this." He puts his hand on my shoulder. "We're a team, you and I, and you're as much a part of this place as I am. Please stay…" he says.

I don't really want to leave either. I belong here.

"You'll find me something else to do?" I murmur. "Because I sure as hell can't keep doing this…"

"I understand that," he says. "I wish you'd come to me sooner, but now I know, we can work it out."

Even though I can't speak for a moment, I nod my head. We stand awkwardly. We've never been the sort of guys who hug, but I think now would be the time, if we were.

"So, what are we going to do?" he asks eventually.

I look up at him. My confusion must be obvious.

"Not about the job," he clarifies. "As long as you're staying, that doesn't matter. I mean what are we going to do about Megan? I want to help."

"What can you do? What can *I* do? I think she made it very clear she wants nothing to do with me. I asked her if she wanted me… she shook her head. She could barely look at me. And she was so cold about everything… She wouldn't even acknowledge the baby to me."

"Luke, don't take this the wrong way… but how do you even know there is a baby? The whole thing might have been concocted by her dad to get money from you."

"You gave him money?" Grace asks.

I nod my head. "A check, yeah."

"How much for?"

"Twenty-five thousand dollars."

"Jeez, Luke," Matt says. "That's a lot of money when you've got no proof."

"Is it possible Megan's pregnant?" Grace asks.

"Yes. It's very possible. And before you say anything, Matt, I know… I should've been more careful."

"I wasn't gonna say anything… but couldn't it be someone else's, if she is?" he asks. I glare at him. He holds up his hands. "Don't lose it with me again. I'm just trying to think of all the angles here."

"No," I say. "It couldn't be someone else's."

"How can you be so sure?" he asks. "She might have been with another guy just before you all left for France. She wouldn't necessarily tell you about something like that, and the timing could still work…"

"You're my best friend, and you always will be, but you're pushing your luck." I take a deep breath. "I know it's mine, because… I was her first…" I can't help the crack in my voice.

He whispers, "Oh, fuck," under his breath and closes his eyes for a moment.

"Luke," Grace says, tears forming again. "This is all so wrong. You should be with her. She needs you."

"Except evidently, she doesn't." I don't have any more words. Matt goes and sits on the couch with Grace, pulling her into his arms and, after a moment, I join them. Silence fills the room for a few minutes. I can't even think straight. None of it makes sense to me anymore. My head's spinning.

"Do you know what I really don't understand…" I say eventually, "Megan promised me at the airport… she agreed that if she was pregnant, she'd get in touch. I told her the deal to end the relationship was off if she was pregnant. I told her I wouldn't stay away. She definitely agreed with me. So why didn't she contact me? Hell, she didn't even say anything to me today – not really – and I gave her enough chances."

"*Could* she say anything though?" Grace asks leaning away from Matt.

I turn to look at her. She sits up, wiping her cheeks with the backs of her hands. "I saw her outside, by the lifts."

"Was she okay?" I move forward in my seat.

"I'm not sure."

"Well, did she say anything?"

"She just said, 'I'm sorry. I'm so sorry'."

"Why would she say that?" Matt asks.

"I don't know," Grace replies. "It struck me as odd at the time. But my point is that her father was controlling everything. He wouldn't let her talk to me. Perhaps he wouldn't let her talk to you either." She twists to face me. "Her dad was pulling her around. She looked scared. I've seen that kind of fear before, Luke… I used to see it in the mirror, when I was married to Jonathan." Grace is talking about her first husband, the violent piece of shit, who beat the crap out of her. *Oh… fuck.*

Suddenly, nothing else matters except that I have to find Megan. Now. I need to know she's okay, and if she isn't, I need to do everything I can – whatever it takes – to get her somewhere safe. Even if she doesn't want me anymore, I have to make sure she's alright.

I jump off the couch and head for the door. As I open it, I realize Matt is right behind me. I turn to him.

"What's wrong?" I say.

"Nothing. But you're not doing this on your own. I'm coming with you." I feel relieved. I know he'll help; he'll stop me going insane, if nothing else.

I glance at Grace, who's still sitting on the couch behind us. "Well then, you'd better give your wife a hug first. She looks like she needs one." He goes back across to her and pulls her into his arms once more. He keeps her there for a long moment, then she pulls away and kisses him.

"Take care of him," she says as he comes back across to me.

"I will," I tell her.

"I was talking to Matt," she replies.

Megan

We've been some time in the bank. There were identification formalities and the money took a while to organize. My dad wasn't worried though… for twenty-five thousand dollars, I'm not surprised. I had no idea Luke had written a check for that much, not until the man in the bank handed it over.

"Marco." My dad's voice sounds saccharin-sweet. I'm driving the car that he borrowed from his friend Lenny and we're headed back to my dad's place. I don't call it 'home' – I haven't since I was old enough to understand what a real home should be. Besides, we've lived in so many places over the years, I've learned it doesn't pay to get too attached. "Hey… there's no need for that… Hear me out, man… I've got your money," he's saying. "Yeah… all ten grand of it. Yeah, in cash." He pauses. "Well, come on over in an hour and you can pick it up…" While we're stopped at a red light, they finalize their arrangements for whoever Marco is to come around, then my dad disconnects the call.

"You owe this guy ten thousand dollars?" I ask, as the lights turn green.

"So what if I do? Who's fault is that?"

"Mine, I suppose."

"Who else's? If you'd stayed here, instead of giving yourself airs… The only reason I agreed to you going to college was 'cause you convinced me you'd be able to earn more money if you had a degree… Well, I've not seen nothing yet, except you spreading your legs."

I don't bother to argue, or remind him that I gave him some money on the day I arrived… a quarter of my earnings from the photo shoot. We drive on in silence until we get back to his condo.

I go straight to my room and lie down on the bed, curling into a ball. I can hear my dad on the phone through the closed door, but I want nothing to do with him. I never did before, but after this morning…

I shut my eyes, trying to block out the memories of the scene in Luke's office, but they're even more vivid. I don't think I'll ever forget the expression on his face when he realized I'm pregnant and that I hadn't contacted him. I told him I would and I didn't. And it wasn't because I didn't want to. I did… but I only found out a couple of days before coming to visit my dad. I thought I'd get this visit over with, get used to the idea myself, and then get in touch with Luke. How was I to know I'd start being sick? Well, I suppose I should have done. It just didn't occur to me at the time. I was probably too wrapped up with thinking about Luke's reaction when I told him… Now, I'll never know how he feels about it.

I hear a knocking on the front door and my dad talking to someone – Marco, I assume. He doesn't stay long… just long enough to collect his money, and probably sell my dad some more drugs, I guess.

Once he's gone, the apartment falls silent, just for a while. I know this usually means my dad is getting a fix… and it's best to stay out of his way.

The door opens unexpectedly. "C'mon," he says. I look up.

"Why? Where are we going now?"

"I'm taking you to the abortion clinic."

I sit up, clutching my knees to my chest. "No. I won't do it."

He moves toward me. "I've already called them. They're expectin' you."

"I don't care." I've never stood up to him like this… I guess it's maternal instinct or something. "I'm not doing it."

He's standing over me. "There's two choices," he says. "Either you come now and I'll take you to the clinic; or…"

"Or what?" What else could he threaten me with? Actually, I don't want to know…

"I'll find a way to do it myself."

I stare at him. "You… you wouldn't."

"Don't push me, girl."

He walks back to the door. "Five minutes," he says. "I'll be waiting in Lenny's car. You choose."

He slams the door behind him and I'm alone. God, I'm so alone.

He wouldn't really abort my pregnancy himself, would he? Would he even know how? I know he's mean and angry and violent, but surely that's too much, even for him.

Can I afford to take the chance? If he does it, he could kill me, or make it impossible for me to have children in the future. At least if I go to a clinic, they'll know what they're doing… But it's Luke's baby. I can't…

I try to think; there's got to be a way out of this… There's no landline here and I've got no phone. If I had either of those, I'd contact Luke, or Erin, or the police… anyone. Except there isn't anyone else.

Slowly, I push myself off the bed and, without thinking about what I'm doing, I grab my bag, pull it over my shoulder and walk to the front door. As I close it behind me, I look down to where he's sitting in the car, waiting, tapping the steering wheel. He pokes his head out through the open window. "Get a move on!" he yells.

The waiting room is sparse. The clinic is sparse. From the outside, it looks like a down-market office building; on the inside, it's not much better.

My dad left me half an hour ago. On the way over here, he told me not to bother coming home until I'd had it done and stupidly, I replied that worked fine for me… I just wouldn't go home again. He pulled the car up at the side of the road, leaned over, and put his hand around my throat. Then he told me that if I tried that 'game', he'd go back to Luke's office and stick a bullet in his 'pretty' head. I nodded my understanding, and he carried on driving… and then he told me the next part of his plan.

"I've decided you're not going back to your friends in the city… you're gonna stay here with me,"

I turned to look at him. "I'm not."

He had a slight smile on his lips… the kind of smile that's always made me shiver. "Yeah… you are," he muttered. "We did good today… and now you've discovered your calling in life, you're gonna keep on doing good."

I had no idea what he was talking about and I told him so.

He let out a half laugh. "Yep… just as dumb as your mother." We stopped at red lights and he turned to face me. "We're gonna find ourselves some rich suckers… You're gonna let them fuck you and then tell 'em you're pregnant… If we go for married guys, they'll pay double." He laughed. "We can make a killing…"

I didn't have an answer. I just stared at him… the lights went green and he drove me straight here, not saying another word.

I wondered if I'd be able to tell a nurse what's going on; maybe get her to call the police, or Luke… but the only person I've spoken to so far, is the receptionist, who's about the most unsympathetic person I've ever met. She huffed a lot when I completed my forms. It being a Friday afternoon, I think my being here is inconvenient for her… And right now, there are three other women ahead of me, so I think I'll be here a while, which gives me more time to think. I don't need to sit here by myself, I don't need time to think. I just need Luke.

Chapter Sixteen

Luke

We're in my car, because I want to at least feel in control of something. But we're still in the parking garage, the engine ticking over, because there's a problem… I don't know where to go.

"I don't know her address," I say, feeling stupid.

Matt looks at me and rolls his eyes, then pulls his phone from his pocket. He scrolls through his contacts and waits until the call connects. "Pamela," he says. He's talking to his secretary. She's only worked for him for a few months, but she's so much better than her predecessor, Mary. She was efficient, but she hated me, and Grace, and pretty much everyone else. What none of us realized was she was in love with Matt… it was beyond awkward. "Can you do something for me?" he continues, and asks her to go through the most recent accounts files. "We just made a payment to Megan Ford, about three weeks ago," he says, "Can you check to see if we've got her address on file?" He waits, then turns to me. "Get this thing going," he says. I reverse out of the space and cruise slowly around toward the exit. There's no point in hurrying yet… I don't know which direction to take. He sits forward all of a sudden and punches a zip code into the SatNav, then when the screen changes, he starts adding the address. "Thanks, Pamela," he says and hangs up. "Move it, Luke," he says.

"Where are we going?" We're underground so the SatNav isn't working properly yet.

"South – I-93."

I floor the gas pedal and Matt shoots back in his seat. "I'd like to get back alive, if that's okay with you," he says.

"Sorry."

"Do you want me to drive?" he asks as I pull out onto the street and speed up.

"No. I need to do something," I tell him. "Besides, you hate driving my car."

"Only because it's damn dangerous.

"And because it's a stick, not an automatic."

"There is that," he agrees.

"And it's not dangerous… Not when you get used to it."

"It's got massive understeer and it twitches… I don't like cars that twitch."

"You just don't like it because it makes a better noise than yours." I turn the corner in the direction of the interstate, accelerating again.

"Nothing makes a better noise than my car."

"Yeah, right." Matt drives an Aston Martin DB9; I drive a Corvette Z06. We bought them around the same time, and it's been a running joke ever since. Although I'm not in the mood for jokes, the banter is good. It's distracting me from worrying about Megan and what her dad might be doing to her…

"Wait a second." I hit the brakes. Luckily there's no-one behind us. "What?"

"We're going to Megan's place?"

"Yeah…"

"She won't be there, will she? She's at her dad's."

"Shit. And we have no idea where he lives…?"

I pull the car over to the side of the road. "No."

We sit for a minute. "What about Will?" Matt asks.

"He's on an assignment. I can't contact him."

"Okay." He pulls out his phone again and goes through his contacts. What does he think Pamela can do this time? "Todd?" he says, once the call's connected, "I need a favor." Todd is a friend of ours – well,

Matt's originally, but ours now. He's a cop. "I need you to try and find a guy called Martin Ford." There's a pause while Todd speaks, although I can't hear what he's saying. "It's to do with Luke. I don't really have time to explain. The guy has a daughter. She and Luke are involved… No, it's nothing like that. It's different this time. The thing is, she could be in trouble…" He waits again. "Her name's Megan. Apart from that, we don't know anything."

"Wait!" I tell him. "I have her cell number. Will didn't tell me where he got it, but it might have been registered to her dad's address… would that help?"

"Did you hear that?" Matt says into his phone. "Yeah… give me the number," he says to me. I get my phone out of my jacket pocket and look up her details, handing it to Matt. He reads the number to Todd. "Thanks," he says and hangs up.

"Try calling her," he says, giving me back my phone. "Who knows, she might answer."

I press the call button and put the phone to my ear, but all I get is a message, telling me the call can't be connected.

"It won't connect," I tell him.

"Maybe she's turned it off."

I hope that's all it is.

"What did Todd say?"

"He'll get back to us."

"Should we sit here, or go back to the office?" I don't want to, but it seems ridiculous sitting at the side of the road. We could be here for hours.

"I don't—" Matt's phone rings, interrupting him. "Todd? Man, that was…" He goes quiet. "Okay." He glances at me. "Okay." He leans forward and starts putting details into the SatNav again. "You sure?" he says. "We'll see you there, then," and he hangs up.

While the SatNav does its calculations, I turn to him. "Where am I going?" I ask.

"North. I-93."

I check the mirror and pull out.

It takes just under half an hour to reach the address and, when we do Todd is already there, leaning against his car. As I pull up behind him, he walks back, coming up to my window. He rests his hands on the top of the car and bends down low so he can see both of us.

"You know, don't you... if you bought a proper car, I could get in the back and we could talk, like normal people."

I look at him. Ordinarily, I'd answer back. Right now... I'm not in the mood. He's in the way and I need to get out.

"Why are you here?" I say to him. He glances at Matt.

"Call it back up," he says.

"Do I need back up?"

"In this neighborhood... probably."

I glance around. The apartment block is shabby, but I've seen worse. Hell, I've lived in worse. Unless Matt's told him – which I doubt – Todd knows nothing about my childhood, which was spent in much worse places than this.

"Can I get out now?" I ask him, trying to open the door.

"In a minute," he says, holding my gaze. "Look, I don't know what's going on here and I don't think you've got time to tell me... But, I'm coming in there with you and you *will* do what I say. Or, Matt will keep you here and I'll go in on my own. Is that clear?"

I stare at him. The thought of Matt keeping me in my car if Megan's in trouble is laughable, but I nod my head because Todd has a gun, and I know it's the only way I'm getting out of the car any time soon. "Okay," I say. He steps back and I get out and take off my jacket, throwing it onto the seat. He goes around to Matt and they talk. Matt stays in the car. I raise my eyebrows.

"No need to spook the guy by having all three of us march in there," Todd says and we start to walk. "So, you've met Martin Ford before?" he asks as we climb the steps to the entrance.

"Yeah. He came to the office this morning with Megan."

"His daughter?"

"Yes." We go inside the building. There's no elevator. "What floor?" I ask Todd.

"One up," he says and we take the stairs. "And Megan… Are you and she…?" he asks.

"It's complicated." He doesn't say a word, and he doesn't push for any more information.

We get to the top of the stairs and open the door that's straight ahead of us, going down a corridor. Todd stops when we get to the apartment numbered twelve.

"This it?" I say, lowering my voice.

He nods his head and, to my surprise, he goes to take his gun from its holster.

"What are you doing?" I say, putting my hand over his. "I don't want guns involved."

"Neither do I," he replies and gives me a look that says I'm a little dimwitted. "There's a reason I could find this guy so fast, Luke. He's got a record." That's not a surprise.

"I get that, but you don't understand… Megan's pregnant."

His mouth opens, just slightly. "Yours?" he says. I nod my head. "Okay." He drops his hand again and thinks for a moment, then moves to one side, so he's out of sight. "You knock."

I raise my hand and tap loudly on the door, then wait. Within a few seconds, the door opens and Megan's dad stands in front of me. He's not wearing the leather jacket anymore and I can see his arms are covered in tattoos. He stinks of strong liquor.

"If you've come to get your money back, you're too late," he sneers.

"Where's Megan?"

"I told you this morning. She doesn't want nothing to do with you. Now fuck off." Just as he goes to shut the door in my face, Todd nudges me to one side and puts his foot in the way. He's holding up his badge about two or three inches from Megan's dad's face.

"Now, that's not very polite," Todd says.

"You brought the fucking cops?" Ford lurches in my direction.

"Yeah… he did." Todd grabs hold of his right arm and twists it behind him, turning him at the same time, and holding him up against the wall of the hallway, his other arm pressing on the back of Ford's neck. "Now… where's your daughter?"

"You're hurting my arm."

"You mean like you were hurting Megan's this morning?" I say to him, coming to stand beside Todd.

"You mean you're beating up on your daughter, when she's pregnant?" Todd hisses into his ear.

"Well, she won't be pregnant by now," Ford says, his lip curling into a cruel smile.

"What do you mean?" I ask... although I think I already know the answer.

"I mean I took her to the clinic a couple hours ago... I imagine it's all over by now." He starts to laugh. I take a step forward and, even as Todd moves his hand to stop me, I grab Ford's hair, pull his head back and slam it hard into the wall.

"Luke!" Todd yells.

"What?" I'm breathing heavily.

"That won't help."

"It'll help me."

"No it won't. You need to know where she is. He can't tell you if he unconscious."

I stop in an instant. He's right.

"If you think..." Ford slurs. "If you think I'm gonna tell you..."

Todd loosens his grip just enough to turn Ford around so they're facing each other.

"I may have called him off," Todd says, getting in his face. "But don't think I'm the nice guy in this. If you don't tell us exactly what we want to know, I'm gonna fuck up your life so bad, you'll be begging my friend here to beat you into oblivion."

"I won't be beggin' him for jack shit."

"Oh, really?" Todd seems almost amused by that response. He takes a deep breath. "I know exactly what you are, Mr Ford, and who you deal with. So, you either tell me where your daughter is, right this minute, or I'll put the word out on the street that you're working for me."

Ford pales. "No-one would believe you," he blusters. Todd lets him go and Ford slumps to the floor.

"Fine," Todd says, and turns away. *What's he doing?* "I'll make a few calls… you'll be at the bottom of the river before I even get back to the precinct." He takes two steps.

"Wait!" Ford yells, trying to sit up. "She's at the Women's Health Clinic on Briar Street."

Todd turns to me. "Go…" he says, and I start running.

"You're too late," I hear Ford yelling, but I'm not listening to him anymore.

I go down the stairs two at a time and sprint to my car. Matt leaps out when he sees me, and leans on the open door.

"What's happened?" he asks.

"I know where she is," I say, grabbing my jacket from the seat, throwing it across to the passenger side, then getting in behind the wheel. Matt jumps back in beside me, putting my jacket on his lap. I switch on the engine and turn to him. "Sorry, man," I say to him. "I need to do this by myself." He looks at me, clearly confused. "Megan's at an abortion clinic," I explain. "I don't know if…" I can't finish my sentence.

Matt opens the door and climbs out, leaving my jacket behind. He leans down. "Call me later," he says. I nod, put the car into gear and take off down the road.

The building is anonymous, like an office, or factory… That thought makes my blood turn to ice. I park up close to the doors and walk in. There's a woman on the reception desk. She looks at me over the top of her glasses.

"Yes?" she says, her voice nasal and disapproving.

"I'm looking for Megan Ford."

"Is she a patient?"

"Y-yes."

"We can't give out patient details."

"I'm not asking you to. I only need to know if she's here. I need to speak to her."

Just then, a door to my right opens and a woman comes out. It's not Megan. The woman makes for the main entrance. She's got her head down, and she looks pale. The door she just came out of takes a while to close behind her and as it does, I see her… Megan, sitting in a chair, clutching her arms around her, staring at the floor between her feet.

"Megan!" I call. She looks up just as the door closes again.

I don't hesitate, not for a second. I start to walk over.

"Wait… Sir!" the woman behind the desk calls out. I turn and glare at her and she closes her mouth. I open the door and go straight over to Megan, standing in front of her. She's gone back to staring at the floor again.

"Hey," I say. She doesn't look up. I kneel down in front of her, reach out and place my finger under her chin, raising her face a little so she has to look at me. "Hey," I repeat. Her eyes are red-rimmed, her cheeks stained with tears, and there are more brimming. She's never looked so damn beautiful.

She kind of falls forward into my arms and we kneel together, holding each other tight and swaying slightly from side to side. Her shoulders are shaking and I can feel the wetness of her tears seeping through my shirt onto my chest.

"It's okay, baby," I murmur into her hair once I know my voice can be trusted.

She shakes her head. "No it isn't… it isn't okay." I can barely hear her, but I know I'm too late. I got here too late. It hurts more than I thought it would. I've never really wanted fatherhood and it's only been a reality for a few hours, but now it's been taken from me, I'm surprised by how lost I feel without it. *Don't let her see that, Luke. Don't make it worse for her.*

"I'm sorry," she whispers, clinging to me. "I'm sorry, I'm sorry, I'm sorry." I pull back from her just a little, placing my hands on her cheeks and looking into her eyes.

"It's really okay," I say.

"Please forgive me."

"There's nothing to forgive."

It's like she hasn't heard me. "I'm sorry," she repeats. "I'm so sorry, for all of it. Please understand. I didn't want to come here."

"I know."

"He… he forced me. He told me if I didn't, he'd find a way to do it himself."

I'll kill him. How could he threaten her with that?

"I thought coming here would be safer," she's saying. "But this isn't what I wanted, please believe me. Coming here… it wasn't my choice."

I know she's telling the truth. It doesn't make it hurt any the less, but I know she didn't want it any more than I did.

Megan

He's here. It's like all my prayers have been answered. How he found me I don't know, and right now, I don't care. His arms are around me, I'm crying into his chest and it feels like nothing can hurt me… unless he can't forgive me.

"I'm sorry." I can't stop saying it, because I want him to know I didn't mean to reject him, and I never meant to put him in harm's way… it was the one thing I was trying to avoid right from the beginning… And I need him to understand I'd never have set foot in this place if it had been left up to me.

"Megan," he says, staring into my eyes. His are so soft, I melt into them. "Please stop apologizing."

"But…"

"Stop. It's me who should apologize."

"Why?"

He sighs and leans back a little, but I grab hold of him, pulling him back. "Don't," I say, "please." He smiles and holds me again.

"Shall we sit?" he suggests. I nod and he lifts me to my feet, and we sit down on the chairs, side by side. Now we're here, I think I preferred it on the floor. He could hold me properly there. This way, we feel separated. "I'm sorry," he continues, "because I should never have acted that way in my office. I should have told everyone to leave so we could speak alone. I should have found out from you what you wanted, not listened to your father. And I should never have been so cold, or have offered you money. I should have offered you myself; even if you didn't want me."

I turn in my seat and stare up at him. "I know I shook my head when you asked me if I wanted you, but I didn't mean that... I'm sorry. I—"

"Enough apologizing."

"I've wanted you since the day we got back." I tell him the truth. "And I've been praying you'd find me... wishing you'd work out where I was, ever since my dad found out I was pregnant. I've never needed anything as much as I've needed you these last few days."

He leans into me and rests his head against mine. "I take it your dad is the reason we had to break up?" he asks.

I nod my head. "Yes. He didn't want me having boyfriends. He didn't really like me having friends at all. It was partly because he didn't want anyone to have any influence over me – that way he could control everything. But also because he didn't want anyone getting close to what he was doing... the drugs, the guns, the thieving... and God knows what else..."

He lifts my face to his. "I'm not afraid of your father, Megan."

"You should be. He threatened to kill anyone who touched me... He broke the jaw of the only guy who ever kissed me. I didn't want him to hurt you."

"He won't."

"Luke, he brought a gun to your office. It was down the back of his pants."

He smiles and looks up at the ceiling. "Oh... so that's what he was doing... I thought it was an odd time to worry about tucking his shirt in."

He seems so calm. Doesn't he realize what I've just told him?
"Luke..."

"Megan, I couldn't give a damn if he brought an assault rifle to my office. The point is, he brought you." He looks down at me. "I'm sorry," he says. "I can't do this." Oh… What's he saying? I suddenly feel sick again. "I can't talk to you like this… you're too far away." He picks me up, putting me on his lap and holding me tight against his chest. "That's better." He's right. It is. With his arms around me, it's perfect. "You okay there?" I nod my head.

"He's dangerous, Luke," I murmur into him. "That was why I didn't speak… why I didn't react to you, or admit how much I wanted you… He told me he'd kill you if I stepped out of line. He scares me." Luke's arms come around me a little tighter.

"There's nothing to be scared of, not any more." I look up at him. "I didn't find you all by myself," he says. "I had help from a couple of friends of mine… one of them's a cop. I left him and your dad talking – well, kind of talking."

I can't help but smirk. "Oh. I can't imagine he was very happy about that."

"That's one way of putting it. He got a lot of satisfaction from telling me you were here, though. I'm afraid I introduced his head to the wall for that… sorry."

"Don't apologize," I tell him. "He deserved it."

"Yeah… he did."

We fall silent for a moment. The thought that my dad might be out of my life – even if it's just for a while makes me feel almost light-headed. Or maybe that's just the realization that Luke's here; I'm in his arms and I'm finally safe.

He leans back a little, puts his hands on either side of my face and looks at me. His eyes are intensely blue, like they've gone a shade or two darker. "I understand your fear of your dad and why you broke us up… Well, I kind of do. I really wish you'd told me about it before, though, because then I could have explained to you that there isn't a man on this earth who scares me half as much as the thought of spending another day without you. I haven't thought about anything but you since we got home. I loved you since the first time I saw you,

Megan. I've never stopped loving you. And no matter what happens…
I never will."

He loves me… I feel the smile spreading across my lips. I hope it
tells him enough, because I know my voice won't work. A tear drops
onto my cheek and he wipes it away with his thumb.

"I know we've got things we need to work out," he says, still not
taking his eyes from mine, "and I'm not saying it's going to be easy, but
can we start again… please?"

I open my mouth to speak, but I still can't, so I just nod my head.

Chapter Seventeen

Luke

She's nodding. I keep my eyes fixed on hers as I close the gap between us and kiss her, real slow and tender, on the lips. She leans into me, lifting her arms around my neck and I know in that moment, that whatever else has happened, whatever else we've lost today, I'm the luckiest man alive… because I've got her back. I can taste the salt from her tears and I guess, after what she's gone through, it could be a while before she stops crying. That's okay, though. We're together now and I'll hold her until it stops hurting so much.

I want to get her out of here; we need to be somewhere else… anywhere but here.

I break the kiss. "How long do you have to wait before they'll let you go home?" I ask her, keeping her close.

She leans back in my arms. "What do you mean?"

"Well… do you need to see someone, or get discharged or anything?"

"No. Why would I?" A look of understanding crosses her face. "Oh… You think I've…" She nestles into me again. "I haven't had anything done, Luke," she says. "When it came to it, no matter what my dad had threatened, I couldn't do it. He told me not to go home until I'd had it done, but with what he had in mind, there was no way I was ever going back there again. I couldn't contact you… and I didn't want to lead him back to Erin… so I've just been sitting here trying to work out what to do.."

She's not making a lot of sense… "Why couldn't you contact me? You've got my number."

She shakes her head. "He took my phone and smashed it when we left your office. He left me here with no money… nothing."

"In that case, I'm a little confused."

"Why?"

"If you didn't go ahead with the abortion, why have you been apologizing?"

"Because I rejected you… because I'm here. I didn't want you think this would have been my choice. I'd never have come here voluntarily… I'd never willingly have an abortion, you have to know that. He made me…"

"It's okay, baby, I know." I sit her forward on my lap so I can see her properly. "So, this means you're still…"

"Pregnant? Yes." She nods her head, but there's an uncertain look on her face.

"Thank God for that."

"You're pleased then?" she seems surprised. "I mean it wasn't exactly what either of us intended, was it?"

"Of course I'm pleased. I wouldn't have loved you any less if you'd had the abortion, but yeah… I'm pleased you didn't." I can't seem to stop smiling. "So… we can go then?"

"Yes, we can go."

I stand with her in my arms and carry her out through the door, into the reception area, past the woman at the desk, who's looking even more grumpy now, and out the main entrance. I put her down by my car.

"Really?" she says. "Bright yellow?"

"What's wrong with bright yellow?"

She stifles a laugh. "It's just not what I would have expected, I guess."

I open her door, take my jacket off the seat and place it around her shoulders, and hold her hand while she sits, then close it and go around to my side.

"Well, don't worry too much about it," I say, climbing in. "I'll have to change it soon." She looks across at me. "You see anywhere in here for a baby seat?"

"But I'm guessing you like your car?"

"Nowhere near as much as I love you." I put my hand over hers and lean across, kissing her gently.

As I pull back from her, I look up at the building again. Something's bothering me… "Just now… you said your dad had something in mind for you… and you were never going back there." I look across at her. "What did he have in mind, Megan?" She stares at me for a minute, then turns away. "Tell me." I need to know.

She doesn't look back, but whispers, "He'd decided he could make good money out of me being pregnant. He wanted to pull off the same stunt as today… but with different men."

"I'm sorry?" Did she just say what I think she did?

She turns back and faces me. "I didn't actually have to get pregnant… just pretend to be."

"And then he'd extort money from… from the guys you'd slept with?" Because she'd have to sleep with them to make it work…

She nods her head, just once. "He seemed to think it'd be quite lucrative."

I can feel a rage burning inside me, like I've never felt before… not even when my dad used to beat up Will. This is beyond anything I've ever experienced.

"Please, Luke…" Her voice just about breaks through the red mist. "I'd never have done it. Please believe me."

"I know," I manage to say, although my voice sounds anything but normal.

"You're angry," she whispers.

"Yeah… but not with you." I look into her eyes and see a lifetime of sadness and hurt. There's something else there too… It's fear. I bury my anger and lean over, pulling her closer. "I'll never be angry with you. And you have nothing to be afraid of… not when you're with me. I promise."

She closes her eyes and my lips are almost touching hers, just as my phone starts ringing. She pulls back. *Damn.*

I check the screen on my cell. It's Todd. I connect the call and put the phone to my ear, but keep Megan's hand in mine.

"Hey," I say.

"Luke. You alone?"

"No."

"You caught up with Megan, then?"

"Yes."

"Good… I just wanted to keep you in the picture," he says. "We're taking her dad back to the precinct. He won't be going far. We found a lot of weapons at his place… not to mention some drugs, and some stolen property. He's a piece of work, Luke."

"Tell me about it." I pause for a moment, glancing at Megan. I don't know how she'll feel about me telling Todd, but I need to tell someone and it might help the case against her dad… "I'm not sure if you can use this," I say, "but Megan's just told me he was gonna pimp her out—"

"What the fuck?" he interrupts.

"He had this idea that she could sleep with guys – presumably wealthy guys – and pretend to get knocked up by them… and he could play the aggrieved father, like he did with me today, and demand money from them…"

"Did he actually do this? Or just threaten it?" Todd asks me.

"He threatened Megan with it. Like he threatened to terminate her pregnancy himself, if she didn't go to the clinic."

I hear him let out a long sigh. "It's all threats, Luke. I don't know if I can use it, but I'll bear it in mind when I'm questioning him… And I won't go easy on him… not even remotely. I can promise you that." He pauses for a moment. "Did you pay him anything?"

"Yeah."

"Cash or check?"

"A check… made out to cash."

"There was some cash in the apartment – a couple of thousand dollars. How much did you give him?"

"Twenty-five."

"Twenty-five *thousand?*" He's shocked.

"Yeah."

"Fuck." He goes quiet for a moment. "Well, it's gone – or most of it is but, judging from the amount of drugs I found at his place, I think I know where most of it went."

"Is he a user, or a dealer?" I ask. I couldn't care less about the money.

"Both, I think."

"Nice… Did Matt get back okay?" I'm sick of talking about Megan's dad.

"Sure. I got a squad car to take him back to his office."

"Thanks."

"Is… is Megan okay?" he asks.

"Yeah… well, she will be." I squeeze Megan's hand. "Thanks for everything, Todd." I tell him. "I owe you."

"You can buy me a beer."

"Sure… just not this weekend. I'm gonna be busy… real busy…"

He's still laughing as we disconnect the call.

"Was that your friend?" Megan asks.

"That was Todd," I explain. "The cop." She looks at me expectantly. "It sounds like he's got a fair amount on your dad. I think he'll be behind bars for a while." She slumps into the seat and I can feel the relief pouring off her.

"Thank you," she whispers.

"What for?"

"For rescuing me from him."

"I didn't, not really. The fact that your dad is out of your life is down to Todd, not me."

"But you brought Todd with you…"

"No, that was Matt's idea. If it had been left to me, I'd have gone barging into his apartment by myself… and I'd probably never have found you… because I'd have beaten your dad senseless first."

"Or he'd have killed you."

"I doubt that, Megan."

"You don't know my father."

"And you don't know me… well, you do, but not in that way," I glance across at her. "Don't let the suit fool you, baby. The kind of people I grew up with… let's just say I learned early on in life to take care of myself… and the people I love."

"He has guns, Luke, lots of them. However good you are with your fists, it doesn't matter if the other person is pointing a gun at you. That was why I had to split us up. It's why I was trying to protect you."

I run my finger down her cheek. "Hey, it's not your job to protect me…"

"You don't understand. My dad is never unarmed. At the very least, he always wears an ankle holster…"

"He'd have had to get to it first." I lean in real close. "Look, the point is, you're safe. You're with me now, and that means nothing can hurt you… but don't thank me for rescuing you, because you owe that to Todd, and Matt."

"And there you go, giving the credit to everyone else again."

"Just telling it like it is." I pull her close and hold her. "I need to just make one quick call. Is that okay?" She nods her head. "It won't take a minute. There's someone I need to speak to."

"It's fine," she says. She twists in the seat, curling up a little.

I go through my contacts, and wait for the call to connect. He answers after one ring. "Luke. Where are you?"

"Hi Matt, I'm outside the clinic."

"And Megan?" I can hear the anxiety in his voice.

"She's with me."

His sigh is audible. "Wait a second. I'll put you on speaker. Grace is here." I wait.

"Luke?" It's Grace.

"Yeah."

"Are you okay?"

"I'm fine."

"Is Megan…?" She doesn't finish her question, but I know what she's trying to ask.

"She's fine too… Hold on." I put my thumb over the mouthpiece and turn to Megan. "Can I tell them?" I ask her. "About the baby?"

"Who is it?" Her voice is sleepy.

"Matt and Grace."

She nods her head. I squeeze her hand again and put the phone back to my ear. "Megan's still pregnant," I say. "She couldn't go through with the abortion, even though her dad threatened her."

"Oh… Thank God," Grace says.

"Her dad is one serious head-case," Matt adds. "You should have seen the hardware the guy had."

"Todd's just told me," I reply. "Matt," I say, taking a breath. "I owe you an apology."

"No, you don't," Matt says.

"Yeah… I do. I behaved like an asshole today."

"No… you were in a really bad place, and I wasn't being a very good friend. What happened was my fault, Luke. Not yours." I hear him chuckle.

"What?" I say.

"I assume you still want your job… the old one, that is?"

I'd forgotten about that. "Um… yeah. I think I can handle it now."

"Looking at Megan in lingerie won't be such a hardship anymore, then?"

"I'll cope."

"Still want me to take your meeting with Frank on Monday? I don't mind…"

"No, it's fine. I'll see him."

"Try and get some sleep over the weekend, won't you? I know you've got a lot of catching up to do, but I don't want you giving Frank a huge discount just because you're too tired to think straight."

"I'll be fine. I'm sure I'll fit in *some* sleep… at least a couple of hours, anyway." He laughs.

"Luke," Grace says, ignoring our juvenile banter, "you need to stop talking to us, and get that poor girl home. We can catch up on everything else next week."

"Yes, Ma'am," I say, then add, "Thanks, guys," just before I disconnect the call.

I turn to Megan. She can barely stay awake now. "Shall we go?" I say.

Her face is troubled. "Where to?"

It hadn't occurred to me that she wouldn't want to come to my place, but I suppose it might be too soon for that. Maybe she needs some space, some time to herself.

"Where do you want to go?" I ask her.

"Would you mind... I mean... Can we go to your house?"

"Mind?" I say, putting the car into reverse and pulling out of the parking space. "I was hoping you'd say that."

She nestles back, pulling my jacket around her and, before I'm even on the freeway, she's fast asleep.

Megan

When he told me on the beach in Antibes that he lived in a prison, he wasn't kidding. The gate and surrounding walls must be eleven or twelve feet high. He has a code to get in through the gate and another for the front door, as well as a key.

It was only when we got here that I remembered he lives with his brother, but he's away, evidently, so we've got the place to ourselves... and what a place. It's all on one floor, very modern and very masculine.

Once we get in, he takes his jacket from my shoulders, putting it on the countertop in the kitchen, then removes his tie and puts it on top, and undoes the top two buttons of his shirt, before taking my hand and showing me around. Off the entrance hall, there's a gym, which is impressive in itself.

"Will likes to keep fit," he explains.

"And you don't?"

"I like it more now than when I was younger. I still prefer running though," he says. "I like being outdoors."

He leads me back into the kitchen, which has glossy black units and a granite countertop. There's a huge refrigerator, and a double oven with a five-burner hob, next to which are lots of bottles of oils and vinegars, a salt and pepper mill, and a few tubs of dried herbs.

"Someone likes to cook," I say.

"We both do."

I remember him telling me that when Will first spoke to him after their mother's death, it was about what Luke was cooking for their dinner.

"You used to cook for your brother, didn't you?" I say.

"Yeah, and then I taught him… He needed to take care of himself when I left for college."

At the far end of the kitchen is a closed door. He points to it. "Through there is Will's office," he says. "It's locked now, because he's away. Just a word to the wise; if he's here and the door's closed, knock before you go in. If it's open, then it's fine to wander in and out." I look up at him. "He's very secretive about his work. He has to be, I guess…" He shrugs and puts his arm around me and turns me, leading me past a modern, angular dining table and chairs, then down three steps into the living area. Here, there are two big gray, overstuffed sofas, a coffee table, a TV and some bookshelves. Bi-folding doors lead out to a deck beyond, but there's no garden that I can see.

"Do you want a coffee?" he asks.

I shake my head. "No, thanks. It makes me feel sick at the moment,"

"Oh. Sorry."

"Don't apologize. It's not your fault."

He moves closer. "Well, it kind of is."

I can't help but smirk. "I suppose."

"Water, then? Or juice? Or tea?"

"Water, please."

He goes away and returns a minute or two later with a glass of sparkling water, then he takes my hand, leading me to one of the sofas and he sits in the corner, putting his legs up, with me between them, leaning back on his chest. We just sit like that for a long time. I know there are probably things we need to say to each other, but at the moment, I don't want to think… I just want to enjoy feeling safe.

"You must be hungry," he says eventually.

It's not something I've really thought about for a while, but now he's mentioned it… "Yes, I am."

"I'll make us something," he says and eases himself out from behind me. He goes into the kitchen, rolling up his shirt sleeves as he walks. I can see him from where I'm sitting and he moves around easily, getting things from the refrigerator, chopping, slicing and then stir-frying. Before long, he comes back, with two bowls, resting on thick cotton serviettes. "It's nothing much," he says, "just some chicken stir-fry."

"Nothing much?" It smells delicious. It tastes better. "You really can cook."

"You've already tasted my cooking," he says.

"I probably wasn't concentrating on the food at the time."

He smirks. "What were you concentrating on then?"

"Er… you."

"Well, if I remember rightly, when I first cooked for you, you thought I was gay, so that's not necessarily a good thing."

"Please don't remind me of that."

"Why? I didn't mind. And it brought us together… eventually."

I fork some more chicken and vegetables into my mouth.

"Can I ask you something?" he says eventually.

I chew and nod at the same time.

"Why didn't you come to me?" he asks. "When you found out you were pregnant, I mean. We had an agreement. Why didn't you get in touch?"

I put my bowl down on my lap. "I would have done. I promise, Luke. I only took the test a couple of days before I went to visit my dad. I intended to call you when I got back from there. I just needed a little bit of time to get used to the idea myself. If I'd known what was going to happen…"

He reaches across and runs his finger down my cheek. "It's okay," he says.

"I wasn't going back on our agreement, I promise."

"I know, baby."

When we've finished eating, he takes the bowls out to the kitchen, then returns with a glass of red wine for himself and another mineral water for me.

"Are you okay with me drinking?" he asks. "It's just wine."

"It's fine," I say. He takes a sip, then pulls me closer. I rest my head on his shoulder.

"Alec's drinking bothered you, didn't it?"

"Yes. It reminded me of my dad."

"I can see that now." He pauses. "What about your mom?"

I feel a cold shiver down my spine. "She left… Well, kind of left."

He stiffens. "What do you mean 'kind of left'?"

"I was five years old when she went. I only vaguely remember her. My dad's always told me that she… she screwed around and he ran her out of town. For all I know, he could have killed her. I certainly never heard from her again." I don't tell him how much it still hurts that the person who was meant to protect me and love me – no matter what – left me with a man she knew to be violent and abusive… and didn't even look back.

He puts his wine down on the table next to my glass of water, then turns us so we're lying down, me on top of him. "Surely he couldn't really do that. I mean that sounds like something he'd say just to keep you scared… not something real."

"I don't know." I lay my head down on his chest, listening to his heart beating and feeling the rise and fall as he breathes.

"Do you want to?"

"Do I want to what?"

"Do you want to know what happened to her?"

I look up at him. "How?"

"I can get Todd to try and find out… if you want."

Do I? No. I don't think I do. She left me. She abandoned me to him… I don't think I could ever forgive her for that. "No," I say to him.

"I don't think it'd help.... I'd much rather leave it in the past and forget about it."

"I get that," he says "We can leave it, if you want."

"Thanks."

"You need to remember, though... whatever your dad says, he's just a bully. Nothing more, nothing less."

"He's scary, Luke."

"Bullies can be, but you have to stand up to them."

"That's not always so easy."

"I did it." I look up at him. "After mom died, my dad used to drink too." I had no idea. I bring my arms up around him and hug him tight.

"I'm sorry," I say. "I didn't know."

"Why would you? It's not something I talk about. He wasn't on the same level as your dad, but he'd get drunk and he was good with his fists..."

"Is that where you learned to fight?"

"I learned to fight all over the place."

"What did you do? About your dad, I mean?"

"I hit him," he says simply. "Hard. He didn't get up for a long time. I was fifteen; I was bigger than him."

"And he never tried to hit you again?"

"No... He finally did the world a favor and drank himself to death about two years after Will left home and came to live with me."

"And Will?" I ask... "How did he cope?" Does he have no idea? Being twelve and scared – or five and scared – is very different to being fifteen and strong.

"He didn't do so well. When you meet him, you'll find it hard to believe. Now, he's like six feet plus of solid muscle, but back then, he wasn't. My dad used to go for Will quite a lot. I'd defend him, when I was there, stick up for him... you know."

"I wish..." I wish I hadn't started that sentence.

"You wish what?" he asks.

I guess I have to tell him... "I wish I'd had someone to stick up for me," I whisper.

"Did your dad hit you?" He pulls me up his body, so we're face to face.

"Sometimes… not that often."

"Do you want to talk about it?"

I've never told anyone about my childhood, and I'm not sure I want to start now. "I don't know," I say, honestly.

"You don't have to. Not if you don't want to."

"Can we leave it for now?"

"Sure…" He kisses me, then pulls back. "I'm here, whenever you wanna talk. And I do understand," he adds. "I get that it's not so easy for everyone."

I'm so tired, I can't stop myself from yawning.

"I think you need to go to bed," he says. "You've had one helluva day."

I can't deny that. "You have too," I say to him. "It's not been an easy day for you either."

"True. But I'm not pregnant."

I roll slightly onto my side and put my hand over my belly. "Yes, you are," I say. "This is all yours in here." He smiles down at me.

"Thank you for saying that," he replies, kissing me gently. "It means a lot." I try to stifle another yawn. "But I'm not the one doing the work." He gets up and offers his hand, pulling me to my feet. He keeps hold of me and leads me through the house, turning off lights as we go. We walk down a corridor and stop at the first door. He turns to face me. The only light is from the moon, shining through the glass panels on either side of the front door. It's just enough to see him. He puts his hands on my hips.

"Where do you want to spend the night?" he asks. "This is my room." He tips his head back toward the door behind him. "Or there's a guest room down the hall. It's up to you. If you want to take things slow, that's fine with me. Don't misunderstand," he adds quickly, "I love you… and I want you. I *really* want you. I've missed you so much, baby." He rests his forehead against mine. "But I'm not taking anything for granted. If you need time, I'll wait."

"I don't need time," I tell him, without hesitating for a second. "I just need you."

He smiles and reaches backwards to open the door to his room.

Then he turns and flicks a switch and the lights beside the bed come on, giving off a dim, subtle glow. It's enough to make out the room, which has a pale gray carpet and white walls, three floor-to-ceiling windows, draped with white sheer drapes on the far wall, and an enormous bed, with white covers and mid-gray throws, at the foot of which is a darker gray couch. It's elegant and stylish, and I can't help but gasp.

"Oh… It's nothing like my dreams…" I say, and then clasp my hand over my mouth. That was not meant to come out.

He pulls me into the room and closes the door. "What dreams?" he asks.

"It's nothing."

He stands right in front of me. "What dreams?" he asks again, his voice more serious. He's not going to let up.

"I've been having dreams…" I say.

"Good dreams?" his mouth twists up into a smile.

"No."

The smile fades very quickly. He keeps hold of me and doesn't move.

"You wanna tell me about them?" he asks.

"I'm not sure…"

He waits for a second. "I'll tell you mine, if you tell me yours… but you have to go first, because you brought it up."

"You've been having bad dreams too?"

He nods his head.

"About me?"

"Yes… you first."

"Can we sit down?"

"Sure." He leads me to the bed and we sit on the edge.

I move back and pull my legs up, clasping my knees to my chest. He turns to face me. We're not touching, but maybe it's better that way. I start wondering how best to put this. "Do you remember the flight attendant?" I ask.

"Which one?" he asks. "We took quite a few flights together."

"The first one… on the flight from here to Paris."

"Um… No."

"Really? You don't remember the redhead?" He's looking at me blankly.

"I remember you sticking your nails in my arm, and the way you stared at me, and I remember how sexy you looked and maybe feeling just a little bit in love with you, even then."

How can I not love him when he says things like that? "And you don't remember the redhead, who offered you a drink, completely ignored me and made it clear that you could have anything else you wanted?"

"Nope. A lot happened after that flight… I might have registered her at the time, but if I did, she's faded from my memory."

"You'll have to take my word for it then."

"Guess so." He runs his fingers up my arm, from elbow to shoulder and I shiver. He must be aware of my reaction, because his lips part, just a fraction. "Tell me what happens in your dreams," he says softly.

"I'm standing at the doorway to a bedroom… It's always the same bedroom and I've assumed it was yours, but now I've seen this…" I glance around the room. "Well, I know it isn't. This is so different…"

"And?" he urges.

"And she – the redhead – is on the bed. She's… she's not wearing anything, except a smile. Then you come out of the bathroom, and… well… you know." I can't say the words.

"I have sex with her?" he says.

I nod my head. "And I'm standing there, screaming at you to stop."

"And do I hear you, or do I just carry on?"

"Both. You hear me, and turn around and tell me I had my chance and I got what I wanted… and then you carry on. And then I always wake up…"

"But I don't even remember this redhead."

"Oh, it's not always her in the dream."

"Who else is it then?"

"Sometimes it's one of the blonde receptionists from the hotel in Paris, or a woman who wouldn't stop looking at you when we went out for dinner in Keswick… there are too many women to list, really."

He looks down at his lap. "They're just dreams, Megan. None of it's real…" His voice fades to a whisper.

"I know… but whenever I have them I always wake up convinced you've found someone else." He pulls me into his arms and we lie down on the bed, facing each other.

"I haven't," he says gently. "I don't want anyone else, and you've got nothing to fear," he adds. "They're just dreams."

"They feel so real."

"But they're not, are they? The room's different; I'm not with someone else… you're here, no-one else is. No-one else has ever been here."

"Never?"

"No." I lean up and look at him, very confused. "I've never wanted to bring a woman to the house. I told you, I've never had a relationship. Not once. I've never felt the need."

"Need?" The word surprises me, coming from him. He doesn't seem to need anyone very much.

"Yes. Need. I need you, Megan. That's new to me." I can't help but glow.

We lie for a minute or two while I think about that. It's a good feeling to be needed.

"Okay," I say eventually, "I told you mine…"

"Hmm," he says. "I guess it's my turn now." He flips me over on my back and props himself up on one elbow, looking down at me. "Some of mine have been considerably nicer than yours." He grins.

"Considerably nicer…" I stare into his eyes, not saying a word. "I dreamt of making love to you in places we visited – not necessarily in places we actually made love though. My imagination worked a little overtime on that." I don't say a word. "Do you want details?" His mouth forms into a smile. I bite my lip and he laughs. "Remember the château?" he asks.

"Of course." How could I forget?

"Remember the parapet around the garden?"

"Yes…"

"Well, in one of my dreams, I'm leaning back against it, holding you up in my arms. We're both naked and I'm buried deep inside you." I can feel the heat building inside me at his words. "You've got your legs around my waist and your hands on my shoulders, your head rolled back and you're screaming my name…" He closes his eyes. "It's heaven."

"Why didn't we do that?" I ask before I can stop myself. His eyes pop open.

"We did something real similar in the shower in Provence and in our room in Carcasonne."

"I know, but it sounds like it would have been… fun." I hesitate for a moment. "Doing that outside, I mean."

"We made love outside… in the pool…"

"I know, but I was still wearing my bikini top."

He laughs. "So, you like the idea of being completely naked, outdoors?" I nod my head. "I offered you the chance at Buttermere… you chose the hotel."

"Only because someone might have seen us…"

"Okay… so, naked, outdoors, but private. Leave it with me… I'll work on it." He grins.

"It seems like you've had much better dreams than me," I say to him.

"No, not always. Sometimes they were awful." I wait. He takes a breath. "In some of them you left me," he says simply. "They were really short, quick dreams, always about somewhere that we'd been happy. The setting would vary, but the end result was the same – you walking away."

"I'm sorry," I say.

"Shh. They're just dreams."

"Except… except that was kind of real though, wasn't it?"

"No it wasn't. I was the one who walked away. Remember?"

"Only because I made you."

He doesn't reply, because we both know it's true. "That's the past," he says eventually.

He's still quiet. "Is there something else?" I say. "Something you're not telling me?"

"There was one other dream," he replies. "I only had it once. The others repeated, but not this one… Thank God."

"Tell me," I urge him.

"I'm not sure I should."

Chapter Eighteen

Luke

From the look on her face, I know I'll have to tell her. She thinks it's a dream about another woman. It's so much worse than that.

I stare down at her. "It's not about sex," I say to her. "There are no other women in any of my dreams." She turns her head away from me, but I reach across and pull it back, so she's facing me again.

"Am I that transparent?" she asks. *Well… you are to me.*

"No…" I say. "But you need to remember that even if I can only have you in my dreams, you're still the only woman I'll ever want." She brings her hand up and caresses my cheek. I close my eyes, leaning into her touch. *Get it over with, Luke.* I open my eyes again. "I dreamt you were in the bath," I say, "but it wasn't like you were in the hotel in the Lake District, all bubbles and suppressed passion…" I shiver, remembering the intimacy of what I did to her and how that made me feel. "In the dream, I found you, lying in a bath of cold, red water, your head to one side, your eyes wide open and blank, sightless… and a razor blade lying on the floor where you'd dropped it." She chokes back a gasp. "I recreated the scene, in my dream, but with you in it, not her… My screams woke Will that night." Her mouth drops open a little. I guess she's struggling to imagine me losing it like that… I'm glad she didn't see me in my office after she left this morning.

"You didn't tell him about the dream though…"

"No. I couldn't. I could never remind him about that. I just said you were dead in the dream, but I didn't give him the detail."

She looks surprised. "Have you told him about me – about us – then?"

"Of course. He's known about you all along."

"Do you always confide in him?"

"No, I never have before. But you're different. I was confused by that."

"Good confused or bad confused?"

"Oh, good confused," I say. "I didn't know what to do."

"Really?"

"Why does that surprise you?"

"Because you're so self-assured."

"Except this is new territory for me. I needed to say a few things out loud to someone. Will was there... You don't mind, do you?" It suddenly dawns on me that she might object to him knowing.

"No. I think it's good you have each other." She pauses. "Your dream..." she says. "I'd never do that, you know that, don't you?"

"Yeah, I know." I can't explain to her that the dream has nothing to do with the act itself, but with my stark, cold fear of her abandoning me, like my mom did. "Now, enough about dreams... Let's put all that behind us, and look to the future."

"I like the sound of that," she says, yawning again.

"You're tired." I push myself up to a sitting position, then get up off the bed and hold out a hand to her. She places hers in mine and I pull her to her feet. I undo the buttons on her blouse and let it fall from her shoulders onto the floor. Then I reach behind her, unclasping her bra, pulling her arms through the straps and releasing her breasts. They look larger... her nipples a little darker and I really want to kiss them, but I don't. I kneel, pop open the fastener on her jeans, lower the zipper and pull them down, together with her panties. Taking her hand, I hold her steady while she steps out of them, then I stand and bring her back to the bed. I pull back the covers and sit her down on the edge, then lower her head to the pillow and raise her feet, tucking them under the comforter, which I pull back up over her again. I sit next to her, stroking her hair.

"Sleep," I say to her. She looks a little confused. "Everything else can wait." She smiles and closes her eyes. I lean over and kiss her forehead, then get up, pick up her clothes and put them on the couch. I get undressed and climb in next to her. For a moment, I think about leaving her to sleep where she is, but I can't. She's back. She's here, and I need her in my arms. I reach across and pull her into me, her back to my front. I'm hard as steel and she moans, pressing her ass into me, even as she sleeps. I can't wait for the morning…

"Please, Luke," she whimpers, shuddering slightly.

"Hush, baby…" My fingers circle gently over and around her clitoris. She's on the brink, but I'm keeping her there, slowing the pace whenever she gets too close. I've held her here, right on the edge, for nearly half an hour, but neither of us can take much more.

"I… I need you…" she cries, raising her hips again.

I need her too. God, do I need her. I shift, kneeling between her legs, parting them with mine, then lean forward and gently push the head of my cock between her drenched pussy lips and into her welcoming entrance.

"Yes," I hiss between my teeth as she takes my length into her body. I pull out, then push into her again… and again, until her moans become cries, filling the room. I want her deeper though; I want more. I want to claim her… make her mine again. Keeping us connected, I change position. I kneel back a little and grab her legs, pulling them up onto my shoulders, before lowering myself again and holding completely still. She's wide open to me, pinioned, restrained by my body and my need for her. I'm so deep inside her, nothing could fit between us, and she's staring up at me, her eyes shining.

"Ready?" I say.

She nods her head, and I start to move, pulling out, then plunging all the way back in, taking her deep, keeping the rhythm slow and steady.

"Oh… oh, God… That's so good," she mutters. I increase the pace just a little. "Harder…" she says. "Please, Luke… harder…" That's all

I need to hear and I give her what she wants, pounding into her. She utters a throaty groan with every deep thrust, forcing her hips up to take me deeper still.

I can feel the ripples of her orgasm beginning and then she grabs my arms, throws her head back, and screams my name, her body convulsing around me in a massive orgasm… and I let go, filling her with everything I've got; and all the emotion, the longing and the pain of the last three weeks just pours out of me.

"You're still shaved," I whisper.

She's lying on the bed, her legs still parted, her arms above her head. I'm leaning back against the footboard, looking down at her. I'm not completely sure I can believe she's here, so I'm not going to let her out of my sight.

"Hmm." She raises her head, smiling at me. "I like it."

"So do I." I move forward, crawling up her body. I kiss her thighs, one at a time. She moans, but I continue moving upwards, licking and gently biting on each of her nipples, then further still, until my lips meet hers. She opens to me and our tongues dance gently. I grind my hips into hers, letting her feel my arousal.

"Again?" she whispers into my mouth. "Already?"

"Yeah, already. I've waited so long for you… Right now, I think I could keep going forever. Why? Don't you want to?" I pull back, grinning down at her.

"Of course I do." I sense there's something she's not saying.

"What? What's wrong?" A thought occurs… "I wasn't too rough, was I? I'm sorry, it's just, you're so sexy, and…"

"Luke, I'm fine. I liked it… a lot."

"Then what's wrong? Something's wrong…"

"I'm hungry."

I laugh. "You're hungry?"

"I'm pregnant… I get hungry. Especially in the mornings."

I roll onto my side next to her. "Isn't that when you're meant to be sick?"

"I don't get that every day. Most days I'm just nauseous…" She hesitates. "I guess I was just unlucky that my dad caught me being sick."

I don't want to talk about her dad. Even thinking about him makes me want to punch something. "And today?"

"I'm fine… I'm always fine, until I get up."

"Then don't get up." I smile down at her, kiss her nose and sit up on the edge of the bed. "I'll bring you breakfast."

She giggles. "That won't work," she says. "I need the bathroom… and the nausea will start as soon as I stand up."

"And you'll still want to eat?"

"Yes. It helps."

"And how long does this go on for?"

"I'm lucky… I'm usually fine after I eat something, and always within a couple of hours. For some women, it goes on all day."

"No… I meant does this go on throughout your pregnancy?"

"Oh." She smiles. "No. Evidently, unless we're really unlucky, it usually stops around sixteen weeks, so keep your fingers crossed."

I love how she's including me in this. "Well, how long is it till we get to sixteen weeks?" I ask.

"We're at eight weeks now."

So, another eight weeks of nausea and occasional sickness… I wonder what comes after that.

"When's it due… he… she. What do I call it?"

"It, I guess… at least until we know for sure. And it's due at the beginning of March. That's what the doctor said, although we need to wait for the scan to get a better date. And now," she says, "I really do need to pee." She clambers off the bed and runs into my bathroom. When she returns I'm still sitting there.

"Is that another pregnancy thing?" I ask. "The urgent peeing?"

"If the last couple of weeks are anything to go by, then yes. And it's not just urgent… it's urgent and frequent." She gets back into bed.

I nod my head. I've got a lot to learn.

"So…" I say out loud. "What do you want to eat?"

"Well, being as I'm now feeling a little queasy, probably just toast would be best."

"Toast it is. But no coffee… right?"

She smiles. "Right."

"Tea?" I ask.

"Tea's fine."

I lean over, putting my hands on the pillow, either side of her head. "It might take me a while," I say, "but I'll get the hang of it." I kiss her, hard, then go to the kitchen.

We showered together after breakfast. Best. Shower. Ever. No contest.

We haven't bothered to get dressed… well, not really. I'm just wearing a pair of jeans, but no top, because Megan pulled my t-shirt off within about ten minutes of me putting it on. And Megan hasn't got any clothes here anyway; the things she wore yesterday are in the washer. She's wearing one of my shirts – a pale blue one. It comes down to just below her ass; she's not wearing panties, because they're in the washer too, and I can't help touching her… she's irresistible. The clothes we are wearing are a little pointless… We're going to rip them off each other any minute.

Megan

The weekend has been amazing. It's better even than it was in the Lake District, because we're not facing the imminent fear of breaking up. I know Luke loves me now; he tells me all the time, and I love him more than ever.

He's washed and dried my clothes, but I'm not putting them back on yet. I like walking around in his shirts – and he likes it too.

"Come outside with me," he says, holding out his hand to me.

I look up at him. He's still just wearing jeans… he didn't even bother with the pretense of a t-shirt today.

"Why?" I ask.

"Humor me?" He's smiling at me… but his eyes have got that dark intensity which makes me quiver deep inside. I take his hand and he leads me across to the bi-folding doors, opening them and letting me pass through ahead of him. There's a deck which seems to wrap around the house, with a high wall surrounding it. A big, heavy-looking semi-circular sofa, with soft white cushions and a glass-topped table is arranged at one end. He leads me over and I think we're going to sit down, but instead he takes me around the back of the sofa and leans up against it, pulling me close in front of him. He looks down at me, his lips curling up a little.

"You wanted to try something, if I remember…?"

My breath catches and I place my hand on his hard chest. "Can we?"

"Sure… why not? It's private enough out here."

I glance around, even though I can't see anything beyond the high walls. "Won't someone hear?"

"That kinda depends how much noise we make, but do I look like I care?"

Well, no, he doesn't… not at all.

He undoes the buttons of the shirt I'm wearing, pushes it off my shoulders and lets it fall to the floor. I'm naked… and we're outside. The light breeze plays across my skin, like a long, slow breath. It's so arousing, my nipples harden and I'm wet before Luke's even touches me.

I reach forward and unfasten the buttons of his jeans, one by one. He lifts his behind off the sofa and pushes them down, stepping out of them and freeing his erection. I take it in my hand, my eyes on his; they widen and darken as I start to move up and down, squeezing gently with each stroke. After a few minutes, without a word, he grabs my hand, breathing hard, and holds it in his until he's calmed. Then he puts both my hands on his shoulders and lifts me into his arms. I wrap my legs around his waist and, with one hand beneath me, he uses the other to guide himself into me. I gasp as he enters me and he stills, waiting. Then slowly, using both hands to support me now, he lowers me onto him. He adjusts his position, leaning back a little, his feet planted firmly on the ground, and then he starts to move me, up and down, slowly to start, but then building the speed until I'm finding it hard not to moan. I'm biting my lip, struggling for control.

His head drops forward slightly, closer to mine. "Let go, baby," he says. "Go ahead… shout, scream… Be yourself, Megan." He nips at my neck and I groan, quietly at first, then louder, until I'm crying out for him.

"That's it, baby," he mutters and, as he pulls me onto him one last time, we both climax together… and loudly.

Luke's cooking the dinner and I've just had a shower. I guess it's time to get dressed and return to the real world. I pull on my jeans and blouse, and leave my hair to dry naturally, then go out into the kitchen. Whatever he's cooking, it smells delicious. He's just putting something in the oven.

"What's that?" I ask him

"It will be baked pasta with tomatoes and olives," he says. "It just needs fifteen minutes in the oven." He turns. "You're dressed," he says, clearly disappointed.

"Yes." I suddenly feel more self-conscious than I did when I was just wearing his shirt – or nothing at all. I put my hands in my pockets. "I have to go home." I'm sure he's going to be upset, or even angry. He's done so much for me, and I'm grateful, but I need to go home. I also need to explain it to him. "I have to check my e-mails, and there are some things I need to do… and I've got no clothes here, and… well, you'll be going to work tomorrow, so I can hardly stay here by myself. I mean… what if your brother came home and found me here? Besides, I wouldn't feel comfortable—"

"Megan," he interrupts, coming over and standing in front of me. "It's fine. I didn't expect you to move in with me straight away, not that I'd mind if that's what you wanted to do, but I get that you've got a life; you've got things you need to do. And a lot's happened to you in the last few days; you need some time in your own space to adjust to everything… and this isn't your space. At least it isn't when I'm not in it with you. Is that right?" I nod my head. "I get it, baby…" He leans down and kisses me gently. "We'll have something to eat, I'll grab a shower and then I'll take you home… Okay?"

"Thank you."

"You don't need to thank me," he says. "You could set the table, if you like, while I pour some drinks, but you really don't need to thank me."

It's Erin's night off and when we get back to the apartment, she's curled up on the sofa in her very short pink pajamas, watching a movie, with a large bowl of popcorn balanced on her lap. She takes one look at Luke, who suddenly seems very interested in something outside the window, and bolts to her room, returning just a few moments later, wearing jeans and a t-shirt.

"I'm sorry," I say to her. "I'd have called, but I don't have a phone right now."

"No, but I do," Luke says. "We should have called ahead."

Erin ignores our apologies. "What happened to your phone and… I'm not being rude, but why are you here? You're meant to be at your dad's still, aren't you?" She motions for us to sit down on the sofa, turning off the TV.

"Um…what about you?" Luke asks her just before he sits.

"I'm fine on the floor," she says, and lowers herself, cross-legged in front of us.

"So?" she says, grabbing a handful of popcorn from the bowl on the table. "Help yourselves, by the way."

I get the feeling we're about to be even more entertaining than the movie…

Luke coughs. "I should probably introduce myself," he says.

"Oh, you don't need to," Erin says. "I know you're Luke." He looks at her, raising an eyebrow. "Let's just say you've been a hot topic around here for a while." She grins and a smile forms on his lips. She sits up a little and reaches out a hand to him. "I'm Erin, by the way." He shakes her hand.

"Nice to meet you," he says.

Then Luke takes my hand in his, gives it a squeeze and I start the explanation, telling Erin about the pregnancy test to start with, because nothing else will really make sense unless I do.

"You're pregnant?" she says, looking from me to Luke, then back again.

He's staring at me. "She didn't know?" he asks.

"Of course not," I tell him. "I wanted you to know first."

"Quite rightly," Erin adds. Luke leans over and kisses me, like Erin isn't even there.

"Thank you," he whispers.

"Except of course, my dad found out before you."

"He did?" Erin says.

"Oh yeah," Luke replies. "He sure did." And he explains the scene at his office.

"What Luke hasn't told you," I add at the end, "is that my dad went there with a gun."

Her mouth is wide open now. "So, let me get this right," she says. "Your dad found out you're pregnant, and bullied you into telling him Luke's the dad, then he came up with this genius plan to extort money from Luke and, just to make sure it worked, he took a gun along with him?"

"That about sums it up."

"And you paid him?" She turns to Luke.

He nods his head. "It wasn't my finest hour," he says.

"He paid my dad twenty-five thousand dollars," I tell her.

She drops the popcorn she's holding all over the floor. "How much?"

"The amount is irrelevant."

"I'm assuming you've canceled the check?" she says.

"He can't. It was made out to cash... and my dad cashed it straight away. He had people he needed to pay off."

"I guess it's good to know some things never change." She starts picking up the stray pieces of popcorn, putting them in a neat pile on the table. "So, you've lost all that money?" she says.

"I don't care about the money," Luke replies. "After her dad dragged her out of my office, I had a long talk with my boss… well, kind of business partner, kind of boss. Actually, I quit my job…"

"You did what?" I say, loudly, turning toward him.

"It's fine," he replies, soothingly. "He didn't accept. I'm still gainfully employed."

"But why did you quit?"

He twists in his seat and looks at me, taking both my hands in his. "A couple of reasons, but mainly because staring at photographs of you every damn day was killing me."

I reach over and caress his cheek. "I'm sorry."

"We covered this earlier, didn't we? You have to stop apologizing." He leans down and kisses me gently.

"Enough canoodling… You can do that later. First you need to finish the story," Erin says.

"Where were we?" I ask her.

"Luke was still employed, and your dad cashed his check…"

"Right, and then he took me to the abortion clinic—"

"He did what? So you're not pregnant?"

"No, she is," Luke replies. "She couldn't go through with it."

"And Luke found me there," I add. "And took me back to his place. I've been there all weekend."

"But how did you find her?" Erin asks, taking more popcorn… I knew we'd be better than the movie.

"I have a friend who's a cop," he explains. "He helped."

"And where's your dad now?"

"In jail," I say.

"Finally." She sits back a little. "My life's so dull by comparison."

"Give me dull any day."

"Let me get you guys a coffee," she offers, leaping to her feet.

"Not for Megan," Luke replies before I can say anything. "It makes her feel sick."

"Oh, what other pregnancy cravings and fads do I need to know about?" she asks him.

"I am here, you know. You can talk to me…" I answer.

"Yeah, but it's more fun talking about you," Erin says, over her shoulder. "I'll make you a hot chocolate instead."

Because that's what friends are for.

We've drunk our drinks and Erin has gone to bed early, leaving Luke and me alone in the living room.

"Shall we go to bed?" I say to him, checking the time. It's already ten-thirty and I know he's got work tomorrow.

"Um… I can't," he says.

"Why not?"

"Well, I guess I can come to bed with you, but I can't stay…"

"But… but, I thought you'd be sleeping here tonight."

"Then you should've said, baby, if that's what you wanted."

"I assumed…"

He laughs. "We're gonna need to communicate a little better, and be more organized," he says. "I'd love to spend the night with you," he continues, "but I've got a breakfast meeting tomorrow and I didn't bring any work clothes with me, because I didn't think I'd be staying… I won't have time to go home and change in the morning."

"Oh."

"I didn't realize you'd want me to stay."

"Why wouldn't I?" I ask.

"I thought you wanted some space."

"Not that much space."

"I think maybe we should have had this conversation before we left my place," he says. "I assumed you'd wanna slow things down, date for a while, not necessarily sleep together every night, but maybe stay over at the weekends, or something… Sorry, I don't know what couples normally do. I've never done any of this before."

"Neither have I. But does it matter what other couples do? Can't we do what we want to do?"

"Sure we can." He smiles. "What *do* you want to do?"

"I want to spend the night with you," I whisper.

"Every night?"

"Yes… every night. But not always at your place. Like we were saying before, I'd feel awkward being there on my own when you're at work."

"That's fine. We'll work out a rota or something, and make sure I've always got some clothes here and you've got some at my place."

"And tonight?"

He thinks for a moment. "I'll stay," he says. "If I leave at five-thirty, I'll just have time to go home and have a shower and get into the office for seven."

"Are you sure?"

He leans down and kisses me. "Yeah, I'm sure."

I've had a productive morning – well by recent standards anyway. Luke left at just after five-thirty. He tried not to wake me, but I wanted a kiss… which led to more than a kiss, so he was a little late leaving. He wrote down his number for me before he left, so I can contact him if I need to.

I've been grocery shopping and I've bought a new phone. On the bus, on the way home, I text Luke:

— *New phone, new number. Text or call when you have time. Hope the meeting went well. Mxx*

His reply comes in straight away.

— *Glad you got a phone already… Now I can annoy you with text messages. Meeting was dull, but productive. Can I take you to dinner tonight? L xx*

— *You could never annoy me. I'd love dinner tonight. Shall I meet you somewhere? Mxx*

— *You might not be saying that when I've texted you 100 times a day. No. I'll pick you up. Dress casual. L xx*

— *Bring it on ;) Okay. Can't wait. Mxx*

— *Just so I know… where are we sleeping tonight? L xx*

— Mine? Mxx —

— Okay, I'll bring clothes for tomorrow. Pick you up 6.30. Love you. L xx

— Love you more. Mxx

— Not possible. L xx

— Wanna bet? Mxx

— Yeah… and I'd win. L xxxxxxxxx (see, all the kisses prove I'm right)

I laugh out loud, and the man across the aisle on the bus stares at me. And I don't care.

The phone only rings once before he picks up.

"Are you okay?" he asks.

"Yes." I hear his sigh of relief. "I just wanted to let you know I've made an appointment with my doctor for Thursday. I haven't actually seen her since I found out about being pregnant… I wondered if you want to come with me?" I know this could wait until tonight, but I want to check with him while he's at work, and got his calendar in front of him.

"Of course. What time?"

"Eleven. But if you can't make it…"

"I'll make it," he says. I can hear him clicking on keys, presumably on his computer. "Oh…" he says.

"If it's a problem, I can go by myself."

"No… It's fine. I'll be there."

"Luke… You don't have to arrange your life around me." I let out a sigh.

"Yeah, I do. Anyway, I can get Matt to take the meeting."

"No."

"Yes. I'll speak to him now."

"I feel guilty."

"Don't. I love you." He hangs up before I can argue any more.

I put on some laundry and check my e-mails again. I still haven't heard anything about the job at the library. Not that I think I'd get it now anyway. I'll have to tell them I'm pregnant; and who'd want to take on someone in my position? It's a problem – another one.

My phone beeps. It's a message from Luke:

— Matt's happy to take Thursday's meeting. I've got the morning off. See… it's no problem. L xx

— I still feel guilty. M x

— Only one kiss? I'll make you feel better later. Promise. L xxx (there's an extra one for you) —

— xxxxxxxxxx (is that enough?)

— No such thing as enough, but it'll do until tonight. L xx

Chapter Nineteen

Luke

We've settled into a kind of easy routine over the last few weeks. On Monday through to Thursday, I stay over at Megan's, because it's easier for her to be there when I'm at the office. Then on Fridays after work, I pick her up and we come back here for the weekend. Erin's been fine with me staying there; we get along well.

Megan and I went for her doctor's appointment and her first scan is due this coming Monday morning. I'm going with her – obviously. Matt's been great about me taking time off; he's been ducking out of the office himself from time to time. I'm guessing Grace might be seeing a doctor too, as they're often gone together, just for a couple of hours; and there's lots of whispering between them. They'll talk about it when they're ready and they've got something to say.

Megan's interview with the Boston Public Library didn't go too well. Not surprisingly, once they heard she's pregnant, their initial enthusiasm cooled. They said they'd be in touch; and she hasn't heard from them since. Still, it's under a week now until we start the fashion shows, and because Megan's barely got a bump at all, she's still doing them. We're traveling to New York first, then we go to London, then on to Milan and finally Paris. I already checked when we visited the doctor, that Megan can travel, and it's evidently fine. Megan won't be the only model we're taking, because one model can't handle a show by herself, but she'll leading, so she's been coming into work with me on a few days over the last two weeks, to learn the basics from Melissa, who's one of our most experienced catwalk models. It's been good having her here, having lunch together and snatching odd moments alone in my office.

It's been a long week… The lead-up to the shows is always a bit stressful; Megan's tired and I'm starting to get worried about Will. I know he said he couldn't contact me while he was away, but he's been gone for weeks – much longer than normal.

I'm glad it's finally Friday and we can take off to my place for the weekend. Megan's been at the office today for her final lesson with Melissa. She says Megan is a natural, and now I've seen her on the catwalk today in the run-through, I have to agree. She had everyone mesmerized. I couldn't help but feel proud of her.

"Shall I order take-out?" I ask her as I help her from the car. We're later than normal, and it's already getting dark. "I don't know about you, but I just want to shower, change and watch a movie."

"Hmm, I'd like that." She leans into me and I put my arm around her as we walk to the front door.

I let us in and leave Megan's bag in the hallway. Switching on the lights, she goes straight into the living room and curls up at one end of the couch, while I go into the kitchen. The take-out menus are in the drawer by the sink. "What do you feel like?" I ask her.

"I don't mind," she replies, "as long as it's not too spicy."

"Chinese then?"

"Sure."

"Er… hello." I spin at the sound of Will's voice. I didn't hear him come out of his office, but he's leaning against the doorframe, his arms folded across his chest.

"Will! When did you get back?"

"About an hour ago."

"And you didn't call me, or even turn on a damn light?"

"I had some work to finish off," he says, glancing into the living room, where Megan has now stood up and is looking a little embarrassed.

"Come here," I say to her and she walks over. I stand her in front of me and put my arms around her. "This is Megan," I tell Will. "Megan, this is my brother, Will."

He steps forward, holding out his hand to her. She takes it and they shake a little awkwardly. This feels weird. "Nice to meet you," he says, then looks at me, his eyebrows raised. *Yeah, I know it's a first, but try and act cool.*

"We were just going to order a take-out... Wanna join us?" I ask him.

"Sure."

Keeping hold of Megan, because she seems as uncomfortable as my brother with the situation, I turn and open the drawer, pulling out the menu. "Choose whatever you want," I say to her, "then you could go take a shower while we wait for it?" She nods her head and goes through the menu, before handing it back to me and telling me what she'd like.

"I'll be out in a while," she whispers. Then she gives me a quick kiss on the cheek, grabs her bag and disappears into my room.

I turn to Will. "What's wrong?" I ask.

"Nothing."

"Yeah, right... Come and sit down." I nod toward the living room and he closes the door to his office before we start walking. We sit together at opposite ends of the couch, looking out onto the deck. "So?" I say.

"What?"

"Do you have a problem with Megan being here?" I ask.

"No. Of course not. I'm just surprised."

"Why?"

"Oh, come on, Luke. After all these years and all the hundreds of women you've slept with, I'm not meant to act surprised when you finally bring one home... and seem to be acting all domesticated with her?"

"I told you before; she's different."

"She's beautiful. I mean she looked beautiful at the airport, but she was sad then. Now she's..."

"I know. But are you okay with it?"

"Sure."

"She's been staying here at weekends for a few weeks now. I stay at her place during the week. And don't worry, I've told her about your set-up… you know, the closed door rule."

"Good… now you just need to remember it yourself."

"Haha, little brother." I throw the menu at him and get up. "Decide what you want to have, then get us both a beer, will you? I'm going to see if Megan wants some water."

"Water?"

"Yeah… she doesn't drink. It's a long story. We'll tell you all about it over dinner."

"Okay." He buries his head in the menu, and I go through to my room. The door's not closed properly and I push it open, and it feels like my heart has stopped pumping. Megan is sitting in the middle of the bed, her knees pulled up to her chin. She's rocking back and forth and there are tears streaming down her face. Something real bad has happened. I go to her, but she moves off the bed, standing on the other side to me. *What the hell?*

"What's wrong?" I ask her.

"Everything," she says.

"I don't understand."

She stares at me through her tears. "What number am I then, Luke? A hundred and something? Five hundred and something? How many hundreds is it exactly?"

For a second, I wonder what she's talking about, and then I understand; and the whole fucking world stops spinning. She overheard Will's remark.

"Well?" she says.

"It's not what you think." *Really? Isn't it?*

"Oh, really?" Her words mirror my own thoughts. "How can I trust you?" she says, raising her voice. She's mad with me. "How can I believe anything you say? You lied to me."

"No, I didn't."

"Yes. You. Did."

I move around the bed, standing a couple of feet from her. "No, Megan. I didn't tell you about my past. That's not a lie... It's an omission."

"A deliberate omission... which is the same thing as a lie." She stares at me. "Why didn't you tell me?"

"Because it's the past; none of it matters."

"You still lied," she murmurs.

"No. I. Didn't."

"You kept secrets, then."

"And you didn't?" She stares at me. "C'mon, Megan. Right from the beginning, you held out on me. Right back at Antibes, when I was telling you about my mom, and Will, you did your best to tell me damn all about yourself. You got me to agree to your casual, no-strings relationship, but forgot to point out you were a virgin... and even when I was begging you to stay with me in the Lake District and at the airport, you still wouldn't tell me why we couldn't be together." I take a breath. "We both kept secrets, Megan."

"Not such a big one as this," she hurls at me.

I take another step, so we're just a few inches apart.

"You really think this is as big as you not telling me your dad was threatening to kill me? Because a piece of information like that might have been useful to know."

"I was protecting you from him," she yells.

"You didn't have to," I yell back. "And if you'd just been straight with me from the start, you wouldn't have needed to. I could have dealt with your dad, and we could have stayed together... For Christ's sake, Megan... You put us both through hell, and I haven't once said anything to you about not telling me the truth... not once. Even now, you still haven't told me about your life with him... and I never pressure you. Never."

"That's irrelevant."

"Oh, really?"

She sobs again, choking on her tears. I reach out to her, but she steps away from me. "Why can't you see?" she mutters.

"See what?"

"That this just proves I can never be enough for you, Luke? I can't ever hope to compete..." *What is she talking about?*

"You are enough." I whisper. "You're all I want. And why do you need to compete? You've got nothing to compete with; not any more. It's all in the past now."

She raises her head again. "And what about when I'm out to here?" She puts her hand out in front of her. "What about when I'm nine months pregnant and enormous? What chance will I have against all the stick-thin women who throw themselves at you all the time? It's bad enough now; what's it going to be like then?"

"I'm not interested in other women," I say, trying to keep my voice as soft and calm as possible, even though I'm starting to panic on the inside. "I just want you... and I don't care how big and pregnant you get. I'll still want you."

"You don't know that... you don't know how you'll feel. Besides, if sleeping around is how you lived your life, why would you stop now?"

"Because I'm in love with you, that's why."

She wipes at her cheeks with the palms of her hands. "Answer me one question..." she murmurs. I nod my head. "How many women is it, Luke?"

Shit... "I don't know," I say quietly, not taking my eyes from hers.

"So it's a lot then?"

"Yes..."

"Thousands?"

"No. Not thousands... Low hundreds." *Well, low-ish hundreds.* She swallows hard.

"And you're... you're seriously expecting me to believe that you've never brought any of them here?"

"Yes. You can ask Will if you don't believe me – which you clearly don't. Why the hell do you think he was so surprised to see you just now? Because it's the first time he's ever seen me here with any woman... that's why." She goes to speak, but I hold my hands up to stop her. "Look, what does any of it matter? It's ancient history. It's not important how many women I've slept with, because from the moment I met you, I only wanted you." She lowers her head, staring at the floor and I feel like I'm losing her again. I can't lose her... I can't... not for a second time. "You do believe me, don't you?" She doesn't reply. "Megan?" She still doesn't reply. She's slipping away from me, and instinctively, without even thinking, I drop to one knee in front of her.

"What are you doing?" she says, finally looking at me.

"I'm proposing."

"Why?"

"Because you're the only woman I want. Marry me, Megan."

She stares at me for a moment and then her lips start to curl upward, her mouth opens and she laughs, quietly to start with, then louder. "This is ridiculous," she says eventually.

"Clearly." I get to my feet. Now I can't look at her. She knows who and what I am and, in her eyes, I'm laughable, I'm contemptuous...

She's stopped laughing, which is a relief, but she's still mad. "How on earth could you think of proposing now?" she says. "What are you trying to prove – and more importantly, who are you trying to prove it to?" I don't have any answers for her. "I mean... the timing, Luke——"

"I get the message, Megan. You're not interested in my proposal – you've made that much very clear." She stills, and looks down at the floor.

We stand in silence for a while. "I think I'd like to go home," she says, eventually.

"Are you saying we're... over?" I ask, my voice cracking.

She hesitates for a frighteningly long time before replying, "I don't know what I'm saying, except that I need some time to be by myself, so I can think."

"What do you need to think about?"

"Us. I need some time to think about us. Can you call me a cab, please?"

"No. I'll take you home."

"You don't have to."

"Don't do this, Megan."

"Do what? Ask you for some time to myself because I've found out you're not the man I thought you were?"

"No!" I yell at her. "Don't make this into something it isn't. Don't push me away. Don't go all distant and defensive on me… I'm exactly the man you thought I was. I haven't changed toward you, have I? I'm no different to when we met, am I?" I don't let her answer. "If you want to go home, I'll take you." I'm breathing heavily.

"Thank you," she whispers.

"You're welcome." She grabs her bag from beside the bed. "Do you need anything else?" I ask her, holding the door open. She shakes her head as she passes through into the hallway, but she won't look at me. "I'll just get my keys." She waits by the front door, while I go into the kitchen and fetch my car keys. Will is still sitting on the couch. He looks up at me, but I shake my head at him. I'm not talking now.

The drive back to her place is silent and tense. In a way, I'm grateful. It gives me a chance to think. I'm not really sure what's going on. She wants time to think about us, which suggests she's not giving up. But at the same time, her rejection stings… actually it cuts… like a knife. A really deep knife.

After I've parked outside her apartment block, I help her from the car.

"You don't have to see me to the door," she says.

"Like hell I don't."

She walks away, but I follow a few paces behind.

When we get to her door, she takes out her key and, as she's about to put it in the lock, I grab her hand and hold it in mine. "You're gonna make me walk away again, aren't you?" I say. She doesn't reply. "Okay… I'll do it. I'll do it because it's what you want, not because I think you're right. I'm not giving up on us, though, and I'm not giving you any promises to stay away… and I refuse to accept even the chance that we're through." I bring her hand up and gently kiss her fingers. "I know you're hurting and I know you think that's all my fault… and I'm sorry. I want to show you how sorry I am and spend the rest of my life making it up to you… but you have to let me… you have to want that too." She lets out a sigh, staring into my eyes and I feel just a spark of hope at what I see there. "I know you don't trust me" I continue, "and I know you feel like everything's changed. But I promise you can trust me, and absolutely nothing has changed. I want us to have a future together, Megan. You've asked for time and space to think. I'll let you have that. I'll let you have just enough time and space to work out that a future with me is what you want too." I let go of her hand. "I'll call you tomorrow," I tell her, "not because I'm hassling you, but because I love you. You're the most important things in my world – both of you – and I have to know you're okay."

I take a few steps away from her, but then turn and look back. She's still staring at the spot where I'd been standing. "I'm not losing you over this, Megan," I say, and then I walk away from her… for the second time.

I sit in my car for ages before starting the engine. I'm not stupid; I know she's not going to come out and tell me it's all fine and she's changed her mind. I just want to look at the window of her apartment, where the light's now on, the blinds drawn. Knowing she's up there makes me feel connected to her. Even so, it feels like the past I've been striving to forget, and the future I've been longing to create are colliding, and I'm in the middle, being crushed – again.

Eventually, I start the engine and slowly drive home.

Will comes out of his office as soon as I get in.

"What happened?" he asks as I walk through and sit in the living room, on the couch, in the darkness.

"She found out. She overheard… when you said about the hundreds of women I've slept with…"

"You hadn't told her then?"

"No. That's not the kind of thing a woman wants to hear. Even I know that much. I can't change it, but I sort of hoped she'd never find out."

"It's my fault, isn't it?" He comes over and sits opposite me, turning on the table lamp.

"No. She'd have found out eventually."

"So, did she break up with you?"

"I don't think so. She just asked to go home. She said she needed time to think things through."

"That's not breaking up then, is it?" He sits forward. "You're not going to give up on her, are you?"

"No. I can't. I mean I couldn't have done anyway, but it's out of the question now…" He looks confused. Of course, he doesn't know. "She's pregnant," I explain.

"What?"

"Yeah."

"When… I mean… how? I mean when did that happen?"

"When we were in France."

"I thought you were always so careful though," he says.

"Usually I am… I mean I was. I keep telling you; she's different."

We sit and talk for hours. I tell him about Megan's dad; the scene at the office; my fight with Matt; finding Megan again… the whole story.

"How did it feel when you found her again?" he asks at the end of it.

"Like everything finally made sense. All of it. I could see everything clearly, for the first time in my life. Megan's the only thing that makes sense to me. She's… she's just it for me – she's all of it." I lean forward. "I have to get her back, Will."

"You'll do it," he says. "I know you will."

"I don't have a choice. I have to. She's my future."

Megan

"He's still there," Erin says. I've been home for nearly an hour and Luke's still parked outside.

"What's he doing?"

"Just sitting in his car, staring up here."

She comes away from the window.

"How could he do this?" I say, more tears falling down my cheeks. Erin pulls a Kleenex from the box on the coffee table and hands it to me.

"What is it you think he's done?" she asks.

"He lied to me… and he slept with hundreds of women, of course," I repeat to her. I've already told her this.

"Since you've known him?"

"No, of course not."

She looks at me pityingly. "Okay," she sighs, "so, before he even knew you; and before you even knew he existed, he slept around a bit…"

"A bit?"

"Megan, it's just numbers. How do you know his brother wasn't exaggerating, like brothers do. He might have been joking."

"Even Luke admitted he's got no idea how many women he's slept with, but it's in the low hundreds."

"So?" I glare at her. *She's got to be kidding…* "What does it matter? I mean, isn't it more important what he's done since he met you? What he does in the future?"

"Well, since he met me, he's lied to me…"

"Has he?"

"Erin… I told you this. He didn't tell me about his past."

"Which is perfectly normal. A lot of people don't talk about their past, especially if it's not particularly happy. I don't go around telling my boyfriends how many guys I've slept with… It's got nothing to do with any of them what I did before I met them."

"And you don't want to know about their past either?"

"No. Why would I? I mean, if they want to tell me, that's fine… but I never ask."

"Why?" I'm interested.

"Because it's the past. They can't change it… and neither can I. It's best left where it is."

"You sound just like him."

She leans over and gives me a hug. "Maybe that's because neither of us is pregnant… so *we're* making sense…" She pauses. "What bothers you most?" she asks. "The number of women, or the fact that he didn't tell you?"

I open my mouth to answer, then close it again, because I'm not sure. "I don't know," I reply. "So many people have let me down in my life… I just never thought he would." Tears start to fall again.

"Did he?" she asks, passing me another Kleenex. "Think about it, Megan. Did he really let you down? Would you have been happier knowing about his past from the beginning? Would that have made everything alright?"

"No…"

"So it's more about the number of women. And there really is nothing he can do about that, is there? It's ancient history…"

I shrug.

She gets up, going toward the kitchen. "I'm gonna make you a hot chocolate," she says.

"I forgot to tell you… he proposed," I call to her.

"Oh my God." She turns back. "What did you say to him?" I'm starting to regret saying anything, because now I'll have to explain how badly I reacted. "Megan?" she urges.

"I laughed," I whisper.

She comes and sits back down again. "Sorry? Did you just say you laughed?" I nod my head.

"Yes. I was really horrible to him. I feel bad about it now. "

"I should damn well think so."

"But I don't even understand why he did it… I mean, what was he trying to prove?"

"Er… maybe how much you mean to him?"

"He didn't have to propose to do that."

"No… Evidently he just had to re-write history." She huffs out a breath. "Look, I'm not saying his timing was great; I'm not even saying it was the right thing to do… but, given that he probably doesn't have a time machine, and can't go back and change his past, maybe he felt proposing was the only way he could prove to you how much he loves you… And you laughed at him…?"

"Yeah, I know." I do feel bad. And I will apologize. He looked so hurt and he didn't deserve that.

"Are you really prepared to lose him over this?" Erin asks, breaking into my thoughts.

"Sorry?" *Lose him?*

"You know you love him, Megs. You know he loves you. What you guys have is special… Don't throw it away over something that's in the past." She puts her arm around me and gives me a hug, then gets up and goes into the kitchen.

I sit for a minute or two and then curiosity gets the better of me. I go over to the window and look outside. He's gone. I wonder if I should have gone out and talked to him earlier; apologized for laughing at his proposal, at least. But what else would I have said? Erin's right; I don't want to lose him. I love him so much, the thought of being without him causes a physical pain in my chest. But how can I live with his past? It's hard enough living with my own.

I haven't slept much. Partly because my mind is going round and round in circles; and partly because I seem to have to get up to pee about every forty-five minutes. And I miss Luke. I've gotten used to falling asleep in his arms, and snuggling into him each time I get back from the bathroom. Even though he doesn't seem to wake up, he always pulls me in close and hugs me, sometimes even murmuring in my ear that he loves me. He makes me feel better, wanted, safe… Yeah, I really miss Luke.

My phone rings at ten-thirty. Erin's in the shower, getting ready for her shift at the restaurant. I'm not dressed yet. I check the caller ID, although I know without looking it'll be him.

"Hello," I say.

"Hello," he replies. There's none of our easy informality. "How are you?" he asks.

"I'm fine."

He sighs. "I hate this," he mutters. "I missed you so much last night… and I hated waking up without you." He's only saying exactly what I'm thinking, but I can't reply. "Can we talk?" he asks.

"We are talking."

"No, I mean can we meet up and talk."

"I don't think that's a very good idea." I can't see him. I'm still trying to work everything out; seeing him will just confuse me.

"Why not?"

I decide to be honest; I accused him of lying, so I have to tell the truth. "Because I need time, Luke. I asked you for time… and if I see you, I'll get confused."

"I confuse you?"

"Yes."

"Is that a good thing?"

"Not right now, no." He doesn't reply. The time has come to bite the bullet. "I did want to apologize to you though."

"What on earth for?" He sounds genuinely surprised.

"For laughing… when you proposed, and for being so rude to you." He doesn't say anything. The silence stretches. "Are you still there?"

"Yeah."

"Did you hear what I said?"

"Yeah." He still sounds hurt.

"I mean it, Luke. I'm sorry."

"Don't worry about it."

"Well, it was wrong of me. I—"

"Megan, please… can you just drop it."

"Oh… okay." Oh God, I think I've really hurt him. "I'm sorry."

"And stop apologizing. It doesn't matter."

I don't want to say that if it hurts him, it does matter… but it does.

"I'll call you tomorrow," he says. "Same time?"

"Sure… but why are you calling me?"

"I explained this last night." Did he? Last night feels like a blur. "I have to know you're okay," he continues, then takes a deep breath. "I want you back, Megan. I want that more than anything. I get that you need time… and while you're working things out, I'm going to stay in touch, because whatever you think of me, until you tell me differently, you're still mine."

Chapter Twenty

Luke

I don't feel as bad as I did last night. She didn't hang up on me, which I half expected. Okay, so she wouldn't agree to meet me, but then I didn't think she would. There was no harm in asking though.

Will's still feeling bad; as though it's all his fault. It isn't. Like I said to him, she'd have found out eventually anyway. The problem isn't him; it's Megan's perception of me. It's changed. I just need to change it back. I need her to see I'm the same guy I always was with her.

Will and I spend the day doing his laundry – not what I'd planned, but he's been away for weeks, and it's keeping me occupied. He can't tell me where he's been, or what he's been working on, but I gather it's not over yet. He's just been sent back here, because whatever it is, requires him to go 'off-grid' for a while. He's worried, I know that… and not just about Megan. And he is worried about her. He wanted to know how she was when I came off the phone; how the baby is; what's happening. He's going to make a fantastic uncle… if he doesn't have a heart attack first.

I slept better last night than I did the night before, which is hardly surprising, considering I didn't really sleep at all the night before. But waiting until ten-thirty to call Megan again is driving me insane, especially as Will's working in his office, with the door shut, so I'm on my own. I decide ten twenty-five is close enough and dial her number.

"Hello." She picks up after two rings.

"Hi," I say. "How's everything today?"

"Okay." No it isn't. I can tell from her tone.

"What's wrong?"

"Nothing."

"Megan. Either you can tell me over the phone, or I'll come round there and stand outside your door until you tell me."

"I just had another bad night," she says.

"Another?"

"I can't seem to sleep very well."

"Can I help?" Dumb question probably, but I don't know what else to say.

"I don't know…" Well, it wasn't a 'no'.

"You usually sleep okay when you're with me, except when you're getting up to pee every five minutes. If it's bad again tonight, call me. Even if it's the middle of the night. I'll come over and hug you till you're asleep – no strings, I promise, but you need to sleep. Deal?"

She's silent.

"Deal?" I repeat.

"Okay."

"Good. It's your scan tomorrow," I say, because I think she needs a change of subject.

"Yes."

"I'll pick you up at ten."

"You're still coming?"

It hadn't occurred to me that I wouldn't be. I take a deep breath. "I'd like to be there, Megan, but if you don't want me to be, then I'll pick you up and wait for you outside. Then I'll take you home again." It's the best I can offer. She's not going by bus, that's for sure.

"I wasn't sure you'd want to come… after…"

"Megan, which bit of 'I want you back'… which bit of 'I'm not giving up on us' do you not understand?"

"Sorry."

"Don't apologize to me."

"Sor—" She breaks off mid-word

"Try and get some sleep during the day," I tell her. "You're tired."

"Okay."

"I'll see you tomorrow… and call me if you need me."

She didn't call, but then I didn't really expect her to. She wants time and space; having me there isn't going to give her that. I'm not sure she really understands that I'd still give her that. I just want to ensure she's getting enough sleep; that she's well; that she's happy… I don't want anything in return, except perhaps the knowledge that she hasn't given up on us.

I pull up at her apartment block and she's waiting outside. I guess she didn't want me to come up. I get out and open the passenger door for her. She looks beautiful, but tired, and I want to hold her.

"Hello," I say once we're both in the car.

"Hello." I pull out of the parking lot and onto the street.

"How did you sleep?" I ask her.

"Not very well."

"And you didn't call me?"

"It didn't seem fair."

"I meant what I said. I'll come over if you need me. I won't expect anything in return and I'll only stay as long as you need me." She shifts in her seat. "Are you okay?" I ask, glancing across at her quickly. She looks uncomfortable. This isn't promising.

"No."

"What's wrong?" She bites her bottom lip. "What is it?"

"I need to pee."

I stifle a laugh. "We've only just left your apartment."

"I know. But I have to have a full bladder for this scan… The thing is, I don't know if I can hold on."

"Oh." I still want to laugh. Her bladder has ruled our lives for the past few weeks. It's kinda nice to have it back again. "Try thinking about something else."

"Like?"

"You're off to New York in a few days... How about that?"

"I hope there are lots of bathrooms there."

I laugh out loud. "You're not very good at this, are you?"

I turn on the radio and find a music station to try and distract her. It seems to help and she looks out the window, while humming to whatever the track is.

When we arrive, I park up and help her from the car, keeping hold of her hand for a moment.

"Can I come in with you?" I ask her quietly.

"If you want to."

Not quite the answer I'd hoped for. "Do you want me there, Megan? If you don't, I'll wait outside."

She looks at me. "I'd like you to be there," she says, "but only if it's what you want."

God, what's happened to us? "Of course it's what I want."

"Can we go now?" she asks, pulling her hand from mine. "I really can't hang on much longer."

Luckily, once we're inside, they don't make her wait. I guess they know that a pregnant woman with a full bladder isn't a good combination. We're shown into a room with an examination table and a monitor. The ultrasound technician introduces herself as Janette and I stand to one side while Megan takes off her jeans and lies down. A paper cover is placed over Megan's panties, and tucked in a little and then Janette squirts gel over her belly.

"This is sticky," she says, "and cold." Megan squirms and I step closer to her. I want to hold her hand, but I'm not sure what she wants from me, so I stand close enough for her to reach out to, if she needs me. "Okay," says Janette, picking up a device from the side of the monitor. "This is called the transducer and I'm going to rub it across your abdomen." She twists the monitor around a little, as she starts to slide the transducer over the slimy gel.

The images appear almost straight away. "Here's baby's head," Janette says, clicking on one button, then another. "And you can make out an arm, here." She points to the screen, then clicks again. I can feel a lump rising in my throat. I glance down at Megan. She's gazing at the images, tears rolling down her cheeks Her hand is by her side, near to mine… and I don't care anymore, I take hold of it and squeeze. She squeezes back, and I return my gaze to the screen.

"It's moving a lot," she whispers. "Why can't I feel it?"

"It's too early yet," Janette says, her voice reassuring. "You won't feel it for several weeks. Don't worry, that's completely normal." She continues to press buttons.

"What are you doing?" I ask her.

"Taking measurements," she replies.

"Why?" Megan asks.

"I'm just checking baby's developing properly."

Megan glances at me, fear in her eyes. "And?" I ask the question for both of us.

"Everything's just fine. There are no problems at all. Would you like to hear the heartbeat?" We both just nod, because I don't think either of us is capable of speech. Well, I'm not. I have no idea what Janette does, but suddenly, from the monitor, we can hear a rapid beating sound. I no longer have a lump in my throat. I lost control of it a while ago.

"That's fast," Megan says.

"It's perfectly fine," Janette replies. She fiddles around with the monitor again and the heartbeat fades again. "I'll print you a couple of pictures," she says. Megan and I are both fixated by the image on the screen and neither of us notices Janette holding out two small envelopes.

Outside, once she's been to the bathroom – twice – I help Megan into the car and she sits, clutching the envelopes.

When I get in my side, she offers one to me.

"Thanks," I say, taking it from her and opening it. Inside is a still image of what we've just seen on the screen. It's not quite the same as the moving, breathing, living baby we've just been looking at, but it'll do for now. I tuck it into my jacket pocket.

"Can I take you for a coffee? Or tea in your case?" I say to her. She doesn't reply. She fiddles with her envelope, nervously. "Megan…" I say. "It's okay. If you'd rather go home, I'll take you home." She nods her head, just once and, although I'm disappointed, I start the engine and pull out of the parking bay.

It doesn't take long to get back to her place – a lot less time than I'd like, anyway. It's been so good spending an hour or two with her… and seeing the baby for the first time.

I park up and am about to get out of the car, when she says my name. I turn back and look at her. "Yes?" She's staring out the front windshield.

"Can I ask you a question?" she asks.

"Of course you can."

"It's just… I'm trying to work things out in my head… you know, after Friday night, and I need to know something."

I'm a little wary, but I just say, "Okay."

She pauses for a moment. "What makes me so different from all the others?"

"That's simple – I fell in love with you."

"I'm not talking about that. We did so much together," she whispers, "but I'm sure you've done it all before… and more… and probably better—"

"No, baby… not better. Never better."

"But more?" she asks. "Did you used to do more?"

"Not in terms of frequency, no." I'm not sure that's even possible.

"I meant… were they more adventurous…?"

I hesitate, just for a minute, then nod my head. "Some of them, I guess."

"And do you miss that?"

"Miss what?"

"Having more… ad—adventurous sex?" She stumbles over her words, her cheeks turning crimson.

I twist in my seat to face her. "Can I be blunt?" She nods. "I had sex with very experienced women, who knew exactly how to get what

253

they wanted. And I took what I wanted too. It was impersonal… and I don't miss any of it. I love what we have. I love your innocence and that we're learning new things together…"

"*You're* learning?" Her eyes open wide in surprise.

"Yes. I learn from you all the time."

"What on earth do you learn from me?"

"How to feel… how to trust… how to love."

She stares at me and a slight smile forms on her lips. I feel it pierce my chest and the warmth that buds there rises into my throat. She lets out a sigh, then looks around the interior of my car. "You never did have sex with me in the car," she says wistfully, still smiling. I know she's thinking about my comment to her when we were in England… and I wish she hadn't remembered it right now. Things were going so well… and I know what's coming, and I know my answer's gonna wipe that beautiful smile from her lips. "Did you… with the others?" I knew it.

I hesitate before answering, but I can't lie to her. "With some of them, yes."

"In here?"

"Yes." She shifts in her seat. I was right… the smile's gone. She turns, looking out the window. "I'll change the car, Megan. I was going to anyway, but I'll do it today, if you want."

"That's not the point." Her voice is cooler, more distant.

"Then what is?"

"There's always going to be something to remind me about your past, isn't there?"

"Only if you're looking for it." She doesn't answer. I don't understand why she needs to revisit old territory. It's not important anymore. "I really don't want to talk about the past," I say. "But I will try and tell you what makes you different, if that's what you want… if you think it'll help."

She turns back to me. "I need to know. Why me and not someone else? I mean, how do you know you won't find another woman who's even more special?"

I look into her eyes. "Because I'm not looking… not any more. Right from the first moment I saw you, I knew you were different – I just didn't know how different. I knew, even then, there could never be anyone else for me..."

"What do you mean?" she asks. "I can't believe I'm that unusual..."

"Oh... you are."

"How?"

"Well, to start with, you're the first virgin I've ever been with; I've always avoided that responsibility... And we did things that were very different; I forgot the condom, for one thing. I've never done that. Ever. And that bath in the Lake District. I meant it when I said that was one of the most erotic things I'd ever done... It was. It was incredible. The truth is, I've never put so much of myself into sex as I do with you. I let you see sides of me that I've never shown another woman... hell, I've never shown them to another human being. Not even Will. I've never talked about, or shared my feelings with anyone before."

She's crying now, but she she gulps out, "It sounds like you were so impersonal... before, I mean."

"I was. I'm not proud of it. I'm not proud of who I was or how I behaved. But I never knowingly hurt any of them. They all knew the score beforehand. There was never any emotion on either side."

"How could you tell? They might not have said they loved you out loud, but that doesn't mean they didn't. You're easy to love, Luke."

"I wasn't; not then. And you can tell, trust me. I knew you loved me before you told me..." I really hope I don't regret telling her this... "I've fucked a lot of women," I say, not taking my eyes from hers, even when she flinches. "I've only ever made love to one... and that's you. You might think there's no difference between the two things. But there is; there's a world of difference. Fucking is just physical. Making love is physical as well – obviously – but it's also emotional... it's intellectual, sensual, even spiritual, I think. I didn't know that until I met you... until I made love to you. It's the whole of my body joining with the whole of yours. Even when I'm not actually inside you, I still feel joined to you; I feel like I'm a part of you and you're a part of me. I feel like that now, just sitting here. I feel like that when I'm at home, wanting you, and you're here, doing whatever you're doing. There's a connection between us, which is about so much more than sex. For me, it's unbreakable… and *that's* what makes you different."

Although the tears are still falling, she sits quietly for a moment. "Thank you," she says.

"What for?"

"Explaining."

"Did it help?"

"Yes."

I wait, half expecting her to say something else, but she doesn't, so I get out of the car and go around to her side, opening the door and helping her out. She stands in front of me for a moment.

"I don't think I'd have known you back then," she says quietly.

"No," I reply. "But I wasn't worth knowing until I met you."

The models are all due to leave for New York on Thursday for our show on Friday, so it's a busy week, which is probably good. I've called Megan already today to make sure she's okay. She still sounds really tired, and I'm getting worried about her.

"Hey," Matt comes into my office, with Grace following close behind.

"Hi." This looks a little ominous. They don't often come to see me unannounced and together…

"We need to talk," Matt says as they both sit down opposite me.

"Right." I lean forward, resting my elbows on the desk.

"I'm not gonna be able to make it to New York," he announces, taking Grace's hand.

"Okay. You want me to handle it?"

"Yeah." He looks at Grace and she sits forward just a little.

"I need Matt here at the end of the week," she says quietly. I know they're trying to conceive and I'm not sure I want to know exactly why Matt has to be here at that precise time… "I've got to go for a scan," she whispers.

I look at Matt, then back at Grace. "You're pregnant?" It seems the obvious conclusion.

"Well, yes… hopefully." I must look as confused as I feel, because she smiles and starts explaining: "I've been pregnant before, when I was with my first husband. It was ectopic." My face must make it clear I haven't got a clue what she's talking about. "Do you know, I knew you'd look like that…" She smiles. "Without getting technical, the baby didn't grow in my uterus; it grew in one of my fallopian tubes. That ruptured and I nearly died. I lost one tube… so getting pregnant again was risky." This must be the medical problem Matt told me about.

"Grace is booked in for Friday." he explains. "The timing isn't great for New York, but I need to be here too."

"Obviously," I say, because I get that better than ever after yesterday. I wouldn't have missed Megan's scan for anything. "I'll handle New York," I tell him. "And the other shows too."

"No," he says firmly. "I'm not letting you do it all by yourself."

"If this pregnancy is ectopic as well," I reply, looking at both of them, "Grace is gonna need you here for a while."

"And if it isn't, I've still got a business to run."

"Which you can be doing from here – with Grace – while I handle the shows."

Grace sits forward again. "Why don't we decide about Europe once we know the scan results?" she says.

"Okay," Matt agrees and I nod my head.

"Can you keep this to yourself?" Grace asks me.

"Sure."

"I mean, you can tell Megan and Will, but no-one else… not until after the scan, anyway. I don't need the whole office knowing about this."

I look down at my desk, running my finger along its edge.

"What's wrong?" Matt says.

I can't look at him. "It's Megan and me… we're kind of not together right now," I reply.

"What happened?" he asks. Do I really want to do this? Well, I guess they're my friends. They've both been involved pretty much since the beginning…

"She found out who I am," I say eventually.

"What do you mean?" Grace asks.

"She overheard Will and me talking. He made a comment about the number of women I've slept with, and she didn't take it well…"

"What did he say then?" Grace queries.

"Oh… he just made a remark about all the hundreds of women from my past…"

"Yes, but surely Megan must realize that's an exaggeration. Surely you can explain…?" She looks from me to Matt.

"Except Will wasn't exaggerating," he tells her.

She turns back to me. "You mean you've really had that many…?"

I nod my head.

"Oh."

"Yeah… oh. And I don't think it helped that she felt I'd deceived her…"

"How?" Grace tilts her head to one side.

"By not telling her before."

"About your past?" Matt asks. I nod. "Sorry, but how the hell were you supposed to do that?"

I shrug. "There was never gonna be a good time, but she feels I was keeping secrets… which I guess I was."

"And her not telling you about her dad… that wasn't keeping secrets?"

"Yeah… we had that argument. It didn't end well." He raises an eyebrow. "She left me," I explain.

"And how are things now?" Grace asks.

"She's at her place, thinking. I'm at home…" I take a breath, "missing her." I swallow down the lump in my throat.

"When did all this happen?" Matt says after a long enough pause for me to get myself together again.

"Last Friday."

"Why didn't you say something before now? You should've called me at the weekend. I'd have come over."

"I know. But I just wanted to keep myself to myself for a while. I've been talking to Megan still. We're not completely over… Well, I don't think we are. I've spoken to her every day, by phone. And we went for her scan together yesterday." I let out a long sigh.

"Don't give up on her," Grace says quietly.

"Oh... I'm not. But I don't know if she wants me enough to live with my past."

"She's been through a lot, Luke," she continues. "What with her dad and everything."

"Yeah," Matt joins in. "Give her some time."

"She can have as much time as she needs. I'm not going anywhere. I just wish I had a clue what I was doing."

"What do you mean?"

"Just that if I knew my way around relationships, I'd have known it was a mistake to propose—"

"You proposed?" Matt's incredulous.

"Yes."

"And what did she say?" Grace asks.

"Nothing, really. She laughed."

"Ouch." Matt leans forward. "That had to hurt."

"Yeah... just a little bit."

"Why did you propose?" Grace asks and both Matt and I turn to look at her.

"Why do you think?" I say.

"Was it just because she's pregnant and you thought it was the right thing to do?"

"No... I only proposed on Friday."

"Oh... so it was after she found out about your past?"

"Well, yes." Where's she going with this?

"And you needed to prove a point... that you've changed; that you're not the man you were before. You wanted to keep her, not give her a chance to leave... Is that right?"

"Well... yes, I guess. But I also proposed because I love her. I want us to spend our lives together." If anyone had told me six months ago that I'd be talking like this in front of my best friend and his wife, I'd probably have punched them. Now, none of that matters anymore.

"And you told her that?"

I think for a moment. I can't actually remember if I did at the time. I was so desperate for her to stay; so scared she was going to leave me for good… "It wasn't the most romantic proposal, no."

"Luke, every woman needs to feel wanted, loved, cherished, needed. But when you're pregnant, you can multiply that by a factor of about a million. She's going to be feeling so insecure, so uncertain. In Megan's case, given your past, she's probably wondering if she'll ever be enough for you… And to add to all of that, her hormones will be all over the place." She gets up and comes around to my side of the desk, leaning against it, next to me. "Whatever she says and does, she loves you, and she needs you, Luke…"

"God, I wish that were true."

"It is. You have to trust me on this one… and don't give up hope." I look up and she's smiling down at me. "You two are good for each other."

Megan

Erin's at work, so I'm here by myself, and at the moment, all I'm doing is staring at yesterday's ultrasound image of Luke's baby… our baby. I run my finger over the outline of the head. It's odd, it looks like he or she is sucking their thumb, but I can't see how they can be doing that at this stage. Having Luke there was so special and I'm glad he came in with me; it would really have spoiled the whole thing if he hadn't been included.

I keep thinking about my future, and the baby's future, if I can't work this out. It's not something I really want to contemplate. I wonder how I'll cope doing most of it on my own. I'll manage, because I'll have to, but it won't be easy. My dad raised me by himself, and look how lousy he was. I put the photograph on the table, and, for the first time in a long time, I think about my mom. I wonder if she missed me when she left. Of course she didn't; she never once got in touch. Not even with a birthday or a Christmas card. She left me with him, and I never heard from her again. It's no different really to Luke's mom... just maybe less traumatic at the time, I guess.

I place my hand on my stomach. "I'll never abandon you," I whisper.

I'm leaving for New York on Thursday, for the show on Friday. Luke will be there and I really need to try and work things out before then, one way or the other. I know I'll be seeing more of him over the coming weeks and it's not fair on either of us to leave things in limbo. I miss him so much, but I need to know I'm gonna be safe with him. All my life, I've been let down by everyone I've ever trusted. I need to know that if I trust him, and let him back into my life, he won't let me down again... I need to know he won't go back to his old ways... that the man I love is the *real* Luke. I've lived a life of insecurity and I can't do it anymore.

So, I've decided I'm going to speak to Will. He's the only person who really knows Luke. And apart from Luke, he's the only person I can ask.

The problem is, how to get hold of him. I don't have his number. The only contact details I've got, apart from Luke's, are for the office. So I call them, and ask to be put through to Grace. I just hope she'll talk to me. If he's told his friends what happened on Friday, she might not be too keen to speak to me... I've hurt her friend.

"Megan?" she says when the call is connected. "Are you okay?"

She sounds genuinely concerned. "Yes, I'm fine."

"I think someone's made a mistake, putting your call through here... Did you want Luke? I've just left him talking to Matt, but I can interrupt them."

"No. It was you I wanted to talk to."

"Oh?" Now she sounds genuinely surprised.

"I need a favor," I tell her.

"Okay…"

"I need to speak to Will. But I don't have his number."

"Hang on a second," she says and then gives it to me. "He doesn't always answer first time," she says. "If not, leave a message. He'll call you back."

"Thanks."

There's a moment's pause. "Are you sure you're okay?" she asks.

"Yes. I just need to speak to him."

"And not Luke?"

"Not right now."

"Okay," she says. I get the feeling she wants to say more, but she doesn't.

Grace was right, Will didn't answer when I called, so I took her advice and left a stilted, awkward message. He called back within ten minutes and, like Grace, his first concern was that I was okay. He also wanted to be sure there's nothing wrong with the baby. Once we'd ironed that out, and established that I wasn't trying to get hold of Luke, he agreed to meet me for coffee – well, tea. So I'm sitting waiting for him in a quiet corner of the Starbucks opposite Boston Common. Will arrives about five minutes late.

"I'm sorry," he says, sitting down across from me. "I couldn't get parked." He looks at my cup of tea. "Can I get you another?"

"No, I'm fine."

"I'll just…" He points toward the counter and gets up again, returning a few minutes later with a herbal tea.

"I assumed you'd drink coffee," I say. "That's why I suggested here."

"I do normally, but Luke said it makes you feel sick right now. I thought the smell might…"

He's obviously just as considerate as his brother, even though they look nothing like each other.

We sit for a moment, both staring at the table. This could get awkward if one of us doesn't speak soon.

"Thanks for coming," I say, because I can't think of anything else.

"That's okay."

"I… I need to ask you some questions. About Luke."

"Right."

I can't think how to phrase this… "What's he… I mean… what's he *really* like?"

He raises an eyebrow. "You know him better than any of us, Megan. You tell me what you think he's like."

I hadn't expected that. "Um… Well, he's kind, understanding, thoughtful…"

"Yep," Will says, then he leans forward. "He's all of that. But I don't think that's what you really wanted to ask, was it?"

He's perceptive. I shake my head. "He says he's different – well, he says I'm different. And he says he's changed. But I need to know if that's true… if it's for real, or if he's going to go back to being that man again."

"God, no. He won't go back to that way of life. Not now."

"How can you be so sure?" His certainty is astounding.

"Because he loves you too much, that's how. You're the only person I've ever known who's really gotten on the inside of Luke. I include myself in that, Megan. He took care of me when our mom died, he put me through school, fed me, kept a roof over our heads, he did everything for me… but he was always very closed off. He never spoke to me about how he felt… He never shared any part of himself with me, or Matt, or Todd. Then, he met you and, for the first time ever, he really started talking to me. He told me how he felt about you. It was a new experience for both of us."

"But his past…" I mutter.

"What about it? None of that matters to him now. There's something you need to understand… He wasn't happy living like that, Megan. He really wasn't. I'd go so far as to say that, at times, he was desperately unhappy. He knew that, and so did I."

"Then why did he do it?"

"You'd have to ask him that, but in my view, it's got a lot to do with our mom… We were both very close to her. She was the guiding force in our lives. And then she wasn't there anymore. She didn't leave a note; so we've never known why she did what she did, and Luke had to grow up overnight. He became responsible for everything, from paying the rent, to feeding and clothing both of us, getting me to school, helping with my homework, all of it. I think he probably felt angry and abandoned, let down by her, as well as being sad and missing her. On top of that I always thought he felt he could have done something to stop her. He couldn't have done, but I think he believed he could… And that's a lot of emotions to deal with, especially when you're fifteen. He felt he had to hide it all, for my sake, and I'm not sure he ever resolved most of it. I think he just decided to isolate himself so that no-one would ever get close enough to hurt him again."

"But… he let me in…"

"Yeah. You broke down his defenses. And he let you. No-one else has ever done that."

"And I still hurt him…" My voice is little more than a whisper.

He looks at me, and there's a gentleness in his eyes that reminds me of Luke.

"Yeah, you did… but that doesn't mean he doesn't want you back."

"And how… how is he? Really, I mean…"

"You've spoken to him every day. How do you think he is?"

"I don't know. He seems tired, I guess. But he keeps our conversations about me, so I don't really know…"

"He's in a kind of emotional oblivion," Will says, and I gasp because that's where I am too. "Just like you are." I stare at him for a moment. *How does he know that?* "He's waiting for you to decide what you want." He sighs, takes a sip of his tea, winces and pushes the cup away. "That's revolting," he says, then looks up at me. "Look, I'm not going to tell you what to do… it's your life, your future, and you have to decide what you want, but you asked to meet me because you wanted me to tell you about Luke. So, I'll tell you… He's been there for me for the last sixteen years. If I need him, he stops whatever he's doing and helps me. He's the most honest, decent, selfless person I know and he never lets people down. Luke's a good guy, Megan. And despite what you think about his past, he always was a good guy. He's just an even better guy when he's with you."

Chapter Twenty-one

Luke

Matt and I have been in a meeting all morning with Paul, finalizing the plans before Paul leaves tomorrow morning. This means I'm back to where I was… looking at pictures of the woman I love and can't have, wearing sexy lingerie; staring at images of the places we made love, or where I thought about us making love. It's torture and I'm hoping we can break for lunch soon, just so I can escape.

We've just finished going through the revised running order when my cell rings and I go around my desk and pull it out of my jacket pocket. It's Megan. She hasn't called me at all since she left; our communications have all been one way. I don't even apologize to Matt and Paul. I pick up the call.

"Megan? Are you okay?"

"It's not Megan. It's Erin." I feel like everything has stopped, including my own heart.

"What's wrong?" I manage to say. I'm vaguely aware of Matt getting up from the couch where we've all been sitting, and moving toward my desk.

"I'm sorry," Erin says, "I'm sure you're busy…"

"Erin… tell me what's wrong."

"Megan's really upset. I can't get anything out of her. Something must have happened, but I don't know what…"

"I'll be there in twenty minutes," I tell her and hang up. I grab my jacket and keys.

"What's—?" Matt asks.

"I don't know." I shrug on my jacket as I head for the door. "I'll call you."

I don't know what his reply is; I'm already running down the hallway to the stairs.

When I arrive, Erin opens the door.

"Where is she?" I ask.

"In the living room." She stands aside to let me through. "I've got a school meeting before the semester starts next week. I'm already running late, but I couldn't leave her like this. She's too... distraught."

"Okay. You go," I tell her. "And thanks for calling me."

"I didn't know what else to do."

She pulls on a sweater, giving me a kind of pained look, then heads out the door.

I go into the living room. "Megan?" I say, just to let her know I'm there. She's sitting curled up on the sofa, her knees bent up to her chin and she's sobbing real hard. I go over and sit beside her, but I don't touch her. "What is it? What's happened?" She doesn't reply. I wait a little while and still she sobs. I get up, take my jacket off, throw it over the back of the sofa and sit down again. I think I could be here some while. "Megan," I say calmly. "Tell me what's wrong." She looks up at me and the sight of me just seems to make it worse. Her sobs become howls. "Talk to me, baby," I say gently. "Tell me. Whatever it is, I'll try and make it alright again."

"You can't," she gulps out.

"Try me."

"I'm lost, Luke." What the hell does that mean? I wait, hoping there's more to come. "I'm tired. I didn't sleep at all last night... and I'm so confused. I've got to pull myself together though and get ready for the trip. I mean, we leave tomorrow morning and I haven't even packed yet... but then how am I going to cope with everything when

I'm so tired? I look awful and I know I'm going to forget what I'm supposed to do… and then I keep thinking, if I can't cope with a few fashion shows, how am I ever going to handle a baby waking up every four hours to be fed, morning, noon and night? It's all too much… I'm going to be such a terrible mother, Luke."

"Hey…" I say. "No you're not."

"But what have I got to base it on? I've got no role models, no experience…"

"I don't think it works that way. All you'll have to do is be yourself, and you'll be great. You're just tired… really tired. And you're worried about the shows."

"And I can't work out what to do…"

"About us, you mean?" She nods her head. "Then forget about it for now. Do the shows, get them over with, and think about us when you get back. I'll still be here."

"I can't do that. I need to resolve it, one way or the other, before we go. I can't keep living like this." I'm not sure I like the sound of 'one way or the other', but I try to stay focused.

"This isn't healthy, Megan." I take a deep breath. Maybe if I try and talk it through with her… "Talk to me about us. Tell me how you feel… what you're struggling with."

"It's the deception, Luke… that's what I'm struggling with."

"So, it's not my past itself?"

She looks at me for a long moment. "I guess it's that too. But it's mainly the fact you didn't tell me."

And we're back to where we started on Friday. Except she's too vulnerable right now for me to remind her she kept so much more from me… And anyway, I'm not sure I care about that anymore. I just want her back.

"I'm sorry," I say simply. "I didn't mean to hurt you."

"I'm so scared, Luke." She starts crying again and it's more than I can take. I move closer and pull her into my arms. She doesn't resist, but rests her head on my chest.

"What are you scared of?" I ask her. "Tell me…"

"So many things… I'm scared of being hurt. I'm scared there are other things from your past you haven't told me… I'm scared that I'll have to come face-to-face with it one day and I won't be able to handle it."

"How do you mean?"

"Well, what if we were out one day, in a café or restaurant, or just out for a walk somewhere, and a woman came up to us and she was someone you'd slept with before… I'd find that really hard."

"Are you saying you'd be happier if I'd only had one or two relationships, but they'd been more serious? What if I'd been in love with someone else before I met you? How about if I'd been deeply in love with another woman and she'd left me, and I'd never really gotten over it? Would that be better?"

"No… but there'd be less chance of meeting her than the many hundreds of women you've been with."

"But that might never happen… And what would it matter? I never had any emotional connection to any of them. It was just sex… And you're so much more to me than that." How many times do I need to tell her this? "You're worrying… you're making yourself ill over things that haven't happened yet, and about the past, which none of us can change."

"I know… but I can't help it. I wish I could."

She looks up at me and it's like she realizes all of a sudden that I'm holding her, and that being in my arms isn't where she wants to be. She pulls away abruptly.

"Megan," I say, "do you still love me?"

She hesitates, but not for very long. "Yes, I do… but…"

And suddenly the realization hits me that there are only so many times I can tell her and show her that I've changed, that I'm not that man anymore; only so many times I can tell her that I love her, that I only want her and no-one else. We're going around in pointless fucking circles.

"I'm sorry," I say. "I always wondered if I'd be good enough for you." Her eyes dart up to mine again and she starts to shake her head.

"I tried to tell you… on the beach at Antibes, when you were singing my praises, that I had absolutely nothing in my life to be proud of. Maybe now you know the truth about me, you get what I meant." I stand up and take my jacket from the back of the sofa, folding it over my arm. "I'm not going to keep having this discussion with you. I can't keep looking back… If you want us to be together, you need to accept my apologies for what's happened, understand that I'll never hurt you again and that I will keep you safe, and leave my past where it belongs: in the past. It's down to you to make your own decision, and from now on, I'll leave you alone to do that. I won't keep calling you anymore. Bear in mind that whatever you decide, I'll always be here for you, and our baby, Megan. You'll never have to cope by yourself… I'll be with you, and I'll help, even if we're not together. You won't be on your own for any of it. You can call me anytime you wanna talk, or if you need anything. As far as I'm concerned, I'm still joined to you. Before you ask, whatever happens to us, I'm not gonna start fucking around again. That's the old me, and I don't want that life anymore. More than anything, I want my future to be with you. If you want that too, let me know… and I'll be here. I'll never be far away. If you decide don't want to be with me, then I'll have to learn to live with that, and somehow find a way to live without you. Take as long as you need, Megan, and then tell me what you want to do. I'll go along with whatever you choose."

The shows have been going really well and, considering the state I left Megan in at home, she's been amazing on the catwalks.

I felt guilty the moment I closed her apartment door. And I wanted to go back, but she needs to decide what she wants and I didn't think I was helping the situation anymore. I spoke to Melissa as soon as I got back to the office and asked her to watch over Megan and call me if anything happened… so I wasn't backing off, not really. But I couldn't keep laboring the point either. I've argued my corner. Now she has to make her choice… I'm just terrified of what her final answer will be. She might be feeling overwhelmed by my past, but I'm real scared of the prospect of a future without her in it, because that's no future at all.

As we've traveled around Europe, I guess maybe a part of me has been hoping that, if she spent some time away from me, without me calling her every day, she might miss me enough to want me back. I don't know whether she has or not, but I've sure missed her... pretty much every minute of every day.

I haven't really seen her, other than on show days, and then only from a distance. She's been very professional; doing her job and doing it brilliantly. This season's styles are proving popular, so I've been kept busy, sometimes until late at night, wining and dining the buyers. We're on the last leg now, and Matt's joined me in Paris. Grace's scan was fine and their baby is growing in the right place... He and Grace are overjoyed and I'm really pleased for them. They kept their celebrations quiet, I think because they felt guilty about my situation with Megan. We talked about the shows when I got back from New York and, although Matt was okay about coming to Europe, I could tell Grace wanted him to stay with her for a little longer. So, I offered to handle London and Milan and he said he'd come to Paris, which means he's only away from Grace for a few days. He got here the day before yesterday and we've caught up on what's been going on... which is that we've had the best season ever.

The show finished about an hour ago and I've come to a conclusion. After three weeks away from home, only seeing Megan in passing, I need to speak to her properly. I know I said I'd leave her alone, but I really do miss her and I need to find out if she's any further forward with her decision.

She's due to fly home tomorrow – along with everyone else, including Matt. I've got a couple more days here, having meetings, and I'll fly back at the end of the week. I'm hoping I might be able to persuade Megan to stay with me... not in the same room, of course, but just to spend some time together. Now the shows are over, and as we're away from home and back in France, where it all began, we might be able to talk and work things out... that's what I'm hoping, anyway.

I go to her room and knock on the door. She answers, opening it just a fraction, then wider when she sees it's me. That feels promising.

"Have dinner with me tonight?" I ask, not bothering with small talk, or even saying 'hello'.

Her eyes widen a little. "We're flying home tomorrow," she says.

"I know you are. I won't keep you up late." I step over the threshold of the room, to get closer to her. "I need to talk to you," I whisper. She stares at me.

"Okay," she says.

"I'll pick you up at six-thirty." And I leave, before she can change her mind.

In the dining room, we're sat close to the window, looking out over the Paris skyline. It's a different view from the one at the other hotel, but that can't be helped. It's still beautiful, but not as beautiful as Megan.

She's wearing her hair up, with just a little makeup, and a fitted dark blue cocktail dress. Because I haven't seen her properly for so long, I think I can detect just a hint of a bump, but maybe that's just because I'm looking for it.

"You've been amazing," I tell her once the waiter's taken our order. "Paul's really pleased with how well everything's gone. So is Matt. We've taken more orders than ever before."

"That's good," she says. "I'll just be glad to get home for a rest."

"It's tiring, isn't it?"

She smiles, nodding. "It's like being on a carousel."

I put my hand across across the table, giving her the chance to take it. Very slowly, she edges hers forward until our fingers are touching. It may be only the slightest of touches, but it feels so good.

"I wanted to apologize," I say to her.

"What for?"

"The way I was before we left… that morning at your apartment. I was very abrupt."

"It was fine," she says. "I deserved it." That sounds even more promising. I decide to take my courage in both hands.

"I've missed you so much," I tell her. "The last three weeks have been hell."

She looks around the restaurant and lowers her voice. "I've missed you too... I—" She stops, then turns and looks out the window. "This is gonna sound odd," she says suddenly, "but are we in a different hotel?" She's turned her head back and is looking straight at me now. "I've been in such a daze since we got here, I hadn't noticed... but the view, the restaurant... it's different to when we were here in the summer, isn't it?"

All my hopes and optimism disappear before my eyes. I didn't even get to ask her to stay with me... Is this what it's always gonna be like? Is she always going to find reminders? Only if we're together, I guess... and that's looking less and less likely now.

"Yes," I reply, and even I can hear the misery in my voice.

"But I thought you said to Emma that the company always uses the same chain of hotels when traveling... Is there a reason we're here, and not at the other one?" she asks, her eyes narrowing, like she already knows the answer.

"Yeah, there is."

"Which is...?"

I look straight at her. "You said you were scared of coming face-to-face with my past. That won't happen here..."

She stares at me for a moment. "But... but it might have done at the other hotel?" I nod my head. She pulls her hand away and sits back in her seat. "Who, Luke?"

"Sorry?"

"Who did you sleep with from the other hotel?"

"I'm not going there, Megan. I told you before we left, I don't want to keep living in the past."

She lowers her voice. "Oh, God... Was it the receptionist, the one in my dream?" It's like she hasn't even heard me.

"No. I don't even remember the damn receptionist."

"Then who?" I don't reply. She sits for a moment. "Wait a second... Was it more than one woman?" Again I don't respond. It was... but

I'm not telling her that. I'm getting really fed up with dissecting ancient history. "But… We didn't stay in the usual chain of hotels in New York, or London, or Milan… Are you telling me you slept with women at each of those places?"

I swallow before replying, "Yes." I can't sit in silence forever.

"Please… Just tell me who it was," she mutters.

"No!" I get to my feet. My voice is loud enough that the people sitting around turn and stare at us. "I'm sick of talking about this, Megan. I thought we might have a chance… I was gonna ask you to stay on here with me, so we could try again, but how can we? You want to live in the past still… and that's never gonna work, not if we're gonna have any kind of future together. Why can't you leave it alone? I've done what I can to protect you from it and still you want to keep digging and digging… I don't understand… and I'm not sure I ever will. Hell, I'm not sure I even want to anymore." Her mouth is open and she's staring up at me. I lean over, so I can whisper, "You're having my baby, Megan… you're creating our future right there, inside you… why the hell do you have to keep dwelling on the past? I'm sorry… I can't do this anymore…" I hear my voice crack on the last few words and I walk away from the table, and leave the dining room. On the way out, I pass Matt.

"What's wrong?" he asks.

I stop, run my fingers through my hair, and look back at Megan, who's watching us. Even from here, I can see she's crying. I want to go back to her, and hold her… I want to make it better, but I can't. I turn back to Matt. "Look after her," I say to him. "And make sure she gets home alright. I'm out of here for tonight."

I go to leave, but he grabs my arm. "Don't do anything dumb," he says.

"Like what?" I ask.

"You know what I mean, Luke. Whatever's happened between you two, don't screw it up now."

I can't help but laugh. "I did that years ago… before I even met her. I can't possibly make it any worse."

"Yes, you can," he says, trying to hold onto my arm, but I wrestle it free from him and head to the elevators.

I know Matt thinks I'm going to hook up with the nearest pretty-looking woman under the age of thirty-five, but he's wrong. I don't want that anymore. I don't want to be that guy anymore. I despise him. Because of him, I've lost the only woman I ever loved.

Megan

When he asked me to dinner, I felt that familiar quiver deep inside me for the first time in ages. It was like being back in Antibes, and I thought maybe we could spend the evening together, and talk. Seeing him from a distance while we've been here has been torture, reminding me how much I miss him and that living without him is just too hard. I'd already decided to ask him if we could try again and his invitation to dinner seemed like the perfect opportunity.

I hadn't realized he was going to ask me to stay here with him. If I'd known, I'd have said yes... except he didn't get to ask, because I screwed up. Again.

When I realized we were staying in the wrong hotel, and he explained the reason, it was a shock. It was the thing I most feared... and it was coming true. I know I over-reacted... I should have let him explain and then left it, but I couldn't. I was jealous of a past I don't understand, and I had to keep pushing him and pushing him, until he cracked.

He wants a future; that's all he's ever wanted. And from the very first day, I've denied him that... He's given me so many chances, but I think I've pushed him too far away this time to ever get him back.

I'm on the flight back home, and Luke's still in Paris. I didn't see him again after he left the restaurant last night. I have no idea where he went. But I guess what he does has nothing to do with me now… and that's all my own fault.

Melissa is sitting next to me. We get along well, but I think she knows I'm not in the mood for talking. We're about an hour out of Boston now and I can't wait to get home to my own bed – even though I know all I'll do is toss and turn and worry about Luke, and fret over what I've done… and whether I'm ever going to see him again. Well, I suppose I am, because I know he'll be there for the baby… but that's not what I want. I want him to be there for me…

"May I swap seats for a little while?" Matt asks Melissa. Oh God. I wish she'd say 'no', but I doubt she will.

"Sure, boss," she says – I was right. She gets up and goes to sit in his seat, one row back and across the aisle.

Matt sits next to me.

"How are you?" he asks.

"Fine, thanks," I lie.

"I wanted to ask if you've got anyone collecting you from the airport."

"No. I'll make my own way home. It's fine."

"No it's not. Luke asked me to make sure you got home safely." *He did? Maybe it isn't too late… maybe he doesn't hate me…* "I'll take you," Matt adds.

"You don't have to do that,"

"Yeah… I do." We sit in silence for a while. I keep expecting him to go back to his own seat, but he doesn't. Eventually, he turns toward me, lowering his voice. "Tell me to butt out, if you like, but what happened between you two last night?"

I sigh. "We had a disagreement… about the hotel."

"What was wrong with the hotel? I thought it was okay."

"Oh, it was. I don't mean it like that… What I mean is, Luke had told Emma and me when we went to Paris before, that your company always stays at one particular chain of hotels…"

"Oh… I see," he says. "And you wanted to know why we weren't staying there this time?"

"Yes. And Luke told me."

He nods his head. "Well, at least he was honest. He could've told you it was my decision. He could've said they messed up the booking."

"I suppose... Instead of that, he told me he's slept with women at each of the other hotels."

"Yes, I know he has. And he didn't want you meeting them."

"Well, I'd said I didn't want to meet them. It was one of the things we'd talked about. I didn't want to keep bumping into his past."

"And he arranged that you wouldn't. It was all very last minute. He went to a lot of trouble over it – to protect you from his past." He stares at me and tears start to fill my eyes, but I don't want to cry in front of Matt; I barely know him. "Megan," he says, "you're his future; that's so much more important than his past. That's everything."

"That's what he told me."

"Then maybe you should listen to him."

And suddenly, I want him to answer one of the unasked questions that's been burning at me since the night we broke up – one of the things I've been dying to know, but have been too scared to ask Luke.

"Can I ask you something?" I say to him.

"Yeah, sure."

"I know he's done all of this before, but how many other models did he sleep with? Before me, I mean. Am I just one in a long line?"

He snorts. "No. He didn't sleep with any of them."

"How do you know?"

"Oh. I know. I had a rule. Well... I still have a rule."

"What's the rule?"

"Putting it bluntly... the rule is 'no screwing the models'."

"Well, he didn't pay much attention, did he?"

"Ahh, but he did... until you."

"How do you know?" I ask again.

"If Luke had slept with any of the models before, I'd have heard about it. The whole purpose of the rule was to keep the peace, really. I can't afford to have any of the girls upset by anyone – and it's not just Luke; the rule applies to Alec and everyone else too... including me, before I met Grace. Luke beat himself up over getting together with you, just because of the rule. I understand it was Will who convinced him that the rule didn't apply if he fell in love." He stops for a moment. "When your dad brought you to Luke's office and I found out what he'd done, I gave him such a hard time. My God, the things I said to him…" He closes his eyes for a moment, then opens them again. "I was very unfair to him. He was going to quit his job, give me back his shares, blow our friendship… because you mattered more to him than anything."

"I still can't see how you know for sure he obeyed your rule…"

"Because I didn't… obey it, that is," he says.

I turn, my mouth opening in shock.

"It was before I met Grace," he says. "A long time before I met her… But if you want to talk about someone's past costing them dearly, you only need to look at mine. Mine nearly cost Grace her life… and me mine."

I can't stop staring, and I know what I really need right now is Luke sitting next to me, reminding me to breathe.

"It's a long story," he says, "But the model I chose to fool around with turned out to be a psychopath. Luke was there… he saved my life, but I'll bet he's never mentioned it. Ask him to tell you about it one day, assuming you don't make the biggest mistake of your life by walking away from him."

"I don't think that's my decision to make… not anymore."

He looks at me, real closely. "You really think that?" he asks.

"When he walked away last night, he told me he couldn't do this anymore. He was quite final about it. I don't blame him… I've pushed him too far."

"Don't be so sure," he says. "Yeah, he was angry, but he'd take you back in a heartbeat."

"I don't think he will… not this time. I've given him such a hard time over keeping his past from me, when I did exactly the same thing. I've been completely unreasonable… an utter bitch… ."

"And he'll still take you back." He's smiling.

"Why? Why would he want me back? I've been nothing but trouble to him…"

"Because he loves you."

"You make it sound so easy."

"Because it is."

"Then why are those women always here?" I tap the side of my head. "I love him, but I can't seem to come to terms with his past, no matter how hard I try."

"Then try harder… he's worth it… and so are you." He takes a deep breath and looks out the window. "We'll be landing soon," he says. "I'd better get back to my own seat." He gets up, but leans over just before he moves away. "Everyone has a history, Megan… all of us. Me, Grace… Luke… and you. It's what you learn from it that matters. For both your sakes, please don't make the penalty for his past something neither of you can live with."

Chapter Twenty-two

Luke

She's gone home. Paris is a damned lonely city when you're on your own. I know; I've been here on my own plenty of times before… and I've taken plenty of women to bed, just for the company. Not this time though. I've had three offers… one from the waitress at breakfast the morning after everyone else left, one from the receptionist, and one from the girl at the coffee shop, who wrote her name and number on my paper cup, which I threw away, without drinking the coffee. In the past I would have filled my spare moments over these last two days with all three of them, but not any more. I've kept my head down, done my meetings, ordered room service – it's less hassle than fighting off the unwanted attention. All I can think about is that when Megan left, we weren't talking. For the first time since we got back to Boston in July and I walked away from her, I really do feel like it's all over. She can't seem to accept what's gone before; or move on from it. And I can't change it to be how she wants. It's a stalemate. I don't see how we can work this out, not if she's always gonna have one eye in the past. I can't live like that.

I keep going over all the things I could have done differently; and I can't think of any, except not sleeping around before I met her. But I can't take that back.

I'm flying home this afternoon and, much as I want to, I'm also dreading it. It feels like the flight marks the beginning of the end.

I'm standing on the balcony of my hotel room, looking at the Paris skyline and the future feels really bleak. I'll be there for Megan and the baby, of course I will; but I can't imagine ever letting anyone into my life again, not like I did with her. Will I go back to screwing around? I don't think so. It's been weeks since I had sex… and I don't even miss it. I just miss Megan. One day, I guess she'll meet someone else; she's too beautiful not to… I stare up at the cloudy sky… oh, God, the thought of her with another guy, sharing herself with him; the thought of another man touching her, kissing her, making love to her… I can't even contemplate it.

It's not that late when I get home. The cab drops me off in the pouring rain. Somehow it feels appropriate to my mood. Will's working, so I knock on his door to let him know I'm back.

"How was it?" he asks. He looks tired.

"I don't really want to talk about it."

"Oh." He looks so forlorn, I have to tell him something; he'll only worry if I don't.

"Megan worked out why we'd switched hotels; and she wanted details."

"You didn't tell her…" his voice tails off.

"No… But we argued. She wouldn't let it go… and I kinda lost it with her."

"Luke… what did you do?" I can hear the disappointment in his voice.

"Nothing. I just told her I'd had enough."

"Oh dear."

"Yeah. I think it might be over."

"But the baby…"

"I'll still be there for them… I'm not going anywhere; I'm not a complete asshole – well not now – but she can't seem to get beyond my past… at least not enough to want me in her future."

"I wonder if she's feeling insecure, Luke. Maybe she's worried she's not enough, after all the others, not when there were so many."

"That's what she said, but it's bullshit."

"Not to her, I guess."

"But if she won't let me in enough to help her feel secure, what am I supposed to do? She so obviously doesn't trust me."

"I think her past has a lot to do with it…" he says.

"How?"

"You said her mom left?" I nod my head. "Think about it, Luke. Think about how that feels."

I stare at him for a moment, then I turn around. "I'm gonna grab a shower and head off to bed."

"Okay," he says. "I'll see you tomorrow. Just don't give up on her…"

"I'm not." I'll never give up on her. I can't.

"Or yourself," he adds.

I don't reply.

Even being in my own bed, combined with exhaustion and jet lag aren't enough for me to get off to sleep. Will's right. Megan is feeling insecure. I've thought it through and her abandonment issues are no different to mine. Not really. Then there's the pregnancy and her fears about that, her hormones going crazy, like Grace said… and then my past, which I know was a shock for her. It's too much for her to handle… I get it. I really do. It's a shame I'm coming to understand it so late… After the way I spoke to her and left her in Paris, I doubt she'll ever want to be with me again. I feel desolate without her, but it's my own fault. I should have tried harder…

The bed is too empty without her. No… My life is too empty without her.

I must have gone off to sleep eventually, but the clicking noise of my door being opened, and then closed again, wakes me with a start.

"Will?" I say. It's been years since he had a nightmare… I can't believe he's come looking for me… And then I smell it… her scent. I mean, she doesn't wear scent, but she has her own fragrance. I'd know it anywhere. I turn and flick on the lamp beside the bed, then turn back and, sure enough, she's standing about two feet inside the closed door, wearing a long raincoat and trainers, with her hair down around her shoulders, and she's fidgeting with her fingers. "Megan?" I say, sitting up a little, "what's wrong?"

"I needed to see you," she murmurs. "I'm sorry it's so late."

"How did you get here?" I ask.

"I borrowed Erin's car."

"And how did you get in? I mean, Will's security…"

"He let me in," she explains. "I had to come."

"Why?"

"Because I couldn't get off to sleep… Does your offer of help still stand?"

She looks so helpless. "Well… I meant I'd come to you, but sure. Take your coat off and come over here." I pull back the cover and move across the bed to make room for her. She steps forward, then kicks off her trainers, turns around and slowly undoes the coat, letting it fall to the floor.

"Jesus Christ, Megan," I jump out of bed. I'm rock hard already – but then she's not wearing anything, so I would be. For some reason I'd assumed she'd be wearing pajamas, or something under her coat… "You can't do this," I say to her.

"What?" she turns to face me and I feel my mouth go dry. The bump is definitely there; her breasts are much larger and more rounded and she's beautiful… utterly, breathtakingly beautiful. And I don't know what's happening. What's she doing?

"You can't turn up here naked," I tell her.

"Why? Don't you want me?" she asks. Her face has fallen. She's hurt.

I walk around the bed and stand in front of her, not touching her, because I don't have her permission to do so. "Of course I do. But we need to talk, not… I mean, I don't know what you want from me, Megan."

"I just want you," she says simply.

I smile at her. I've wanted to hear her say that for so long. "And I want you too," I reply, "but what does that mean?" She tilts her head to one side. She doesn't understand me. "What I'm trying to say is, do you just want me for tonight? Is this just about a hug to help you sleep? Because if it is, I'll put on some shorts, and I'll find you something to wear, and I'll hold you for as long as you need me to…"

I wait for her to answer me. "No," she whispers eventually. "I don't just want a hug."

I take a breath. "Do you want to have sex?" I ask her. "Because if you do, I'm sorry, but I can't do that. I can't have sex with you." She wraps her arms around herself and her head drops. "Not because I don't want you," I add quickly. "I want you so much, I ache. You're the other half of me and I want to be whole again, but if I can't make love to you properly, knowing we've got a future together, then I'm sorry, I'd rather not make love to you at all."

She doesn't say anything, but looks up into my eyes.

"What do you want?" I ask.

"You."

I move a little closer to her. "You already said that. Can you elaborate?"

"I love you," she says.

"I love you too."

"And I'm sorry, Luke. I'm so sorry… for everything. I was wrong about you. I was wrong about all of it. I judged you based on your past; I shouldn't really have judged you at all, but if I did, it should have been based on your present… on how you've treated me. I know I've behaved badly, I know I've hurt you, but can you forgive me… and can we please try again?" I close the gap between us so we're almost touching. "Please… just kiss me…" she whispers.

I put my hands on her cheeks, my fingers sliding into her hair, and tilting my head, I cover her lips with mine. My tongue delves deep into her mouth, finding hers and her moan fills me, combining with all my love, need and longing. I can taste her salty tears and I break the kiss and pull her into my arms. "Don't cry," I whisper into her hair. "I'm here…"

She runs her arms around my neck, holding on tight. "It's so good to feel you," she murmurs. "And I'm sorry for all the times I've hurt you."

"I don't want you to be sorry… I just want to know you're back for good this time."

Megan

He lays me back gently on the bed, lying beside me, raised on one elbow, and looking down at me.

"Tell me you're back for good," he reiterates.

"I'm back for good."

He lets out a sigh of relief. "Thank God for that. Breaking up with you is hard… really hard. I don't ever want to do it again."

"Neither do I," I whisper, and I feel a tear roll down my cheek.

He leans down and kisses it away. "God, you're beautiful," he says.

"So are you."

He smiles. "Talk to me," he murmurs. "Tell me what you're thinking."

"That I love you."

"And I love you," he replies. "And I want to know why you changed your mind."

"Who says I changed it?"

"I do… C'mon, Megan, you made it very clear you were more bothered about my past than our future… so what changed?"

"Does it matter?"

"Yes. It matters… a lot. I need to know; I need to understand."

"Why?"

"Because I need to be sure you're doing this for the right reasons."

I move away from him slightly. "What do you mean?"

"If you're coming back to me for the baby... because you're still worried, despite everything I've told you, that I won't be around for both of you, then you're wrong. I will be. You have to do this for you, Megan. Because it's the right thing for you and for us – and for no other reason, otherwise it won't work. Doing it for the baby isn't enough."

"I knew you wouldn't abandon us," I tell him. "You told me so many times – and after the scan, I knew it for sure." He reaches over to his nightstand and grabs something, then shows me the photograph of the ultrasound image.

"I look at it all the time," he says.

"So do I. I keep mine beside the bed too." We stare at the picture for a while. "My decision had nothing to do with the baby," I say eventually. "It was a combination of things..."

"Such as?"

"I had a talk with Will before we went to New York..."

"You did?"

"Yes. Didn't he tell you?"

"No."

"I asked him to meet me," I explain. "I wanted to know more about you; about what you were like before you met me."

"What did he say?"

"Don't look so worried," I say, laughing. "He was very complimentary."

"Hmm."

"He was. He told me you were a good guy."

"Right..."

"But that you're a better guy when you're with me."

"Well, that much is true."

"He also told me you weren't happy living your old life, and that he thought you only did it to keep from getting involved with anyone." I pause for a moment.

"Go on," he says quietly.

"He said your mom doing what she did made you feel abandoned... and angry and guilty, and you didn't want to let anyone close enough to to hurt you again."

"He said that?"

"Yes."

"I never knew he'd worked it out."

"So it's true?" I ask.

"Yes. Until I met you, I kept everyone at arm's length… even Will. I took responsibility for him and I helped him out, but I never let him see the real me. I didn't want the emotional hang-ups of relationships. I didn't ever want to have to feel again. It hurt too much when I lost her." He pauses and takes a breath. "Letting you in was weird, because it just happened; it wasn't something I had any control over… it was the most natural thing in the world. All my barriers were just gone, and none of it mattered. I just wanted you, more than anything… and even the fear of being hurt wasn't going to stop me."

"But I did… hurt you, didn't I? And I kept on hurting you…"

"Well, yeah. But it's okay. I understand why."

"You do?"

"I think so. I think you've got similar issues to me. I think your mom leaving you made it hard for you to trust people too." He touches my cheek with his fingertips.

"It wasn't just my mom," I murmur.

"No… it was your dad too, wasn't it? The two people you're meant to be able to trust more than anything… and they both let you down."

"Yes. That's it exactly, but how did you work it out?"

"I can't claim any credit. That's down to Will again. He put the idea in my head… You don't have to tell me about it, if you don't want to."

"Yes, I do." He pulls me into his arms. "You were right," I begin, "my dad's a bully. And maybe if I'd been older and stronger, I could have stood up to him… but I was five."

"I know…" he whispers. "I was wrong when I said it was easy. It isn't… not for everyone."

"He used to leave me… sometimes for days at a time…"

"On your own?"

"Sometimes with a neighbor, but sometimes on my own."

"Where did he go?"

"I've got no idea. There was always some scheme or another. Usually they didn't work out and he'd come back, angry… frustrated…"

"And he'd take it out on you?"

"Sometimes… or he'd just get high, if he had enough money for the drugs." I snuggle into him a little closer, enjoying the feeling of his arms around me.

"Why did you go back there?" he asks me. "Once you'd gone to college, you'd escaped him… so why go back?"

"He told me if I didn't go back… if I didn't give him money, he'd come and find me. That might have meant Erin getting hurt, so I did what he wanted." I lower my head, murmuring, "I always did what he wanted. I was too scared not to."

"Well, not any more," he says, raising my face to his. "You've got nothing to be scared of now. And you don't have to protect anyone… ever again. That's what I'm here for."

I let out a sigh. "I like the sound of that."

"Good… because that's how it's gonna be, from now on."

He holds me for a long while before either of us speaks again. "It looks like it was Will who worked it all out then," he whispers.

"Yes. I suppose we should go and thank him."

"I guess so. But we can do that in the morning… he'll wait." He smirks, then leans down and kisses me gently.

"My talk with Will got me thinking," I say once he breaks the kiss. "I don't know whether I'm a good person or not, but I know that everything in my life is much better when I'm with you. And I mean *everything* – even the bad things are better when I'm with you. I've been sitting at home on my own these last few days, while you've been in Paris, thinking about your past and how much I hate it – and I do hate it, Luke – and then I'd think about your words, about how you told me the difference between me and all the others…"

"That's all true. Every damn word of it. And I hate my past too – the point is—"

"We can't change it."

"Exactly." He's grinning at me. "At last… she gets it…"

"Eventually. And… well, you have Paris to thank for that. Paris, and Matt."

"Paris?"

"Hmm. Your reaction at the hotel…"

"Oh, God… Don't remind me. I was horrible to you."

"No, you were honest. You've always been honest. But I think I realized I might have pushed you too far. And the consequences of that were… frightening."

He leans down and kisses me again. "You didn't push me anywhere, baby. I just lost it. I'm sorry."

"Oh, don't apologize. I needed telling. I was focusing far too much on the past… and nowhere near enough on the future… on our future. That's what Matt told me too."

"How did Matt get involved?"

"He talked to me on the flight home from Paris. He gave me the hope to come here tonight. I thought you'd given up on me after Paris, but he told you'd take me back… because you love me."

"Damn right I do," he smiles.

"Matt also he told me about his own past," I tell him. "He said it nearly cost him everything. He suggested I ask you about the rule he broke? The one about sleeping with the models?"

"He's talking about Brooke," Luke says.

"Who's Brooke?"

"She was a model we used once – and I mean once. That's how Matt justified fooling around with her. She wasn't one of our regular girls, which made it okay to have a relationship with her. This was ages before he even met Grace. He and Brooke dated for a while… Except she turned out to be crazy. When he broke it off with her, she pulled a knife on him."

"What?"

"Yeah, it got ugly. She ended up in prison, but only after she'd nearly ruined Matt in court. Anyway, she was released eventually and turned up at Matt and Grace's place, and tried to kill them both."

"Oh my God, what happened?" I ask.

"She set the whole thing up; she got her brother to tell Matt I'd been in a car crash, so he left Grace at their apartment and rushed to the hospital. Luckily, Will happened to call Matt, and told him I was at home, not hurt at all. That was when we realized what was going on… and that Grace was on her own, with Brooke. I left at once and went over there. Will called Todd and he and I arrived just in time. Matt had got back there first; Brooke shot him, but he recovered and Grace was physically unharmed."

"And mentally? I mean having something like that happen… in your own home…"

"Grace is a resilient woman. She's had to be… but that's a whole other story, which I'll tell you later…"

"He said you saved his life."

"No, that was Todd, not me. The guy was like ice… I just held a cloth against Matt's wound until the medics arrived."

"And that wasn't saving his life?"

"It wasn't any more than the next guy would've done."

I look up at him, running my finger down his cheek. He's never willing to take credit for his actions. But he'll admit to, and take the blame for, the bad things he's done… that's so wrong.

"What happened to Brooke?" I ask eventually.

"Todd shot her. She died. It was bad… real bad. Matt beat himself up about it for a long time," Luke says and I know he's remembering. "It was a tough few months for both of them. But they've put it behind them now… Oh, and Grace is pregnant."

"Really?"

"Yes. Their baby's due a few weeks after ours, so you'll have someone to go through all this with," he says. "That might help a little… take away some of your fears." He puts his hand back on my tummy. "It's showing more, isn't it?" he murmurs.

"Yes."

"It's incredible, to think our baby is growing… inside you."

"Yes… growing is the right word… I'll be fat soon."

"And still beautiful."

"Luke," I say, "I've got a lot to learn. I need to stop looking backwards and try harder to look to the future."

"I can help you with that," he offers. "You've never really had anything to look forward to, so what was the point? But you've got a future now. We all have. I meant what I said in Paris... at least a part of it. You're making our future, Megan, right here." He leans down and kisses my stomach.

"I still feel insecure, I know I'm gonna make mistakes..."

"Me too. I'll get it wrong... all the time. I know damn all about relationships, so I'm gonna screw up – a lot. And I've got no idea what you're going through. We'll just have to remember to talk to each other."

"And I need to learn not to be so jealous."

"Oh... I don't know. I kinda like the idea of you being a little bit jealous." He grins mischievously. "As long as you know you've got no grounds for it."

"It's the women who throw themselves at you that I can't handle."

"Have you looked in the mirror lately? Whenever we've been out together, pretty much every man around us has his tongue hanging out... looking at you."

"And you don't feel jealous of that? Not that I'm saying they do it, but doesn't it bother you?"

"Are you going to run off with another guy?"

"No, of course not. I'm not even aware of anyone looking at me."

He smirks at me. "Then no, I'm not jealous of other men. If anything, they're more jealous of me. I'm the one who gets to call you mine; I get to hold you naked and take you to my bed. And, on top of all that, you're having my baby..."

"I don't have the kind of self-confidence where I can think like that. I expect you to be attracted to the other women."

"Why? I want you... just you. Remember, I'm yours. I'm not going anywhere. Ever. It's like I told you, even when I'm not with you, I'm joined to you."

"That's a lovely thing to say."

"It's the truth," he says.

"I know."

"Good. Don't forget it."

I lean up and kiss him. "Can I ask you a favor?"

"Of course… anything."

"Do you remember, you said your friend might be able to find out about my mom. I think it might help me move forward if I knew why she went away; why she left me with my dad, when she knew what he was like… and why she ignored me for so long. Do you think he'll be able to help?"

"Sure. I'll ask…" He thinks for a moment. "Although Will might have more luck. I'll see what he says in the morning."

"Thank you."

"You don't have to thank me. I'll do anything for you. You know that."

I yawn, because I really am exhausted. I haven't slept well for so long, and the trip to Europe is still taking its toll.

"You're tired," he says. "Move up the bed and settle down…" I do as he says, putting my head on the soft pillow. He gets up and walks around to his side of the bed, getting in and switching off the lamp, then pulling me in close. "I've just thought of something," he says.

"What's that," I ask, nestling into his arms.

"There's one kind of sex I've never had… not ever in my whole life."

I turn to look up at him in the moonlight. "What's that?" I'm suddenly intrigued.

"Make-up sex." He grins. "I'm reliably informed it's the best kind of sex there is. But you're tired right now, so maybe we can try it in the morning."

I reach up and caress his cheek with my finger. "I'm not that tired… and I don't want to wait till the morning. Besides, I've got a lot of making up to do…"

"Me too, baby… me too." And he rolls me onto my back, so we can find out just how good make-up sex really can be.

Epilogue

Megan

We've just finished eating Thanksgiving dinner and I'm lying on one of the couches at Grace and Matt's beautiful lakeside house, my head in Luke's lap, his hand on the bump… the bump which now has a name. Daisy is the name we've chosen for our daughter. We found out she's a girl a couple of weeks ago, at the second scan, having both been uncertain whether we wanted to know. But when the doctor offered us the chance to find out, we just nodded our heads together.

"Man, for a girl, she can sure kick," Luke says, rubbing my stomach gently. "Are you sure it doesn't hurt when she does that?"

"No. It's like a kind of fluttering. It's weird, but I like it." I put my hand on top of his and he kisses my forehead.

"I pity the poor guy who wants to date your daughter," Todd says from across the other side of the room. "You're gonna give him such a hard time."

"Date her?" Luke says. "Daisy isn't dating anyone until she's at least thirty."

"I knew it," Todd replies. "Overprotective father alert."

"You can't wrap her in cotton wool." Grace and Matt have just come into the room, catching the end of the conversation. Grace looks more pregnant than I do, although she's a few weeks behind me. We're great friends now, and she's helped me so much – actually, we're more like sisters than friends.

"Absolutely I can," Luke replies.

"No you can't," I tell him. "She'll end up repressed."

"And if I don't, she could end up with someone like me… I mean, how I used to be."

He hugs me just a little tighter as he says the words. "She'll be far too sensible." I reply, then I turn and kiss him.

"I'm so gonna enjoy watching you two flounder around in fatherhood." Todd's laughing as he speaks.

"It'll happen to you one day," Matt says. "And then *we'll* be the ones laughing."

"No, it won't," Todd replies, suddenly serious. I don't know why he's so against relationships, but I'll try and remember to ask Luke when we get home…

Speaking of which, Will is very quiet today. He's sitting in a corner by himself. He's worried about the job he's working on. He doesn't talk about it to either of us, but it's been going on since before we came back from France in the summer and I get the feeling something's gone wrong. It doesn't help that Luke and I are moving into our own place next weekend. It was always going to happen – well it was once I saw sense and realized I couldn't live without Luke, but that doesn't make it any easier for Will. He's always had Luke with him.

"I'm going to talk to Will for a minute," I whisper to Luke.

"Okay," he says and helps me to sit up.

"Everything alright over here?" I ask Will, lowering myself to the floor by his feet. Getting down here is fine… getting up might be a whole other story.

"Yeah, sorry. I'm not very good company today."

"Can I help?"

"It's work."

That's Will-speak for 'I can't talk about it'.

I figure I may as well come straight to the point. "You are okay with us moving out, aren't you?"

"Sure," he says.

"And why is it I don't believe you?"

"Really, Megan. It's fine. You need your own space, with the baby and everything." He's right, we do need somewhere of our own.

"We're only half an hour away."

"I know." His voice is flat, emotionless. Luke had wanted to get somewhere closer, but he's got a lot of money invested in Will's house; he can't expect Will to sell it, just because we want to move, so we ended up looking out of the city to get something affordable.

"You'll have to come visit your niece and teach her how to use a computer," I say, nudging into him.

"Yeah, sure," he says. I glance across at Luke, who's staring at us, and give him a slight shake of my head. Something's not right with Will.

Luke comes over and gives me a look, which tells me he's going to try and speak to his brother, to find out what's wrong. He helps me to stand up, then takes my place on the floor and I go back to the couch. He starts talking quietly to Will, and soon their heads are close together and they're deep in conversation. If anyone can help Will, it's always going to be Luke.

Matt and Todd are talking, and Grace is resting on Matt's lap, so I sit and watch Luke for a while. He's been incredible since we got back together. He looks after me, supports me, and helps me all the time. I've given up trying to find work for now, but Matt's asked if I'll model the company's new range of maternity lingerie, and we're starting the shoot for that on Monday. It'll be quite nice to have something to do. Not that I'm idle. Getting everything ready to move house is taking up enough of my time.

If only Luke would propose again, everything would be just perfect. But I'm not sure he ever will. I don't blame him – having your proposal laughed at isn't what most men hope for... I guess I shouldn't be greedy. I've got him. I'm having his baby; we're moving to a beautiful new home, my dad's in prison, and for the first time in my life, I'm surrounded by friends. Life's good... really good.

"I know it's Thanksgiving and everything," Matt says to Luke a little later, "but can we talk about work, just for a few minutes?"

"Okay," Luke replies. "Should we go into the kitchen?"

"No. This concerns Grace and Megan too."

"Oh?" I sit up a little, but Luke pulls me back down into his arms. I really like the fact that he's so affectionate in front of his friends. I know, after my conversation with Will, it's another thing about us that's 'different'.

"The shoot starts on Monday," Matt says.

"We know this, darling," Grace replies patiently. "Megan and I have been talking about it for a couple of weeks now."

"Yes." He kisses the top of her head. "And I know I promised Luke I'd never make him do another shoot, but…"

"You want me there?" Luke asks.

"Yeah."

"We can manage," Grace says.

"I know you can. You can manage the design side; hell you could even take the photographs if there wasn't going to be so much ladder work involved. But…"

"Alec?" Luke says.

"Yeah."

"So I'm there as the guard dog again?"

"Yes. He won't listen to Grace – probably about anything. I can't be there – I'm booked solid. And it's only for two days… I promise, no agency hitches this time." Matt grins.

"It's fine," Luke says. "I don't mind."

"You sure?"

"Yeah. The previous problem doesn't exist now, does it?"

"What was the previous problem?" I ask.

"You… And Matt's rule. Keeping my hands off you was a little challenging, to say the least."

"I don't think Matt's rule applies to us though, not any more." I lower my voice. "Especially not when you, and your hands have already been pretty much everywhere." I look up into his eyes.

"Wanna bet?" he whispers.

"Where haven't you been then?"

"I'll show you later." He leans down and I smile into his kiss.

It's late by the time Luke drives us home. Now he's changed his car for a Range Rover, we're all together... Will sitting in the back. But the journey is quiet... actually, it's silent.

"Is everything okay?" I ask him as he pulls up outside the house.

"Yeah... well, no." He gets out and comes around to my side of the car.

"What's happened?"

"Nothing," Luke says, "but we need to talk to you."

"To me?"

"Yes." He takes my hand and leads me into the house. Will follows, closing the door behind us and switching on the table lamps, so there's a dim, subdued glow in the livings room. "Come and sit down, baby," Luke says, and I start to worry.

"What's going on?" I ask him.

He sits beside me on the couch, holding my hand, and Will takes a seat opposite. Luke looks at Will and nods his head. "You start," he says.

Will leans forward, resting his elbows on his knees, his hands clasped together. "Luke spoke to me when you got back from the shows in Paris and asked me to check out your mom," he says. "I've been busy with work things, so it's taken a while, but I've found out what happened to her."

"Right?" I say, and I feel Luke's arms come around me, as he pulls me in close to him. This feels like it's going to be bad.

"I don't have all the answers," Will says. "But I do know why she left your dad, why she didn't take you with her, and where she went... She rented a small apartment just over a mile away from your dad's place."

"That close?"

"Yeah."

"And is she still there now?"

"No. I'm sorry, Megan…"

I feel myself shiver, and I know what's coming. Luke holds me closer still. "She died, baby," he says. "I'm so sorry."

"How?" I ask.

"A car accident." Will replies. "I got hold of the police report. She was crossing the road…"

"Was it a drunk driver?"

"No."

"Oh, God… It wasn't my dad, was it?"

"No," Luke says.

"Then what happened?"

"She just wasn't looking where she was going," Will continues. "According to the police report, the eyewitnesses all said she was distracted."

"What on earth distracted her so much she didn't see a car coming at her?"

"It wasn't a car, Megan… It was a truck. And she was distracted… well, I think she was distracted by you."

"Me?" I don't understand.

"Yes." Will's face is pale. "The accident happened right outside your school."

"When was this? I don't remember it."

"It was about three months after she left your dad, so you'd still only have been five or six at most. According to the police report, all the children were taken back inside the school straight after the accident, because…" He leaves his sentence unfinished. I still don't remember it.

"Why was she there? She didn't collect me from school. My dad got the neighbor to do that… Mrs Cutler. She'd pick me up and give me something to eat and watch me till my dad came to get me."

Will sighs. "I found your mom's old address. She rented the apartment with another man… Peter Williams?" He looks at me like the name should mean something. I shake my head. "I managed to track him down and I've been to see him. He told me what happened. He and your mom had an affair. It started when you were about two years old and eventually your mom decided to leave your dad. He used to beat her and she'd had enough… She loved Peter Williams and she thought she could have a new life with him. She planned to take you with her, but your dad came home from work early and caught her packing. He threatened her and told her to go. He said that if she came anywhere near you, or tried to contact you, he'd find Peter Williams and kill him, and then he'd kill you. She said she'd stay, leave Williams and give up her chance of happiness just so she could keep you, but your dad didn't want her anymore and told her either she had to leave on her own, there and then, or he'd kill you. I don't know whether he'd have actually done it, but he knew her weak spot, Megan… it was always you. So, she left without you, because she thought it was the only way to keep you safe.

"Williams told me, from that day on, she was never happy again. She missed you so much. She wouldn't move too far away, because she wanted to see you, and she got into a daily routine that never altered. She'd leave the house early in the morning, go and sit by your school and watch you arrive, then she'd do the same in the afternoons when you left." I can feel the tears falling down my cheeks. "Williams worked, so he wasn't there with her, but he knew that's what she was doing. She made no secret about it. He made no secret about how much he loved her. He gave me a photograph. He thought you might like it," he says, getting up and going into his office. He returns a moment later and stands beside me. "She was beautiful, Megan." He hands me a faded photograph. He's right. Even in a grainy black and white image, she's stunning, and there's something about her eyes…

"This is her?" I say.

"Yeah. No-one really knows what happened that afternoon. As I say, all the eyewitnesses just said she was distracted – she was staring at the school and she walked straight out in front of the truck. There was nothing the driver could've done to miss her."

"Did she suffer?" I ask.

"No," he replies. "She died straight away."

"Promise? You're not saying that just to make it seem better."

"I promise."

"And Peter Williams? What happened to him?" I ask.

"He met someone else a few years later. He's married now, with a couple of kids, but he's never forgotten your mom. He was happy to help when I contacted him. He was a nice guy."

I sit in silence for a while, Luke's arms tight around me. Will has sat down again opposite us.

"How do you feel?" Luke asks eventually.

"I don't know. I've always blamed her… I assumed she left me. But she didn't – or at least she didn't want to."

"No. And she kept an eye on you the whole time."

"Yes, but at what cost? I think I'd rather she'd just left – then at least she'd still be alive."

"Megan," Will says and I look up at him. "Your mom loved you very much. She died looking at you. I don't think there's anything better, if you have to die, than doing it looking at someone you love."

He gets up and comes over. "I'm sorry," he says. "I really hoped I'd find out better news for you."

"Oh, Will. I'm so grateful for what you've done," I tell him. "Thank you. Is this why you've been so quiet all day? Have you been worried?"

"I didn't know how to tell you," he says. "I was worried about upsetting you… with the baby, and everything…"

I get up and give him a hug. He stiffens, but eventually hugs me back, awkwardly. "You're such a lovely man," I tell him.

He reddens and shakes his head, then walks to his office, closing the door behind him.

I sit back down with Luke and he holds me a little longer. "You did a good job with Will," I say. "And you're going to be an amazing dad."

"Are you still worried about not being a good mom?" he asks. "Because I don't think you need to be, not anymore."

"No… I've got you and Will… and the memory that she loved me. It's not perfect. But it's better than it might have been… it's enough."

Luke

The timing for this shoot isn't exactly ideal. We're moving at the end of the week, and it's been a difficult weekend, after Will's revelations on Thursday night, but Megan's determined to go ahead with it. The studio's booked, and everything's been organized. She doesn't want to let Grace down. I called Grace on Friday and told her what had happened, so she's prepared if Megan can't handle anything. And I'll be there.

Alec is as grumpy as ever – if not more so. He remains to be convinced that there's anything sexy about pregnant women. I'm reminded of my own attitude a few months ago – and I've completely changed my views now. Megan's body turns me on more than ever.

The first shot of the day is on a bed, which is set up in the middle of the enormous studio space, surrounded by lights. It's made up with white silk sheets, and there are red rose petals scattered across it. Megan comes out of the changing room wearing a lacy black bra, with pearl embellishments, and matching briefs. I'll admit the straps are wider than on our normal bras, but apart from that, it's just as sexy and Megan looks hot.

"Lie down on the bed," Alec says.

"Good to see you too," Megan replies and I smile. She's still giving him as good as she gets.

"Very funny," he snaps. "Lie on the bed."

I take her hand and lead her over. "Which way?" I ask him.

"On her back. You're used to getting her on her back, Myers."

"Piss off, Alec," I say to him, and I wink at Megan. "Lie down, baby," I say to her, lowering her onto the bed, just as Grace comes in, with a bag slung over her shoulder.

"I'm so sorry I'm late," she says. "Oh good, you've started already."

"Yeah," Alec says. "Move further onto the bed, so you're lying in the middle at an angle." I help Megan to move. "Now, raise your right hand above your head." She does. "Good. And rest your left one across your stomach. Now twist slightly, and bend your right leg up across your left, just a little." Megan gets herself into position, seeming to know exactly what he wants. "That's it," he says, coming across. He pushes me. "Get out the way, Myers." Grace's mouth drops open, but I shake my head at her and move. It's best to choose your fights with Alec. Him pushing me around isn't important; I'm here to make sure he behaves himself with Megan and Grace. He straightens the sheet, then stands above Megan, and grabs a few more rose petals from the box on the floor, dropping them over her strategically. He tilts his head from side to side, then nods, and climbs up the ladder which is at the end of the bed. Leaning over, he starts taking pictures from above. "Look at me like I'm Myers," Alec says.

"Not a chance," Megan replies, chuckling.

"That's good," Alec says. "Do that again." He takes a few more photographs, then stops and climbs down.

"What next?" I ask him.

"She has to stand up, so I can get shots of the back, then we can add the kimono," he says… and the day progresses.

At just after four, Grace tells us it's time to go home for the day.

"We can get at least two more sets done today," Alec moans.

"No. Megan's tired. I'm tired. We're stopping," she says.

"For f   "

"Leave it," I growl at him, pulling rank for the first time today. "We'll easily get finished tomorrow."

He looks at me, shrugs, and starts packing his gear away. Then he grabs his jacket and leaves.

"How did you do that?" Grace asks. "I thought he'd argue a lot more."

"Luke hit him when we were in France," Megan tells her. "I think he's scared."

I'm stunned. "How did you know about that?" I had no idea she knew about that little scene.

"I heard what he said."

"You did? God, I'm so sorry."

"Why? You defended me. And when he was offensive, you hit him." Grace is looking at us.

"I'm not going to ask what that was about," she says, smiling.

"Best not," I reply.

"Now… before we all go," she says, "I've got something I want to try out." Megan and I look at each other, then back at Grace. "I needed Alec to be gone," she adds glancing at me, "because I knew you'd never agree to my idea with him being here." Now I'm really intrigued. She turns to Megan. "How would you feel about putting the first pair of briefs back on… but without the bra?"

Megan's eyes widen, and I think my mouth probably drops open. "You want me topless?" she questions.

"Not in the way you're thinking," Grace says. "No one would see anything. It'd be a three-quarter shot, and you'd have your hand over the only visible part of your breast." She demonstrates what she means on herself.

"But who'd take the picture?" Megan asks.

"Well… me, if you're okay with that?" Grace says. "Luke will still be here."

"Oh…" Megan looks at me. "I guess I'm okay with it."

If she is, so am I. "Is this for the website?" I say, "because if it is, I'd want to see the images before they're used."

"Of course. I'm not even sure I'll use them yet. It's just an idea."

"Okay. But nothing gets used without my and Megan's agreement," I tell her.

"Absolutely."

Megan goes back to the changing room and returns a few minutes later, wearing the black lace briefs, with her arms clasped around her chest, hiding her naked breasts.

"Come on over here," Grace says, her tone much softer than Alec's.

She positions Megan where she wants her in front of the lights, with a gray backdrop behind her, and takes a camera from the bag she brought in with her, then starts shooting. After a while, Grace steps back. "Something's not right," she says. Then she turns to me. "Luke," she says, "How do you feel about a bit of modeling?"

I laugh. "I'm all for equality, but I'm not putting those panties on, if that's your idea."

She giggles and reddens. "That's not what I had in mind at all. Would you mind taking off your t-shirt though?" I notice Megan smirking.

"I'm virtually naked here," she says. "Why should you still be fully clothed?"

I shrug. "Okay." I've got no idea what Grace is planning but I pull my t-shirt over my head and let it drop to the floor.

"Good," Grace says, not really paying me any attention. "Now, can you go and stand behind Megan, then put your arms around her and place your hands on her bump."

I shake my head, simply because I can't believe I'm being talked into this, but I do as I'm told, standing behind Megan and folding her into my arms.

"What do I do?" Megan asks.

"Nothing. Just stay as you are," Grace says, looking at us through the viewfinder of her camera. "Now, relax and act like I'm not here…"

"You are kidding, aren't you?" I say to her, smiling. "Megan's not wearing a lot… If you really weren't here, we'd be on that bed."

She laughs. "Don't mind me," she says.

"I'll pretend you didn't say that," I reply.

Megan tips her head back to look at me and we lock eyes for a moment before I kiss her gently. "You wouldn't dare," she says.

"Wouldn't I?" I reply. Then I whisper into her hair, "I've been looking at you semi-naked all day, which means right now, I'm as horny as hell. So, yeah… I'd dare."

"You think you're horny?" she mutters back. "Try having my hormones."

I kiss her neck and she leans back into me.

"Okay," Grace says, interrupting us. "I've got everything I need." She starts packing her things away. "I'll leave you two to it." She grins across at us. "I think I'll go and find Matt… He should be finishing work soon." She's gone before we can even say goodbye.

"See… horny hormones," Megan says. "Grace has got them too."

"I don't need to think about that," I tell her. "And I'm not making love to you here. So, go get changed and I'm taking you home… and we're having a shower together. A long one…"

Today, Megan and I arrive before everyone else and I open up the studio and put on the coffee machine, while she goes into the changing room.

"Hey, Luke," she calls, "come in here."

I go to her. "What's wrong?" I ask as I walk through the door.

"Look." She's pointing to a large, square parcel, wrapped in brown paper. "It's got our names on it," she says.

"Then open it."

We stand together, my arm around her shoulders as she rips off the paper and reveals a framed photograph. It's of Megan and I. It's in black and white and it's very atmospheric, and utterly beautiful. It's a three-quarter shot of us, so we're not quite sideways on to the camera, and I'm standing behind Megan, with my arms around her, my palms resting flat on her swollen belly. The angle of the shot, my arm and Megan's hand between them just about conceal her breasts from view. Her head is resting back against my chest and she's looking up at me, with such an expression of love in her eyes, my breath hitches in my throat. Her mouth is smiling and slightly open and I'm staring down at her, about to kiss those perfect lips. It's captivating and really intimate.

"You look so erotic in this," I tell her. "So sensual, so passionate… and so full of love, but there's something else." I think, just for a second. "You look happy," I say. "You look real happy. This is you, Megan… This is all of you."

"It is. And I am happy. Look, Luke… look at the way your arms come around both me and Daisy," she says. "It feels like we're safe, because you're holding us…"

"You are safe, baby… both of you. I promise you'll always be safe."

"I know." She leans into me, then looks back at the photograph. "But there's more to it… you're strong, but at the same time, that look in your eyes…"

"What you're seeing there is need…" I whisper. "A need to be inside you."

"I see more than need, Luke. I see tenderness, and trust and so much love…" She runs a finger along the part of the photograph where my arm is touching her breast, then down to the waistband of my jeans. "And I've gotta say, with all this muscle on show, you look so damn sexy."

There's a note. Megan opens it, reads it and passes it to me. I notice there are tears forming in her eyes.

"How did she do that?" she says and I pull her close as I read what it says:

> Megan and Luke,
> The photographs I took last night were never intended for Amulet. They were leading up to this, which I wanted to take for you both to keep. I wanted you to always remember yourselves as you are now, to each see yourselves as the other does, and to never forget the strength and the love you share… and to know, however much pain there has been in the past, the future is always worth it.
> Love,
> Grace. x

I turn Megan in my arms and, with my thumbs, I wipe away her tears.

"So, how did she do that?" she repeats.

"Do what?"

"Say it so perfectly? And how did she take a photograph that shows the best of both of us…"

"Grace has a past too, baby. She gets it… probably better than most people. And she just captured what's always been there." I lean in a little closer. "You once said that you wished I could see the man you were seeing – well that goes both ways. You need to see the beautiful, sexy, strong, passionate woman I see every time I look at you." I glance back at the photograph. "And now you can."

"And we have the photograph to keep forever."

"You've always had me to keep forever." She looks at me. Oh, to hell with it. I was going to wait until we'd moved into the new house; I had it all planned out and everything... The last time I spontaneously got down on one knee, it didn't go well, but I'm prepared to risk getting burned a second time... because she's so damn worth it. I drop down in front of her and her eyes widen, her lips part, just slightly.

"Luke?" she whispers.

"Shh..." I murmur. "This isn't how I planned this, and I don't have the ring here... it's at home, but I can't wait any longer. Please... please, Megan... say you'll be mine forever... say you'll marry me..."

She nods her head, tears now flowing down her cheeks, even though she's smiling.

"Say it out loud."

"Yes," she murmurs.

I stand and pick her up, holding her along the length of my body and I spin her around and, as we twirl, Daisy gives a big kick. Big enough for me to feel.

"Looks like your baby girl approves..." Megan says as I put her down again, holding her in my arms.

"She's got no choice. I'm marrying her mommy." I grin down at her. "And then we'll see about a brother or sister..."

"What? Wait a second... I don't know—" I kiss her, partly because it stops her arguing, and partly because it's everything I want to do right now... and the rest of what I want to do can wait until I get her home.

The End

Keep reading for an excerpt from book three in the Series...
Finding Will.

Finding Will

Escaping the Past: Book Three

by

Suzie Peters

Chapter One

Will

"I'm not happy about this." I've said it three times now and Jack's still not paying the slightest bit of attention. But then he doesn't have to; he's my boss.

"Your happiness is not my problem, Will," he says. That much has been obvious for months. "We're getting nowhere right now and we need to find out who leaked the information."

"I get that." I'm not stupid, although the way he's looking at me, it seems he thinks differently. "But you seriously want to put cameras on six of our agents? *And* you want me to hack their cell phones?"

"Yes. And it's not something I *want* to do. The hardware's being put in place as we speak. All I'm telling you to do is monitor it. By your standards, that's a walk in the park."

"*All* you're telling me to do? I know these people, and they have a right to their privacy, Jack."

He gets up, walks around his desk and stands in front of me, like I'm meant to feel threatened by him, or something. It's not working. "And the people on the streets have a right to feel safe in their own homes; they have a right to believe the men and women who are employed to protect them are doing just that – not selling their country's secrets to the highest bidder." He sounds like he's reading from a script. He puts his hands in his pockets. "You've been real quick to forget what happened," he adds. That bit didn't come from any damn script.

"No, I haven't," I snap. How could I forget? The memory of that day will haunt me until I die.

"So the lives of three of our agents don't mean anything to you?"

Now I stand up and it's his turn to feel intimidated. I'm a couple of inches taller than him, at least fifteen years younger and a lot fitter. "How dare you!" I bellow at him. "You weren't there. You didn't have to listen to the whole thing going to shit… I did."

He swallows and takes a step back. "Sorry," he mutters and goes back around to his seat. "Look, I understand that you're not happy, Will. But this is happening with or without you. And I really need it to be with you, you know that. I've got no-one else. You've been on this since the beginning." *Yeah, don't I know it.* "You're the best man we've got, so don't let me down when I need you most. Nobody inside the department can know what we're doing. That's why we're meeting here and not at the office." He looks around his study. The wall to my right is lined with photographs of him, glad-handing various dignitaries, grinning at the camera, and the one behind me is full of books that I'm fairly sure have never been touched, let alone read. Between us is an enormous oak desk, with a red leather inlay, which matches his red leather chair – personally I find it grotesque.

"I'd worked that much out for myself." I sit back down and put my head in my hands and he takes this as a sign of my acceptance of the position he's put me in.

"Now," he says, leaning forward, "I'm sending someone to help you."

"What?" I look up at him. "What do you mean?"

"Will, you can't monitor all the devices we're talking about on six subjects, twenty-four hours a day, for an indefinite period. It's not humanly possible."

"So you think you can just send someone to live at my house for an 'indefinite period' instead?" He nods his head. "Like hell you can."

"Do you have to argue about everything?"

"Why can't you just set them up remotely too?"

"There's the minor detail that you've already got an incredible set up at your house, so why waste the department's money duplicating it... Plus there's less chance of any further leaks," he says. "If you're working together, in the same room, there'll be no comms to intercept."

"You think I can't set up secure communications between me and another agent?"

"I didn't think one of our own would sell us out, Will..." He doesn't need to finish that sentence.

I take a deep breath. "Okay, okay. Who is it?"

"A new operative."

"Oh, great – this just gets better. You're sending me a rookie?"

"A rookie with a Master's in Analytics from Northeastern."

"The same as me...?" I'm impressed.

"Yes. You'll make a good team."

"And this rookie... you expect them to stay at my house, do you? What if it's not convenient?"

"Like I said, I need watertight security on this, and it's not a big ask, Will. It's not like you don't have the space, now your brother's moving out."

I sometimes forget they know my life better than I do.

"I meant, what if it's not convenient for them?"

"It is," he replies.

"It looks like you've thought of everything."

"That's how it tends to work, yes."

"Hmm... when it works." He raises an eyebrow at me. "When can I expect this whizz-kid rookie, then?"

"I'll text you all the details when I get into the office," he says. "The flights haven't been confirmed yet."

On the plane home to Boston, I sit back and close my eyes. I'm determined not to remember that afternoon in August, even though my ears still ring with the sound of the explosion, and the screams of agents, maimed and dying... made worse because I was remote from it, listening in, watching the cameras, seeing and hearing it all unfold and unable, helpless to do anything about it. Someone had warned the terrorists we were targeting; they'd got out, and booby-trapped the house… Of the five guys who went in, three died, one lost a leg, the other had superficial cuts and burns, but he hasn't worked since and none of us are sure he ever will. Despite everything Jack says, it's not a day I'll ever forget.

Since then, on Jack's instructions, I've been working on my own at home, trying to discover who leaked the intel. Someone must have… but I've not been able to find out who. If Jack had just agreed to a full-scale investigation – like I wanted from the start – this would probably all have been dealt with by now. But when it's just me, working on my own and reporting to Jack, it's gonna take time…

This plan of his to spy on the only six people in the department who had enough knowledge of the op to impart it to the terrorists, doesn't sit well with me. I'm going to be listening to and watching them at home and at work, with their families, their wives or husbands, their kids. It feels wrong… especially as I've got no information telling me that any of these people are responsible, which means I think we should start to look elsewhere. I've already told Jack this; I've been telling him the same thing for weeks now, but instead it seems we're doing the opposite. We're focusing everything on people I'm convinced are innocent… I just need to work out why.

Of course, one reason behind it could be the stone cold certainty I've got in the pit of my stomach that this rookie is coming to have a long hard look at me. I told Jack right from the beginning that no-one should be above suspicion; now it seems that, on this point at least, he's decided to listen. Yeah, it needs more than one person doing the surveillance, but they don't have to do it from my house; they can do it from anywhere. Whatever Jack says, secure comms can be arranged, and my equipment isn't that expensive. If it was, I couldn't have afforded to put it into my place at my own expense. I'm being set up… I just became his next target. Jack can't get cameras into my house, so he's doing the next best thing and putting another agent in instead.

I think I just got the nudge I needed to help me toward a decision I've been contemplating for a while now – even before the explosion and its aftermath… namely to get out. I can't keep doing this job. It's too destructive.

When we land, I make my way to the parking garage and turn my phone back on. I've got two messages. One's from Jack:

— Expect Jamie Blackwood approx. 2pm Tuesday. Jack

Well, at least it won't interrupt the weekend, and I'll need that time to prepare. I don't bother to reply to him.

The other message is from my brother, Luke.

— Everything's moved. Dinner our place (new place), 7pm. I know you're busy. Please try. L

I check my watch. It's four-thirty. I can easily make it. I tap out an answer to him.

— Sure. I'll bring wine and beer. W.

He replies immediately.

— Good. Megan will be pleased – to see you, not so much about the wine and beer ;) L.

I pull up outside Luke and Megan's home, alongside his new Range Rover. He drove one in Europe in the summer and, when he needed to change his car, decided this was what he wanted. I haven't had a chance to drive it myself yet, but it looks good, especially in black.

I stand and stare up at their house for a moment. Even in the dark, it's beautiful; although right now, I think every light in the house is switched on, so it's not all that dark around here. It's a wooden-clad Colonial property, with a wrap-around porch, an amazing eat-in kitchen, and four bedrooms, near Belmont. They brought me to see it a couple of weeks ago, because Luke wanted me to see that it's not too far away, to reassure me they'll still visit and I can call in anytime, and stay over if I want to. He's the most incredible brother. He's cared for me since the day our mom died and I owe him everything, including the house he now insists I now call my own. He bought it about six years ago, when his friend – well, our friend – Matt made him a partner in his firm. I then made it secure, adding the systems I wanted and the fencing and gates and, over the last few years, we've done a lot of work on the interior of the property, which we've paid for jointly. But he knows I can't afford to buy him out, so rather than sell it and force me to live elsewhere, he and Megan have moved out of the city, to get the size home they want for them and their new baby, Daisy, who's due in about three months' time.

The door opens and Luke comes down the steps to greet me.

"Will… You okay?" he asks.

I nod my head. "Sure."

"How was the flight?"

"The flight was fine… it was the meeting that sucked."

I open the back door of my Jeep and get out two bags, one of beer, one of wine, handing the beers to him. "I don't suppose you're gonna tell me about it," he says, because I'm renowned for not telling anyone about my work – for obvious reasons. We start walking toward the house.

"For once, I might," I tell him and he stops and turns to me.

"Has something happened?"

"I can't tell you what's happened, but I need to talk to all of you about something that's going to happen."

"This sounds worrying," he says, and we start walking again.

"Much more so for me than for you," I mutter as I follow him up the steps and into the house.

The front door opens onto a wide hallway, with a staircase in the centre, leading up to a galleried landing. To the left is a huge living room, which I know has doors at one end, leading out onto the porch, but which is currently full of boxes. To the right is the kitchen, which goes through to the dining area, set in a fully glazed sun room, and then the deck is beyond that. In the summer, this is going to be spectacular. We go through, to find Megan standing by the island unit, her hand on her now obvious bump. She comes round and gives me a kiss on the cheek.

"Hello, you," she says. She's beautiful... maybe even more beautiful now than ever. When I first met her, I'd just got back from that disastrous assignment. She was very newly pregnant with Luke's baby, but it didn't show then, and she was stunning, but now – she's positively glowing with the expectation of motherhood. I put the bag I've been carrying on the countertop and look around.

"This is lovely," I say to her.

"Isn't it? Matt and Grace are picking up dinner on their way here."

"And Todd?"

"He'll be here soon. He called about twenty minutes ago."

Luke puts the beers on the countertop and goes to stand behind Megan, bringing his arms around her and kissing her neck. She leans back into him and I look away... Luke is very openly affectionate with Megan, and I find that awkward... maybe even embarrassing. I know it's my problem, not theirs, but that doesn't make it any easier.

Matt and Grace arrive just over half an hour later, roughly ten minutes after Todd. I'm not sorry he's here – being the lone single guy would have been difficult, especially as Matt and Grace are just as doting over each other as my brother and his fiancée. Grace has become a really good friend to me since she got together with Matt; she's a really good listener and I can tell her just about anything – although there are some things that I'd never discuss with her. I'd never be able to. These are the things I've never even told Luke, so how could I possibly tell Grace?

She's nearly as pregnant as Megan, although I think she looks more so – her bump is more rounded; and while they unpack the food onto the table, the two of them discuss how Megan's going to decorate the nursery upstairs.

Todd comes over to me. "We're better off free and single," he says.

"Absolutely," I reply, because it's what's expected, and I clink my beer bottle against his.

"Yeah, right. Like you two wouldn't really love to have what we've got," Matt says, grinning at us. He's right. Now I've seen how happy he and Luke are, I'd love it – I don't understand it – but I'd love it... Still, it's not going to happen – not for me.

The girls call us over for dinner and we all sit around the table, dishing up the food onto earthenware plates, which – together with the wine glasses – seem to be the only things Luke and Megan have unpacked.

"So, Will," Luke says once we're all settled, "tell us what's going on…"

Everyone looks at me and I can feel myself redden. I hate being the center of attention. "What's this?" Grace asks.

"I went to see my boss today," I tell them, taking a bite out of my spring roll.

"Right," Luke says.

I finish chewing. "I'm sorry, guys, I can't tell you what we talked about, but the result of it is I've got someone coming to stay at the house for a while."

"What for?"

"I can't tell you that either. It's just part of an ongoing assignment. I need some help with a job I have to do."

"And how long is 'a while'?" Luke asks.

"As long as it takes."

"So basically you're telling us you've got a strange guy coming to stay with you for an indefinite period of time?"

"Yeah, that about sums it up."

He glances at Megan. "You okay with that?" he asks me. He knows I'll find it hard sharing my space.

"I wasn't really given a choice."

"What's he like?" Todd asks.

"I've got no idea – he's new to the department. I guess he's quite young, though, since this is his first assignment. Apart from that, all I know is he went to Northeastern, like me, and his name's Jamie… oh, and he's arriving at two on Tuesday."

Grace is looking at me. "Why are you telling us?" she asks. "You don't normally talk about your work. I mean, even if one of us dropped by, the very worst we'd assume is that you had a friend over."

"Or a boyfriend," Todd says, smirking. They've never seen me with a woman, so I guess it's a natural assumption to make.

I look at him for a moment, then Luke says, "And that's precisely why Will wanted to tell us, I guess…Because the cop in the corner can always be relied on to jump to the wrong conclusion."

"It's a habit I have," Todd replies, and winks at me.

"No, guys, the reason I'm telling you is that I need you all to stay away from the house." I need some time alone with this guy to see what he knows about me, what his instructions are, and what he's going to do about it. I don't tell them that part.

"How long for?" Luke asks. "Not indefinitely, surely."

"No, probably just a few days… I'll call you when you can come over." I look at him. "I know you've still got the pass codes and your key; and I wouldn't normally mind you just letting yourself in; but for the next few days, can you just… not."

"Sure." He doesn't ask for an explanation, because he knows I can't give him one.

After the meal, I excuse myself and go to the bathroom. On the way back, I take the chance to have a better look around the house, which is perfect for Luke and Megan. It's not as large as Matt and Grace's place, but Luke wouldn't want that anyway. They've bought some new furniture, which I know is being delivered tomorrow, and then they've got a lot of unpacking to do. I'm so engrossed in looking around, that I'm not paying attention to what's being said as I walk back into the kitchen.

"…But that's just what I meant," Todd's remarking. "And, in any case, there's nothing wrong with being gay, is there?"

"Who's gay?" I ask, and they all turn to look at me.

Megan stares at Luke. She looks a little startled, and he glares at Todd, then says, "I… I was just starting to tell the story of how Megan thought I was gay."

"What?" I say, starting to laugh. "When was this?"

"When we first met," he replies, smirking a little.

I look at Megan. "You seriously thought *he* was gay?"

"I think it's quite an easy mistake to make," Matt puts in, laughing.

"Thanks for defending me." Megan smiles at him and gets up to start clearing the dishes.

"But…" I'm lost for words. How anyone could think that Luke Myers, serial womanizer – before he met Megan, that is – could be gay, is beyond me. "Why? How?"

Luke looks at me for a moment, then grabs Megan around the hips and pulls her down onto his lap. "She didn't understand why I wasn't responding to a few women, who were throwing themselves at me…"

"So she thought you were gay?" I'm still struggling with this concept.

"Well, I was fighting my attraction to Megan at the time," he says. "But she didn't know that, so I guess it didn't make sense to her."

"And that just makes me seem so conceited… You're making it sound like I assumed you'd be attracted to me," Megan replies, nuzzling his neck.

"The man's got a pulse, hasn't he?" Todd says and Luke turns to him.

"And?" he asks, smiling.

"Just saying…" Todd shrugs.

"Just saying what?" Luke stands Megan up again and gets to his feet. I can't help smirking at the idea my brother could be jealous – even if only in jest. It's just not his style.

Todd stands as well. They're about the same height; they're both very useful with their fists. I'm not getting between them and from the looks of it, neither is Matt. He's sitting, holding Grace's hand, a broad grin on his face.

"Just saying, I wouldn't have fought the attraction, that's all; I'd have gone with it," Todd says and moves the chair to one side so he can make a quick getaway.

"Yes…" Megan's voice is quiet as she puts her arms around Luke and kisses him, even though her eyes are fixed on Todd. "But the difference is, you wouldn't have got anywhere." And everyone laughs… even me.

Jamie

"Are you going to be alright with this?" Scott asks me, for probably the tenth time. "I mean… It's Boston."

"Yes, I know that – I told you about it, remember?"

He looks at me. "I'm just concerned about you," he says defensively.

I stop packing and go over to him. He's leaning against the wall, just inside my bedroom door. "I'm sorry," I tell him. "It'll be fine."

"But you haven't been back there since…"

"I know." I put my hand on his arm. "And it'll be fine."

He shakes his head. "And if it isn't?"

"It will be. Stop worrying about me. It's not your job."

"You're my sister, of course it's my job." I'm touched. "So, how long will you be away for?"

"I have no idea." I go back across to the bed and carry on packing. "I'm sorry, but I may not be back before Christmas."

"That's okay," he says and I look up. He's grinning. "I was going to ask if Mia could come over for the holidays anyway, once her exams are over. She can't afford the fare to get back to her parents' place and I don't like the thought of her being all by herself."

"No, of course you don't." I smile at him.

"So, she can come?"

"Yes, she can come." He walks over and hugs me.

"Thanks, sis… And can I have a few of the guys around for a party… or two?"

"Scotty…" I pack some extra socks in my case… I remember Boston being really cold in December.

"Please. I promise we'll behave."

"Hmm." I hold up two sweaters – one's blue and fluffy, the other pink and more delicate. "Which one?" I ask him.

"Can't you take them both?" he says. "They're real pretty."

"I'm flying, not driving. I've got two others already, but I can't fit much more in."

"Blue, then…"

I do as he suggests. Scott has good taste.

"And the party?" he pleads.

"Alright…" I say. "But I have neighbors, so keep the noise down; and no-one – no-one, Scott – is allowed in my bedroom. Do you hear me?"

"Yes. I promise, no-one will use your bedroom. Not even to sleep in." He smirks.

"I suppose I should take a dress," I say. "If I'm there for Christmas…"

"A dress? Are you sure?" He looks at me.

"I do wear them… occasionally."

"But I didn't think you did anymore." He stops speaking. "I haven't seen you—" he mutters.

"You're right," I say. "I'll take my black pants and the pink sweater instead. It's probably safer."

"No," he says. "Take a dress, if you want to. If they can't handle it, that's their problem."

"I'm not sure any of my dresses fit anyway," I tell him. It's an excuse – but a valid one. "I'm still a little bigger than I was before…"

"So, buy a new one when you get there. They do have shops in Boston, remember?"

"I'll take the pants anyway, just in case."

"What about your exercises?" he asks. "You won't have your bike…" He nods at the exercise bike in the corner of my room.

"Maybe I'll find a local gym…" I say, packing my purple sports gear.

"You haven't used a public gym since you left the hospital… that's why you bought the bike." He's right. We both know I won't look for one, and I'm just packing the shorts and top the sake of appearances.

"Well, hopefully I won't be gone for long enough that it'll make a difference," I tell him, although the thought of how much pain I'll be in has occurred to me too.

He comes over and stands next to me. "I'll miss you," he says. "I only got here yesterday, and you're leaving tomorrow."

"Yeah, and your girlfriend is coming to stay in a few days... you won't even notice I'm not here."

He smiles. "She doesn't make pancakes like you do."

"That's only because I've been making them longer... and I use mom's recipe. If you went home occasionally, you could have mom's – they're even better."

"But then I'd never get to see Mia – or you."

And he'd argue with dad, like he usually does, but I won't bring that up now.

"I'll make some for breakfast tomorrow," I tell him. "I'm not leaving until ten."

"Hmm... that's worth getting up early for."

"You mean you wouldn't have got up early just to see me off?"

He looks at me for a moment. "Nah..." he says, grinning. "I've got a lot of sleep to catch up on."

"Well, thanks for that."

"Anytime." He sits down on my bed next to my case. "Why are you going?" he asks.

"You know I can't tell you that."

"No, what I mean is why do you have to go to Boston instead of working from your office. It's a bit dumb, if you ask me... they just gave you an office, and now they're sending you away. It doesn't make sense."

"Of course it doesn't make sense – it's the government. And I still can't tell you why. It's just the way it is."

"It's not dangerous, is it, Jamie?"

"No. I'm just gonna be sitting in a room, looking at screens all day." That's not strictly true, but he doesn't need to know the other reason I'm going, and I can't tell him anyway.

"In Boston?" he asks.

"Yes, in Boston." I don't tell him that I've spent the last four days installing cameras and listening devices at various addresses around

Virginia. Scott doesn't like to think of me doing any actual field-work, so I never mention it… it's not like that's the bulk of what I do anyway. It's just on this occasion, no-one else could do it, because no-one else is allowed to know what's going on; Jack Fielding was adamant about that.

"And this guy you're going to stay with… what's he like?"

"I've got no idea – except he went to Northeastern, like me." I haven't had time to read his file yet. Jack only handed it to me an hour or so ago, together with my unofficial instructions: to find out if Will Myers has a reason to sell out his fellow agents.

"You're staying at his house, though, right?"

"Yes."

"Does he have a family?"

"I don't know. I'll find out when I get there." *Or when I read his file, assuming I get to do that before I arrive.*

"Well, if he doesn't, and he's single… and he tries anything…"

I smirk at him. "I won't call you, Scott… You'll be too busy with Mia."

He grins up at me. "Fair point," he says. "But…" A shadow crosses his face.

"I can take care of myself, you know."

"Call me?" He sounds concerned. "If you need to talk."

"Yes, I will."

"Can we go out to dinner?" he asks. "As it's your last night…?"

I really should read this file, but I guess I can do it on the plane. "Okay. But we can't be late back."

Scott enjoyed his pancakes this morning. I didn't have any. I hate flying at the best of times, but when I woke up and saw the gray clouds, I decided that eating wouldn't be a good idea. I was right. I managed to survive the flight, but only because I had nothing in my stomach. I didn't get to read the file though; I was too busy trying not to be sick.

I've picked up my rental car, a horrible bright green Chevrolet Spark, which is tiny, but sufficient for my one suitcase and me. I put some music on, plug Will Myers' address into the SatNav, and set off.

There's a fair amount of traffic, but I'm familiar with the roads, and I make good time, getting to his house at just before two. At least, the SatNav says I've arrived at his house, but all I can find is a high wall, with a huge solid metal gate… This can't be it, surely?

Printed in Great Britain
by Amazon

28018605R00185